FLASHTIDE

FLASHTIDE

THE SEQUEL TO FLASHFALL

JENNY MOYER

HENRY HOLT AND COMPANY

NEW YORK

Henry Holt and Company, *Publishers since 1866*
Henry Holt® is a registered trademark of Macmillan Publishing Group, LLC
175 Fifth Avenue, New York, New York 10010 • fiercereads.com

Library of Congress Cataloging-in-Publication Data is available.
ISBN 978-1-62779-483-1

Our books may be purchased in bulk for promotional, educational, or business use. Please
contact your local bookseller or the Macmillan Corporate and Premium Sales Department at
(800) 221-7945 ext. 5442 or by e-mail at MacmillanSpecialMarkets@macmillan.com.

First edition, 2017 / Design by Liz Dresner
Printed in the United States of America

10 9 8 7 6 5 4 3 2 1

For my boys—
Caden, Landon, and Kai.
I'd cross the cordons for you.

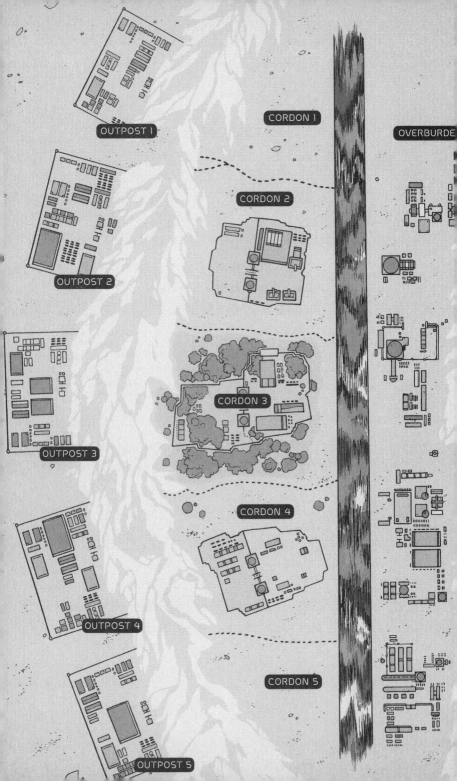

OUTPOST 1

OUTPOST 2

OUTPOST 3

OUTPOST 4

OUTPOST 5

CORDON 1

CORDON 2

CORDON 3

CORDON 4

CORDON 5

OVERBURDE

PROLOGUE

A HUNDRED AND fifty years ago, our sun turned on us. At first, observers noted the largest solar flare in recorded history, an X29 that they later changed to the first-ever Y-classified flare. Still, it was nothing to cause alarm—our sun was approaching solar maximum, a cycle that had repeated every eleven years for millennia.

Scientists with NASA and NOAA reported the approach of a CME—a coronal mass ejection. They predicted a disturbance to spacecraft and aircraft navigation systems, as well as potential damage to power grids, all caused by the burst of electromagnetic radiation impacting our atmosphere. But what came hurtling toward us was nothing at all like they predicted. An unprecedented solar event.

The world changed in an instant—a flash of radioactive electromagnetic particles that invaded our atmosphere and hangs here still, a visible reminder of humanity's vulnerability.

And adaptability. For some of us, anyway.

They called it a flash curtain and watched as it turned cities to rubble in the space of a breath. It altered landmasses, raised water levels, made islands where none existed before. Then seventeen more fell in the following days. The US, UK, Europe, Asia—no place was unaffected.

And the world broke apart.

ONE

WE MOVE THROUGH the forest like we're being chased.

Dram and I don't speak, both of us listening for the drone of Inquiry Modules, or things less mechanical, coming after us. The mountain provinces, once a haven, are now a trap closing. Each day new Mods are added to the small, autonomous hovers patrolling this region in low-flying grids. The Congress is desperate to find me before I can finish what I started on the other side of the flash curtain.

And since we can't go back to the cordons, that leaves only the protected city—from which Subpars are exiled—or the lawless outlier regions on its far side. Either place could hold Dram's father. Or maybe Arrun Berrends is as dead as the rumors suggest.

The branches of a pine tree slip through my fingers, the stiff needles scraping against my palm. One touch from a Conjuror, and it could transform into something that would shield us from the Congress's trackers.

Of course, under my hand it's just a tree. Which really doesn't help with our current dilemma.

"Hurry, Rye," Dram says. "We're almost there."

I lift my feet, trying to place them in the snow-packed steps his boots have made. My breaths feel heavier up here in the mountains, and each exhale clouds the air.

Everything looks and feels different beyond the flashfall. Especially the air.

People have a name for the place we came from. Westfall. This side of the flash curtain is considered Eastfall. Dram and I grew up with only the five outposts and the five cordons as boundaries, but here there's the Overburden, the mountain provinces, Alara, and the outlier regions. Apparently, being closer to safety gives people time to name things.

And apparently, we Subpars weren't given that much space.

I grasp another branch as we shuffle past, our steps carving a path through the snow. Living with the Conjies has taught me to see nature as something *more*. Alive, radiating with energy similar to mine. Even the dirt and rocks. I didn't understand that before.

Or maybe I did.

"Wishing you could conjure?"

I look up at Dram, pine needles slipping through my fingers.

"The way you're holding on to that tree—it's the third one you've grabbed."

Words crowd my mouth, but the only true answer is—

"Yes."

I want the ability so badly that at times I think I can feel elements transform when I watch a Conjuror at work. More likely, it's jealousy stirring in me, a creature inside my soul roused by equal parts gratitude and resentment.

"Me too." Dram touches the branch and grins ruefully. He sighs, and the branch snaps back. "You ready for this?" he asks, drawing his hood over his dark hair. A chill snakes down my spine as the camo-cloth shifts, altering shades of white, adapting until he blends with our surroundings. In an instant, my Subpar-who-looks-like-a-Conjie is gone. Dram doesn't look like a Strider—he's not wearing their electrified armored suit and flash weapons—but still, he doesn't look like the caver I've known all my life.

He looks like someone who belongs in Eastfall.

I'm glad he can't see my face as he slips the gun from his thigh holster and checks the ammo clip.

"I wish you would use a gun, Orion." He looks at me now, and I'm not fast enough to hide my revulsion. Guns, like camo-cloth, are tools of the Congress. It's enough that I'm wearing their stolen cloak.

"I'll be fine." I reach to free the pickaxe on my back. "I can handle a couple of vultures." It's the same words I said to Bade when I convinced him to let only Dram and me go after the creatures. None of the free Conjies have ever faced down a flash vulture. Except for the two Conjies they found in pieces. Stiff black feathers with thorny protrusions were discovered beside the bodies.

Dram and I knew at once what they were—and what they meant. Flash vultures. In the mountain provinces.

I adjust my grip on the axe handle, but it still feels foreign— this is Dram's pickaxe. I left mine—my mother's axe—in

Outpost Five. Its handle was split, just a few swings away from cracking apart. I couldn't justify the extra weight, though I've regretted the loss of it ever since.

I regret the loss of many things.

"Orion," Dram says softly. "We're going back for them. We'll get them out."

My fist tightens around the handle. I wish my thoughts weren't so transparent to Dram. Sometimes I want to cling to my aches without him knowing.

"How many blades on you?" he asks.

"Three." I can't see the knives tucked in my arm holster, but I feel them beneath the lightweight cloak. I wear another, larger knife at my hip and a slim blade inside my boot. But I don't tell Dram. Telling him I brought five knives would reveal I'm more worried about this than I pretend to be.

We used to hide from the flash curtain's altered creatures. Now we're hunting them.

I wish I could unsee what happened to those two poor Conjies. They fought hard, but they didn't know what they were up against. Beasts with wings so tough they can withstand the flash curtain. Talons that pierce your skin before you've even registered that there's a beak aiming for your jugular.

"They were sighted near the boundary," Dram says, "about thirty kilometers from the curtain."

I draw the hood of my cloak over my head. I don't need to see the flashfall to know we're getting close. The past months with the Conjies have only increased my sensitivity to the elements, to the altered particles that have always called my name.

He turns without another word, and I follow. Adrenaline surges through me like the silence is a cue. This is when Dram and I are at our best—when our actions supersede our words, and we talk to each other with the language we developed down tunnel nine.

Our boots push at the snow, and my hand tightens around my axe handle. White camo-cloth drapes us, and with the snow swiftly falling, I lose Dram at times, even though he's just ahead of me. It is strange to follow when I have always been out front, but we are east of the curtain, and he is the better leader here.

Snow crunches behind me, and I whirl. At first, there's nothing but snow-dusted scrub brush, but as I look harder, I can make out a face in the conjured concealment. Roran.

"I told you to stay back," Dram says.

Roran barely moves. His dark eyes shift toward Dram and away. I don't say anything. Roran hasn't spoken to me since he stumbled into our camp a week ago, half dead with flash fever. When he finally spoke, it was to Dram—to tell him—

I press the point of Dram's pickaxe against my palm and distract myself with the pain. Some pain is easier to take than other kinds.

"Let him stay," I say.

Roran doesn't look at me. The path that once connected us is as gone as the people who made it.

Wind blows up through the pass, rattling bare branches above our heads with a clacking and sifting of snow. A narrow twig the size of my finger lifts from where it's twisted in Roran's black hair. He brushes it absently, and tiny white flowers bloom.

I wonder if he even knows that he's conjuring, or if it's reflexive, a sort of magical respiration. He catches me looking and turns, striding ahead of us. A petal slips to the ground, and I pick it up.

They are for Mere. I can make myself acknowledge that much. Mere, the Tempered Conjie, my friend, his mother, is likely dead. Dram knows how. A flashburst in Cordon Five, Roran separated from the others . . . He parcels out pieces of the story in moments when he thinks I can take it. The truth is like exposure to the flash curtain's radioactive particles. It kills me slowly, over time. All at once, and I'd be nothing more than dust.

Hers is the only loss I accept. I must do that for her. For Roran. If he is ever to heal, then he must grieve. He can blame me, hate me, but I won't leave him alone. I don't wear a Conjie talisman woven in my hair for Mere, but I made her this promise.

The talisman I wear is on the inside. A hollow place that aches like a bruise, that steals my breath when memories sweep in. Especially the good memories. The sound of her laugh is fresh in my mind, and I—

"Rye," Dram says, "I can't fight these things alone. I need you here." Wind gusts throw his brown hair into a fury around his face. A faint jingle reaches my ears.

I touch the tiny silver charm woven into a lock of his hair. One I'd never noticed before.

"Maybe you should take this out," I say. "It might warn the vultures we're approaching."

"No. That one's important."

"They're all important, aren't they?" He wears numerous talismans: tiny bits of shell, a narrow strip of bark, the top of a green acorn. It's not the Conjie way to speak of talismans. But we are not Conjies, and I'm filled with a sudden need to know.

"Yes." He clasps my hand against his head, trapping my

fingers. The charm pushes against my palm. It is strange to think of Dram keeping something important from me.

"Is it for a memory or a promise?" I ask.

"Both."

I lift my camo-cloth hood. "Lead the way."

We step over fallen trees, our steps slower, cautious. We catch up to Roran, where he stands like an extension of the trees around us. "I hear them," he whispers.

We stand unmoving, ears strained for the sounds I'm already dreading, sounds that wake me at night when my nightmares take me back to the cordons.

I hear the faint jingling of Dram's talisman and the clacking of beads from Roran's sash. Then, the guttural, drawn-out hissing of agitated flash vultures.

Roran leans in close. "The vultures in the provinces eat only dead things. They don't attack people."

"These aren't normal vultures," I whisper.

"There," Dram says, pointing to a snow-dusted tree. "Five of them."

Five, when once no flash vultures existed beyond the flashfall.

They shift on the branches, like the tree is too small to contain them. Wings extend, the span longer than Dram is tall. These are the largest I've seen. Their bones don't protrude like those of their siblings in the cordons. Perhaps they've found prey to feed their appetites. I watch them arch their necks, black eyes fixed on us, and know that whatever they've been filling their stomachs with, we are what they hunger for.

"How are they getting through?" Dram asks.

I don't have an answer. Not one I'm willing to share yet.

"Bade says he's seen tunnel gulls—"

"Tunnel gulls?" I'm so shocked I lower my axe. "Where? They nest in stone." I have a hard time imagining gulls surviving beyond the caverns. They don't have the flame-resistant wings of flash vultures.

"Maybe he was wrong," Dram says.

Or maybe the curtain is altering things again.

"Get ready," he says.

My grip tightens, my palms sweating despite the cold. I find the dark shapes of the vultures in the tree, but my gaze strays beyond them, searching for the flash of a silver-white wingtip. A flash like the blade of a knife. If tunnel gulls survived the destruction of the Barrier Range and made their way here, we are in more danger than I thought.

But the sky is overcast, the clouds so low I feel like I could climb up and touch them. They are a shroud, keeping the rest of the world veiled.

A twig snaps, and we both whirl, Dram with his pistol in hand. I'm the only one who still uses a pickaxe. A soft whistle comes from the wood, and we both relax. Conjuror. A girl emerges from the tree, her hair braided like a crown around her head.

"What is it, Meg?" I whisper. Her face is whiter than the snow.

"Newel sent me to find you," she says. I try to imagine what could compel the older leader of the free Conjies to send her after us. "To warn you," she adds.

"What's happened?" Dram asks, and it's his commander voice—the new one that sounds more like his father, Arrun, and less like the boy I searched caves with.

"Trackers found us just after you left. He said to tell you he'd meet you—"

Two vultures drop to the ground behind Meg. They fan their massive wings, like they're barring our escape. She stiffens, but I can tell she's not afraid. Not like she should be.

Dram takes aim, cocking the hammer back with a click. "Don't move, Meg," he orders softly.

"They're just birds," she says. But she snaps a bead from her bracelet, grasps it in her palm in preparation to conjure.

"If you conjure," Dram says, "make it something you can hide behind."

Wings beat the air behind me, the sound taking me back to the cordons, to memories of blood and burning. I don't have to turn to know at least two more have dropped in. I glance at Roran. He slides a wooden ring from his finger and conjures it into a shard of rock, sharp as a blade.

"Rye," Dram says, and it's more a breath than a sound.

"Yes," I whisper. I am ready.

"Now," he says. I pivot and swing my axe at the nearest black body, while shots fire one after another from Dram's gun. I dive at the second screeching creature. A third shot. I throw all my weight behind my axe and—

Wings. Pain shoots up my arm. I wasn't prepared for the resistance, and my axe tumbles from my fingers. I reach with my left hand to free a knife while the vulture recovers from my failed attack, grunting and twitching under the force of the blow. It's on me before I've freed my knife. The beak pierces my skin through my coat, and I cry out. It holds fast to my flesh, digging and tearing. I fall back, light-headed, searching for my blade.

"Orion!"

The last vulture drops from the sky and lands heavy on me. A beak jabs, glancing off my ribs. I scream from the pain, from the shock of facing these beasts this far from the cordons, in a place that should be safe from the flash curtain's horrors.

"Stay still, Rye!" Dram's voice, deadly calm. I force myself to quit struggling so he can get a clean shot. I wait for the report of the gun, but all I hear is a click and Dram's curse. He drops the pistol and dives toward me, to where I shake on bloody snow that surrounds me like a target.

Dram wrestles the vulture off me, and it shrieks in protest. Two more fly toward him, circling, their bodies so massive that Dram's camo-cloth ripples with shades of black. I can only listen as he rolls and grunts—and then his breathing changes, and I know he's in control just before he levers his body atop the creature and beats it with my dropped axe. He's up on his knees a moment later, a blur of motion, with an overhand grip on two knives. The beasts fly at him, wings extended, and his camo-cloth responds with matching ebony, then they shift away, launching themselves skyward. His cloak absorbs him into the winter woods again. I roll onto my side, clasping the torn skin that burns and pulses in time with my pounding heart.

It smells of blood. With my eyes squeezed shut, and my body numb from shock and cold, that's all I sense. The smell weighs on me, heavy, like two flash vultures pressing on my chest. I gasp into the snow, needing the clean air to flush out the taste of death.

Dram pries my hands away to look at the wound. I refuse to cry, to give in to the despair I feel tearing into me as sharp as talons. Somehow our nightmares followed us through the flash curtain.

We're not free yet.

"It's not deep," he says, stanching the blood. "But it might need stitching." He winds a bandage around my ribs, and I hiss as he cinches it tight. "Where else?"

"Shoulder." I grit the word out between clenched teeth. He lifts aside my camo-cloth and peels back my torn coat. A Conjie curse slips past his lips.

"Something's wrong," he murmurs. "Your wound—"

I crane my neck to see what has him frozen in shock. A shallow gash, no wider than my palm, bleeding steadily. But as Dram lifts the cloth, my breath stutters. The blood . . . shimmers. The gash glints with opalescent shades of pink and aquamarine, as if the flash curtain took hold of me and left its handprint behind.

"It's spreading," he says. Iridescent streaks fan from the wound, illuminating my skin in ominous rays.

As if the sight of it tripped a signal in my brain, I suddenly feel it—pain catches up to my senses, and I scream behind my teeth.

"Worse than orbies," I gasp, knowing Dram will understand. Whatever this is, it hurts more than the tiny glowing organisms that chewed through our skin down tunnel nine.

"Clean it," Meg says. She leans past Dram with handfuls of conjured water and scrubs at my skin. "It's still spreading!"

"Do you think it's some kind of venom?" Dram asks, his face grim. This, too, he's familiar with. He drew flash bat poison out of my body twice down nine. A look of resolve crosses his face, and he leans toward my wound.

"No!" I shove his head back, my body screaming with pain. "You're not putting your mouth on this thing. This isn't . . . flash bat venom." My voice shakes, but my gaze is steady. I tell him more, without words, the silent communication that saved our lives hundreds of times down the tunnels. Whatever the flash vulture did to me, it's worse than anything we faced on the other side of the curtain.

"Cut it out of me," I say.

"I'm not *cutting* it out of you—"

"Cut it!" I throw all the authority of a lead ore scout into my voice, though my designation means nothing now.

"You'll bleed to death!" Dram says.

"Then burn it!"

Dram's wild eyes meet mine. "There's not time for a fire. The wood is wet—"

"Flare," I gasp. And I know, flash me, I know what this pain is like. "It's making me sick," I murmur. "Whatever it's done to me—I can feel it!"

"I'll help," Roran says, kneeling beside me. He holds me steady while Dram yanks a flare from his pocket.

"Her Radband's changing!" Meg's voice.

I shift to see my Radband glowing pale yellow at my wrist. It darkens as I watch. Dram's stark gaze collides with mine, then shifts to my shoulder. "What if this doesn't work? We don't know what this is—"

"Dram." I bite his name out, a brittle command. A moment from now, I won't be able to speak.

He lights the flare and sets it to my skin.

Pain. Burning. Radiating. Like a piece of a star pressing

against me. My eyes squeeze shut, but colors explode behind my eyelids.

Tremors rack my body, the chill of shock on the heels of fire.

"It's gone. We got it all." Dram's voice shakes. "Breathe, Rye," he murmurs.

Air slips unsteadily through my nostrils. Burning flesh. I choke on the smell. My skin burns so badly I fight the urge to vomit. I shake uncontrollably, as if the rest of my skin is trying to escape from the source of pain. I count to five and push up onto my hands and knees.

"What are you doing?" Meg asks. "Let us tend your wound."

"There are at least two more of those vultures out there." I gasp the words, panting past the pain.

I clasp Dram's hand and tell him the rest with my eyes. He nods grimly. We are back to relying on our tunnel talk. I bite back a cry as he tows me to my feet. Blood spatters the snow like cavers' marks. I think of flash vultures seeing them. *This way to an easy meal.* If more come now, I'm done. I'm already dizzy from shock.

"Let's move, ore scout," Dram says, tucking his axe into his belt. I didn't realize I'd dropped it. He scoops snow into his hands and rubs it between his palms, cleaning them of the vulture and Orion blood. "Still with me?" he asks, giving my hands the same treatment.

"I'm fine," I murmur. We head toward the camp, my staggering steps no longer quiet. I make it a dozen meters before I collapse against a tree. Dram lifts me in his arms.

"Tomorrow I teach you to shoot," he mutters.

He trudges behind Meg and Roran over snow-covered trails, and I will myself to be lighter, less a burden. At least he's not injured. Just me—the girl who can't let go of her caver's ways. The Westfaller.

Snowflakes whirl down from the heavy blanket of sky so thick I can watch their lazy descent. It makes a hush fall over everything, and I imagine it helping us, covering our tracks, shielding us from the Congress's trackers.

Then, a glint of silver through the flakes—and I blink the snow out of my eyes to look harder.

Beyond the sounds of their footfalls, the creature calls, *Mew, mew, keow.* Dram heard it too; I can see it in the tensing of his jaw. I'm suddenly too aware of my hair, dangling past his arm, and Meg's braids—wound like the nest this monster would use them for.

Mew, mew, keow, the tunnel gull calls again. I slide my knife free and grip it tightly, eyes fastened on the sky above us.

I will learn to shoot tomorrow.

TWO

THUNDER RUMBLES THROUGH camp, and I'm grateful for our conjured tree shelter. Most nights, Dram and I sleep under the stars, but the winter has brought snow. And snow, this close to the flash curtain, can be deadly.

Particle snow exposes us to radiation as surely as a breath of cordon air. It shouldn't reach us here—we're camped beyond the flashfall—but I feel a shift in the atmosphere, as if it's pushing past boundaries along with the vultures and gulls.

Another rumble, and I give up on sleep. Usually I sense the approach of a flash storm, the deepest parts of me awakened to the curtain's particles. A bead of sweat trickles down my back, and I realize it's not a storm that woke me, but a premonition, a tingling sense of dread I can't ignore.

I push up my sleeve, and my Radband casts a glow on the woven branches on either side of us. My eyes water from staring at the indicator. It turned yellow while I was imprisoned by King in Cordon Three. Even then, starving and half mad with fear, I marveled that it wasn't red after the days I'd spent in the cordons, so close to the flash curtain I could feel its song pulse through my body. My father's compound saved me, preserved my life long enough to get him the elements he needed to create a cure.

But no one's heard from him in weeks.

Dram stirs, and I glance down to find him studying my face. He gently clasps my wrist, blocking the light of my Radband. He despises the biotech all Subpars wear from birth—indicators of approaching death by radiation.

But we're safe from that now. So long as we don't get close to the curtain again. And as long as we take shelter from any storms that carry its radioactive particles to us. I weave my fingers through his, and our callused palms press together, hands scarred from years of mining and fighting the creatures down tunnel nine.

Tension creeps into his eyes, and I turn up the lantern before he has to ask. I need the sky above me, and Dram needs light in dark spaces. We both carry demons from Outpost Five. He sits up and gently checks my wounds. I didn't need stitches after all. He trails his finger beside a row of butterfly bandages.

"You in pain?" he asks.

"No. Looks worse than it feels." I pull my shirt back over the angry red gash marking my ribs.

"Glenting vultures," he mutters.

"Glenting out-of-practice axe skills," I say.

He grins ruefully and draws me into his arms. "What's got you flighty, ore scout?"

Lately, Dram speaks more and more like the Conjies who've taken us in. I feel the rings on his fingers as his hands move over my skin—another bit of Conjie adornment, like the matching cuffs we both wear. But the rest of him is all Subpar. His lips brush mine, and I lean into his kiss, weaving my fingers through his dark hair. My hands skim his shoulders, the hard muscles that mark him for the caver he was, the boy who climbed down tunnels every day after me.

"Orion?" He senses my tension, like there's a line stretched between us that he can feel when it pulls too tight. But how do I tell him what I'm uncertain of myself? "Is it the curtain?"

Four words that state perfectly the nature of our existence. If we Subpars live, it is because the curtain stayed far enough away, that it yielded enough of its cirium to provide a shield, but not so many radioactive particles that it killed us. If the curtain reaches toward us through winds or storms, though . . . we become flash dust the Congress can use to fuel its weapons.

Is it the curtain?

When you live this close to the flashfall, it is *always* the curtain. But Dram knows there's more to it for me.

"I feel it . . . *pressing*," I whisper.

"We're more than thirty kilometers from it," Dram says. "Beyond the flashfall." I can't stand the tension drawing his brows together. I should tell him that I barely sleep at night, that in my dreams the curtain rolls and undulates in waves, an iridescent sea of pink, green, and violet—and it moves. Toward us. Toward *me*, as if I am tied to it so strongly I have the power to bring it with me wherever I go.

I shiver, and Dram slips his blanket around my shoulders. "Talk to me, Rye. What's going on?"

Something. Something bad. But since I don't have any answers, I clasp him around the neck and kiss him. He makes a soft sound of surprise, but then a moment later, his arms wind around me. We fled the cordons, found our way to the freedom of the mountain provinces, but this is our true escape—the places we find together where fear can't follow.

Thunder shakes the ground, blocking out the sounds of our breaths, our soft words. Not thunder.

Engines.

"Dram!"

He shoots up, letting go of me to reach for his guns. Outside our shelter, Conjies shout, a child cries.

"Weapons and warmth," Dram commands, shoving his feet into boots. "The cold can take us as fast as their flash weapons."

We snatch up every weapon that's not already strapped to us, and he tosses me my coat.

A Conjie ducks inside our shelter. "Inquiry Module at the edge of camp—"

We follow him, gliding down a conjured slide to the ground. I gasp. Particle snow. I sense it even before I touch the fresh white powder.

In the feeble dawn sunlight, Conjies flee from the earthen shelters they've conjured; others leap down from the woven branches of tree forts. None of it offers sufficient protection from the Congress's trackers. The orbs swarm in the distance, their sensors glinting with light. If we can't evade them, they'll bring the Inquiry Modules racing to collect us.

Our band of Conjies is small—twenty-six men, women, and children. Fewer than half have fighting experience—but they know how to hide. Trees twist up around us, sending snow and pine needles cascading. Conjured rock juts from the ground, and Dram grasps my arm before I collide with the sudden barrier.

"Camo-cloth," Dram says, digging his cloak from his pack.

I yank mine over my head and thrust my arms through the sleeves. We thread through the trees, blending with the snow whipping up around us.

A Conjuror sends a wall of snow flurries arcing over our camp, shielding us from view of the Inquiry Module approaching from the east. We don't have the kind of weapons necessary to take down one of the unmanned hovers. Bade's the only Conjie I know who can make fire in his hands and throw it, but he's not here now.

It rumbles, nearing, and the Conjies still. They are suddenly tree or rock, nothing but elements the Mod's roving sensor won't see. It drones above us, so low it knocks snow from the treetops.

Buzzing metallic cylinders drop from its hold.

"Pulse trackers," Dram murmurs. These don't need to see us to find us. "Everyone—get wet—they track body heat!"

"The spring's a half kilometer—"

"Get in the snow!" I shout.

They look at me, eyes wide, deciding which danger is worse. If the Congress captures us, we'll be processed and sent into the cordons. The particle snow might not kill us—not right away, anyway.

With Bade away, everyone looks to Dram. And right now, he's looking to me.

His brow creases beneath his cloak's hood. He doesn't want to ask me to take the risk—but he's never had to. I tug my glove off with my teeth and crouch. My heart hammers in my chest, urging me to stop. I thrust my hand into the fresh powder, closing my eyes to better sense the—

Burn. Like paper taken by flame, the way the fire curls the edges before it turns black . . . I breathe past the pain, wedging my hand farther, into the deeper layer of snow. My hand freezes, numb with cold, but that is all.

"Is it safe?" Dram asks.

My eyes meet his, and he curses. "Flash me. How bad, Rye?"

"We need to get deep," I call. "Don't let the fresh snow touch your skin." We're resistant to the curtain's radioactive particles, but not immune. And it's the recent snow the curtain has gifted with its particles, brushing our camp like a radioactive caress.

The pulse trackers whine toward us, drawn to our body heat.

"Get under the snow!" Dram calls.

We burrow, digging ourselves under blankets of fresh powder. The cold soaks through, and I shiver, burrowing deeper. I lie back, gasping when wet droplets snake down my collar. The trackers hum above us, whistling through the air. Roran lifts his hands, cupping dirt, and snow flurries lift from his palm, giving us cover.

We are cold enough that the machines don't register our body heat, but parts of us are on fire. Beside me, in a hastily dug trench, a little girl whimpers.

"Where does it hurt, Briar?" I whisper.

"My hands," she says, shivering. "They burn."

Particle snow. At this elevation, we experience it more than we did down in the outpost. Like the rains and wind that herald a flash storm, they carry with them the deadly particles of the curtain. We should be far enough from the flash curtain to avoid any of its fallout. More proof of what I fear.

"This isn't right," Roran says, shifting in the snow. "It

shouldn't burn like this. We made camp ten kilometers from the boundary marker. We're beyond the flashfall."

"Maybe you read the marker wrong—"

"I didn't read the glenting marker wrong, Meg!"

"Then why is there *glenting particle snow* burning my arms?"

"Quit scrammin' or we're all slayed!" Dram hisses.

"It's shifting," I announce softly. In the hush that follows, I hear wind whining through bare branches. They know I have a connection to the curtain, even if they don't understand it. These are Conjies—people so tied to nature they can transform it at will. They don't question my scout's senses. But it doesn't make them any less afraid.

"What do you mean, it's *shifting*?" Newel asks.

I try to think how to describe what I've been sensing for days. I close my eyes, letting the snow around me numb all outside distractions—shut out the rational side of me that wars with my instinct.

"Pulses," I whisper, and my blood—my Subpar, adapted blood—seems to echo the sentiment. I sit up, and the Conjies watch me like I'm a creature they haven't yet named. "Pulses of energy, like it's testing for holes, pockets of energy that have dissipated. That's why it's worse at night—when the Earth's turned away from the sun. Like it . . . frees the curtain, to stretch, to reach . . ." I'm babbling, I realize, throwing out half-formed theories in an effort to help them understand how much danger we're in. Their wide eyes fasten on me like I'm something that came from the flashfall, something feral.

I *did* come from the flashfall. And I am more a creature of the caverns than they will ever understand.

"Trackers are gone," Dram announces. We dig ourselves from the snow, wet and shivering. "No fires," he says. "Dry clothes and pack up. We need to leave within the hour."

The Conjies set about their tasks without further instruction. This is how they've evaded the Congress for generations. One hour. They will be ready in half that time.

I don't go to collect my gear with Dram. Instead, I jog to the base of the nearest ridge and start climbing.

————

Rock scrapes my palm as I reach past the ledge. My injuries throb, and a sheen of sweat makes my hands slip. I don't have to climb anymore—I'm no longer the ore scout the Congress forced me to be. But I need to see the flash curtain, need to know why its song started humming through my veins again.

I shove my fingers into a shallow crack, scraping the back of my hand. I repeat the action with my other hand and lever my body higher. If I were a Conjie, I'd just weave a vine from rock and pull myself up. But that is not how the curtain affected my people.

How it affects me.

My breath hitches, and the scent of pine winds through my senses, reminding me that I'm beyond the ash of Outpost Five. I let the memories linger as I climb, until the ghosts of the cavers I loved propel me past my limits.

I reach the top, grasping tree roots to hoist myself up.

I have to do this before Dram leads us farther east. He doesn't look back—only forward. He doesn't ever look west beyond this perimeter of mountains, toward the flash curtain. From this vantage, I can make out shifting violet and green hues, stretching like a wall of light from the ground upward as far as I can see. Rivulets of aquamarine shimmer down, as if an artist dripped paint over a canvas. The colors bleed together as I watch.

The sight of it, after two months of living beyond the flash-fall, steals my breath away. Back at Outpost Five, I'd climb the Range and stare out over Cordon Five, catching glimpses of the curtain beyond the sulfur clouds. It strikes me suddenly that I've missed the view.

I have never hated myself more.

This thing destroys everyone I love. It is killing Subpars and Conjurors forced to mine the burnt sands, even as I perch here, safely beyond its reach. And yet . . . it hums a tune inside my soul that I recognize.

I close my eyes and let the wind buffet me, let the sounds of the air whining through the pines block out the sounds of my self-recrimination. Tears streak down my cheeks—from the cold, the wind, I tell myself.

But I know it's shame. I promised them freedom. Even if the cavers I left behind didn't hear me say the words, I know they've heard stories of the Hunter, the Scout who will find a way out for everyone. Months have passed, and we haven't gotten any closer to finding the leader of the resistance—Dram's father, Arrun—and now we've lost contact with Commissary Jameson, the only connection we had to my father somewhere inside Alara. It's taken all we have just to survive, to outrun the Inquiry Modules.

Now this. The curtain is changing. I can sense it, even if I don't understand what's happening. For 150 years, it's been a constant horror that wipes out all life within its perimeter. As bad as it is, at least we've adapted to it, found ways to survive even within the flashfall. But now, all that could change. I feel it deep inside myself, like a cup filled to overflowing.

"I thought I'd find you here." I whirl, surprised to find Dram pulling himself over the ledge. "I've watched you slip away for days now, Orion. Like you have a secret." I don't say anything, and he walks to my side, takes in the view. "Alara's the other way, you know."

I smile, but I can feel tears in my throat. During our first weeks of freedom, I climbed for views of the protected city. I'd watch the sunset reflect off its cirium shield.

"Why aren't you saying anything?" he asks softly.

"Because it's useless to lie to you." And the truth is too terrifying.

"You know something about the flashfall. Why it's changing."

"I couldn't tell you *why* it's happening."

"But it is," he says, asking the question more with his eyes than his words.

"Yes." I turn back toward the horizon, the bands of color shifting in the distance. Green, pink, faintest red. Red is rare. Or it used to be.

"What does that mean for us?"

I don't answer. I just watch the red bands bleed across the sky. He hasn't asked the most important question.

"Fire," he curses. "What does this mean for Subpars left in the outposts?"

My stomach twists. It didn't take him long.

"Fire," I answer, repeating his word that is both curse and truth. It means fire.

Not a literal fire with flames licking the air, but an internal one, that burns from the inside out. The kind of burning our Radbands monitor in shifting shades of green to red. Fire that swept away my beloved mentor, Graham, in a gale of cordon wind, and fire that burned our friend Reeves in pieces, a day at a time.

Exposure to the radioactive particles of the flash curtain takes many forms, but it all ends the same. And it leaves only ashes behind.

———

Conjies have stories.

When we dare to risk firelight, we huddle close, weapons at the ready, satchels packed—ready to flee at the first rumble of an Inquiry Module, the faintest hum of a tracker. Singing and dancing are saved for special occasions, but storytelling, to Conjurors, is like food. Essential. Life-sustaining.

Tonight, I lean against Dram's legs, watching flames flicker. The cadence of Newel's voice lulls me deeper into the tale he weaves as artfully as a song.

"The sun was reaching solar maximum," he says. "But this was not the eleven-year cycle scientists had come to expect, nor the hundred-year cycle they had predicted. These solar storms didn't fit any known pattern. They were the largest on record—sixes and sevens on a five-point scale, and the velocities they traveled were unprecedented."

Conjurors are rarely still. Maybe it's something to do with the energy within them, or their connection with the elements, but as we sit listening, I watch them. I think of Roran and the rock he always clutched in his fist, how he was constantly—secretly—altering it. *Practice*, his father had told him. I wonder if it's more than that, though. Like maybe, on some level, they need to conjure, need to maintain an exchange of energy with the natural world.

He sits apart from the rest of us, on the fringes of the camp. Firelight dances over him, leaving the rest in shadow. He stares into the woods, and I wonder if he's watching for flash vultures or maybe for his mother to suddenly emerge. I used to do that with Mom. An entire year after seven collapsed, I still looked for her in the caves. He conjures something in his hand. Dirt morphs into white flowers, which turn to ash before the petals have unfurled, and back to dirt. Dirt-flowers-ash, over and over, while he stares toward the darkness.

I wonder if Dram senses the energy crackling between the Conjurors. The air feels alive tonight. With memories, with magic.

Newel continues his story, speaking of our past, but I'm struck suddenly with a sense of our future. It stirs in me, like a creature waking. Possibility.

"What if we use the Mods against them?" I say.

Heads turn, and on many faces are the looks I've grown accustomed to. Expressions that ask unspoken questions.

"How do you mean?" Newel asks.

"They come from behind the shield, they return there. What if we could . . . harness one? Without them knowing?"

"We're hunted as it is," Newel answers. "We can't risk provoking the Congress further."

"We've lost connection to my father. Maybe from inside Alara it would be possible to—"

"We survive because we hide," Newel says.

"What about those with no place to hide? Subpars and Conjies trapped in the flashfall?"

"We help when we can. Bade and Aisla are tracking Arrun. We wait."

Wood pops, and sparks lift into the air. Arguments collide in my mind, reasons why we cannot simply *wait*. Mainly, the names and faces of my friends left behind.

"When was the first Conjie Tempered?" I ask.

Newel studies me, as if searching for the hidden meaning in my question. "A hundred years ago. After the first rebellion."

"A hundred years," I say. "And you want to wait more?"

"We're not the revolutionaries we once were."

"Maybe we should be," a voice calls. Bade strides into camp, covered in mud and leaves. Branches weave around his arms—he looks more tree than man. I realize it's intentional, conjured concealment. Another figure pulls away from the forest, mud covering her blond hair. Aisla. Beneath the bark and branches, they wear guns.

I look past them, hoping to see another person wander in from the trees.

"Did you find Arrun?" Newel asks.

"No." Bade holds his palm against his arm, and the branches morph and dissolve to dust he brushes away. "The outlier regions are overrun with Striders. The Congress set guard towers along the pass. We barely made it out."

"So we have no word from him."

"I didn't say that." Bade hands Newel what looks like a packet of leaves. "One of his men managed to get us this message."

Newel conjures the leaves away, then holds up an object that doesn't belong in a camp of free Conjies. "What does it mean?"

Bade shakes his head. "I have no idea."

———————

MORIOR INVICTUS.

Death before defeat.

I stare at the words emblazoned on the patch. Dram grasps it tightly, the only message from his father. No note. No instructions. Just this patch torn from a Strider's uniform. In the months we've been in the mountain provinces, this is the first we've heard from him.

Morior invictus. The Latin words arc above the symbol of a coiled snake with fangs bared. I try to imagine how Arrun got hold of it. Striders wear electrified armor.

"This was all he sent?" I ask.

Bade sighs. "If there was more to this message, it's been lost."

Dram presses his lips together in a tight line, probably holding back the words we're all thinking. Whatever Arrun's been doing in the outlier regions, it's likely to cost him his life. There are scorch marks on the jagged bit of cloth. And blood. He breathes a curse and shoves it into his pocket.

"It's a sign he's still alive," Bade says.

"That's one way of seeing it," Dram mutters.

"Our coms system is compromised," Bade says. "We can't even get through to Jameson right now. Not with Alara on lockdown as it is."

"What about Orion's father?" Dram asks. "Any word from him?"

Bade's features tighten further. "Nothing. I'm sorry."

Two months with no word.

Dram and I thought we could save our people. So far, we've only put them in more danger.

———

We crouch beside Alara's shield, camo-cloth draping us head to foot. Dram shifts beside me, and the cloth ripples in shades of moonlight-touched silver. I wouldn't have known he'd moved if I weren't pressed against his side, if I hadn't felt his armored body brush mine. It's a move I recognize—something we did crawling through tunnels back in Outpost Five. A shift of weight, a stretch of muscles to keep legs from going numb.

We need to be able to move—to run—at a moment's notice.

We haven't spoken in over an hour, since we took our places here. I can't even read his eyes. We wear the camo-cloth draped over our faces, so that when I look in the direction of his head, I see only the cirium shield reflected back at me. I touch my own with a camo-cloth glove, just to make sure I haven't disappeared. We've gotten so used to hiding that at times I lose myself.

It's the only tech we allow ourselves. The Congress has tracked every screencom, every device. With the commissaries secured somewhere within Alara's Central Tower, we've been cut off from Jameson. From my father.

From our plans to get a cure to our people.

The moon rises in a cloudless sky. I look up at it, feeling a mixture of wonder and trepidation. Wonder, because I never saw it from Outpost Five—the cloudlike layer of flashfall blocked the sky from view. Trepidation, because we risk capture with this plan.

First night of a full moon. According to Bade, it's when Jameson positions one of his Striders at the third shield entrance. I am not absolutely positive that it's not the *second* night of a full moon. What if it is? I glance at Dram, but see only a thin outline of a shape slightly incongruent with the shield. I want to ask him, How do we know this is the right time? For that matter, are we certain this is the third shield entrance?

I don't ask. Dram is desperate for word of his father, as am I. He has become more like me—moved to action and less to thought.

We track time in constellations, slowly trekking across the sky. Two hours. Four. Finally, a narrow passage opens beside us a meter from Dram's hand. I hear the click of his gun. He lifts it, hidden under the cloth—just in case.

A Strider emerges, electrified armor humming. Dram tenses.

The Strider mutes his armor, then slowly scuffs his boot across the ground, forming a mark: two slanted parallel lines. Still, we don't move. Even Alarans know this symbol now—a caver's mark that's become a rallying cry for Subpars and Conjies, anyone oppressed by the Congress. An easy enough trap to draw us out.

"I can see your heat signatures," the Strider says, looking in our direction.

"Can you see my gun aimed at your head?" Dram asks.

The Strider lifts his face shield. "If Bade trained you, then I'd expect nothing less."

We push back the hoods shielding our faces, but Dram doesn't lower his gun.

The Strider stares at me until I begin to fidget under his close scrutiny. "I can't believe you risked coming here," he says.

"Tell me it was worth it," Dram murmurs. "Do you have a message from Jameson?"

"They're coming after you with something new. Something worse than trackers and Inquiry Mods."

"When?"

"He's already out there, tracking you."

"He?"

"A Conjie that escaped from the prison cordon. They say he caught Orion once before."

Dram swears beneath his breath. I can't speak. I can't breathe.

It's not possible. The Congress dropped flash bombs on that compound. I barely saved Dram in time—

"His name," Dram demands softly.

"King," the Strider answers. "He calls himself King."

My mind floods with images, memories buried in the deepest parts of myself. The man sizing me up alongside his gang of dusters, cannibals thrilling to the scent of blood. I hear an odd wheezing sound and realize it's coming from me.

"He's just one man, Rye," Dram says.

"Three," the Strider says. "He leads a squad of three Untempered Conjies. They wear cirium tracking collars—that's how you'll know them."

"Why would he help the Congress?" I ask.

"They captured and interrogated him, then sent him off to hunt you. His life, in exchange for the Scout." The Strider glances at a screencom on his wrist. "I'm out of time. One last thing—" He activates his armor, then lifts his voice over the hum of the current. "Within the next few days, a Skimmer will deviate from its flight path and drop supplies in grid echo six. I don't know what the cargo is, but Jameson says you're going to want to be there." He lowers his helmet visor and turns toward the shield.

"Wait," Dram says. "Did he say anything about our fathers?"

"If Jameson knows where they are, he's not entrusting that information to anyone. After you two, they're the most wanted Subpars in the city-state."

THREE

I TEAR MY hood back the moment we reach the trees. It's thin cloth, but I suck in air like I was suffocating. Dram lifts his hood, and I can see the storm in his eyes.

"Go ahead," I murmur. "Tell me we'll be fine. We handled King before, we will again." Dram releases a shaky breath and drags a hand through his hair.

Moments pass. He doesn't offer me any false assurances.

"He doesn't know the provinces," Dram says finally. "Congress might've supplied him with tech, but he won't know how the free Conjies move, or what our camps look like."

He's right. Free Conjies use their abilities to blend with nature. Not even Dram and I would've found them on our own. They aren't usually seen unless they want to be seen.

"He's not a free Conjie," Dram adds. This, more than anything, assures me. Conjurors born free—beyond the bonds of Alara—are raised attuned to the elements and develop abilities beyond those of their counterparts in the protected city.

"Conjuring ability won't matter," I say. "If he gets close enough, he can use tech."

"Then we don't let him get close."

We lift our hoods back over our heads and blend into the night.

———

I sit beside the fire, my knife within reach. Newel posted extra Conjies to stand watch, and I've stayed up with them, feeding logs into the fire.

"Let him come," they say, with a sort of nervous anticipation.

They don't understand King. It makes me think of when Meg found us hunting flash vultures and tried to assure us they were "just birds." King is just a man, a Conjie, but he is also something feral, with the hunger of a flash vulture.

Dram, Bade, Aisla, and Roran surround me—in ways not meant to seem obvious. Dram must've told them some of the story, about cages and dusters and a place called Sanctuary.

Fear can be helpful, Graham would say. *Keeps us from staying in one place too long. Sometimes it nudges us in the right direction.*

I sit sketching, putting an idea to paper. The more details I add, the more I convince myself it's real.

"What are you drawing?" Aisla asks, looking over my shoulder.

"Working on a theory," I say, shifting so she can see the map I've sketched. "This is Cordon Five—" I point to one edge of the paper. "This is where the Barrier Range was before the Congress blew it up, and these are the places where I think the tunnels are. If they didn't all collapse."

"What's so important about tunnel six?" she asks, skimming her finger over the place I've filled in with the most detail.

Roran lifts his head. He doesn't look at us, but I watched his shoulders tense when I mentioned Cordon Five. I haven't shared this with him—not even with Dram. I didn't acknowledge the idea to myself at first, either, but it kept circling my thoughts, fighting past my shock and grief.

"It's where my friends are, if they're still alive."

"Why do you think that?" Aisla asks.

"Water." I speak the word like a prayer, a hopeful belief, too fragile to throw out carelessly. Like the shell on display in the lodge at Outpost Five—small and chipped, yet powerful enough to make us believe in a place we'd never seen.

It's like the word is a summons. First Dram, then Bade and even Roran lean in to see what I've drawn. I feel suddenly like Dad, having to explain equations I haven't finished solving.

"The Sky," Dram murmurs, his gaze skipping over the sketch, reading it like a caver. Suddenly his eyes widen, and I know the moment he latches onto my idea. Blue eyes meet mine over the tops of heads.

"What do you think?" I ask.

"If Owen or Roland survived, then it's possible. If the cavern held."

"Somebody translate their caver's code," Bade grumbles.

"Survival," I answer. "With Roran gone, the first thing they would've gone after was a water source. There's nothing in the cordon, so they would've had to go back in the direction of Outpost Five—but just as far as the rubble of the Barrier Range. Specifically, tunnel six."

"How do you know?" Bade asks.

"Most cave water isn't safe to drink—the bacteria will make

you sick. But down six is a pool of blue water, a secret memorial cavern that every caver knows how to find—the Sky."

"Wouldn't Roran have seen them?"

"Cordon Five is clouded with flashfall—it's one of the things that make it a good place to hide. If they were sheltering underground from flashbursts, I can see how they might've lost each other. They wouldn't have spent more than a day searching for Roran—" I glance at him. "I'm sorry, but Owen wouldn't have let them. He knew you could survive, and he would've had to think about keeping the others alive."

"Owen?" Bade asks. "He's a Subpar?"

"Yes, a Third Ray caver, and a scout. He would've been the one to lead them."

"You're assuming they could dig their way down through rock and rubble to this cavern?"

"They could," Dram says.

"They had full caving gear," I add. "Oxinators, rations, medkits . . . If they survived the flashburst—and if the cavern held—there's a good chance they're alive."

"It's been two months," Aisla murmurs. "If they ran out of rations . . ."

"Tunnel gulls," Dram and I say at the same time.

"It's how the forfeit survived," he says. "Subpars who were sentenced down tunnel four for noncompliance weren't supplied with rations."

"There's more," I say softly. "This cavern, it's . . ."

Sacred doesn't seem like the right word. I'm not sure I can put the Sky into words.

"It's like a talisman," Dram says. "If a place could be a talisman."

Bade studies us for a long moment. Finally he nods. "Then you have to go after them. Somehow."

I lift my gaze to the young boy standing so still. Too still, like the wrong word might make him shatter. "I don't want to give you false hope, Roran. I could be wrong about all of this."

"My mom would've stayed," he says, his voice thick with emotion.

"I know." Maybe this is why I didn't share my thoughts earlier—because he's right. It's possible Mere would've died searching the cordon before she gave up trying to find her son. Her mother's instinct is stronger than her survival instinct. My eyes fill with tears. I drop my gaze, but too late. Roran runs off.

"Let him grieve her," Bade says. "We don't have any real reason to believe she's alive. That any of them are."

"Just a fragile hope," I murmur.

"No such thing," Aisla says. I meet her green eyes, which are filled with some emotion I can't interpret. "Dram said the Sky is a talisman. I'd say that's pretty powerful."

———

The screams sound inhuman.

I jolt upright, still caught in the foggy remnants of a restless sleep. It's dark; the fire has died. I listen for the sound that woke me. Was it a vulture? It sounded like a man. A man in pain. The ground shifts beneath me, and I shove my sleeve up and use the glow of my Radband to see it. At first, I don't understand how the pine needles and dirt seem to be melting. Then, suddenly, I do. *King.*

"Orion!" Dram's voice, but garbled, like he's drown—

I sink. Mud surrounds me, sucks me deeper. I scream, and it fills my mouth. I struggle to lift my arms above my head. It's like lifting my caving gear. Mud oozes into my ears, my eyes. I thrash but barely move.

How like King, to kill us horribly rather than trading us for freedom.

All at once, the mud evaporates. I flop forward onto a carpet of grass, coughing, spitting mud. My arms weigh a thousand pounds, but I drag them across my eyes so I can see. Roran crouches at my side, his hands still pressed to the ground. He grits his teeth, and the mud pushes back.

"Stay down!" he shouts.

He saved us. I can't speak. Dram drags himself across the ground to my side. He holds his pistol out to Roran, who grasps it and conjures away the mud without looking. We scan the darkness for our attackers.

King laughs, the sound lifting from the trees a few meters away. Dram levels his gun at the shadows.

"Ah, how I've missed you, Orion," King says. I stand, shaking, mute, caked in mud. My lungs ache. Part of me is still drowning. "The Congress promoted me," he says.

"You're still wearing their collar," I mutter.

They leap from the trees like wolves, all three of them at once. A wall of clashing matter collides as free Conjies rush to meet them. Energy pulses around us, exchanges of matter so rapid it makes my head spin. A scent on the air, verdant, like grass pulled up from the roots. Then fire, smoke, and electricity in the air like lightning.

Gunshots rip across the night, the sounds reverberating over the mountains. Birds scatter from the trees, children cry. Men shout, and I can't tell if they are ours or theirs.

Bade rushes by, arms swinging, fire launching from his

hands. He catches one of the men in the chest, knocking him off his feet. The man yells, and I recognize the sound that woke me. He conjures the flames to water, then lurches up, aiming a weapon unlike any I've seen. Something illuminates Bade's hands, like the ionic marks trackers use, then twin bolts launch toward him. Webs of metal wrap around Bade's hands. Cirium binders.

"The Congress gave us toys to play with," the man calls.

I run to Bade's side, reaching for a weapon. My knife. I left it back beside the fire. It's somewhere deep beneath the earth, in mud that isn't mud anymore.

"Rye!" Dram shouts. He throws his pickaxe, and I catch it.

I grasp Bade's bound hands and shove them against a rock. "Don't move." Every metal has its breaking point. Even cirium.

"You can do this?" Bade asks, his eyes wide.

"I'm really good at this." I focus on the loose links and swing my axe. The metal shatters apart. Bade frees his hands, muttering Conjie words I don't know. Then he conjures a spear of rock that sails across the clearing into the man's chest.

"Conjure *that* to water," Bade mutters. The man collapses to the ground.

Suddenly, King grabs me from behind, his hands around my throat.

"Stop!" he shouts. "One move—from any of you—and I conjure a branch right through her neck."

Everyone stills.

"Weapons down." King slides a glance to Dram.

Dram reluctantly drops his gun, his gaze fastened to King's hand on my throat.

"The Congress wants the Scout and Berrends. Alive. We're going to take them, and you're going to let us."

"No."

We all look to see who dares refuse the mad Conjie. Aisla. Bade's bonded mate. She walks toward King as if he's not about to spear me with conjured bark. She extends her left arm to Bade, and he grasps her forearm. I stare in shock as he conjures away her *skin*. A blue Codev glows in its place.

"You can conjure a Codev?" King asks. Even he sounds impressed.

"Ordinance gave me this," Aisla answers. "Bade just helps me hide it."

"You see that symbol on her arm?" King's man calls. "She's a *Vigil*! We need to get away—"

"CEASE!" King roars. "I have the power here! I'm not afraid of some Gem."

"You should be," Aisla says. She shifts her arm, and the collared man jolts, then drops like a stone.

King's hand loosens, and I lurch from his grasp. He conjures a rock wall and dives into the trees. Bade and Aisla sprint after him. Dram retrieves his gun and jogs to my side. He pulls me into his arms.

"They'll have announced our location to the Congress," Newel calls. "We move. Now!"

Dram and I turn to gather our gear, and Newel stops me with a hand on my arm.

"I haven't seen Aisla's Codev since she was a child," he says. "You must be very special to her."

"She's special to a lot of people," Dram says.

"Yes, but Aisla risked more than her life by revealing herself like that."

"They'll come after her?" I ask.

"Not the Congress," Newel says. "Ordinance."

"She's not a Conjuror, then?"

"No. She was sent to hunt us, years ago. We adopted her instead." He looks at the Conjies hurriedly loading supplies. "I suppose that's the nature of secrets. Apply enough pressure, and they unravel. Nothing stays hidden indefinitely."

———

Bade and Aisla meet up with us hours later, slinking in from the woods, once more looking like they're part of it.

"The Congress picked him up before we could get to him," Bade announces grimly. He conjures away their camouflage, and I see that Aisla's Codev is again just a smooth patch of skin.

"Thank you," I tell her. I glance at the other Conjurors, hard at work constructing a new camp, even more concealed than the last. "Did they know about you?"

"Yes. Conjies are good at keeping secrets."

"What you did to that man . . . Can all Gems do that?"

"No. Vigils are genetically modified for a specific purpose."

"King probably told them what you did," I say. "They know your secret now."

"Not all of them," she says softly. "This world is changing." She looks up toward the flashfall, visible in the distance. "Not even the provinces are safe anymore. The flash curtain, the Congress—it's all so unpredictable." She crouches and draws an inverted V in the snow. "Only Vigils bear this mark," she says. "If you ever see this symbol on a Codev—run."

FOUR

41.6 km from flash curtain

I SLING MY pack over my shoulder, and it drags across the flare wound. I groan aloud, shoving the pack off and dropping it on the ground. I sink to a rock, peeling back my cloak and shirt as the burn pulses in time with my heart.

I don't want to look at it. I've seen enough burns that I know what it looks like, and how the skin will eventually heal into a puckered scar. But this wasn't a normal wound; this was the flash curtain, reaching across boundaries to brand me.

Dram's checked it each day, to make sure the strange luminescent streaks didn't come back. I turned my head away each time, too afraid I'd see the flash curtain's imprint on my body again. I can feel it oozing now, the skin torn open from our fight with King.

"You have a bad owie."

I glance up. Briar stands over me, her conjured cloak dwarfing her small frame.

"Yes," I whisper, trying to muster a smile. I slap a handful of snow over my wound, hoping to numb the pain.

"Mom says aloe for burns." She kneels beside me and digs in the snow until she uncovers a green shoot. I wonder if she sensed it was there, like Subpars sense cirium in stone. She peels off her mittens and cradles the blade of grass. The grass quivers, like it's waking up. It grows, stretches, as if spring just announced its arrival.

My pulse quickens. I never tire of watching Conjurors in that moment when they shift matter to something else. I realize I'm stretching my hand toward that shivering plant, like I'm somehow part of its alteration, as if I can feel the energy making it something new. It widens, splits; spines ripple along its length, and pointy fronds burst from the center.

"Aloe," she says, breaking off a spiny leaf. She squeezes the juice along my wound. I hiss from the touch, but moments later the cool liquid chases away the burn. She snaps another pad from the plant and dabs it over my skin, humming softly.

She is a child of nature. Everything we Subpars have sacrificed was to protect the remnant of natural humanity inside the city, but I wonder if our society has been looking at it wrong this whole time.

"It will heal now," she says.

"Thank you," I murmur.

Healers. These people are healers, and the Congress is exterminating them.

I think of all the wounds torn open by our city-state—the families ripped apart in the outposts, and the miners burning in the cordons. A Protocol that preserves some people and not others.

I wonder if Alara could ever heal.

Maybe. If we use our abilities to transform what is into something new.

––––––––

My wound still aches as I jog from our camp, but instead of slowing me down, it propels me, a warning of a single truth that can no longer be ignored. The flash curtain is expanding its reach, and if we don't act soon, it will take hold of us all.

"Orion, wait!" Roran calls. His gaze travels over my pack to the climbing harness I'm wearing. "I know you're planning something. I want to help."

"It's too dangerous."

"As if things around here are ever *safe*." He lifts his wrist to show the flash vulture feather he wears as a cuff. "This is my fight as much as it's yours."

"No."

"How long have you been hiding from the Congress?" he asks. "A few months? I've been running from them my entire life."

"I'm going after a Mod."

Words die on his lips, and he simply stares. "What do you mean 'going after'?"

"I'm going to climb a charging station and bolt onto one of them. Ride it straight into Alara."

A smile spreads across his face. "The camo-cloth . . ." I can see him mentally piecing together my plan. "But the platform is fifty meters high. How do you plan to—"

He breaks off when I shift my coat to reveal the climbing harness strapped tightly around my waist and thighs. From my belt sways Dram's old climbing bolt gun and a dozen bolts.

He shakes his head. "Not good enough. Those platforms are alive with current. Even if you made the climb without attracting attention, I'm sure your charred corpse would hinder the rest of your plan."

I glare at him.

He shrugs. "You need to think like a Conjie."

"Fine. What would a *Conjie* do?"

"It's better if I show you." He shoves two handfuls of dirt into his pockets and strides ahead of me, in the direction of the one remaining charging station.

————

We're silent the first few kilometers, stealthily trekking through the woods. Then we pass through the trees at the top of a ridge and see it rising from the ground like a finger balancing a plate. I was never really aware of the charging towers before. Not with the visceral awareness thrumming through me now. Seeing them and knowing you're about to climb to the top of one are very different things. I step forward, before fear paralyzes me.

"Wait." Roran catches my arm. "Not much cover once we head down the ridge."

"Except what you conjure."

"True." He plucks a pinecone off the ground and closes both hands around it. Seconds later his fingers spread apart, revealing the shiny skin of an apple. He hands it to me and conjures water. "There won't be time for rations once you anchor onto that Mod."

I crunch the apple down to the core, not even tasting it. I don't tell him that my stomach is a twisting ball of nerves. Instead, I hand him my loaded gun. "In case of flash vultures."

"You've seen more of them?"

I consider lying, just to spare him, but I can't think of a time that has ever helped any of us. I nod.

His features harden, like water turning to ice. "Let them come," he murmurs, lifting dirt from his pocket. The soil bounces in his palm, twisting on an invisible wind current, then suddenly explodes in thick spikes of wood, a five-pointed star with tips sharp as blades. "Keep your gun," he says.

"Promise me—if something goes wrong, you'll get out of there."

He conjures the wood back to dirt. "They won't catch me."

We race down the ridge at the same time.

"I should warn you," I call, "this plan has a lot of holes." *Foolish, reckless, headstrong.* The words pass through my mind on a loop, sometimes in Dram's voice; other times it's Graham, shaking his head at me with a caver's whistle clamped between his teeth. *Stop, Orion. Think.*

Fire sparks inside me, the way it did in Outpost Five when I climbed the sign that hung before the tunnels. WE ARE THE FORTUNATE ONES, it said. I had beaten the words with my axe like a battle cry.

And the Congress punished every Subpar for my noncompliance.

But this is different. I'm not just reacting in anger. I'm going to do something that will help everyone.

Beneath my resolve unease tingles, like I'm stretching my hand toward an electrified fence. We run toward the station, and all the while anxiety dances in my belly to the tune of *foolish, reckless, headstrong.*

I press my fingers against my flare burn, and pain answers, overriding my thoughts, my senses.

"What are you doing?" Roran asks.

"Reminding myself."

"Of what?

"That doing nothing isn't an option."

FIVE

35.3 km from flash curtain

THE CHARGING STATION towers above the treetops, a solitary metal pole. Even from the ground we can hear its disk-shaped top buzzing with current.

I tip my head back, but I can't see much from the forest floor. My mind fills in the parts of my plan I can't see—from the times I watched Inquiry Modules drone through and land atop these stations. This is one of the few that Conjies haven't destroyed or disabled. Mostly because it's too close to Alara, and not worth the risk. Ideal for my purposes.

"You're really going to do this?" Roran asks.

In answer, I adjust my camo-cloth cloak, lifting the hood so it conceals me.

"What if getting close to it shocks you?" he asks.

"I won't touch the charging pad—just the Mod."

"So you secure yourself to the outside of the pod and ride it back into Alara. You do realize the drones are kept in the military compound?"

"Which I've been to once before, so it's familiar to me." I

don't mention that Bade and Aisla are the only reason that Dram and I escaped with our lives. I strap a water bottle to my side and fill my pockets with nuts and dried fruit, conjured food I've been saving for the past few days.

"And then—if you're still miraculously alive and uncaught— you're going to sneak into the central part of the city? And track down your father?"

"The last time I had contact with him, they were testing the cure. He had *done it*, Roran—finally created a way for all Subpars and Conjies to live free within the flashfall—and then no communication from him for two months. Something's off. I don't trust . . ." For some reason, I don't say his name. Jameson. The commissary playing both sides of the fence. He has a habit of helping me and betraying me at the same time.

But there's more to it. He and I have Mom in common. He knew things about her—about her past and her life before Outpost Five. Before Dad and me. I'm not sure how, but it connects us in ways I don't want to think about.

"How exactly are you going to find your father?" Roran asks.

"That's the part of the plan with the holes."

"Great," he mutters. "When Dram kills me for letting you do this, I'm going to blame you."

"Just conjure the tree, Roran."

He twists a wooden bead from his sash. A moment passes, and it trembles in his palm. Roots burst, twining around his hand before he drops it and it explodes into the ground, the roots growing, pushing up dirt.

"Better step back," he says.

I duck as a branch thrusts from the trunk, twisting, shooting upward. He presses his hands against the bark and closes his eyes. This tree isn't free to grow however it wants. I need it to reach the charging platform.

The benefit of unmanned Inquiry Modules is that they lack sense. A machine won't think anything of a tree growing exactly parallel to the charging station, nor branches that reach conveniently above the platform. Sometimes a Mod's scanner feed is directed back to techs inside Alara, but that's only if Conjies have been detected. I don't plan to be detected.

Roran's arms shake against the tree as it grows and twists beneath his touch. "Tell me when it's tall enough," he calls.

"Another few meters!" Leaves burst from the ends of branches, and the verdant smell lifts around us. He laughs, a carefree, happy sound I haven't heard from him since Outpost Five. Then, above the sound of wood cracking and snapping—rumbling. I peer up past the branches. "There's a Mod approaching! About five kilometers away."

"Get climbing!"

"The tree's still forming—"

"Climb!"

I leap and grasp the lowest branch and hoist myself up. The tree moves, stretching toward the sky as I climb. My arms disappear from view as the camo-cloth adapts to exact shades of bark and leaves.

"I can't see you," Roran calls. "How high are you?"

"Halfway." I'm leaping now, thrusting my body upward.

"That Mod is less than a kilometer away. You're not going to be able to climb the rest fast enough."

"How about you conjure me some steps," I mutter. If this were rock, I'd have made it to the top already. But this is a shifting, morphing Conjie tree, and one false step will send me plunging over the side. I've slipped twice already.

"How much do you trust me?" Roran shouts.

"I'm thirty meters off the ground in a tree that sprouted from your hands!"

"Right. I'm going to try something. Slip your hood off so I can see you."

I feel the approach of the Mod, a subtle vibration beneath my fingers. "No more talking! Its sensors are activated!"

"Fine. Just—hold on tight!"

Vines shoot up around the trunk of the tree, curling around me, lifting me as they climb up through the branches. I pull free when I reach the top and tug my hood up. I want to shout with elation. I want to tell Roran his idea was brilliant, but I must stay silent. Invisible.

I stretch out along the branch as the Mod rumbles above the platform. I'm in place. Ready. As it begins its descent, I turn my head, squinting against the beam of light from its scanner. I force myself to breathe steadily. In a few moments, it will dock and then I'll secure myself to the backside of its rounded body. I unholster Dram's old climbing bolt gun and wait. Just a few more seconds. The Mod approaches, its thrusters kicking the leaves into a frenzy, pushing at me so powerfully my limb sways. It descends past the platform.

I stare at the bit of sky where the Mod should be. Why didn't it dock? Nearly all Mods charge here before returning to Alara. A sick feeling blooms in the pit of my stomach.

Roran shouts.

"NO!" I thrust my cloak back and wave my arms, but the drone has zeroed in on Roran.

It takes me too long to descend the tree. Bark scrapes my hands, my face, as I direct my body in a guided fall to the ground. Beneath me, Roran fights.

We survive because we hide, Newel said. But he wasn't speaking for Roran.

I'm halfway down when the metal arms stretch toward him. He conjures rock—midair—so that a boulder slams down atop one of the clamps. The machine whirs and lifts, disengaging from its trapped claw.

Branches snatch at my hair as I drop the last five meters.

"Roran!" I shout, running toward him.

A needle speeds toward Roran, and he conjures a wall of rock so fast it slams into it, snapping off. But another metallic arm seizes him from behind, pinching him around his waist and lifting him into the pod.

I take the stance Dram taught me and empty every bullet I have into the Mod. Holes pit the metal, but the lid seals shut, muffling Roran's shouts. Then the thrusters engage.

"Fire, oh, fire!" I pound my fists against the metal, but there's no lever, no visible way for me to unlock the opening. It begins to lift.

I don't stop to think. By the time it leaves the ground, I've anchored myself into the side of the craft with climbing bolts and rope knotted to my harness.

We climb—not high, maybe a dozen meters off the ground. Usually Mods streak across the sky as if they are a part of it. This one lurches like it's being kicked out of the air. Perhaps my bullets affected it after all. We rise slowly above the treetops, and I strain to make out landmarks. East. We're heading east.

Toward the flash curtain.

I'm latched to the craft, just as I'd planned, but riding this Mod now won't get me to Alara. Occupied Mods take their victims directly to the Overburden for processing. A wild thought streaks through my mind. I could disable the Mod before it can take us farther. I press my cheek to the metal and try to measure the dangers of crashing against the dangers of the Overburden.

All I have to do is imagine Roran with appendages for hands. The scales tip.

I reach for my gun, then remember I've used every bullet. I pat down my sides. What could I possibly use to stop this thing? My axe is back at camp. Knives—useless. My fingers brush the bolt gun.

I snatch one of the last two bolts from my harness and load the gun, pointing at the Mod's thrusters. A horrendous sound rends the air as the bolt collides with the inside of the engine. Metal groans; sparks burst from the thruster port. We drop, the ground rushes up, and then the Mod sputters and lifts, as some kind of secondary power kicks in. I dangle from the belly of the craft, my feet hitting branches as it cuts an unsteady path through the trees.

"Orion!" Roran shouts. I'm surprised I can hear him through the pod's glass. I picture his face in my mind, an expression that begs me to help. One I've seen before.

A gulp of air, then I let go of my handhold. I sway, careening against the metal body of the Mod, but I need both hands free to load the bolt gun a final time. I unclip the last remaining bolt, clasping it so tightly it cuts my hand. I cannot drop it. I can't fail him a second time.

I fit the bolt to the gun, thinking how Dram would do this

without even looking. Only, this was never the way he secured climbing anchors.

I lift the bolt gun a final time, aiming with unsteady hands. I twirl from my rope, and the forest spins around me in a blur. I focus on the smoke seeping from the thruster port like blood. The beast is injured but not mortally. Not yet.

I fire.

A high-pitched whining pierces the air, and the engine screams. It coughs flame and shards of metal. We spiral toward the ground, and I clutch my handhold. Roran yells.

We crash through trees, snapping branches. There's no longer a wisp of smoke, but a plume of black so thick it fills my vision. I don't see the branches the craft collides with, but I hear them cracking in protest as the Mod slams against them.

The craft shudders like a beast in its death throes. My only hope is that it won't explode before I can get Roran free.

I wish I could conjure. I'd weave thick vines to catch us, keep us from hammering into the ground. Suddenly, as if my thoughts brought them to life, branches twist around the falling Mod, catching hold of trees like hands grasping a ledge. I slam against the side of the craft as it jolts to a stop. We sway above the forest floor.

"Hurry!" Roran shouts. He leaps from the cracked pod lid, vines twisting and streaming beneath his hands. I grab hold and release myself from the Mod. I tumble to the ground in a glide of vines and leaves.

Roran lands beside me. We lie on our backs, catching our breath.

We are alive. I can hardly believe it.

The Mod bursts into flames.

I don't even shout at him to run. I lurch to my feet and yank him up by the arm. We sprint as far as we can, then collapse behind a shelter of rock, chests heaving.

"Glenting hell," Roran says breathlessly. We watch smoke plume, and even at this distance, the crackle of fire reaches us. "It would've taken me for processing."

"Yes."

"You saved me."

"I made us crash. You saved us."

"I can't ever be Tempered, Orion."

"I know. I should never have risked this."

"Still. We took down an Inquiry Module."

I smile. Our eyes meet, his brown. Same brown as his mom's. "You know who would've loved seeing that," I say. It's not a question. We both know. He nods, and those brown eyes shine with unshed tears. But he smiles. The first one I've seen since he found us.

"You're alive." Dram's voice, his tone a mix of shock and stark relief. I whirl to see him on the edge of our rock shelter.

"What are you doing here?" I ask.

"Well you know, *step in my steps* and all that." His bitterness is an unexpected jab. I've never heard him use our cavers' creed like an insult.

"You shouldn't have come after me."

"Oh, right. You wanted me to just sit around while you ran off chasing Inquiry Modules—"

"I had a plan!"

"Your *plans* get people *killed*, Orion!"

His words gouge me. Tear into me like a flash vulture.

"I'm trying to *save* us."

"Fire, don't I know it," he mutters. He checks an ammo clip and slams it into his gun. "There's smoke pouring from a downed Mod a few kilometers from our camp. How long before they send more to scour this area? Did you think *at all*, Orion?"

"That wasn't supposed to happen. I was going to—"

"How did it crash?"

"I shot bolts into the thruster." His eyes widen.

"*Climbing* bolts?" He looks back at the wreckage and drags his hands through his hair. "*Glenting hell*, Orion."

"It had Roran!"

"So when Striders examine that Mod, they'll find it was attacked by someone using miner's climbing bolts. Subpar gear from the outposts. They'll know it's *us*!"

The enormity of what he's saying slams into me.

The free Conjies are hunted, but it's nothing compared to the Congress's relentless pursuit of Dram and me. We are targets on the backs of anyone who shelters us.

"Oh, fire," Roran murmurs. A look of horror crosses his face, and Dram and I turn at the same time. Trackers erupt from the Mod's port. I'd assumed we'd damaged them in the crash. Some of them catch fire as they burst from the crippled Mod.

I think of ore mites, down the tunnels, how the true threat was when you split them open and their parasites emerged.

Foolish, reckless, headstrong.

"We have to warn them." Dram's grim tone hits my blood like ice.

"Roran," I say, gripping the boy's shoulders. "Stay here. Hide."

I turn away while he's still arguing with me. *Please*, I think. *Just this once, do as you're told.* And then, when I hear him racing through the trees behind Dram and me, I think: *I'm sorry, Mere.*

We run through the forest, our boots crunching over fallen branches. Dram activates the screencom on his wrist.

"I thought we weren't supposed to use those."

"I've got to risk it." He lifts the tech to his mouth. "Newel, come in. You've got trackers coming. From the southeast."

"Dram!" Newel's voice crackles through. Static garbles the rest of his words.

"Newel! Did you hear me?" Dram adjusts the com, glancing down as we dodge between trees. "You need to take shelter!" Shouts burst from the com speaker.

". . . already . . . here!" We reach the top of the ridge as he says it. But it's worse than that. We can see more than Newel from our vantage point, and trackers are the least of their problems now. "Mods!" Newel's voice breaks through. "Too many . . . surrounded—"

Dram powers down the com device and retrieves a gun. He loads it with a grim determination I've only seen this side of the flash curtain.

"Did I do this?" I have to know.

"That Mod you destroyed was a signal flare to the Congress!" He turns, and I grasp his arm. "Don't go. If you're caught—"

"*Don't go?* I can't believe you'd ask that!"

"Your Radband—"

"They need us!" He yanks his arm from my grasp and runs toward the camp. Cries lift on the wind, piercing past the drone of trackers. Roran follows in his wake.

"Roran, stop!" I call. "There are too many!" I chase after

them, my lungs squeezing as I fight to breathe past the weight on my chest.

The camp is chaos. People run, but trackers dart through the air, tagging them with ionic paint. Once marked, they'll show up on every sensor. Mods are already approaching to collect them.

"Aim for the trackers!" Dram calls to the fighters gathered at the center, weapons raised. He fires, and a tracker shatters apart. "I need you in this fight, Rye!" He unclips a gun from his thigh holster and tosses it to me.

I fumble with the weapon, trying to release the safety. My mind runs through all the things I've seen Dram do. I point the muzzle at the ground and pull back the slide.

"Flash me!" I can't get it pulled back.

"Use your whole hand," Dram calls.

I drag my sweaty palm against my coat and then clamp it over the slide. It pulls back with a click. I mirror his stance and take aim. The trackers hum through the air in unpredictable patterns, rarely hovering for more than a few seconds. I squeeze the trigger, and the gun jolts in my hands. I stagger back and lift my arms again. It's nearly impossible to pin a tracker in the gun's sights. We need Bade, with his ability to throw fire.

A child cries. A boy with curls of dark hair twisted around stone talismans. A tracker darts after him, and Roran bolts in front of it.

"Get down!" he shouts. Massive crystals jut from the ground, arching over the child. The tracker tags Roran with an ionic mark; we can't see it, but it illuminates on every screencom, every scanner.

"Roran!" I shout.

The forest floor rumbles beneath my feet. A Mod descends, blocking the sunlight. I stand in its shadow and point my gun at its thruster. A tracker explodes beside me, and bits of metal rain down. My ears ring. I turn, disoriented. Smoke fills the clearing; I try to see past it.

"Roran!"

The glade is chaos. Conjies flee in every direction. I search through the haze, but the Mod's gone. So is Roran. I didn't even see it happen.

Another Mod approaches, and I lift my gun.

"Wait." Dram catches my arm. "That one's for me."

"What are you talking about?"

"Rye. A leader stays with his people."

"You're not their leader."

"Bade left me in charge. I need to go with them to processing, do whatever I can to help them."

"These aren't our people."

His eyes soften. "They are. In every way that matters."

They are. I know this, but as I watch Dram slip off his camo-cloth and shove it into my pack, I know I will do anything to hold on to him. Even forsake the people who've sheltered us. Mods descend around us, their engines drowning out the cries of people I've come to know as family.

"This is our fault," Dram says. "I won't abandon them."

"What if Jameson can't get you out?"

"Then you'll have to."

"Like I did for the others?" My voice breaks.

"You'll find a way." He pulls something from his pocket and

shoves it into my hand. The bloodied Strider patch his father sent. "Keep this," he says. "In case it means more than I think it does." I stuff the patch into my pocket and grip his arms.

"Your body can't take more exposure!"

"I've got one more light." He lifts his wrist, where his Radband pulses a faint amber.

"I've lost *everyone*!" I bite the words out. "Don't ask me to give you up, too." His lips are cold as he presses his mouth to mine.

"Find Bade," he says. "Then find us." He cups my face. "Find me, Scout." *Scout.* A name he's called me since the day it became my title back in Outpost Five.

But now it means something more.

He walks toward the smoke of burning, whirring trackers, the cries of Conjies being restrained and taken up into the droning crafts. I bite my lip to block the scream I feel building in my throat. Everything inside me urges me to run after Dram, to drag him back to safety.

We spent our whole lives mining the deadly tunnels to earn our freedom, and the Congress sent us to die in the cordons when we discovered it was all a lie. We survived and made our way beyond the flashfall. Now Dram's going back, willingly giving himself up. If anyone can show them how to survive, it's him. And if anyone can find a way to free them—

It's me.

I stand frozen, tears streaking my cheeks, as a Mod's light beam swings over Dram. He stills, his broad shoulders hunched as his gaze drops to the ground. He doesn't watch the pod descend upon him.

"No." My voice is a whispered cry. Trackers whirl past me,

swirling about the chaos. I drop, crouching in the snow, but not a single drone comes close. Maybe they sense the ice inside me, the parts of me deadening as I watch Dram swept off his feet by a metal arm. The machine tackles him to the snow, and all the breath leaves my chest, as if my lungs are linked to his. He flinches, from the particles in the snow and from the metal clasping his wrists behind his back. A syringe plunges into his arm, even as another metal appendage draws a sample of his blood.

He twists his head around and meets my eyes. I can barely see him through the blur of my tears.

"Subpartisan," the machine drones. A faint voice answers, maybe a tech on the other end of the com.

"Reanalyze," the voice commands.

Dram gasps as a narrow tube pierces his vein. His blood spatters the snow, and my gut clenches.

"Subpartisan," the machine announces.

The drugs in Dram's system make his head sway, but his eyes hold mine as he mouths a word. I squint, trying to see, and he says it one last time.

Run.

He's yanked off the ground, and his head flops forward, his long Conjie hair covering his face. With a start, I realize I've taken the stance we developed down the tunnels. I've got an overhand grip on a knife, and I'm tensed, waiting for his cue to attack. If my caving partner changes his mind, I'll dive after the Mod with everything I have.

The machine sweeps him into the collection pod, and a metallic door grinds shut. Through the windshield, I see clamps fasten over his arms and legs. His head tips back, and I feel his panic like it's my own. He hid his fear from me before, but it erupts from him now.

He fights the restraints, his mouth open on a yell. The lights die a flickering death as the hover wobbles in the air, battling interference from the curtain.

Dram's in the dark, restrained and sealed in an unsteady, droning craft. No chance of light—only the blistering heat of the flash curtain as it carries him back toward the burnt sands and the starving creatures birthed in its shadow.

I drop to the ground as the hover lifts, pressing my face to the snow. The icy crystals burn, even as they numb my cheeks and forehead. I embrace the physical pain, because I cannot bear the agony tearing open my heart.

The Congress has Dram.

With no one left to hear, I give in to the scream. I shout into the snow, into the particles I sense more than anyone else. The curtain sings to me, and I used its melodies to find my way out. I will use it to find a way back.

But first, I have to find Bade. And my father. Or we all die.

I stand, shielding myself in the folds of the camo-cloth. The Mods shoot upward, ascending in a growling chorus of engines. Sunlight glints off the machines as they disappear overhead. All at once I'm alone in a glade spattered with blood.

I tuck my cloak around me and run.

SIX

I'VE GONE LESS than a kilometer when I find the craft, half buried in snow. I know the hover's one of ours by the parallel lines—a caver's mark—painted on the side. It's small, just a four-person Skimmer, but smoke pours from it, and as I approach, I hear the crackle of fire. The flight and nav systems should have been safe this far from the curtain's interference, but just like the particle snow, the flashfall is extending beyond its normal parameters.

This must be the Skimmer Jameson told us to expect. This isn't the coded location he mentioned, but it's close—within a few kilometers. A bloody hand suddenly pounds against the viewing window. I run forward, shocked anyone managed to survive the crash.

"Hold on! I'm here!" I boost myself atop the metal fuselage and pound on the glass. Flames lick the sides of the craft, and I know they'll draw any nearby Mods like a beacon. "Move away from the glass!" I shout. I balance on my knees and raise my axe. I swing it down, and the windshield cracks. Heat bleeds off the wreckage, bringing tears to my eyes and making my skin burn. Two more swings and I've made a hole. I holster my axe, wrap my hands in my jacket, and reach through.

"Watch the glass," the man calls around hacking coughs.

A jagged edge catches the inside of my wrist and I gasp, more surprised than pained. "Flash me," I mutter, ripping the sleeve of my cloak free and hastily wrapping it over the cut.

"Grab my hands," I say, reaching through the glass. The man grasps my hands, and I give him the leverage he needs to pull free of the smashed cockpit. He wears a medkit strapped across his chest. Through the smoke and snow, I can't see him clearly, just enough to see that he's pulled on extra layers of clothes— maybe the pilot's—to protect himself from the burning heat.

"What about the others?" I ask.

"Just the pilot," he answers, his voice muffled behind a thick scarf. "I did what I could for him—"

"Then we need to get away from here. Trackers will be here any second." We stumble through the drifts, and I barely notice the sting of the particle snow.

"Let me look at your wrist," he calls. I glance back and realize I've left a trail of blood.

"Damn." I sway on my feet, staring at the spots of red, stark against the snow. This will lead Striders to us as surely as marks on a map. I tear more of my cloak free, my fingers shaking—more from shock than cold, I realize dimly. I must've cut myself deeper than I thought.

The man wades toward me, his steps hampered by the snow and extra clothing. He's unwrapping the scarf covering half his face. "Stay there, I'm going to apply pressure." As he nears, I see that his sleeve's soaked with blood.

"You need a physic," I murmur, trying to connect the suddenly disjointed thoughts rambling through my mind. "You're bleeding—"

"This isn't my blood, Orion. It's yours." Without the scarf shielding his face, I recognize the man I pulled from the hover, but it's his voice I knew first.

"Dad," I whisper. The world tips beneath me and the snow is everywhere.

I am numb and all is white.

———

"Orion."

I fight my way through the chemical haze clouding my mind. "Dad?" There's something in his tone that makes me feel like a little girl, frightened by the panic I hear in his voice.

"You need to see this."

"Mmph." I bite my lip to keep from being sick. My wrist is opened up, skin pulled back, tendons exposed. He woke me too soon.

"I'm sorry, Orion, but you need to see this for yourself. You might not have believed me if I told you later."

The glow of a lantern illuminates sutures and clamps and bloody gauze. I'm on a ledge of rock. "What are you doing?" My Radband is dangling off my arm, the biotech partially removed. I can't believe he would attempt this surgery.

"I had to remove part of it to suture your wrist. You nicked your radial artery." He lifts my wrist, and I flinch. "Look at your biotech. Four lights, not two." He lifts my Radband. "The indicators don't function properly."

"It broke?"

"It never worked."

"What are you saying?"

"Your radiation levels are higher than the tech indicates. You're sick, Orion. We all are. They just don't want us to know it." He works the biotech back over my wrist and inserts the sensors into place. I don't feel anything. I am numb, inside and out.

"Four lights," I murmur. "I'm at gold." Too soon to feel the effects of radiation. My gaze shifts to Dad. "What about you?" My fog-filled mind runs the math, the years more radiation he's been exposed to.

He doesn't answer and my eyes rove over him. "It's nearly impossible to remove the biotech," he says. "Not without irreparable damage. But Jameson found someone in Alara. He was the one who told me about the indicators." He lifts his bare left wrist, and I see just how much he was willing to risk for the truth.

"How many lights, Dad?" I don't recognize the strangled voice choking past my lips.

He hesitates. "Five."

Orange. My dad's at level orange. There's only one light after that.

"I'm putting you back under, Orion," he says softly. I barely notice the sting of the needle; my mind is grasping at scattered fragments of thought. There is something . . . something important. Heaviness settles over me, and I struggle to keep my eyes open. Red. An orange indicator means a Subpar is actually at red.

A whimpering cry pushes past my lips.

"Sleep now," Dad murmurs. "I'll be done soon. You're going to be fine."

"Dram." I slur the name, but I hear it echo a thousand places inside myself. "Dram's . . . orange."

Dad doesn't answer—or if he does, I don't hear it. I can only hear that name, echoing in the halls of my heart, along with one other word.

Red.

SEVEN

31.2 km from flash curtain

WE SURVIVE THE day in a cave. My emotions swing wildly, between relief that Dad is alive and the terror I'm reminded of every time I move my wrist. Dram's Radband is giving him a false sense of security, an indication of time he doesn't actually have. Plans shape and reshape as I lie on the ground, anchored to consciousness by my tether of pain.

Dad wakes, and I ask him only the essential things. We keep our words to a minimum, but he shares enough to give me an idea of what's going on.

A map forms in my mind. Not a tunnel map of caverns and depth readings, but a map of this Eastfall world with more spaces filled in. Places like the Overburden, a land of tapped-out mines. Dad doesn't know much more than the Conjies do—that the original outposts and cirium there are gone, but the cordons of the Overburden are mined for flash dust.

"We developed a cure," he says. But there are tears in his eyes when he says it. Because he couldn't hold on to it. Dad perfected the cure to the radiation poisoning, and the Congress took it. Not to save people, but to keep them enslaved. "Workers in the Overburden are given a rationed, daily dose," he explains. "In exchange for service. And compliance. Jameson tried to—"

"Stop," I say. "Don't tell me any more." Because all the hollow places inside me are filling too fast with horror, devouring me from the inside, like I'm being pumped full of orbie water.

Dad studies my face, then doses me with Serum 129. It's only a temporary relief from physical pain, but maybe it'll grant me just enough oblivion to keep the orbie water from drowning me. Slowly, the tether holding me eases and I float up

up

up.

"Rest, Orion," Dad says. I think I hear him tell me that he loves me and that we'll find a way.

Dram said that, too. Just before the Mod took him.

I doze in snatches of time, my ears pricked for the drone of trackers. My mind stirs, restless, shaping my fractured thoughts into a single realization. The flash curtain isn't finished with me yet.

I crawl to the edge of the cave and watch the stars arc across the sky. I wonder if Dram and the others can see them or if they're already under a flashfall sky, where the air has teeth.

I shoulder our gear, being careful of my injured wrist, and hoist Dad to his feet. We trudge through the forest as the sky lightens to palest pink. *Like the inside of a shell*, Mom would say. Then she'd go on to explain shells and oceans, and I'd want to leave Outpost Five even more than I did before.

"Orion?"

I realize I've stopped. I let go of my wrist, the reassembled

Radband glowing up at me. Dad managed to reattach it, though it's not adhered as it once was.

"Why did the Congress do this to us?" I ask.

"Protocol," Dad answers. "The principle Alara is built upon—in order to preserve natural humanity, radiation exposure must be kept 'as low as reasonably achievable.' Better that *some* die, instead of *all*."

"I hate them."

"Most Alarans don't know what's happening to Subpars and Conjurors on the other side of the curtain."

"They know they *mine*. They know people *die* to keep them shielded in their glenting city!" I taste salt and realize I'm crying. It stirs my rage. We cry—and it doesn't matter. We bleed—and nothing changes. It has been this way for 150 years. Subpars mine and die. Alarans live. Protocol is preserved.

"Orion. You're stronger than this."

I glare at him like he's standing inside the protected city. "Maybe I'm sick of having to be *strong*!"

"We're tired. Let's—"

"*Tired*?" I practically shout the word. "We're *dying*, Dad! The Subpars—if there are any left—are mining *cordons*. Owen and Marin, and Mere and Winn—my friends are waiting for me to s-save them! And Dram—" I break off, swiping my eyes. "Dram's at RED!"

His arms steal around me, holding me as I shake. I'm drowning in my own weakness, my inability to save the people I love. He rocks me, like he did when I was nine and Dram's sister crawled out of seven, the only survivor from Mom's team. He's speaking softly—fragments of sentences.

"My brave girl . . . see your strength . . . You're just like her . . ."

His voice slowly replaces the sounds of my hitched breaths. Words that don't mean anything.

That mean everything.

He clasps the sides of my head. "There's a reason she named you for the stars. And not just any constellation. One of the brightest."

Tears slip down my cheeks. "I don't know what to do. Back at Outpost Five, each day was the same. I knew how to survive the tunnels. Here, everything's different. It's constantly changing."

"Then change with it." He smiles, a sad tilt of his lips.

"It's not changing me, it's *breaking* me."

"Maybe we are meant to break. Maybe that's what makes us stronger."

———

I stare at Bade across the campfire. Tension fills the space between us, thick as the wood smoke. We found him and the others sheltered near echo six and staggered into their hidden Conjie camp an hour ago. I can't seem to ask him to forgive me for going against him and accidentally drawing the Mods. I'm not sure it would matter. Some things "sorry" can't fix.

"Seven Conjies were captured," he announces, his voice gruff with emotion. I realize he's counting Dram among the Conjurors.

Six Conjurors will lose their hands and their freedom because of me.

It was a well-intentioned idea. Roran and I nearly succeeded.

Roran. My stomach lurches. One of the six.

I take a shaky breath and level my gaze at Bade. Sometimes the forgiveness you need is too big to ask for. Sometimes you skip it and go straight to penance.

"Let me get inside the Congress."

Bade lifts a brow. "Oh, are you *asking* me this time?"

I wade past his bitter tone. "The curtain is expanding, creatures are escaping the flashfall . . . our Radbands are a lie. If we don't act, then everyone who's not behind the shield will be dead soon. You know it's true."

"We're not ready to bring a full-fledged fight to them," he says. "We don't have the numbers. That's why Arrun's been in the outlier regions—trying to assemble a secret army."

Arrun. Arrun and his cryptic, useless message. I retrieve the patch from my pocket. A memory stirs, painful, like a thorn tearing across my skin. Dram pushing this into my hand. *Keep this. In case it means more than I think it does.*

My thumb brushes the stitching, the metallic thread stained with blood. I've considered it from every angle, even unraveled a bit of the outer stitching to see if it concealed another message. Nothing. Just this Strider patch, the motto twining above a snake. *Morior invictus.* Death before defeat.

Is this really Arrun's message to us? Die trying? Bade says it traveled by at least three different carriers. I consider the effort. There must be more we're not seeing.

I study the letters. *M, O, R, I, O, R*—the second *R* is dark with dried blood. *I, N, V, I, C, T*—the last three letters are stained. It reminds me of our caver's suits in Outpost Five and all the nights Dram and I sat in the Rig, a bottle of vinegar between us, scrubbing bloodstains off our uniforms. I recall the times, exhausted from mining, I just wanted to toss the clothes into the fire pit. Especially when it was someone else's blood. I glance down at the patch again. Something's off. I stare so hard my eyes begin to water. The motto swims up at me.

The motto.

"Hand me a stick," I say. I drop to my knees and smooth my palm across the ground. I clear an even patch of dirt and take the stick Dad hands me.

"Orion?"

"We kept it clear," I mutter. "The Subpar motto, on the front of our caver's suit. Even down the tunnels—if it got dirty, we wiped the words clear. It was tradition—or superstition— like touching the sign supports before entering the tunnels. Something only cavers knew about."

"I don't follow," Dad says.

"Arrun didn't know who to trust, so he sent a message only a caver would catch."

I draw the bloodstained letters into the earth. *R, T, U, S.*

"What is it?" Bade asks, crouching beside me. I thrust the patch at him. "Look at the blood on the letters." He lifts a brow. I huff my breath in frustration. "It's wrong. Blood sprays, or drips, or smears. It doesn't . . . skip letters like this. This marking is intentional."

"You think those letters hold a message?"

"I think all of it's a message. One that only a Subpar would see." I rearrange the letters. *R-U-S-T.* No. *T-R-U-S.*

"Holy fire," I murmur. "If we use the *T* twice—" I draw the word into the dirt.

Trust.

I glance up, but Bade's staring into the middle distance,

like his thoughts are as far away as Arrun. He shifts and looks at Aisla.

"It makes sense," he says. She nods.

"What does?" Dad asks.

"Arrun went to the outlier regions to raise an army. He didn't tell us his plan in case—"

"Striders?" I ask, my voice choked. "His plan is *Striders*?" Memories surge: fear, shock, the heart-tripping effects of electrified armor.

"Think of it," Bade says. "If he can infiltrate the Congress's soldiers, turn some of them to our cause, it would leave them defenseless. We could breach the city—and anything we wanted inside of it."

"We told you," Aisla says. "Arrun's good at stealing things—" *"Armies?"*

Bade grins. "Take them down from the inside. It's a good plan."

"Why would Striders support a rebellion?"

"Because Arrun's not recruiting them from Alara. He's in the outlier regions—the Trades. If there's a place beyond the flashfall to inspire resentment against the Congress, it's there."

"The Trades?" I ask.

"A series of compounds along the coast," Bade answers. "It's where Alara's youth are sent when they come of age. They train and test to earn a place in the protected city. It's brutal. I've heard stories—"

"What if you're wrong about the message?" Dad asks. He motions toward the patch. "What if it's just blood?"

"Then we move forward anyway," Newel says. "We do what we can to save our people. We fight."

"Not even Jameson can get close to the cure," Dad says. "Not enough of it. The Prime Commissary moved all major stores of it to an underground compound in the Overburden. It's overseen by a Subpar commissary there." These are details he gave me as we staggered here, leaning into each other, talking when we had the strength for it.

"Even if we were to forge an attack on the council's Central Tower," Bade says, "I'm not sure we could get hold of it. It's the most closely guarded resource in Alara."

"That's why I'm not going to fight my way into Alara," I say softly.

"Where else would you get it?" Newel asks.

"The last place they'd ever expect me to go. The Overburden."

Dad makes a sound and hunches over, his head in his hands. He's barely spoken since I told him my idea. I know it's because his analytical mind is calculating scenarios, probabilities, estimating my chances of succeeding. The fact that he hasn't said anything about it tells me my chances are slim.

"The place you're speaking of is a closely guarded secret," Aisla says. "It's called Fortune. Not even Striders can enter. Only Delvers who've earned their way."

"What are Delvers?"

"They scout paths through the caverns beneath the Overburden," Aisla answers.

Her explanation hangs in the air, an invisible bridge between where we are and where we might be if we choose this plan.

"They could arrest you the moment they figure out who you are," Bade says. A flash of his earlier heaviness returns, flitting across his expression like a shadow. I know he's thinking of Dram—of what the Congress might do to the son of Arrun Berrends.

"Not if I'm valuable to them. I'll get into this underground fortress. I'll find where they've stockpiled the cure."

"It could work," Aisla says.

"It could fail horribly," Bade says. "There are too many unknown variables."

"If we manage to get her inside," Dad asks, "how long will it take you to raise forces enough to get them out?"

Bade glances at Aisla. "A few days, a few weeks—it all depends."

"How long can people survive in the Overburden?" I ask.

Bade lifts a brow and says sardonically, "A few days, a few weeks—it all depends."

Dad's gaze slips to my Radband glowing yellow. He doesn't say anything.

"Past fear lies freedom," I say softly. "Graham used to say that."

"Well, then," Bade says. "Let's find out if it's true."

————

I sit cross-legged on a sunlit, loamy patch of ground. The snow has melted away, and I push my hands into the dirt, allowing my Subpar senses to take in the full spectrum of elements: natural, earthy, and alive.

I am still saying good-bye.

I lean forward and rest my cheek on the ground, squinting as pine needles push against my face. I've seen Dram do this, watched him in secret and laughed inside at his wild Conjie ways. I didn't understand.

I think maybe now I do.

Good-bye.

After a time, I sit up. I reach inside my shirt and lift my memorial pendants. The Conjies have talismans. I suppose these are mine. One at a time, I fill them with this sun-warmed soil, the earth of the provinces, as the Conjies call it. Wherever I go, I'm taking it with me.

A reminder that I have known life beyond the flashfall.

A promise that I am coming back.

———

If I'm going to get myself caught by the Congress, I might as well make it count.

I study the device in my hand, one of the Congress's "toys" we pulled off the Conjies sent to hunt us. *Not as powerful as a flash wand*, Bade told me when he explained how to activate the grenade-like tech. He asked me to create a distraction, something to draw the Congress's attention, so he and Aisla could more easily slip past the boundaries of the provinces into the outlier regions.

I twist the device and it whines to life, gleaming with red light as I throw it toward the charging station beside the tree Roran conjured. I turn and run, Bade's warning ringing in my ears. *Red means dead, so when you see that light, Orion, sprint like hell. You'll have about five seconds.*

Boom!

A concussive wave knocks me off my feet with a sound I feel as much as hear. I cover my head as shards of wood fall around me along with a hail of debris. Wood groans and cracks and melds with the sounds of metal screeching. The ground thunders beneath me as a part of the disk-shaped platform slams into the dirt. Then—

Silence.

From the force of that blast, I'm expecting to look back and see nothing but a scorched pit of earth, so my heart sinks when I stand and see the skeletal remains of the station and the tree.

The device blew apart most the trunk and the base of the Mod station. The tree leans like it just needs a strong push to send it the rest of the way over.

Something sharp to take out that last bit of wood.

I jog toward the station, a smile blooming on my face.

I lift Dram's pickaxe and swing the blade as hard as I can at the tree Roran conjured. Wood chips away as I drive it into that last tether. Branches shudder against the platform. If I take this tree down, it will take the station with it.

With every strike, I replay the moments when the Mod went after Roran.

And when the Mods went after us all.

Thwack! My arms strain against the weight of the axe striking the wood. I think of how I'm using Dram's pickaxe for the very last time, and how fitting this is.

I promise myself that I'll find him somehow in the Overburden, and tell him that the last swings of his axe were made taking down a Mod platform. He'll shake his head, and grin with that dent in his cheek, and I'll know there are still ways I surprise him.

Thwack!

The tree cracks and leans, and I lurch back as its momentum carries it over, slamming against the platform. Chunks of debris hurtle down as the Congress's last charging station tumbles into the dirt.

Come and find me.

The Congress will be here soon.

I don't have to wait long. Beyond the treetops, a glint of metal, a rumble like mountains shifting. Fear dances across my nerves as it descends.

This one's mine.

Dram's words echo through my memories as the Mod approaches, arms reaching. It drops pulse trackers, but I'm not running anywhere. They surround me, whining, glinting in the sunlight. I have never let them get so close. Doubt flitters through my mind, but I force myself to stand unflinching as a tracker marks me. Seconds later, the Mod's arm ensnares me with more force than I was expecting. The jab of a needle, a cold pinch, and then sudden lifting, the ground falling away beneath me.

"Subpartisan," a voice drones. I'm deposited into the craft, my limbs mechanically arranged before bars clamp across my torso and legs. The pod closes overhead. "Cargo secured. Proceeding to processing."

The thrusters rumble beneath me.

I scream into the darkness.

EIGHT

11.6 km from flash curtain

THE POD OPENS with a concussive blast of air.

I blink against the glare of overhead lights. I've landed in some sort of hangar. A Strider reaches inside before my bonds have finished releasing.

"Hurry!" he says under his breath. He taps buttons in the console of the Mod, illuminating a panel I didn't know was there.

"Subpartis—" The machine-like voice seems to melt. He taps more keys, and it stutters into silence.

"Come on!" He pulls me from the pod. I'm so shocked by his demeanor that I don't resist. My feet are numb from the restraints, and I fall against him. My body stiffens in anticipation of a shock that doesn't come.

"My armor's muted," he murmurs. "Can you run?"

I snort-laugh. Flash me, they've given me shock inhibitors. I feel a giggle bubbling past my lips.

"I'll take that as a no," he mutters. He bends, scooping me into his arms.

"This is so strange," I announce loudly.

"Quiet," he hisses.

"Shhh!" I say. Then I turn it into a sort of tune.

"They warned me you might be like this, but I didn't believe them."

"Who?"

"Walsh!" a Strider calls.

My escort dumps me behind a row of shelves.

"What?" he calls.

"Central reported a Subpar contained in the provinces. Should've been in Mod four-five."

"I emptied that pod. Just another Conjie. She's in binders in holding cell two."

I peek from between a row of boxes in time to see the Strider's look of confusion. He turns and jogs back the way he came.

Walsh crouches beside me and pulls a tablet from his sleeve pocket. "Put this under your tongue."

"Why?" My head sways as I study the flat, round pill.

"Because I can't carry you where you need to go. And if you start singing again, we're dead."

I place it under my tongue.

"Good," he says. "No more singing." He fastens a pair of binders over my hands and lifts me to my feet.

"Where are we going?"

"Not holding cell two."

He guides me around a corner, and I gasp. A sign marks the entrance to the Overburden with flashfall exposure warnings.

"Your ride's about to leave. You have a better chance out there together."

"Together?"

"With your . . . what do you cavers call it? Marker?"

Dram.

My heart pounds.

He herds me along a ramp that leads into a large metal-barred containment unit. Striders with flash rifles line the sides, their weapons pointed toward the group of Conjies huddled within. Walsh releases me.

"Run hard," he murmurs.

"What?"

"Something we say in the Trades."

The Trades. I whirl back, but he's already jogging back toward the hangar. The door seals with a hiss and the transport device lurches forward. I'm jostled against the bars as it gains speed over the cordon sands.

"Holy fire."

I turn at the sound of Dram's voice. He stares at me, eyes wide with horror. I wend my way past Conjies hunched in groups and throw my arms around him.

"How did you get caught?" he asks.

"I chopped down Roran's tree with your pickaxe and took out the charging station." He mutters a series of Conjie words. I bracket his face with my hands, wishing I could erase the hollowed-out look he's wearing. "I pulled my dad from a crashed hover. Our Radbands are lies. You're at red, Dram." Tears slip down my cheeks, faster than my rambling explanations. Because this, more than anything else, scares me. That whatever we do—if we manage to get the cure out of the Overburden—it won't be fast enough. Not for Dram.

Cordon winds filter between the bars, and I shudder as

particles abrade my skin. I taste ash on my tongue. I'm start-
ing to think that what Graham said was wrong—that what
lies past my fear is simply death. And worse—the deaths of
people I love.

Over Dram's shoulder, between the bars, I can see the red
tents Mere once told me about, and pitted metal signs marked
PROCESSING. I rise onto my tiptoes and pull his head down so
my lips are at his ear. "Your father's in the Trades. Raising an
army of Striders." He pulls back, stares at me with wide eyes.

I can give him this, at least. A bit of hope. His father is still
alive. Still fighting.

"The patch," he murmurs. I nod. *Morior invictus.*

We have a chance.

If we can just survive what comes next. And the days
after that.

———

The bars slide open, and Striders march us toward processing.
They funnel us through a set of fences, and I throw my hands
up, guarding my face against a gust of cordon wind. My survival
instincts root me to the ground.

The soldier motions for me to move, but I stand, fixed in
place. I haven't done this since I was nine and Graham had to
rescue me from where I'd frozen in fear, mid-climb, above my
first orbie pool.

"The green acorn," Dram calls from beside me, lifting his
bound hands toward the talisman swaying near his temple.
"It's a promise. One I made to my father." I realize he's trying
to distract me, the way he did down tunnel nine whenever my
fear took hold. "A promise that I wouldn't give up finding him
until I saw his body or his ashes."

He walks forward, slowly, and I follow. One foot. Two.

Step in my steps.

"We're not here to die," he says at my ear. "We're here to finish what we started, right?"

I nod. *Step. Step.* "I'm sorry, I—"

"Don't apologize for being afraid of things we should be afraid of."

I step. Breathe. It's getting easier to walk.

"And the new one?" I ask, looking up at his talismans. "The metal charm?"

A soft smile spreads across his face. "That one's for a promise I made to you."

"What was the promise?"

His smile grows. "You'll just have to wait and see, ore scout."

NINE

7.4 km from flash curtain

A MAN IN a gray uniform walks the length of our group, his eyes bouncing from one face to the next, like he's analyzing some invisible data. He murmurs something to a Strider.

"All men, come with me," the soldier calls.

"No—" I grasp Dram's hand through the chain links of our binders. "Your Radband," I gasp. The men are being ushered toward the curtain, and I'm terrified for him. His body can't take more exposure.

"Orion—" Dram leans down, his voice low, urgent. "Take off your bonding cuff first chance you get." I stare at him, derailed by his train of thought. "They think we're Conjies."

"But—"

"They'll *cut off your hands*, Orion!"

He drags his bound hands through his hair and tears free the bit of birch wood, then the acorn. His kohl-lined eyes meet mine, and I don't tell him that he still looks exactly like a free Conjie. He pulls at the sash tied at his hips, tears it off with a rending of silk. I glance at the bits of shell and carved wood

I sewed on it myself, crushed underfoot as I'm jostled away from him. He shoves back and reaches for me. Cold metal presses my cheeks, and the cirium links pinch my skin as his bound hands draw me close.

"Find a way out," he says, and then he's gone, swallowed by the crowd.

Dram. We've been pulled apart before, but this time there's a finality to it. This time, he's wearing an amber Radband and heading to a processing tent in the cordons.

They steer me into a line where a grim-faced Gem walks from person to person, unlocking our binders. My fingers go to my bonding cuff. I haven't taken it off since the day Dram placed it on my wrist. I follow his movement through the crowd as he's herded toward a processing tent. He turns, and my gaze collides with his.

His bonding cuff drops to the dirt.

Take it off, he mouths.

My fingers fumble at the interlocking bands. I remember when he twisted them into place. The night he showed me the stars.

Hurry. Dram's worried blue eyes follow me as I'm suddenly pushed forward.

My cuff falls to the ground, and I watch as it's trampled into the dirt.

Step in my steps? I'd asked Dram that night.

Always, ore scout.

I search for him, but he's lost from view, surrounded by Striders. Men shout and a current of unease ripples through the processing station. Men and women, dressed in uniforms I've never seen before, patrol the loading docks before the hovers. They don't wear Radsuits or headpieces, and their sleeves are cut away to reveal the glowing symbols in their forearms.

Gems. And yet . . . different. They carry no visible weapons, but the threat they emit is stronger than the Striders'.

"What are they?"

A girl at my side leans close and answers. "Vigils. From Ordinance."

Vigils. I remember Aisla drawing an inverted V in the snow. *If you ever see this symbol on a Codev . . . run.*

A pair of them walk past, and they read each face like a screencom. I get the impression they're evaluating data the rest of us can't see. I duck my head, my heart pounding.

Striders urge us toward the red tents, and all at once, I smell it: burning flesh. Bile rushes to my throat. I stumble, and the woman at my heels slams up against me.

"Keep moving," a Gem in a gray suit orders.

I struggle to move, my legs two numb sticks, because now I can hear the screams. Mere told me once, in halting, spare words, of the day she was Tempered. It was the only time I saw her strength diminished, as if the weight of the experience was still too much for her to bear. I could barely stand to listen as she described the physics in red uniforms, the smell of cauterized stumps, the liquid burn of cirium injected through tubing into arms.

Beside the canvas entrance, people lie on the ground where they've fainted from the procedure. I weave on my feet, unsure I'll even make it that far.

"I'm not a Conjuror," I whisper. But my terrified murmur is lost to the wind and screams filling this dead place.

The woman behind me slumps to the ground. They force us forward, and she's heedless of the feet crushing her hands, legs knocking her head. I crouch and grasp her hands. Hands she won't have much longer.

"I have friends who went through this," I say, helping her up. "We'll make it through."

"Noncompliant Conjurors," a man calls from a platform. He wears red bars on the sleeves of his uniform. "As Constable of the Overburden, I order you processed according to your crimes," he announces, his voice flat, like he's said the words so often they no longer have meaning. "After your Tempering, you will be given the opportunity to serve Alara and earn remediation for your noncompliance."

My ears prick at the word *earn*. It is a lie. One the Congress has perfected.

"How can we serve our city-state without glenting hands?" I say, loud enough that everyone around me turns. The constable looks stricken—he's apparently not used to his listeners responding. A Strider winds through the line toward me.

"Tempered Conjies perform a vital role," the soldier says, his voice amplified behind his face shield. "They make up the squads that head into the cordon. Since you're eager to know, I'll move you to the front of the line." His gloved hand clamps around my wrist and I'm towed forward.

They are going to cut my hands off. They will shove tubes of cirium up my arms and cauterize the stumps. I am next in line. But somewhere between tearing off my bonding cuff and listening to the constable, my anger bubbled up past my fear. I'm so full of terror, there's no room to contain my rage.

We are close enough to the flash curtain that I sense its

reach and pull. Even now, the flash curtain sends tendrils of energy snaking past its boundaries. And no one here has any idea.

The Strider stands so close to me that his electrified armor lifts the hairs on my arms. And then, suddenly, it doesn't. The low hum of his suit stutters, like a hover engine stalling out. I leap at him, and he falls back, taken off guard by my attack. He hits the ground hard as my weight slams into his chest. His eyes widen, and he gasps for air.

"Not so tough without your suit," I growl. He makes a wheezing sound, and I lean down into his whitening face. "I will stand at the front of your glenting formation, and lead them right out of the cordon." His hands fist in my hair, but I've got my arm wedged across his windpipe. "With or without my hands!"

I'm pulled off the Strider. Rough hands shove me forward, and the electrified armor hums to life once more. Now tackling a soldier like that would kill me. But it was enough. The curtain interfered with their tech just long enough for me to make a point.

As I'm pushed toward the processing tent, white flowers float down, petals twirling on wind drafts like snow. Small white blossoms—Roran's flowers—like the one I handed to Mere through the fence of Cordon Four. My Conjie family knows the story, and someone here used their last moments of conjuring to send a message.

Hope.

I search among the faces and find Roran. He nods once, his expression solemn. Whatever happens next for all of us, this isn't the end. We will find a way.

I'm swept toward a processing tent, my boots crunching over bloodstained sand.

"Move, Conjie," the Strider orders. He shoves me, the edge of his armored sleeve brushing me enough to shock. My breath stutters, and I lurch between the tent flaps.

Blood. Heat.

It's a visceral wall of sensation. I can practically see remnant pain radiating from the instruments, the table, the bucket of vomit by my foot. The stench singes my nostrils, and I gag. Torment has a smell, and it is its own punishment.

My courage flees, and terror takes hold.

"I'm Physic Conrad," a man says, as I'm steered toward the gleaming metal table. He offers me a brief explanation of the process, his tone gentle, like what he does here is not butchering. He works a cord over my right hand, tightening it so that my arm slides forward, wrist exposed.

"I'm not—" My words catch in my throat. "Not a Conjuror," I say louder. The assistant looks at me, but no one speaks. I suppose they've heard this before.

My scout senses prickle, awakening to the presence of so much flash dust. The incinerator is an arm's reach away, a smaller version of the one we used in Cordon Two to deposit bodies and gain access to Sanctuary. The thought makes my stomach heave. They are going to incinerate parts of my body right in front of me.

The assistant pulls the cord, and my arm slides across the table. "I have pendants," I gasp. "Memorial pendants. Only Subpars wear them!"

The physic's gaze slips to the blue and yellow pieces of glass that once held my mother's and brother's ashes. They look like Conjie adornment.

"Proceed, Strider," Conrad murmurs.

The soldier makes a motion with his hand, some kind of salute, then steps to the table. "For the crime of sedition against our city-state," he says, his voice hard as steel, "by the authority granted by the commissaries of Alara—"

"She's a Subpar!" a voice shouts. We all turn as a man breaks into the tent. "Don't Temper her! She's not a Conjie!" Dram shoves his way forward, and the Strider seizes him. "She's an ore scout—the best there is. You can use her!"

The Strider's head swivels from Dram to me, like he's assessing a foreign threat. One of the Ordinance soldiers—a Vigil—leaves her post and walks toward me.

"She's got a Radband!" Dram shouts, fighting the soldier holding him. He gets one arm free and tears his sleeve up, baring his forearm. "Look at her wrist!" He holds his toward the Vigil, the biotech that's marked him from birth as the Congress's miner.

"Show me her other wrist," the Vigil demands. The Strider draws up the sleeve of my left arm, working the fabric back to reveal my glowing yellow Radband.

"Westfall tech," she murmurs. Her eyes narrow on me. "Who are you?"

My name sticks in my throat. What if Bade is right, and they've heard about me here? What will these people do to the Scout, who crossed the cordons with a cure?

"Orion Denman," I whisper.

The impact of my admission ripples through the soldiers.

They share glances with each other, but not the Vigil. Her eyes are locked on me.

"We found these," says a Strider, walking to her side. He holds our bonding cuffs. Dram's gaze meets mine, then flicks away. If they discover we're linked, it won't take them long to figure out who we are.

"Subpars with Conjie bonding cuffs," the Vigil murmurs, examining our bands. She reads the words etched inside. "*Step in my steps.*" Her brows push together. "What is that?"

"Cavers' creed," I say softly. "Something we say down the tunnels."

"He said you were a scout?"

"Yes."

"Scout," she muses, her fingernail scraping over the words on the cuffs. She strides to the waste bucket and drops them in. "Bring the boy here." Two Striders bracket Dram and drag him forward. "Your name," the Vigil demands.

Dram stares at her like his eyes are weapons. If my name was bad, his is so much worse—son of the leader of the resistance. My name has the power to rally people to hope; his, the ability to tear the Congress apart.

"I don't ask twice," the Vigil says. She grips my arm and pain riots through me. My cry seizes in my throat as I convulse.

"Stop!" Dram shouts, lurching toward me. Blood trickles from my nostrils. I am in agony, my nerves raw, scorched—*too much too much!* Dimly, I'm aware of Dram shouting.

"Fire, stop!" he cries. "It's Berrends. I'm Dram Berrends." The Vigil lifts her hand and I sag, swaying on my feet. Her eyes narrow on Dram as if she's registering something the rest of us can't see.

"Secure them in a Delver's pod," she commands. "I need to alert the council."

The soldiers leap into action, hauling Dram and me away from the others, away from the scents and sounds of agony. I work to regain my footing, as I strain to see past the soldier's shoulder, to see Roran. He's no longer in line. Which means he's facing a physic like Conrad, and a vat of cirium.

"How can you do this?" I hiss at the Strider gripping my arm.

"I don't make the laws."

"You think that since you don't wield the knife, you're not responsible for that butchery?"

"Orion." Dram shoots me a warning look.

"They brought this upon themselves," the Strider answers. "The rules of compliance are clear."

"Where are you taking us?" Dram asks.

"Delver's pod," he replies. "If I let you walk on your own, you going to give me trouble?"

I shake my head, and he releases me, keeping one hand on his gun. "Quit dragging the boy, Nills."

If anything, the Strider's grip on Dram tightens. "You know who he is?"

"I heard the Vigil, same as you."

"This kid's father blew up a squad of soldiers."

"So hurting him's gonna make you feel better?"

"Damn right it will." He presses a sequence into his screencom, and his armor hums to life, buzzing with current. The Striders lift their rifles at the same time. I freeze when my escort steps in front of me.

"Stand down." He levels his rifle at Nills.

The man gapes in shock. "I think you're confused about who's the enemy, Greash."

"Anyone noncompliant," Greash answers. "And right now that's you. The Congress wants these Subpars. Alive." Time suspends itself as we all wait to see if reason will relax Nills's trigger finger.

"You'd kill me to protect this subhuman?"

"I don't have to kill you to stop you."

Nills swears and lowers his rifle. "Don't give me a reason, Berrends," he says to Dram. "Next time I'm not yielding." His gaze shifts to me. "You're the one they call Scout?" Dread tingles along my spine, worse than the cordon embers burning my exposed skin. "You're a lot smaller than I imagined." He makes a sound like a laugh and a sneer mixed. "I think people made up half the stories I've heard about you." He leans in, so close I can smell his acrid breath. "You're nothing here," he says softly. "A girl in a cordon, and you're going to die."

"You'll need more than words to beat me down," I murmur. Nills just shakes his head.

"You're already beaten, Subpar. You just don't know it yet."

TEN

THEY DIRECT US to one of the domed pods that stick up out of the ground in rows. I lean onto the balls of my feet and peer down through the clear roof. I can't make out more than a circular floor and a pair of cots.

"Go on," Greash says, ushering us toward a ladder built into the side.

"What is this place?" Dram asks.

"Safest quarters in the Overburden—other than Fortune. But that's something altogether different."

I descend the ladder, and cool air envelops me.

"Rest up," Greash calls down to us. "Someone will come for you after the council decides what to do with you."

"What's going to happen to us?" Dram asks.

"Nothing good," Nills answers. He tosses a bottle of water and a pair of nutri-pacs onto one of the cots. Then his camocloth shifts from shades of shadow to light as he climbs back up. The dome seals behind him.

Light glows above us, steady and golden, spreading around the room in a narrow ring.

"Halo," I whisper.

"What?" Dram asks.

I collapse onto a cot. "Graham told me once about angels with glowing crowns of light." I point to the pod lighting. "Halo."

"Fire, I think you need sleep even more than I do."

I laugh bleakly. "Or angels. Angels might be helpful right about now."

"No angels here," he mutters, falling with a sigh onto the other bed.

"None that we can see, anyway." I toe my boots off and close my eyes.

"He called this a Delver's pod," Dram says. "What do you think a Delver is?"

"Someone who gets a bed," I mumble.

"Right. Let's hope they make us Delvers, then."

I smile despite my exhaustion. "I think they're already onto us, Subpar. You sort of announced it to everyone when you busted into my processing tent."

"Ah, right. Do you think Subpars get beds here?"

I laugh. "Yes, and castles with cirium shields around them." My cot shifts as Dram eases beside me and draws me into his arms.

"Just in case," he whispers. I close my eyes and sigh against his chest. I listen as the spaces between his breaths grow and wonder if I'll ever get to listen to Dram fall asleep again. We have no idea what awaits Subpars found in the Overburden.

I focus on Dram's arms wrapped around me, the safety I feel in this moment.

Just in case they don't give us castles.

———————

The flashfall wakes me. Streaks of green and yellow wave from the other side of the domed glass roof. All at once I'm reminded that I'm back in a place of death. Dram sleeps on, even after I slip from his arms and sit up. I study his features, my chest tight. It's possible his fatigue is the first sign of radiation poisoning. Other than his Radband indicator. The amber light that is really—

I don't let myself finish the thought. Reeves was at red when we fought our way through the cordons, and his sickness was obvious. Maybe Dram's indicator isn't like mine.

And maybe the Congress is fair.

The latch on the pod lifts, and Dram jolts upright, his hair sticking up.

"You're smiling," he says. His voice is different when he first wakes. Deeper. I hold on to the thought like a talisman. "You remember where we are, right?" he asks, raising a brow.

"You didn't take out the silver charm." I saw it when he woke, tangled beneath the layers of his hair.

"Told you—that one's important."

"The flashfall is red," I murmur.

"I see that." Red aural bands mean Radlevels are high. Today will not be easy. "You shouldn't have followed me into this hell," Dram says.

"Step in my steps." I touch his face, skim my fingers over the thin scars I know so well.

"Let's go," a soldier calls. "Time for your commissioning." It's the same Strider from yesterday. Greash.

We climb up out of the Delver's pod and follow him through the camp. We pass Striders' barracks, an infirmary, and a handful of other buildings lined up across from a massive fence with a corral tower and turnstiles. The seal of Alara waves from a pole beside a Radlevel indicator flag. Greash glances at it as we walk past.

"Try not to breathe any more than you have to," he says.

"Tell me about Delvers," I say. "How can we become one?" Only Delvers have access to Fortune, Aisla said. And Fortune is where the Congress has safeguarded the cure.

Greash eyes me through his face shield. "Delvers are carefully selected, or commissioned in the Trades. They're tested in a gorge at the boundaries of the Overburden for a chance to win Fortune. Delvers with Fortune live inside the compound."

"I thought Fortune was a place?"

"More than that. It's a designation, a ranking higher than Striders. Inside Fortune, the Delvers take orders directly from the council."

"So," Dram says, "as far as commissioning goes, Delvers with Fortune are at the top. What else is there?"

Greash lifts a gloved hand toward a cluster of people clothed in Radsuits and armor. "The squads are made up of Miners and the people who protect them. We call them Dodgers. There are also Brunts."

"What are Brunts?"

His looks away, and I sense his hesitation. "Their purpose is to draw the threats away from the Miners. They're injected with transmitters that attract the creatures."

I stare at him, telling myself I couldn't have heard him right.

"They're bait," Dram says.

"Just until the Dodgers can take down anything that attacks."

My eyes slide shut. I remind myself to breathe.

"The system is necessary. Efficient. Without it, the Miners are unsuccessful."

"How many Brunts die in a day?" I ask, my voice hollow-sounding as I feel inside.

"Many," he says, looking toward the cordon. "But their sacrifice serves a greater good."

"What glenting good is another Subpar or Conjie death?" Dram asks.

"Flash dust," I answer. For the good of everyone in the city. For the good of humanity.

"Flash me," Dram mutters.

"Exactly," I murmur.

Greash directs us toward a small crowd gathered before Gems in uniform. As we approach, he activates his suit.

"Give me more space, Subpar," he says. "Even this setting would do some damage."

"You didn't have your armor charged?" I ask.

Greash shrugs, a barely discernible movement under his ridges of armor. "I only activate it if there's a threat." He gives me a look. "Were you planning to attack a Strider bare-handed?"

Wouldn't be the first time. I have enough healthy fear of Striders to not speak the thought aloud. But the memory filters through my mind. The dust beneath Dad's bed, where I crouched, hiding, as a Strider marched into the room. Glass crunching as we fought; his scream when an ore mite's parasites dug into his skin.

"What does that patch mean?" I ask, motioning toward the patch on his sleeve, beneath the seal of Alara. It's round, with a cresting wave at its center.

"It means I earned my commission in the Trades."

"The Trades?"

"You Westfallers probably don't know much about that."

What I know is it's the last place Dram's father was seen. "What kind of a place is it?"

"It's more than a place. It's a phase of life. It's where Alara's youth are sent. Most of them, anyway. It's three years of instruction and . . . challenges. Age sixteen to eighteen."

"I had thought . . ." I search for words, difficult when all my preconceived ideas about Alara are shifting around in my head. "I used to think about girls my age in Alara. I imagined them safe."

"Then you were half right. The girls in the Trades, though . . ." He shakes his head. "Nothing safe about that. How you perform in the Trades determines your role of service to the city-state. You have three years to prove your worth."

"And if you don't?"

"Then you remain in the outlier regions, which, trust me, isn't something anyone wants to do." He adjusts his armored glove, revealing a cirium hand.

Dram staggers to a stop. "You're a *Conjuror*?"

"Tempered." Greash tightens his glove. "What? You thought all Striders were Naturals?"

"Did you choose this?"

I'm glad Dram's asking all the questions I have, because I'm too shocked to speak.

"Yes. I fought for it. I earned this." He motions to the Strider patch on his arm, the coiled snake and its Latin banner. "Some people in Alara are rich enough to purchase their commissions. The rest of us head to the Trades." He looks out over the cordon. "The Trades are . . ." He shrugs. "You learn quickly that you have to fight for what you want."

"But you at least have a *choice*."

"Choice is relative." The words are softly spoken, but I don't miss his caustic tone. "I know you think you had it bad in the outposts. But there are worse places."

"How can you say that?" I step toward him, heedless of his charged armor. "We watched our friends and family *die*!"

"So did I. How big do you think Alara is, that everyone born there gets to stay? We're all citizens, but a place in the city must be earned."

"Oh, yes, I know all about *earning* a place in Alara!"

"Get. Back." He bites the words out, and I realize how close I've gotten. "The other Striders here won't try to protect you. You come at them, they'll meet you halfway—and laugh as you're shocked."

"Why would you even want to be one of them?"

"Because there's more than this. A city full of life and technology and hope for our future, and it needs to be protected." He directs us into a line of people. "Stay here. They'll commission you according to your abilities."

"Commission," Dram says. "That's a grand word for sorting us into death squads."

"You won't be made Brunts," he says. "They save that for the sick or the old. Or the noncompliant." His words tingle along my nerves, a visceral warning.

I glance at Dram and see that he's thinking the same thing.

They move our line into a square patch of cordon sand, a pen where people are being separated into groups by Gems in gray uniforms.

"Be good, Rye," he murmurs. His gaze skips over the Striders lining the fence with their feet braced, guns held at the ready. My gaze travels back to them as we wait. My vision of them is overlaid by the things Greash told us. I squint, trying to see the expressions of those with their face shields up. A few are young, like Greash, and I wonder if they wear the Trades on their sleeves. If they've earned the viper through a choice that wasn't really choice.

I fought for it. I earned this.

Who or what exactly did Greash fight in the Trades?

Bade showed us maps, months ago, when we first arrived in the mountain provinces. The Trades border the sea. I assumed the region was named after our sanctioned trade zones with city-states like Ordinance. But maybe it's more about trading the life you have for the one you want. I had always considered that a Subpar thing.

We step to the front of the line and stand before a compliance regulator. The Gem examines our Radbands. "Subpars," she murmurs. "Miners, both." The man beside her steps forward and appraises me.

"Are you the one they call the Scout?" he asks.

"Yes," I answer. "I was lead ore scout of Outpost Five."

"She's not just any Subpar," he says to the compliance regulator. "If what I've heard is true, she's a Delver." My ears prick at the word. Only Delvers can earn a place inside the underground compound.

"I'm commissioning her as a Miner."

He leans in. "Meredith will want her alive."

"If what you've heard is true, she'll survive long enough for Meredith to get here and commission the girl herself." She lifts a pile of clothes and shoves them into my arms, followed by a satchel, canteen, and items I instinctively reel back from. A flash dust pail and sifter. "Take them," she orders.

I grasp the pail, staring her down with everything I feel. I can't believe I'm back to being the Congress's miner. I yank the sifter from her hand, but I'm not prepared for the memory that crashes into me.

Mere.

Roran's mother. My friend. The woman who took in Winn with open arms, and in the next moment gave me her only hand so I'd have a chance at surviving Cordon Four. Her appendage was just like the sifter I'm grasping now. A sound escapes my lips, a breath pulled from my chest like it was punched loose.

"What about me?" Dram says, towing me back and stepping between me and the Gem. He darts a glance at me—a look of warning and understanding combined.

"Can you fight?" the man asks, sizing Dram up.

"We both can," Dram answers.

The man hands him a rifle and a pouch of ammunition. "Don't try shooting Striders, Gems, or anyone else. Triggering mechanism on these only recognizes the biometric signatures of vultures, gulls, and other cordon creatures. You aim at anything else, and the Striders will take you down without a second thought."

Dram nods at me. "She's better than anyone you've ever seen fighting the things in the cordons. If you're passing out weapons—give one to her."

"We need a scout more than we need another Dodger."

"A . . . *Dodger*?"

"You avoid all the dangers out there—and you help everyone else do the same."

Dram has the look he wears when he's trying not to curse in someone's face.

"Next!" the Gem calls.

"Wait." I step forward, willing her to be compassionate, because I have nothing—nothing—with which to bargain. "I have a friend here," I say quickly, my words tumbling over each other. "He was processed at the same time. A Conjie. Can you assign him to our squad?" *I am the reason he is here.* I don't say those words. Perhaps my eyes do. There is a black space inside me, widening with every moment—every horrific encounter here—because I know that whatever we're going through, it's worse for Roran. I still have my hands.

"I could mine extra dust, work longer—"

"Your memorial pendant."

"What?"

Her violet eyes drop to my neck. "I've heard that Subpars from the outposts wear them. Do you have one?"

"Two." My voice is a stark whisper.

"Orion—" Dram says.

"Wait." I loosen my coat and reach inside my shirt, like another part of me is going through the motions. I free my glass pendants so that they hang down my chest, one blue, one yellow.

"Don't." Dram bites out the word.

I remember Roran, his hands braced against the tree he conjured, laughing as it wound upward above our heads. I remember those hands touching his mother's arm, in the place she could still feel. *When* she could still feel.

I slip Mom's pendant over my head. Dram curses and kicks the dirt. He won't watch me give this away because he knows it's part of me—as much as my skin, or blood. Maybe more.

The Gem takes it with wide eyes and a look of delight that's out of place on her stern features. "How . . . quaint. We're told your traditions, and there's a Subpar pendant on display in the museum. It holds someone's ashes, right?"

"My mother's," I lie. Now it just holds a bit of dirt from the provinces. If it still held Mom's ashes, I'm not sure I could've given even that small part of her away. With trembling fingers, I grasp Wes's pendant and lift it over my head. I tuck my brother's memorial glass into the Gem's hand. "Please." My voice breaks, which is right because I am breaking apart inside. Her fist clenches around it, and I wait to see if it will be enough.

The Gem slips my pendants into her pocket. I wonder if she has any idea, the worth of them. They are memory and promise and hope bound together and worn as a testament. Invisible threads connecting me to the people at the other end of them, on the other side of this life. They were the last tie I had to my life before, to the girl I was.

"Find your friend." The Gem sweeps her hand toward the lines of Tempered Conjies. "I'll assign him to your squad."

Dram doesn't say anything as we search, but the space between us is weighted with our unspoken words.

I can't believe you did that.

It was all I had to give.

It wasn't something you give away. Ever.

I think of the bonding cuff I tore off my wrist and trampled in the dirt yesterday. I am losing pieces of myself all over this stretch of leached earth.

A crowd mills around between the Striders and compliance officers, most of them cradling their arms against their chests, still coming to terms with severed limbs. Fear pushes through my veins, reminding me that I still have full circulation.

"There," Dram says, pointing at Roran. His back is to us, his dark hair still woven with twigs, tangled now. I can't see his hands. Or whatever the Congress has replaced his hands with.

"Roran!" I call.

"Rye, maybe it's better if I talk to him—"

But I'm steps ahead, pushing past Tempered Conjies to get to him, to—

He knows me at once. I'm so relieved that he's still inside there—that the horror of processing didn't destroy him—that I'm even glad to see the resentment banked in his dark eyes. Hate is better than hollow.

"You're going to be in our squad. We'll look after you—" My words stop. They've hit the wall of Roran's bloodshot gaze. It tells me not to come any closer, that I've already trespassed too much.

Dram clasps his shoulder. "If we're going to fight our way out of this, we need to stick together."

"Step in my steps," Roran mutters.

I've earned it: the mocking tone, those words thrown back in my face. I've led Roran straight into his worst nightmare.

ELEVEN

7.4 km from flash curtain

THE COMPLIANCE REGULATOR eyes Roran over her screen-com. "Dodger," she announces flatly. Her assistant hands Roran a rifle and a stack of gear, tossing a pair of crude hinged hands atop the pile. Dram steps in to fasten Roran's appendages, which is good because the kid looks like he's eager to try driving his metal fingers into their eye sockets.

"Your squad leader is Reuder." She points to a Dodger leaning against the side of a squat metal building, his rifle slung across his chest. "Check in with him. He'll show you to your barracks and rations."

Dram carries Roran's gear and meets my eyes over the top of his head. He's staring down at the things now attached to his body. Dented, twisted metal that has been worn by countless Conjies before him. He unfolds his arms, tries to let them hang at his sides, but these are not hands. And these are not the arms he knows.

A shudder of revulsion rolls through his body. The free Conjie who laughed and spun petals from his hands is gone.

In his place stands a Dodger with hands that are tools made for killing cordon creatures. Everything a boy was, cut down and fitted for a solitary purpose. A person whittled into a weapon.

"You gave away your pendants for me?" he asks.

"I traded the memory of my brother for the one who's still alive."

I wait for him to acknowledge what I've said: that he is a brother to me—as much as Wes was. More, in some ways, because Wes was just a baby, and Roran and I have fought and bled for each other. But the anger in his eyes remains, and he doesn't say any of it.

"You don't need a piece of glass to remember someone," he says. He turns and walks into the barracks.

I press my hand over my heart, where I used to feel glass, warm where it touched my skin.

———

Our squad leader speaks to us with a grumbling reluctance. I barely make out the words *rations* and *follow* before he shoves away from the side of the barracks like it was the one thing keeping him upright.

His hands aren't crude appendages but the perfect, carefully formed cirium prosthetics given to Conjies in Alara.

We descend a set of wooden steps into a rectangular space. The building is windowless, half underground. Even down here, I feel particles tickle my throat, like the feeling just before a sneeze. A few of the squad members lift their heads as we near; most barely look up from their beds.

I have to squint, my eyes adjusting to the murky half-light as we make our way toward a row of bunk beds lining one side of the barracks. Three rows of narrow beds, with gray blankets and flat pillows. There's a rack for Dodgers' weapons, but no space for personal belongings. Probably because nothing here belongs to us.

Still, it could be worse. It could be a cage.

"You're Subpars," Reuder says. It's not a question, but I nod anyway. "You're a long way from home."

I feel the familiar ache at the thought of Outpost Five. My eyes flick to his hands. "So are you," I answer.

He squints, like he's trying to see me through a lens. Dirt and dried blood crack in the creases of his skin. "Name?"

"Orion. This is Dram."

"Your other names?"

I hesitate. It's possible he means our last names. But his dark eyes bore into me, and I know he means the names that have stories attached to them. By now, most of the squad sits watching, listening to our exchange.

"Scout," Dram answers. "She was lead ore scout in Outpost Five. I was her marker. We were Fourth Ray cavers."

Silence greets his explanation. I'm not sure how much of it they understand.

Reuder leans against a wooden support beam. I'm beginning to suspect he has an injury he's trying to ease. "I'm not sure why they allowed you to live and why you're not both headed on a hover to Cordon Two, but I will tell you this: compliance is the key to our survival. It is all that matters. If you step out of line, I will turn you in myself." Reuder apparently believes in using all his words at once, firing them at us like the bullets of an automatic gun. I feel them land, the concussive impact. Anger blooms inside me.

I step toward our squad leader, and Dram catches hold of my arm. "Compliance," Dram says loudly. "Got it." He steps on my toes until I stop pulling away.

There are a few things I'd like to say to Reuder of the shiny Alaran hands. But I have a role to play here. If I'm to gain an opportunity to become a Delver and earn Fortune, then I have to bury my resentment deep as a vein of ore.

"Tomorrow you begin your service to the city-state," Reuder says, and I catch an edge of bitterness in his tone. He may be compliant, but he's not happy about it. "This is your gear." His muscles strain as he lifts two packs from hooks behind him. As he crosses the uneven stone and dirt floor, I notice his limp. I take the pack he shoves into my hands. "These contain your canteens, nutri-pacs, medkits, flash blankets, clothes. Armor's over there."

Dram and I exchange a glance. This is more than they gave us in the cordons of Westfall. We might actually have a chance here.

"We need another pack," I say. "For Roran." I motion to the eleven-year-old sulking in the corner.

"If he wants supplies, he'll have to speak up for himself," Reuder says.

Roran peels himself away from the shadows and saunters toward Reuder as if he'd like to test his spit in the man's face. "Roran. You haven't heard of me. My family's dead. I can't promise compliance, but I'll fight the glenting vultures."

Reuder studies the boy. "Three days, and the swelling will stop making you feel like your arm's about to burst." He pulls one of Roran's folded arms free and adjusts the straps and pulleys of his appendage. "You've got to loosen these every hour.

Helps with the swelling. You've got the fever. That's a normal reaction to the cirium. Sleep it off." He loops the pack over Roran's shoulder. "I'm not going to say you'll get used to it. But it gets easier.

"We take our meals as a squad, at the table. Twice daily, cordon rations." Pouches line the shelves, just like the ones King and his men ate from in Cordon Three. Real food, instead of nutri-pacs. "Fridays off," Reuder continues, "curfew's at ten, and, of course you must be deconned before you enter the barracks—"

"Deconned?" Dram asks.

"Decontaminated." Reuder stares at us blankly. "Did you not have decon units in Westfall?"

"We didn't have *meals* there, either," I mutter.

He shakes his head. "How did you Subpars protect your-selves from exposure?"

Dram shoves his sleeve up past his Radband. "We didn't."

"Well, I guess the stories about you in the Honor Hall are true. The hardy and brave Subpars, who need nothing but their pickaxes and cavers' creed."

"If only I had my axe right now," Dram says.

Reuder grins. "Welcome to the squad, Subpars." He turns away. "You missed mealtime. You'll find nutri-pacs in your gear bags." He joins other squad members at the table, where they're playing a dice game.

"Glenting skant," Dram mutters.

Roran vaults into the nearest vacant bunk and stretches out, one leg dangling over the side. He's not fooling me. I know he's terrified.

Whatever we face tomorrow in the cordons, it includes a

guaranteed march closer to the flash curtain and its creatures. He will have heard all about it from Mere, but stories about the cordons pale in comparison to actually experiencing the burnt sands.

Dram and I choose our bunks, and as I run my hand over the thin blanket, I try to imagine what Mere would tell her son. I want to assure him that the worst is over. Can there really be anything worse than having your hands cut off, your abilities taken?

Then I think of mining flash dust. The burning sand. Suffocating air. Bearing the attack of flash vultures, some with the curtain in their bites. Of watching cordon winds rise up and steal away someone you love until they are nothing but dust in your pail, and I think, *Yes. There are worse things than Tempering.*

"You know what Graham would say, don't you?" Dram asks.

I look at him, lying with his arms pillowed behind his head. I smile because he's right: I know exactly what our old mentor would say. But I miss Graham with a piercing ache, so I don't answer, just so I can hear his words again, even if they come from Dram.

"You can't do his climbing for him," Dram says.

I'm facing Roran, but what I see is the second ledge beneath tunnel eight, stretching into darkness beyond the glare of my headlamp. I see my blistered hands, knuckles bent, struggling to maintain a crimp hold.

I can't do your climbing for you, girlie. Graham's words echo through my memories. *You're going to have to keep going, keep reaching. Just step in my steps.*

I climb up to Roran's bunk. "Hey." He doesn't look at me. "Bade and Aisla know where to find Arrun." I lean closer, lowering my voice. "Help is coming."

"I believed you the first time you said that. So did the other people you abandoned."

"Rora—"

He twists the pulleys and forms his appendage into a crude gesture.

"Clever," I mutter. I set rations on his blanket. "Don't use up all your energy hating me." I tear open the nutri-pac with my teeth, giving him a hint as to how he might do this later, on his own. His wrists are swollen over the edge of the appendages, and sweat sheens his face. "I'll ask Dram to come help loosen your appendages, then you can tell him to go flash himself too."

I drop to the ground and give Dram a look. "Roran needs help, but he'd rather die than admit it. His anger might kill him before the cordon does."

Dram lifts a brow. "I don't think anger is fatal." He climbs up past me. "You're still alive." I give him the same gesture Roran gave me.

I dig through my pack and find a set of clean clothes, then stride to the back of the barracks, into one of the shower alcoves. I step into the pod, and water shoots from a mechanized arm that revolves around me. A scent lifts on the steam, as a cleanser mists my hair and body. Water streams over me, and I will it to wash away some of my anger, too.

The lights suddenly flicker and fade. I duck my head outside the shower and the water cuts off. In the half-light, I can just make out the bare outlines of bunks and tables and gear.

"What's happening?" I call.

"The lights are set with atmospheric sensors," Reuder says. "They change to night-dim as a warning."

That sounds ominous. I drag on clothes without bothering to dry off.

"A warning for what, exactly?"

"Flashtide. Happens most nights around midnight. You don't want to be without shelter when it comes."

I wring the water from my hair and twist it into a knot. I step from the shower and run into half-dressed, dripping Dram. I look up at him, just as a shadow peels away and leaps toward us. It throws something—a blanket?—over Dram, and two more squad members grab hold of him. I jump toward them, my hands claws, prying at their arms.

A blanket drops over my head, pulled so tight my neck bends. I thrash, but arms clamp me around the waist and jolt me off my feet. I yell, my voice muffled. Dimly, I'm aware of Roran's hoarse shouts.

"This will be over soon." Reuder's voice. "The Overburden is different from the cordons of Westfall. Air currents bring the flash curtain's particles to us in ways you never experienced. I could tell you what happens to the air here after midnight, or I could just show you." The person holding me grunts as one of my kicks lands. I'm hauled up the stairs.

"What are you doing?"

"Initiation." The blanket is whisked off me. A girl with more talismans than hair clamps my arms with her appendages. "We all did it."

Roran is yelling, spitting threats at the Dodger carrying him up the steps.

"The night-dimmed lights are the only warning you get. You have to learn to feel the danger."

They push us out the door and bar the entrance.

"Don't let it kill you," Reuder calls.

It's the first time I've ever *smelled* the flash curtain. Ribbons of orange spiral down from the sky, as if they're unwinding from a roll suspended in the stars. We stand transfixed; even when Roran tugs at my arm, I'm helpless to do anything but watch. The smell is so strong I taste it, like ammonia on the back of my tongue.

The hairs on the back of my neck lift, then along my arms. I feel all at once breathless. More ribbons descend, clouds of luminescent amber and orange, the color of Dram's Radband. The sight mesmerizes me, even as I begin to feel the sting, like an emberfly landing on my arm. Waves of orange aural bands collide against yellow and citrine—shades of flashfall I've never seen, never knew existed. They undulate in waves that break over the horizon and cascade toward the cordon like pieces of exploded stars.

Flashtide.

I sense it pulling me, drawing me across the cordon sand. It's a lure, bait at the end of a hook—I realize that on some level, even as it reels me in.

"Scout!" Roran shouts. I hear him, distant. The flashfall performs its dance over the horizon, reaching as high as the flash curtain, and winding down . . .

. . . down—

"SCOUT!" Roran screams in my face, and I'm pulled from the orange spirals. His brown eyes are glassy with tears—anger, fear. They pull me from the curtain's hook, and I stumble with him toward the barracks. He shoves me toward the door, his appendages unyielding against my particle-abraded skin.

I falter down the first couple of steps, gripping the railing so I don't pitch forward. Roran has his appendages grasped around Dram, pulling him toward our refuge. He shouts Dram's name, then a curse, and one of his appendages snaps off at the buckle. They crash into the barracks, barreling down the steps ahead of me. I slam the door and drive the bolt through. All of me shakes. So hard. And over all of it, that odor, like the strike of a match. I make it to the bottom of the stairs and glare at our squad leader.

"That ritual just saved your life," he says. "You needed to fear it. To respect its power. Up there, we could've pulled you back in."

"I notice you didn't."

Reuder shakes his head. "If you thought I'd be willing to die for you, you'd be wrong."

"Yeah, I got that."

"I warned you."

"Not enough."

"Hard to explain the flashtide's . . . draw. Techs in Alara compare it to a fish that lives deep in the ocean. A fish that illuminates a light in order to draw its prey. It consumes them while they're still dazed by the light. Can you imagine scientists giving that kind of animalistic intention to the flash curtain?"

"To what?" I ask. "*Consume* living matter?"

"Or defend its existence."

"You're talking about a solar anomaly. It doesn't have survival instincts!"

"The flashtide didn't start happening until Delvers began

placing devices beneath the curtain. The Congress developed ways to control the flash curtain, and it laughed at us all."

"You speak like a free Conjie. Not everything on earth is *alive.*"

"Then give me another explanation for what just happened to you." He opens a case and withdraws three syringes. "I give you your first dose, but after this, you'll go to the prickers." He administers the serum, one of us at a time. "Each day, when you return from the cordon, you'll file through a tent where you will be given a dose of treatment to prevent radiation sickness."

My father's compound. He succeeded, but instead of freeing us, it's the most successful bondage Congress has ever had over us. We serve, we live. Just like in the cordons. Only . . . my gaze flicks to the door, and I consider what we just experienced on the other side of it. Flashtide.

The Overburden isn't as bad as the cordons I crossed on the other side of the flash curtain.

It's worse.

TWELVE

6.9 km from flash curtain

WE WEAR ARMOR, like we're going into battle. I can't guess why they didn't equip us like this in the cordons of Westfall, unless they just wanted us for flash dust. Here, it actually feels like they want us to live.

Some of us, anyway.

They march the Brunts before us, men and women, a mix of ages. They don't wear armor, though many have tried to fashion protection from pieces of wood and rope—even bits of glass. They hold long spears. The ones with hands, anyway. Most are Tempered Conjies, their cirium-stumped arms still swollen from processing. Others have been fitted with crude appendages, blunted, forklike tines that resemble fingers and thumbs.

I can't tear my gaze from the Brunts. Most are young men; there are a few women, and someone really short, heaped beneath layers of piecemeal armor. Fire, I hope it's not a child. I think of Winn trembling beside me in Cordon Four, wearing Graham's too-big suit over hers for extra protection. There was never enough protection.

Dram turns from his place with the Dodgers, following my gaze, like he's reading my thoughts. He glances back at me and lifts his rifle. He'll do his best to protect them. And me—I'll find the dust as fast as I can so we can collect it and get the hell out of the Overburden.

As we pass beyond the fence, some of them murmur anxiously, but most are silent with terror. Greash said they're tagged with transmitters. I think of the devices I saw in the prison cordon. The towers that drew the emberflies with some sort of tech. Congress adapted that tech to people, to attract cordon creatures and give the Dodgers steady targets to aim at.

I'm in the back of the procession with the other Miners, seven of us assigned to this quadrant. My collection pouch sways with every step. I feel once more like the lead ore scout of Outpost Five, guiding my caving team to the only element that earns us freedom. Only, there was never any freedom then, and there isn't this time, either. There's just exposure in the Overburden and dust that buys us refuge from it.

We trudge across the desolate ground, silent but for our heavy footfalls, and the occasional murmuring voices. A ragtag army come to steal from the flash curtain. I trip over scrub brush that pokes up from cracks in the ground, dead-looking bushes with thorns as big as my fingernails. If we're not careful, they'll tear holes in our suits and leave us exposed to the elements. It's like everything that survives in the flashfall is hostile—even the plants. The Miners don't watch the skies. I'm scanning for flash vultures, but they've barely lifted their heads for the past kilometer.

"Is it all like this, Kara?" I ask the girl next to me.

"Like what?" She doesn't lift her eyes from the sand.

"Covered in these thorny plants."

"The plants?" She looks at me, startled. "Who cares about the glenting plants?"

My gaze darts over the land stretching before us, to the Dodgers just ahead of us, all with their heads bent. "Then what is everyone looking for? There's no flash dust here."

"I've got movement!" Reuder shouts. "Dodgers up! Protect the Miners!" A wall of armored bodies hems us in.

"What's hap—"

They come up through the ground.

It's so unexpected that, at first, I can't make sense of the ridges of sand streaming toward the Brunts like underground bullets the size of my fist.

"Cordon rats!" Kara shouts.

I stare, openmouthed, as the creatures burst from the sand, fast as a dust storm, and launch themselves at the Brunts. Their thick tails are barbed, like spiny branches, and they swing them into their targets, latching on. Brunts scream, kicking and beating at the creatures with their makeshift weapons.

The furry brown beasts are everywhere, clambering up from the sand and attacking the nearest Brunt. They make a squeaking sort of cry as they tear through the thin layers of clothes, rooting for flesh. Soon I can't hear the rats anymore, just the Brunts crying out.

I step forward, and Kara clutches my arm. "Stop," she hisses, and I can see tears welling in her eyes. "This is how they serve Alara. This is how we stay alive."

"Move on!" Reuder calls.

Dram raises his rifle.

"No!" Reuder commands. "Save your ammo, Subpar. There's

nothing to be done for them. The tail barbs are poison, a toxin that paralyzes the prey." Even as he explains, the Brunts stagger, and two more fall to the ground, limbs jerking. "Mark the coordinates, Kara," he orders. She types into a screencom on her wrist.

"Why?" I ask, my voice hoarse.

"You know why," she says.

"I need you to say it."

"We mark the location so we can collect the flash dust tomorrow."

I'm falling down a well of despair so deep, I feel like I'm folding in on myself, my soul collapsing until it disintegrates. I stand in my squad, a dutiful servant of Alara, watching four Brunts writhe on the ground, tossing up cordon sand as they flail, covered in cordon rats. One man's face is bleeding, and as a rat nibbles close to his mouth, he bites it, crushing it with his teeth even as he cries in agony.

I slide back my face protection and vomit. I thought I knew fear in the cordons of Westfall but this is something I didn't know existed—terror that drives you to paint a target on someone else's back.

Kara tugs my arm. "We have to keep going, or it will be in vain."

We march onward, and the cries fade to whimpers as we pass. I stumble over a rocky bit of ground, not looking where I'm going, the stale taste of vomit stinging the back of my throat. I think of the cages in the prison cordon, the machines that moved us toward the curtain and forced us to mine dust for Congress. Machines don't work in the Overburden, so Congress made one out of people.

I see the squads now for what they are: cogs in Congress's wheel, gears in a flash dust factory. I wonder morbidly what hurts worse—the tails or the teeth.

Dram maneuvers himself to my side. A glance at his face tells me he's riding his own waves of shock.

"If that happens to me—" I begin.

"It won't."

"But if it does . . ." I touch his shoulder before he can argue again. "I need to know you have a bullet in there for me." I nod at his rifle.

"They won't fire at a human heat signature."

"Then use your knife," I answer.

He holds my gaze, brows lowering. "Same," he says, and I nod. Teeth and tails won't matter for us.

His gloved hand catches me behind the neck, and he tugs me close, our headgear pressing together. Then he's gone, jogging back to his squad, his place in the machine.

We've promised each other death without suffering, and it's a sign of just how bad things have gotten that I now feel like I can breathe again.

———————

The hours wane, and in the absence of sunlight, I gauge the passing of time by my body's reaction to radiation exposure. It starts with the heaviness in my chest, like I'm breathing with a boulder pressed to my rib cage, then the dryness that travels up my throat until my mouth feels like I've swallowed sand. I probably have—tiny particle dust that leaks past my headpiece. We put on eyeshades, but I feel myself squinting behind them, even closing my eyes, walking blind for moments at a time, just to spare my burning retinas.

"Just ahead," Kara announces, consulting her screencom. "Twenty meters."

My stomach grows hollow, but this is our third collection site. I thought they would need me to help scout for flash dust, but all they need are Brunts and cordon rats.

A small flag whips in the wind above the spot. "Fire," I curse beneath my breath. The Congress loves its glenting flags. And cirium cloth, too. They'll use precious metal for a marker flag, but not as added protection for people. I yank the flag from the sand—somehow I got tasked with this odious job—and jab it into my pack. I wonder if all the teams function this way. *Lead people out to die, mark with flag. Collect flash dust from unfortunate Brunts, retrieve flag.*

I collapse to the ground and sit cross-legged as my squad of Miners holds our position and the Brunts move into place. A few of them limp, having pulled barbed tails from their legs before the venom could take full effect. They lumber over the collection site, visible now as tattered clothing and shoes, scrap pieces of armor and sticks—whatever the curtain failed to consume in the evening's flashtide. There are a few bones, some ashes. And flash dust.

The Brunts move on, strapping on whatever useful bits they scavenged, taking their places as lures to keep the flash curtain's horrors occupied while the rest of us do our jobs.

The Dodgers fan around us as we scurry in with our collection pouches and sifters, scooping the sand on hands and knees, an eye on every shifting line of sand, lest it belong to something with teeth. But this time we need little effort; there is so much dust. I try not to think about how many died here and how their deaths give us another day of living.

The Dodgers keep their rifles angled upward, scanning the sky for vultures. Dram moves so that he stands at my back, a couple of meters away. A knife gleams at his side, and though he's lifted his gun, his eyes trace the sand around me.

The buzzer sounds in the distance.

"Move out!" Reuder calls.

I shove to my feet, securing my ore pouch and sifter as we trudge back toward the camp. An anxious voice carries from the front—the pack of Brunts. I can barely breathe through the shield protecting my face, I can't imagine using my energy to form words. But as I watch, a Brunt pulls away from the cluster and stoops to lift the smaller one I saw earlier. It *is* a child. A boy, younger than Roran.

Oh, flash me.

The man staggers, trying to hold on to the child I assume is his son.

One of the heavily armed Dodgers stops and stares at me. Dram. Waiting to see if he'll need to hold me back.

In this moment, I'm glad they didn't commission me a Dodger. I'm yearning for a weapon, so I can attack the next Strider I see.

"Move, Dodger!" Reuder commands, looking back at Dram.

But Dram holds his ground, boots planted wide against the rising cordon wind. He watches my face.

"Winn," I say, thinking of the child we protected in the cordons. He nods, like he expected my response, and jogs away from the Dodgers, passing ahead of them toward the Brunts.

"Stay with your glenting squad!" Reuder shouts.

Dram slings his rifle over his shoulder and lifts the boy from the man's arms. One of the man's appendages is bent at an odd angle, into a sort of zigzag shape that looks like it could've been someone's idea of a cruel joke. I see now that he's injured—lifting the boy must've opened his wound.

"You can't save them," Reuder says. "Congress made him a Brunt!"

"Flash Congress," Dram says. He drapes his armored vest over the child.

Reuder shakes his head. "Don't do this, Berrends. You're young and strong—you might actually have a chance. But not if they make you a Brunt."

"You know who I am?"

"Everyone knows who you are. There are Striders just waiting for a chance to punish you. Don't give them a reason."

"Already met them," Dram mutters.

"Maybe since you weren't Tempered, you didn't get a healthy dose of fear at processing," Reuder says.

"Did you lose your humanity when you lost your hands, or just your balls?"

Reuder shakes his head. "You've been out here *one day.* Show me how brave you are after a week."

"I never said I wasn't scared," Dram says.

"We don't protect them; we protect the Miners!"

"We can do both." Dram hoists the child onto his back.

"Are you insane?" The Dodger nearest him lurches away. "That Brunt's tagged with a transmitter. You'll draw the creatures right on top of us!"

Dram spears him with a look and walks a few meters away.

"You just put a target on your back," Reuder calls, "and I'm not talking about the kid."

———————

They may have commissioned me a Miner, but I will always be a warrior first when it comes to Dram, and I don't need a Dodger's rifle to defend him.

I've worked my way to the front of the squad, up beside the Dodgers. Reuder glances at me and just shakes his head. I return my focus to the land and air around Dram and the unconscious child he's shouldering. He keeps pace halfway between the Brunts and the rest of our squad, a distance deemed an acceptable risk by the others. They haven't forgotten that Dram's holding a tagged Brunt.

Neither have I.

I'm not the only one watching Dram's back. Roran walks at his side in defiance of Reuder's orders. He doesn't lift his eyes from the ground.

We near the corral tower, and I begin to breathe easier. I push back my headpiece with a sigh. Dram and Roran have theirs off, and their conversation carries.

"You're angry. I get that," Dram says, slinging a look at Roran. "You want to blame Orion for this, I can't stop you. But know that you were two glass pendants away from being one of them." Dram thrusts his finger in the direction of the Brunts.

"Talk to me about it when they cut off *your* hands," Roran says.

"You close yourself off because you've lost everyone. Believe me, I understand. But there is a shortage of people left in this world who care about you, Roran. Be careful who you push away."

"You *understand*? You're a Subpar—one of *the fortunate ones*. The Congress doesn't *Temper* you!"

"You know what's unfair?" Dram asks. "Being born in the flashfall. Wearing biotech that warns you every day that you're in danger and not being able to do a glenting thing about it!" Dram grips Roran's chest plate and drags him forward. "I'm *dying*," he says, under his breath.

His words crash into me, hollowing my chest. I'm the one who told him about the Radbands, but I've never heard him say it. The simple truth I can't bear to face.

Dram looks at me, but I don't meet his eyes. I'm not ready to acknowledge the certainty of his words. To myself, maybe. But not to him.

He walks ahead with Roran, and I follow, close enough to hear his soft words. "I need to know you'll look out for Orion," he murmurs. "When I . . . when I can't." Roran looks at Dram's Radband glowing dark orange.

"Will you?" Dram asks.

Roran nods.

"Then start now. You can hold on to your anger or you can hold on to someone—but not both at the same time. Not very well."

———

Roran mutters beneath his breath, and I glance up toward his bunk, where he's struggling to work a comb through his snarled hair.

"Hey."

"Go away, Scout."

"Will you let me help you?" He glares at me, but there are tears in his eyes. I climb to his bunk and tuck the comb into the curve of the fingerlike ends of his appendage. His right appendage is equipped with pulleys that can be adjusted to move the fingers. I tighten them until they curl around the comb, then guide it to his head. The comb falls the first two times, so on the next attempt, I use my own hand to keep it in place, and together we draw it through his hair.

It's awkward. Me, helping an adolescent boy do something that only a child usually needs help with. And with every pass through his hair, there's an awareness that this is at least partially my fault. But he doesn't pull away.

After a few minutes, I wave my empty hands before him, to show him he's doing it on his own. A look crosses his face. Not relief—the circumstances are too grim for that—more like an awareness that he can adapt, that he's taken a step closer to being the person he was before. Still, there is one thing he can't do.

"What about this?" I touch the talisman discarded at his side. He nods stiffly.

I lift the twig. The white flowers he conjured last have long since wilted and torn free. I twist his hair around it, the way I've seen Dram do.

"Is there a special way I should do this?" I'm crossing into the sacred, the rituals the Conjies do, but don't speak of.

"We usually . . . conjure it . . . into our hair," he says softly. It cost him something to say the word. *Conjure.*

I wind strands of his straight brown hair around the twig, tying them in tiny knots.

"I'm sorry about your pendants," he says.

"You were right—I don't need them to remember my mom

and Wes. It was just . . . a way for me to feel that they were still close somehow. Even though they're not."

"We believe they are." He looks at me, brown eyes solemn. "We are elemental, and the elements are everywhere. Matter and energy change—they don't cease to exist."

Now I understand the depth of his grief. He is suffering more than the loss of his limbs and his ability to conjure. In a single moment, the Congress effectively cut him off from his mother and father, and everyone who came before him. His heritage. The elemental.

"Don't cry," he mumbles.

I turn my head and swipe my hand across my eyes. "If there's a way to restore you," I whisper fiercely, "I'll find it."

He holds my gaze a moment, then nods. With one point of his appendage, he drags a chipped piece of cirium closer. It's a thin shard of metal about the size of my thumbnail. It's not like the ore I mined; this is perfectly smooth, refined. I can't imagine how hard he hit his stump against something to break this off.

"For a talisman," he says. "So you don't forget your vow."

"I'm not a Conjuror."

"You made a promise like one."

THIRTEEN

I STAGGER FROM the barracks and blink owlishly at the washed-out sky.

"We live another day," Dram says. He shoves his face shield up on his forehead, making his brown hair stick up in spikes.

"You sound surprised," I say, pulling my own headpiece on.

"Nah, just disappointed," he says. "I'm exhausted. Eternal sleep would have been nice." He grins at me, and I feel lighter somehow, even though I'm dragging beneath the weight of my gear.

I thrust my sifter through my belt. "Perhaps tomorrow." We joke about it, because fear weighs on us more than our armor and cirium suits. When you don't have a choice about facing death, you make it less of a reaper, more of a punch line.

A few Striders patrol the fence. They wear the seal of Alara on their sleeves like us, but their external dosimeters glow yellow, and they throw glances toward the cordon like they're expecting the flash curtain to come creeping into the camp. Between them, a woman sags on her feet, one of her appendages dangling. I search her features to see if she's one of the Conjies I know.

"Orion," Dram says, his voice low, "time to quit blaming yourself for the Mods."

I drag my attention from the woman and join the rest of our squad at the turnstile. I let go of my regret, because if I don't get hold of my focus, I'm going to lead us somewhere that gives Dram the eternal rest he's been craving.

I sigh, loud enough that Dram turns to look at me.

"This is all temporary, Rye," he says.

"Yes, because we're likely to die at any moment," I mutter.

He grins. We left Outpost Five, but we haven't lost our Subpar humor.

———

We've been gone half the day, and stand regrouping after a flash vulture attack, when Reuder stops to pull some sort of viewing device from his pack. He holds it to his face shield and peers out over the cordon.

"Strays," he calls. "Fifty meters, southwest. A pack."

Our squad moves into defensive positions as three of the creatures approach.

"What are they?" I ask.

"Cordon dogs," Reuder says. "The Congress trained dogs to scent flash dust, and these are the ones that survived and adapted. But they're feral. Deadly." He lifts his weapon.

"Wait," Dram commands, sighting down his rifle. He stares down the nearest dog, finger hovering over the trigger. The stray—a wiry, short-haired thing, more bone than beast, maintains its distance, trotting back and forth, close enough for me to count its ribs.

"Shoot it!" Reuder growls.

Dram lowers his rifle and hands it to me. "Keep it in your sights, Rye." He stoops and grabs a flash vulture carcass, holding it out to his side, knife tucked in his other hand.

"You're insane, Berrends!" Reuder calls.

"So you've said." He walks toward the dog, slowly, broken vulture carcass held like a flag of surrender. The dog bares its teeth, growls low and deep. Dram says something to it. I'm too far to hear him, but I have no problem hearing the stray's snarling response. I've got the thing's head in my crosshairs, fingertip brushing the trigger. *Dram, you are insane*, I think.

He slowly lowers his feathered offering to the ground and backs away, eyes trained on the snarling dog. One step, two . . . the dog follows, like he's through playing and ready to show Dram he prefers the taste of human.

I take a focused breath, ready to exhale and squeeze the trigger. Another dog whines.

Four steps, five . . . Dram's within reach. The dog lowers its head and sniffs the carcass. It occurs to me that it's likely never tasted flash vulture. Looking at it more closely, I'm guessing it eats mostly scrub brush, or maybe cordon rats—though it's probably in as much danger from those as we are.

The dog seizes the carcass, all the while locking gazes with Dram. They're still having a conversation—one with their bodies this time. The dog turns and lopes back to its comrades, black feathers poking from its jaws. Dram turns, grinning like he's had two mugs of outpost ale.

"Well, that's glenting brilliant," Reuder grumbles. "Now they'll never leave us alone."

"That's the idea," Dram answers. He gathers two more vulture bodies and hangs them so they dangle from his belt. "What do you think they've been eating out here? Scrub brush? They know how to kill the damned rats." He takes his gun from me and loops it over his shoulder. "We need them."

"We cut the wings off first," I say, hiding my smile as I stoop to retrieve a carcass.

"What for?" Kara asks.

"Armor," I say, sawing the cartilage with my blade.

"Fire," Reuder curses. "You're both glenting mad."

————

The dogs make another appearance less than an hour later, keeping their distance so we just see them loping along behind us. There are five now. Apparently, Dram's new friend invited a couple more to the flash vulture party.

Reuder looks back and curses. I've decided that for every five words, Reuder uses an equal number of curses. Or maybe Dram and I just bring that out in him.

The lead dog—Dram has taken to calling him Soma— breaks from the pack, treading steadily closer as the cordon winds rise and the whitish light yields to gray.

"I'll catch up," Dram announces. He pulls a—wingless— carcass from his belt and turns toward Soma. I can't catch the words he calls to the dog, but whatever he says brings the animal loping. It's hesitant, long legs crossing forward and back, forward and back, each time a little closer. Dram holds his ground, arms relaxed at his side.

Soma—I still think of it as Stray Vicious Dog—snarls and snaps its jaws. Reuder lifts his rifle. I'm wishing Dram had his knife in his free hand. The dog lowers its head, and its lips peel back, showing its teeth. Dram waits. Stray Vicious Dog whines suddenly, and it sounds like a question.

Dram drops the carcass. He doesn't back away.

Soma barks. Whines. Steps forward. Again.

And Dram calls him that name again and again. I recognize it as a Conjie word, but I don't know what it means.

"Brave," Reuder says, like he's reading my mind. "It means 'brave one.'" And I know, now, where I've heard it. In the lines outside the processing tents, as women held hands for the last time. And before that, when children hunkered in burning particle snow to evade pulse trackers.

Soma. My eyes fill with unexpected tears. Dram and his Conjie heart.

The buzzer sounds. The dogs whip their heads up, and Soma snatches the bird and lopes away. Dram jogs to catch up to us, and he reminds me of that dog, wiry and strong, exhausted but unbroken. Brave.

"Soma," I say, when he's worked his way to the edge of my group. "I like it."

Dram smiles. "Wait till those glenting rats come at us," he says. "Then you're going to *love* it."

FOURTEEN

CONGRESS NAMED THIS the pricking tent, as if we need a reminder of what happens here. We line up according to commissioning status and await our reward for the day's work.

One cc of Dad's cure. Enough to protect us for one day. I watch the needles plunging into arms and go through every new curse word I learned from Reuder. Dram and I nearly died to get this to our people, but not like this. Never like this. The cure for radiation poisoning was supposed to set everyone free, not act as grease for the Congress's flash dust machine.

I study the squad groupings, thinking how clever the Congress was to alienate us from one another by infusing this system of hierarchy. Delvers at the top—I'm still uncertain what they do, as we only ever see them here—then Miners, Dodgers, and Brunts way down at the bottom. Even I have started to view Brunts as expendable—horrifying as it is—but five days collecting their remains has proven it so. The thought wedges in my chest, and I'm glad—glad I can still feel something, even if it's shame. I make myself look at each one of their faces, and remind myself they are human beings with the same desperate hopes I have.

Before I fully realize it, I've stepped out of line, the Miners around me shooting me curious glances. I walk past the Dodgers, to the first Brunt in line. The Brunt, a man with hair just turning to gray, blinks at me like I'm an apparition. I wonder how long it's been since someone looked in his eyes.

"What's your name?" I ask.

He hesitates, darting a glance at the Striders. "Michael."

"I'm Orion."

"I know who you are, Subpar." He peels back the frayed hem of his sleeve. An indicator flashes burnt-orange.

A Radband. "You were a caver?"

"Outpost Four." He turns his wrist, and I see something etched into the black biotech of his band. Two slanting lines. My breath catches. "Not much you can do for us from back here," he says softly, tugging his sleeve back down. His gaze shifts to something over my shoulder. "Better return to your squad now, Scout."

I hear the Strider approach behind me, armor buzzing. I let my gaze slide past Michael to the other Brunts trying to stay on their feet.

"Did you forget your place, Miner?" the Strider calls. A woman's voice. I turn with surprise. I didn't know the Congress commissioned female Striders.

"I know my place," I answer, too loudly. The ghost of a smile twitches Michael's lips. I meet the Strider's eyes, but my words are for him. "I know my place."

There is something off about one of the Miners in my squad. My scout senses break past my exhaustion, nagging at me like a child tugging on my sleeve. She's not a Conjuror, or I'd sense the cirium in her Tempered limbs. No Radband pushes up the sleeve over her left wrist, so she's not a Subpar. A Natural wouldn't survive these Radlevels without a headpiece—and she rarely wears hers.

Reuder assigned us as partners, and we're on our knees, sifting the sand, wedged close together with Dram and the other Dodgers forming a defensive ring around us. I sit back on my heels, studying her as she drags her sifter through the sand.

"It's usually best to ask," she says. "Otherwise, you're only guessing at answers."

"What?" I ask.

She pulls back her sleeve. Blue symbols and numbers glow beneath the skin on the inside of her forearm. A Gem.

"GM"—she points to the first letters—"to indicate genetically modified; one-six, which designates my specific conditioning; and these symbols here, to show my commissioning status." She points to a faintly shimmering symbol. "This means Miner." She says it without a hint of fear or misgiving—in a way that no other miner I know discusses service to Alara. "This is for the Overburden." She touches the symbol beside it.

"What if you don't want to mine the cordons for Ordinance?" I ask.

She shrugs. "They have other uses for me. But I'd never earn citizenship."

Citizenship. "In Ordinance?"

Her violet eyes light up, vibrant as her Codev. "Alara," she says.

"You understand what flash dust is, right?"

"I understand that some must die in order for others to live."

"Well, then, I think you'll fit in Alara perfectly."

"Orion." She grips my arm, giving me a hint of the superior strength in her grasp. "Nature has taken from us the ability to live in a perfectly moral and just society. People would die—either way."

I slam my sifter in the sand. "You're going to blame *nature* for this?"

"The Alaran Protocol is the reason your society survived. The commitment to keep exposure to the curtain's radioactive particles 'as low as reasonably achievable' is the reason your city-state endured while so many others collapsed. To ensure the survival of many, some must be sacrificed."

"Not so great for the people outside the protected city."

"It is justifiable—"

"You see that kid?" I stab my finger in Roran's direction. "The Congress considers what they did to him *justifiable.*"

"Compliance is essential for the preservation of civilized society."

The only reason I don't try to knock her onto her backside is that I'm pretty sure I'd fail. "You do belong in Alara," I mutter. I stand, cordon sand streaming from my suit. "Find another partner." I walk away, stepping past the other Miners on their hands and knees.

Reuder throws me a disgruntled look. "Return to your position, Miner."

"No."

Dram lowers his rifle and looks at me.

"Stay with your partner," Reuder orders. "Work your grid."

Dram gives me the look that tells me some things are more important than my pride, but it's Roran's expression that makes me turn back. A gust of wind brushes my talisman against my cheek.

I'm not a Conjuror.

You made a promise like one.

I drop to my knees and scowl at the horrible half human I've been assigned to. "Just so we're clear," I mutter under my breath, "if I see a cordon rat coming, I'm going to get out of its way and let it have you."

GM16 shakes her sifter with methodical care. "I appreciate the warning, Subpar. But just so we're clear—I have genetically modified blood that repels them."

FIFTEEN

5.6 km from flash curtain

THEY CALL IT the dust trail.

It's the route where all the quadrants intersect, the final stretch of sand before arriving at camp. All the squads travel it, and all have wounded who stop somewhere along the way. The flashtide claims them in the night, and eventually, their remains are scooped up by Miners.

The dust trail.

———————

When the buzzer sounds, calling us from the cordon, our squad marches back to camp. By the end of the day, more than a few people can no longer march. Some can barely walk.

We don't wait for them. Reuder explained this vehemently to Dram and me the first day, when we tried to assist an ailing Dodger. It compromises the rest of the squad's safety, he explained. I told him that not waiting compromised our humanity. The next day, I had to wear a pack filled with rocks. I wore it marching, I wore it mining. I couldn't even take it off to pee.

I didn't question Reuder's humanity again. At least not to his face.

Every time I walk the dust trail—twice daily—I remind myself what I'm really doing here. I'm not a Miner, but a hunter. The Hunter who is finding a way to take apart the Congress. I'll do it with my bare hands if I have to. I make the promise so often, my hair should be weighted with talismans.

Bone, I decide, as we trudge the path on our way toward the curtain. If I were a Conjie, I'd use pieces of these bones poking up along the trail like markers. I'd conjure them into my hair, and they'd rattle and clack together like a skeleton come to life, calling for me to do something—*do something!*

It's possible I'm flash-fevered.

———————

Soma whines again. He turns, shifting his body restlessly, first one way, then another. The other strays respond with yips and whines, and paw at the ground.

"Something's happening," Dram says. He doesn't lower his weapon or shift from the defensive ring the Dodgers form around us.

I watch the dogs as I transfer flash dust into my ore pouch.

"Orion?" Dram calls. "Do you think they sense a sandstorm?"

Somehow I'd sensed the shift in the elements back in Cordon Four—enough to give us a running start on a sandstorm that had nearly swallowed us. I pull off my gloves and push my hands into the burning sand. "Not a sandstorm," I call. There's no current that I can sense, no churning collision of cirium stirring.

Soma paws the ground, tossing sand behind him. The others keep their usual distance from us, but even from here I can see their hackles raised, their short fur standing on end. They scent the air in a way that makes me feel like I should smell the danger too. One by one, they begin to dig.

"Probably cordon rats," Reuder says, but he sounds uncertain. We've never seen the dogs stirred to a sudden frenzy of digging. "It's too early for flashtide."

"What else is there?" Dram asks.

"Flashbursts, but those are usually—"

"Where's the nearest shelter?"

Reuder glances at his screencom. "About four kilometers west. The buzzer already sounded. We need to get back to camp."

"We need to *run* back to camp," a Dodger adds.

Dram glances at Roran, who's limping from an encounter with a cordon rat.

"He can barely walk," he says. "How long till the numbness wears off?"

Reuder shakes his head. "Hours. If you don't leave him, you won't make it back before they lock the gate."

"I'll assist the child," GM16 calls from beside me. "I can carry him."

"You're not a Vigil," Reuder says. "You don't have the strength and stamina to run with him—and that's the only way you'd make it."

Dram watches the dogs burrowing beneath the sand. "We should start digging, then."

"*Digging?*" Reuder says. You're glenting mad, Subpar."

"It's kept *them* alive!" Dram points toward the dogs. "And I'm not leaving him!" He drops his rifle and unclips his pack.

"Roran," I call. He turns, and I toss him my sifter. He'll never dig fast enough with his appendages. He hesitates for a moment, then sets his weapon down and kneels beside Dram. I join them and tear into the sand.

"The rest of you come with me," Reuder orders. "We're going to take the trail at a run!"

GM16 hesitates, her gaze swinging between me and Roran.

"You probably think I'm foolish," I mutter, scooping sand.

She watches me pensively. "That's not what I'm thinking at all." She turns and runs to catch up to the rest of the squad.

Even with my sifter, Roran struggles. "Take mine!" I direct him to my burrow, which is twice as deep as his. He shakes his head, and I pull him into it. "There are things more important than your pride!" I practically growl. I can't believe Dram's words are coming out of my mouth. He has grumbled that same phrase to me more times than I can count. I pull Roran's headpiece into place and secure it, then start shoving sand over him, burying him the way the dogs have buried themselves.

"How do I breathe?" Roran asks, and suddenly he's just a kid again. Scared.

"The air in your headpiece," I tell him.

"I don't want to be buried!"

I look at our supplies, trying to think past the rising Radlevels. "My flash blanket!" I pull it from my suit pocket, and drive my sifter into the ground to tent the top over his head. I wrap the ends around his appendages and twist the pulleys so his fingers close around the fabric. "Hang on to the ends. The wind is picking up!" Even as I speak, sand stirs, lifting around my face.

"Orion!" he cries.

I can't imagine how this must feel for him. He lost his mother this way—all of our friends. "You're safe," I assure him, and I try to say it with all the conviction of a Conjie.

"They come in threes," he says, his voice small. "The flash-bursts."

"Rye," Dram warns.

"I need to dig—"

"No time." He tucks his arms around me and pulls me into his burrow. He drives the muzzle of his rifle into the ground between us and tents his flash blanket over the top.

I can sense the energy churning in the particle-filled air. The air warms and then I feel it: a pulse deep in my veins, like the curtain's joining me inside my skin.

"Dram," I breathe, holding him tight. Our face shields press together, and I watch his face in the light of our Radbands. I wait to see if we will be turned to glass like the sands of Cordon Five.

"The dogs survive this," Dram says. "They survive this."

A sound makes us both jolt, a concussive burst that shudders up from the earth and rattles my bones. It's the sound of a cordon shard slamming against the lodge at Outpost Five. But when I open my eyes, we are not glass. My skin tingles only because of how Dram holds me so, so close.

"Roran says they come in threes," I say.

"Then we wait." Sweat drips down his face into his eyes. It's getting hard to breathe. "At least there's no emberflies," he murmurs.

"None."

"And green flashfall. Mostly."

"Mm-hmm." Green aural bands are like the shifting green of Radbands. Not good, but better than the other colors.

"I don't think the flashbursts will kill us," he says. "Not with our cozy blanket of sand."

"There's always the chance of cordon rats," I murmur. He smiles.

The air in our burrow dissipates all at once, as if the curtain is taking a deep breath in order to blow it all back at us. Dram grips the flash blanket, and we brace for the—

———

Still here. Not glass.

"Dram," I whisper. His eyes open. "I think we're going to make it."

"Only one more flashburst," he says.

"No, I mean this place. All of it."

He looks hard into my eyes. "I believe it if you believe it." Cordon winds tug at the flash blanket, and his shoulders tense around me as he grips it.

"How much air do you think we have?" I ask.

"Enough. If you need more, I'll give you mine." I grin at him, but he's not smiling. "Rest, ore scout. I promise I won't let go."

"I believe it, if you believe it," I answer. I tilt my face shield against his and close my eyes.

———

"My arms are dead."

Dram's hoarse voice draws me from my half rest. I open my eyes, and sand creeps in. It grits between my teeth. I unwind the flash blanket from where he'd wrapped it around his fists. I have to uncurl his stiff fingers and rub feeling back into his arms.

"Fire," he gasps, gritting his teeth.

I push the flash blanket and its hill of sand from atop us, and help him to a sitting position.

"I'll be fine in a minute," he says. Since his hands are still numb, I brush the dirt from his face and comb my fingers through his hair, shaking out the sand. His talisman chimes softly.

My own legs move stiffly, but I pull myself from our den to check on Roran. He sits cross-legged watching us, Soma at his side.

"You're okay?" I ask. He nods and moves his arm from the top of Soma's head to his back, petting the dog with his arm instead of his appendage.

"I can't believe he's letting you do that," Dram says.

"He came for me when it was over. Dug me out." Roran's water pouch lies open beside him, and Soma leans over and laps up water from it.

"We have to get back," Dram says. "Before they lock the gate."

We grab our gear and weapons and head toward the corral towers. The dog lopes beside us.

"Soma, go," Dram commands. Soma runs a few meters away and barks. "Leave us. Find your pack." The dog scrunches its massive body and prances closer, like this is a new game. "Soma. Go!" Dram flips his face shield up so Soma can see his stern expression. "A Strider will shoot you if you follow us into camp."

Soma wags his tail and tenses, long legs stretched before him. Dram crouches and the dog lumbers over.

"Here," Dram says, and he ties his neck cloth around the dog, so Soma can keep Dram's scent even if he can't keep Dram. "I'm coming back for it," Dram says. But I hear *I'm coming back for you.* He turns and runs back to Roran and me. Soma watches.

"Go," Dram calls.

And he does.

———

We half walk, half drag Roran back to camp.

Reuder told us, depending on where the tail spikes hit, the paralyzing effects can take hours to wear off. In Roran's case, it's taken two hours since we dug out of the sand.

The bones littering the dust trail gleam like pearl beneath the evening flashfall. Low-hanging clouds hinder our view, but part just enough for us to catch a glimpse of the fence.

"We made it," Roran says. Dram and I don't say anything. The camp lights are at night-dim.

"Can you walk on your own?" I ask. He nods, and Dram and I release him. He starts running, a rambling stagger that takes him colliding against the turnstile. It doesn't budge.

"Let us in!" he shouts. "Reuder!"

I stare past the fence toward our barracks, my chest tight as I wait for the door to open, for our squad leader to come demand we be let in. But I remember the weight of that bag of rocks he made me carry. *We don't wait for anyone, Subpar. Compliance is the first rule of surviving here.*

Roran bangs his appendage against the turnstile, and the sound clangs out across the camp. We won't survive the night without shelter, not without the serum that keeps the radiation sickness at bay.

The barracks door opens, and Reuder steps out. He watches us, silent, his face drawn in hard lines. *Please*, I think. *Do something.* But who is he to make demands? He's being punished here just like the rest of us.

A figure emerges beside him. GM16, wearing a Radsuit. She strides toward us. "My squad members are back," she shouts. "Open the gate!"

"Return to your barracks," a woman commands. I recognize her as the compliance regulator who commissioned us.

"They were helping an injured Dodger—a child!"

"There isn't time for them to properly decon before flashtide. Protocol demands we not risk exposing others—"

"You can't do this!" GM16 bangs her fist against the turnstile.

"Step away from the gate!"

"No."

"Be compliant, GM16."

"I will not be *compliant*," she says.

The turnstile buzzes, and the web of bars pulls back. GM16 looks stricken for a moment as she looks out at the burning darkness beyond the fence. She turns to the other Gems peering out from their barracks. "They are going to die without our help!"

"Proceed through the corral," the compliance regulator orders.

She lifts her head and pushes through the turnstile.

"Don't close it!" A Gem with twists of blond braids runs from the infirmary.

It's like she's the stopper on a bottle. A flood of Gems jog from their barracks and pour through the turnstile, their Codevs glowing beneath their sleeves. They stride toward us— more than a dozen of them, surrounding us in a circle so close we nearly touch. They form a barrier with their bodies—their genetically modified, flash-protected bodies. Already the temperature feels more bearable, like the air isn't going to sear me from the inside out. A man passes a nutri-pac to Dram. He hands me a canteen of water, smiling, his white teeth flashing against his dark skin.

"Hydrate first," he says. I drink, shaking with relief and the lingering effects of exposure. He shields us with his tall frame, blocking our noncompliant behavior from view of the Striders. Another Gem treats my burns with a salve that feels like water posey. Roran's shaking hard, so I help him get the canteen to his lips. With the adrenaline wearing off, shock is overtaking us.

"Here." The Gem with blond braids sets a tablet in my hand. "Put this under your tongue. It's a restorative we use in the infirmary." *A physic*, I think. The physic of the Overburden ran out here to shield us from the flashtide. Roran can't get his appendages around the tablet, so she helps him with his.

GM16 kneels beside us, her back to the camp. She unzips her Radsuit, and I nearly laugh. She's wearing rations strapped across her body. "Sorry it took me so long to get out here," she says. "Reuder had to make sure it was hidden well." She hands us each a meal pouch.

"Thank you," I say.

"Thank our squad leader," she whispers, sliding free a row of syringes. I recall the small supply of treatment Reuder has at the barracks. Tears prick behind my eyes. We might actually survive this.

The night winds pick up. The Gems shudder against the blast of heat, but it doesn't consume them like it would us. GM16 crouches beside me. She trembles, and a pang of guilt hits me. This is costing them more than a sleepless night. Like us, they are resistant, not immune.

"Thank you, GM16," I murmur.

"I always thought that I would like to be called Megan," she says.

"My mom used to say that names are important."

She nods, a knowing look in her eyes.

"Were you born with it?" I ask. "Your Codev?"

"It illuminates when we turn sixteen," she says, "when we're commissioned for service."

"Do you choose to serve?"

"It was chosen for us," she answers. "The modifications are costly. Parents sign a deed of service on behalf of their altered embryo. Those who survive owe a debt to Ordinance, payable upon their sixteenth year."

"For how long?"

"It depends upon the debt." She traces the line of code. I think of my Radband, with its biotech that resembles a depth gauge, difficult to remove without damaging vital arteries.

"Can a Codev be removed?" I ask.

"Why would I want it removed?" Her violet eyes widen, and I have the random thought that if I could choose genetically modified eye color, I'd pick exactly that hue. Then I wonder how many extra years of service it's costing her. Irises that don't need the protection of eyeshields.

"What happens to Gems who refuse to serve?" Dram asks.

"The Unaccounted," she says. For the first time, there's a crack in her doll's expression. "If caught, they are sent to Cordon Two."

Cordon Two. The prison cordon.

Dram tucks me against his side, like he senses the dark turn my thoughts have taken. "Eat," he says hoarsely, handing me a nutri-pac. I finish it off, but my stomach feels empty. I feel empty everywhere. Is there a way out of this life for any of us? Even the Gems are caught in the Congress's trap.

The flashtide descends, and the Gems brace themselves more tightly around us. To protect us, but also to hold us back. I can feel myself leaning toward those rivulets of color, as if they offer comfort. I want, need, yearn to walk out into the cordon and feel them spiral over me, down, down—

"I've got you," a Gem says to me. And I see that she's clutching my hands, keeping me from taking that senseless walk. Two Gems hold onto Dram.

"Don't listen to its lies," GM16 says.

"Does it not . . . call to you?" I ask.

"It does," she answers, "but we have a stronger ability to resist it."

The Gems close in until we're surrounded so close, I no longer feel the effects of the flashtide. They take turns, resting and sheltering. The man who gave me water—the one with the smile—has burns on his arms. He's bleeding, and it's not luminous or blue or beautiful. It's just blood, same as mine.

Shame settles over me—for the ways I resented them before. The cavers work the tunnels to earn enough Rays to get free.

Gems work the cordons to repay debts and get free. But at least in the outposts Subpars had homes and community.

This . . . this isn't living. Being alive is not the same thing as living.

"Megan?" I call softly. She's staring at something, unseeing. I repeat the name that is not her name, and she looks over. A trace of sadness lingers in her violet eyes. "How old are you?" I ask.

"Twenty."

"How many more years do you have here?"

Her perfect features shift. "Ten."

Dram murmurs a curse. I can only stare and wonder if her genetically enhanced body can endure that much exposure. That's assuming she survives the flash vultures and emberflies.

"My parents wanted to give me a chance," she says, as if that excuses her horrifying sentence here. "My sister—a Natural—died. Things in Ordinance are—" She breaks off, like there aren't Subpar words for what's happening there. "We don't have a shield."

I try to imagine what I'd be like if I'd been born a Gem in Ordinance, commissioned and taken from my family. And I know, with a return of that hollow feeling . . .

I would not wear my Codev like a badge; I'd have tried to cut the brand out of my arm and taken my chances on the run. Like Aisla.

I'd be an Unaccounted.

You are more than what they say you are, I want to tell her. "I like the name you chose for yourself," I say instead.

We are from two worlds, she and I. Even our biology is different. But we are more the same than I ever realized.

The pseudo-sky lightens, the clouds of flashfall rimmed with a buttery glow I can almost pretend is sunlight.

"Flash me, we're still alive," Dram murmurs. He groans as he stretches, like he's ninety instead of nineteen. Roran stirs, and the Gems surrounding us move away.

Dram stands and faces the fence, the outbuildings, and barracks we were exiled from last night. "The noncompliants are still alive!" he shouts.

Roran laughs, and so do most of the Gems.

Dram walks past us. "Where are you going?" I ask.

"Since we're barred from the privies, I'm going to take a noncompliant piss on the corral tower." He continues on his way, my laughter following him.

I take care of business in less dramatic fashion and return to find the Gems passing around rations. I've finally met people who make better thieves than Dram.

He returns singing, a silly, bawdy song that Graham loved. His voice is pitchy, his throat still raw from our encounter with the curtain. I've never heard anything sweeter. He sweeps me into an outpost dance. There's no music and no ale, but I feel like I did on those Friday nights. Free.

He turns me under his arm, and we laugh. We dance well together. Reading each other's body language down the tunnels has given us an innate sense of each other. I catch the sides of his head and bring him down to me. He smiles wider, still singing.

"I love you," I say. He stops singing, and his steps falter.

The noncompliants are still alive, I think, as his lips collide with mine.

The buzzer sounds.

Our barrier of Gems step away, some of them bearing burns, a few coughing from sand and ash. They meet up with their squads to begin another day of collecting flash dust. We follow, shuffling toward the turnstiles.

SIXTEEN

7.2 km from flash curtain

THEY COME FOR us as we stand in the pricking tent, await-ing our rationed dose. Enough Striders enter that their suits give a warning of their approach. Their suits get louder as they near us, a resonant whine, like hovercraft engines powering up. The hairs on my arms raise.

"Don't say anything," Dram warns beneath his breath.

I bite the inside of my cheek, just in case. My last remnants of self-control burned up like cordon sand hours ago. The injus-tice of the Overburden is more than I can bear. I want to fight someone who deserves my anger. Not a cordon creature, but a person who takes up arms to defend what the Congress is doing here. Weary as I am, another part of me is waking up, and it wants to go toe-to-toe with a Strider.

Dram's boot nudges mine. "We're in trouble enough, Rye," he says softly. "Don't make it worse." The Miners and Dodgers around us seem to dissipate, until only Dram and I stand before the med table, sleeves still shoved up to our elbows.

"Dose them," the lead Strider commands the tech. I barely register the needle, but the effects of the compound restore me like a pair of strong hands lifting me up off the ground. Maybe I can reclaim a sense of self-preservation. I roll my sleeve back down, and Dram's words replay in my mind. *We're in trouble enough, Rye.* Still, I catch myself looking into the face of each of the five men. I can't seem to lower my gaze.

Five soldiers for two unarmed Subpars.

"Restrain her," the Strider orders, shoving a pair of wrist locks into Dram's hand. This is how they demoralize us in the Overburden; when we step out of line, they force us to be the source of each other's suffering.

"No," Dram says.

"Restrain her yourself, or I'll have Wellsey do it." The Strider nods at the soldier beside him. "I promise he won't be as gentle."

"Flash me," Dram mutters, unfastening the restraints. I lift my wrists, but the Strider shakes his head.

"Behind your back, Subpar."

I comply, because Wellsey looks eager to test the shock value of his suit. And because I sense a fight brewing inside Dram. I kick his boot like he did mine moments ago. He slides the wrist-bands into place and locks them.

"Tighter," the Strider commands.

"It's already digging into her Radband," Dram says. "Any tighter, and she'll—"

"I'm losing patience, Subpar."

Dram tightens the bands, and I force myself to keep a blank expression. Wellsey grins at me, like he knows exactly how badly the metal is biting my skin.

"You should probably restrain me, too," Dram mutters. "Before I punch him in the face." He slides a glance at Wellsey.

"Oh, we have a different plan for you, Berrends."

At the mention of his name—the one he shares in common with his father—the atmosphere changes. A sense of impending threat invades the space, like the particle-charged air just before flashtide.

Another Strider enters. My stomach twists when he lifts his face shield. Nills. The Strider from our first day. The one who pulled his gun on Dram.

"You interfered with a Brunt," he says to Dram.

Dram doesn't answer. No one does. A few Dodgers cough nervously. The soldiers have sealed the tent entrance, corralled us all in.

"Answer me, Dodger."

"There was an injured boy—"

"A Brunt."

Dram stares daggers at the soldier. "He was in mortal danger."

"So you deserted your position."

"He *saved a child*," I say, ignoring Dram's warning glance.

"So you witnessed this Dodger's actions?" he asks me. A trap. My defense of Dram only confirmed his actions in the cordon. Nills turns back to Dram. "We have a system in place. Compliance is the only thing required of you."

"Compliance at what cost?" Dram asks, not bothering to shield his anger.

"At what cost?" Nills echoes. "This cost." He holds out his hand and another soldier sets a long metal object across his palm. An appendage. "This is yours now. The last owner doesn't need it anymore." He tosses it at Dram's feet. Not just any appendage, but one that's misshapen, the forked tines bent. My stomach hollows as I recognize the distinctly damaged replacement hand.

Ice. Dram's face is a block of ice, the features hard and cold, chiseled there by the same realization.

"You'd better restrain me," he says, his voice raw.

"I have bullets to restrain you," Nills answers. "And that's only if you somehow survive the charge of my armor. Go ahead and attack. Your life is worth nothing now."

"He's the son of Arrun Berrends," I say. "He's worth something to the Congress."

"I know exactly who he is, Subpar. That's why I'm making this worse than it needs to be." His lips twist in a sneer, but it's the pain in his eyes that fills me with dread. "Arrun Berrends blew up a squad of Striders. One of them was my brother." His words are a bomb, the blast ripping through every noncompliant person here.

"On your knees," he orders. Dram hesitates the space of two of my held breaths, then sinks to his knees.

"Don't," he says under his breath. To me.

My hands are fists, fingernails digging into my skin. I don't know how I'll fight unarmed, with my hands bound, but fear is driving away all rational thought.

"Tag him," Nills commands. A Strider steps forward and levels a tool at the base of Dram's head. "Don't worry," he says. "This isn't the part that kills you."

The Strider presses a triggering mechanism, and Dram hisses. I leap forward, and a Strider's arm lifts in front of me, suit humming with energy. It might as well be an electric fence. He looks at me, brow raised. Maybe he's heard stories about me, the crazy Scout from Outpost Five. A girl who might actually take a run at him.

"Dram?" I call.

"Still here, ore scout," he answers, voice strained.

I've felt the shock of Strider armor before, when I fled Outpost Five. Dram's staring at me, hard.

"Bring the child," Nills orders.

The Strider hesitates. "Greash wouldn't approve—"

"Greash isn't here. Do it."

The Strider moves through the cluster of Brunts to where the boy sits propped against the side of the tent. He hauls him forward.

"A demonstration of what it means to be a tagged Brunt," Nills says. "You already know the tag is a beacon that draws the cordon creatures. But it also allows us to put down rebellion simply and effectively. We maintain order and preserve Protocol." He sets a screencom in Dram's hand. He points it at the boy, and the tech projects a string of code. "Press it."

"No."

The Strider aims his wrist at Dram, and a code illuminates over his screencom. "Detag him or I detag you."

"Stop this," I murmur. I look at the soldier holding his arm in front of me. "You know this isn't right." His face is a mask of disbelief, but he doesn't move.

Reuder pushes his way forward. "Let the child go."

"You volunteering to take his place?" Nills asks.

Reuder glances at the boy, the child he didn't attempt to save in the cordon. "Yes," he answers softly.

Nills seems suddenly lost, but recovers his composure quickly. "Well, then. Take his place, Dodger."

Reuder helps the crying boy to his feet and steers him into a Brunt's arms. Then he kneels across from Dram. A Strider tags him. The code above Dram's device changes, the numbers arranging themselves in a different order. Reuder's tag.

"No," Dram whispers.

Reuter smiles ruefully. "Guess I've still got balls, after all."

"I won't do this." Dram's voice shakes.

"Your life or his," Nills says. "You have five seconds, Berrends." His finger hovers above his screencom. "Then I take all your choices away, permanently."

"Press it!" Reuder says. "Press it, or we're both dead."

"No!"

"You can help them. You can do something about this."

"I won't—"

"Give me back my soul, Subpar."

Dram's chest rises and falls. His finger shifts over the screencom.

"*Soma*," Reuder whispers urgently. Brave one.

"*Soma*," Dram chokes, and presses the button. Reuder's body seizes once and falls forward. Dram yells, clutching the man's limp body. He tips his head back and shouts, the sound of a soul torn apart. Then I can't see him at all, as tears flood my vision.

"I'm a Delver with Fortune," a woman calls, shoving her way into the tent. "What's going on here?"

"Cordon law," Nills replies.

She glances at the body slumped on the ground, Dram hunched beside it. "I need the girl. The Westfall scout." She searches the group of Miners. "Where is she?"

"Here," I say. I want an excuse to use my voice, remind myself that I am really here. Alive. Because I think Dram is gone. He doesn't even lift his head as the woman orders me unbound. "Where are you taking me?"

"A Delver died today. Meredith's hoping you have the skill to replace her. But in case you don't, she'll need an alternate. Name the next best Miner in your squad."

"Dram," I answer, nodding to where he sits.

She lifts a brow. "He's not a Miner."

"He was. We were the best in Outpost Five. Fourth Rays."

"That boy is noncompliant. Name someone else."

"He's the best choice—"

"Are you also noncompliant?"

"I'm wearing shackles in the Overburden. What do you think?"

Her eyes widen, and she laughs. "It's possible you'll fit right in with the other Delvers. You have a chance to win Fortune, my dear. Now look at your squad and give me a name."

Win Fortune. I can't think. I barely process her words. All I know is that Reuder's body is being hauled away and Dram's still kneeling there, like he detagged himself.

"I'll stay with my squad."

"I'm not giving you a choice, Subpar—"

"Kara," Dram says, without looking up. "Kara and Orion are the best Miners in this squad."

The woman smiles. "Thank you, Dodger." Her gaze skips over the Miners clustered beside the tent wall. "Kara, come with me."

Kara steps from the line and follows her, but my feet are rooted to the ground.

"Let's go, Subpar."

"Are we coming back?"

"No."

"Go." This from Dram, who's still not looking at me.

"Dram—"

He stands and turns the force of his glare on me. "I'm nothing now. Bait. Food for cordon rats. If you try to help me in the cordon, they'll kill you. Or force *me* to do it!" His voice breaks, and he allows Striders to steer him toward the group of Brunts. "You have a chance to live. Take it! Glenting take it, Orion!"

He turns his back on me, taking his new place beside the other Brunts as if he's accepting defeat. I was angry before, but it was nothing compared to this, a match beside an inferno.

"We have a deal." My voice is steel, harder than cirium.

"Not anymore."

"Scout." Metal tines grasp my arm, and I look into Roran's eyes. "I'll protect him," he says. "I won't take my eyes off him. I'll shoot anything that gets close."

My eyes fill with tears. "Who protects you?"

"My strength comes from a place they can't Temper," he whispers. And I remember all the times Mere said that.

"I believe it if you believe it," I whisper.

Roran nods. "Go win Fortune."

SEVENTEEN

7.3 km from flash curtain

"YOU MAY CALL me Val," the woman says. "I oversee the Delvers."

We stand at the edge of a fissure, a crack in the ground that goes deeper than I can see without dropping a flare.

"What is this place?"

"The gorge," Val answers. "It's a test."

This "test" could easily fit the barracks within its opening. This isn't like any of the tunnel entrances in Outpost Five.

I look at the other people gathered here, the man and two young women who joined us from the Delvers' pods. They gear up with equipment piled in crates. They watch me like I've come to steal their rations.

"How do we pass the test?" I ask.

"Whoever performs best earns Fortune. That person also gets to choose someone to go with them."

I pull on a harness and stare down into the gorge. All I see is Dram's face, when he ordered me to go. "What do Delvers do exactly?"

"They forge pathways beneath the flash curtain."

Her answer startles me from my haze of shock.

"*Why?*" I ask.

"Because the curtain is a caged beast—only so long as we work to keep it contained."

"You think we can help . . . *contain* the flash curtain?"

"It won't take all of you," she says. "Just one. One who's very good. But that's only for the Delvers with Fortune. For now, you have to prove you're capable. This is what you're looking for."

She lifts a handful of dirt from a pouch. It glimmers in the dark. At first I think it's the flashfall lending it the iridescent colors, but as she shifts her palm, I see bits of gems. "The flash curtain emits bursts of energy beneath the surface that we Delvers have named flashpulses. When this happens, it comes from a specific place along the curtain. It's imperative we find these places, delve paths to them, and place these pulse transmitters." She lifts a narrow, cylindrical tech that looks similar to the light bolts Dram used to mark routes.

"If you succeed here, you will gain entrance to a place you can't imagine currently." She says this without any apology, as if simply stating fact.

Fortune is beyond your comprehension. The sun is a star.

"We have technology that helps explain this further, but for now—" She holds up the soil. "Find this. Mark the coordinates in your depth gauge. Bring it up."

"Why bring it back?" Kara asks. "If you just need to find where to place the transmitters—why do you need us to mine the soil?"

Val narrows her eyes, like she's deciding which flavor of

nutri-pac she's going to choose. "It's extremely valuable to the Congress. Eludial soil contains elements unlike anything else. It's believed to have . . . transformative properties."

She goes on about her special dirt and their efforts to delve paths to the eludial seam, the bedrock directly beneath the flash curtain. I fasten my gear, only half listening. A Brunt. Dram is going to have to march out into the cordon tomorrow as bait.

"Miner."

It takes me a moment to realize Val's addressing me. I pull my gaze from the direction of the pricking tent.

"Whatever you think you have to go back to," she says, "it's gone. He's gone. Let it go, so you can move forward."

"I left people behind in Outpost Five," I say. "I keep going *because* of them—not in spite of them." I lift a pickaxe from a crate and tuck it through my harness. "That Dodger you saw—he's the reason I'll do your test. The reason I'll win it."

"These aren't like the tunnels of Westfall."

"I'll try to manage."

Her lips twist in the semblance of a smile, as if they're holding back a secret.

"You'll be equipped with a bolt gun and—"

I lift one from the ground and sling a coiled rope over my shoulder.

"Orion, you'll need a depth gauge to show proof of—"

"Fine." I slap one over my wrist. "I can earn a place inside the compound, underground?"

"In Fortune, yes."

"Fine," I murmur. I should care about the cure, and finally getting a chance to gain access, but right now all I care about is making sure my best friend doesn't die a Brunt. I crouch beside the edge of the gorge. "How much to earn Fortune?" I ask, clicking on a headlamp.

"The most," Val says. "You should know . . . there are creatures down there—"

"Creatures, yeah. I've got it." I thrust my legs over the side and let go.

The cavern is alive.

It breathes with a heartbeat I can feel pounding up through the granite beneath my fingers. My hands begin to sweat as I traverse the wall, even though the rest of me is so, so cold. I keep seeing Reuder's head fling backward, and Dram lurching after him, catching his body.

I find a chalk pouch attached to the harness and dip my hands inside, one at a time.

You have a job to do, girlie.

Fire, don't I know it.

One of the advantages of shock, I've learned, is an immunity to fear. I could stumble across a tunnel gull's nest right now and probably not care. The disadvantage is that my mind is blank, a canvas painting obliterated with white paint. My emotions are contained in a locked box, too volatile to let loose.

I'm a creature of action.

The other Delvers descend, so loudly I can hear their conversation. Whatever caving experience they have, it wasn't down tunnel nine. I hoist myself atop a ledge and tuck into the shadows. I hear the word *scout*, and it splashes a bit of color on my blank-canvas mind. They talk about me. Not in ways that would make my father proud.

"Do you think she knows?" one of them asks. "About what happens down here?"

"I doubt it. She didn't take a locating transmitter."

"She'll never make it out!"

"She's probably already lost."

"If we're charmed."

I follow, setting up a rappel in the lee of a crevice, and descend a few meters behind them.

They are a team, and they've agreed to give Fortune to the other. Now I understand the test Val arranged. It was never about anyone else. She wanted to know how far I'd go to get what the Congress wants. I have no limits. Not anymore. They blew apart the moment Dram pressed that button.

The Orion from yesterday would've approached this differently, but I'm pretty sure I just watched Dram shatter. The kind of breaking that doesn't mend. My breath catches, and I shut my mind to the images that invade, chase them back inside the box. And lock. Them. In.

Keep reaching.

Keep climbing.

Perhaps it's these caverns, or the sway of an axe at my side once more, but I feel the memory of Graham with me, his gruff voice inside my head, my heart.

What is the most important thing we bring with us into the caves? he asked me, crouching down so we'd be eye-to-eye.

Our axes, I said, my young voice full of bravado. But he shook his head.

"Light," I say aloud, now.

And what happens if our light fails?

"We find another source," I murmur, pushing off the rocks. And he taught me, finding our way across a cavern with only our Radbands glowing dimly, to an orbie pool. We carefully filled my water pouch and gave ourselves two hours of luminescent orange light until the orbies began to chew their way out.

Light is the most important thing a caver has, Orion. You could find all the cirium in the world, but it wouldn't matter if you couldn't find your way home.

"I miss you," I whisper. I can't think of Graham without a weight pressing my chest.

Keep reaching.

Something slinks from the shadows. A scuffling sound, like claws scratching against stone, and I twist to see if it's headed toward me or away. It freezes in the glare of my headlamp, and I reel back. A mole of some kind—large, the size of my axe head. I've heard other cavers describe them, though we didn't come across any in Outpost Five. I think it's blind, but the odd tentacles on its nose tell me it senses exactly where I am. The teeth and front claws are massive, like curved shovels.

There's a small knife sheathed alongside my ore pouch, but I don't reach for it. These creatures hunt earthworms. I remain still, watching it test the air with its tentacles. One of the cavers—Owen, I think—told us about creatures in the tunnels beneath the Overburden that could sense seismic shifts in the ground. I hold my breath to make myself very, very still. Soma has taught me to respect the animals that survive the flashfall. Their instincts have saved me more than once.

Suddenly, it darts across the rock and plunges its claws into the ground, pulling up worms in a blur of motion. I'm so startled I lurch back, and the creature freezes. Before I can move, the rock directly beneath its long claws shifts with a crumbling and cracking of granite. It shoots upward, into a wall of stone that separates me from the mole. Rock crumbles beneath it as it scurries away on a bridge of stone that forms as it runs.

I hang from my rope, gawking as the thing disappears into the shadows. What just happened? Val's last warning rings through my mind. *You should know . . . there are creatures down there*—that can what? *Conjure?*

I tip my head back and study the sides of the cavern rising above me. A chill prickles along my spine. It's different. Even without mapping it, I can tell the cavern's various ledges and tunnels have *shifted*.

Holy. Fire.

The creatures down here have more than a sense of the flash curtain's shifts and pulses. They can manipulate organic matter—at least stone—like human Conjurors. As much as I'm stunned by the mole's survival instincts, the analytical part of me I got from Dad is nodding in acceptance. The flash curtain's particles cause living things to adapt in different ways. Why should the human species be the only one?

At once the dangers of this crash into me. How do you find your way out of caverns that are constantly changing—and tunnels that can be closed with a wall of rock if a mole is startled?

I climb with renewed fervor, anxiety propelling me past my exhaustion. The light from my headlamp falls on vines and trees, unnatural in this environment. Plants that can't grow without light and proper soil, and yet they don't need those things because they weren't grown. They were conjured.

How many creatures can do it? All of them? A few? With every meter, my questions multiply. Does Jameson know? Val does—and the Delvers here. Why didn't this happen on the west side of the flash curtain, in the tunnels beneath the Barrier Range?

And then an even bigger thought collides with the others, spinning my mind into a whirlwind: how are they doing it in cirium? Very few Conjurors can conjure this close to the flash curtain and its elements.

What is different about the tunnels beneath the Overburden?

To distract myself from thoughts of Dram and the thought that something coming after a mole snack might find an Orion snack instead, I paint my blank-canvas mind with the sights and sounds of the mountain provinces. Like the multidimensional map that Dram and I once walked through, I overlay everything around me with another place.

"Owl," I say aloud, crimping my fingers around a rock. One of them lived in our conjured tree fort. Rock falls, scattering, but I hear the whir of feathers in my imagination.

Then I realize the wings I hear flapping are real.

My hand shoots up to mute my headlamp. I count to ten, frozen in place. If the gull is feeding, it's focused on something else, and wouldn't have heard me. If it's tending a nest or a youngling, a female will have her talons in me before I reach twenty.

It attacks from behind.

I turn violently and knock it against the wall. It flops to the ledge, stunned. The gull is small, a young female. She blinks at me, her pulse beating rapidly against her chest. A plan forms in my mind, and I hurriedly unclasp the small pack I've got strapped to my back. I empty it in a blur of motion, stuffing rations and med supplies into my pockets.

Foolish. Reckless.

But possibly the means to find my way back.

I drop the pack over the gull, and she tries to flap her wings in protest. My hands shake as I scoop her inside and clasp it closed. She shrieks, a piercing cry that leaves my ears ringing. The roosting male gulls answer.

"Flash me," I whisper, slipping the bag over my shoulders. Male gulls don't normally leave their nests if they're roosting, but I've never before stolen one of their females. She flaps and jerks against my improvised cage, and her beak pokes against the material. Her every movement tugs me backward. She's a young gull, smaller than most females, but still larger than my skullcap. When her weight shifts, so does mine.

Ha-ha-ha! she screeches. A gull's warning call, an attack cry.

"I'm bringing her back," I assure the male gulls under my breath.

I grasp the rope wound through my rappel device and drop. I imagine myself explaining this later to Dram. *Well, I was in a hurry to save you, so I didn't listen to Val's instructions. I didn't take a locator device, so I just took a tunnel gull with me instead. Oh, by the way, the creatures down there can conjure and alter the tunnels—but I didn't think that could stop a gull from finding its nest. I know—a reckless theory.*

I'm counting on it.

Cavern air rushes up, enclosing me in darkness so heavy, it's like another creature fastened to my side. The gull screeches, again and again. It tears at me. Vicious as these gulls are, she's still a mother calling for her babies.

"You'll get back to them," I say, detaching from the rope. "We'll get back to them."

Her cries stir the moles from their burrows, and I follow. I have a theory about them, too.

––––––––

I dump out my ore pouch to make room for the worms. I've mined so much eludial soil that it fills my water bottle.

"Almost home," I murmur to my gull. After the hours we've spent together, I think of her as mine. My responsibility. My only chance of escaping these shifting caverns.

She makes the rumbling cry I've grown familiar with. I drop an earthworm past an opening in the pack. Then there's the clacking sound of her hooked beak, a sound that still terrifies me. I work quickly, breaking open a glow stick and dripping the glowing chemical over her wings while she's distracted. She ruffles her feathers, staring at me with a gimlet eye. Then, with my heart in my throat, I unzip the pack. She flies at me. I hold my arms over my head as she screeches, the edges of her feathers cutting through my suit. Then she turns and propels herself up.

I climb after her, my eyes trained on her glowing feathers, my beacon. I lost count of the number of times moles conjured around me in the past hours. At first, I kept a mental map in my mind, modifying it as they altered the caverns, but as the hours passed, I realized there was no way to keep an accurate map down caves that are constantly shifting—not without tech.

My gull soars up through the gorge, and I can't climb as fast as she can fly, but she's hindered by ledges of rock blocking her path. She'll roost, waiting for me to catch up and hammer through with my axe. As long as I keep her supplied with earthworms, she doesn't seem to want to taste me.

I climb, shaking, my forearms shot. She watches me from

her perch, then suddenly lifts her head. She launches herself from the ledge and flies beneath the ceiling of rock, her beak open with each cry. *Mew, mew, keow!*

Her silver wingtips glow in the stygian darkness, the chemical paint of my light bar illuminating the rock face. Her cries shift, like she's responding to something calling her from the other side of the barrier. She scrapes at the stone with her talons, her beak drilling into the rock with a shallow clacking.

"No!" I shout. She attacks the stone like I've seen gulls attack cavers. She will kill herself hammering that stone.

Blood rushes through me, but I hoist myself closer. She could turn on me in a second—my knife is in my left hand—but her only concern is answering those cries.

I can't believe I'm getting this close to a gull without a cage between us. So close I see blood on her feathers, beside the fading light gel.

"Please don't attack me," I murmur. I'm scared, but—more than that—I want to see her return to the nest I stole her from. She led me out. I can get us through this final step.

My pickaxe cracks against the stone. Granite spits against my face, and I hammer at it again, harder. Rock rains down, and over the scrape and slam of my axe, I hear the gulls on the other side.

They could all attack me. I could be fighting my way to my own death. I check that the knot holding my rope is locked. I can free it in two seconds and descend if I need to. My palm sweats against the handle of my knife.

The mother gull watches me, her pulse fluttering the feathers at her neck. Her eyes are blue-black, slightly clouded.

"It would be really helpful if you could conjure," I say,

slamming my axe upward. Rock falls away; I've broken though. The gulls screech back and forth. She swoops and dives beneath me. Through the crack, I can hear the younglings. It's a sound I know and recognize. Hunger.

I loosen the pouch of earthworms and lift it through the split stone with my pickaxe. The mother gulls darts after it, her sharp feathers scraping the rock as she pushes through. I harness my axe and grip the knot on my rope, heart in my throat. But her only thought is caring for her brood. I mute my headlamp and lever myself through the crack.

My heart trips, and I realize I'm counting down to an attack. If they're going to come after me, it'll be now, while I'm crouched over the side of this gulf, trying to gather my rope.

A sound lifts above my labored breathing. Cooing. I secure my rope, all the while searching the shadows. A faint green glow illuminates a shallow ledge of rock. I can just make out the nest, the bobbing heads of youngling gulls.

I look past the nest, as rock begins to shift in myriad directions. Stone cascades down, even as the ledge beneath me crumbles.

I climb, faster than I've ever climbed, toward the flashfall sky.

EIGHTEEN

7.1 km from flash curtain

I TROMP TOWARD the decontamination pods gleaming in the fading light. The metal pods reflect the glow of the flashfall, mirroring the curtain's violet and green auroral bands. I lift my hand and watch the colors move over my skin. Every once in a while, the curtain reaches out this way, painting us with its hues like it wants to show it can touch us without causing harm.

We know better.

I step into a pod, buckle the straps across my shoulders, and stab the button. The door seals shut, and faint green light illuminates my gloves as I grip the handles. Three days have passed, testing in the gorge. Three days I've spent chasing eludial soil.

"The Congress of Natural Humanity thanks you for your service," a voice says from a speaker. "Commencing decontamination."

A vortex of air swirls around me, whipping my hair upward like a flag. The fan accelerates overhead with a mechanized whirring as air abrades my body like it's going to pull my skin right off. The buckles cut into my shoulders, pushing against the new bruises I wear along the pods' strap lines.

"Particle dust detected," the mechanical voice drones.

I suck in a breath just before a spray mists me, a chemical that adheres to radioactive particles and draws them away. It burns my lungs if I breathe it, so I tell myself I'm underwater, swimming in a still blue pool—anywhere but here.

With my eyes clenched shut, it's easier to see my mom. I think of her in these moments, amazed how much of her former life she hid from us. She never spoke of the Overburden. I never knew about this pod that she stepped into, long before I stepped into her arms. She should have taught me about life east of the curtain; instead she taught me games.

Come and find me, Orion, she'd say. There weren't many places to hide in our outpost cottage, but it didn't matter. I never tired of searching for her.

Found you, Mom.

The air cuts off, and I open my eyes slowly, holding on to her just a moment longer.

"Decontaminated," the voice announces. "Proceed, Delver."

The door opens with a hiss, and I stumble out toward the weigh station. Delvers speak in low tones as we shuffle through the line. We've used most our energy surviving the gorge, and in the quiet I hear each Delver empty her ore pouch onto the scale and the inspector's graveled voice as he relays the weight to the recorder.

Despite our exhaustion, anticipation crackles in the air. One of us is going to earn Fortune tonight.

"Name."

"Orion Denman."

The man looks up from the ledger. "The scout from the out-posts."

"Yes."

He grunts and scrolls a stubby finger over the list of names. "Submit your depth reading." I pass my forearm beneath a scanner until it beeps. I don't need to see the numbers to know they're high. It's written all over the recorder's face.

"Let me see your gauge." He grabs hold of my wrist and turns my arm to study the tech. "This isn't possible. Your mon-itor's malfunctioning."

"It's not." I shake out the contents of my ore pouch. Eludial soil spills onto the scale—five times as much as anyone else had. A few people gasp. The inspector breathes a curse as he leans in to scrutinize my findings. I barely keep myself from smiling. Fortune is mine. The other Delvers never had a chance against a Fourth Ray caver.

"I've never seen numbers this high," the recorder says. Bushy brows lower over his eyes, like he's trying to see through me to the way I tricked the Congress's system. "They say you didn't even have a locating transmitter your first time down. How did you find your way?"

"I captured a tunnel gull and followed it out."

"You captured a . . ." A smile breaks across his face. "Flash me, you *are* the scout I've heard about." He sets a chain on the table. "You've won. This chain proves your commissioning status and will grant you access to Fortune."

"I get to bring someone with me."

The recorder waves his hand beside the names on his list. "Take your pick."

"No, he's . . . not a Delver. He's a Brunt."

The man stares at me, his face more scrunched up than when he took my depth readings. "No Brunts in Fortune."

"But I get to choose—"

"Not a Brunt."

"Please." I grasp the man's arm, and he doesn't flinch from my touch—a fellow Subpar, then. "If you've heard of me, you've heard of him—the Brunt—he was my marker."

His eyes soften, but he shakes his head. "What you're asking for isn't possible."

"Then make it possible. Please!"

"What's the problem?" Val asks, striding forward.

"She wants to share Fortune with a Brunt."

She gives me a hard look. "The noncompliant one? I told you to let go of him."

"The flashtide is still an hour away," I say. "If I find him before then, will you let him share Fortune with me?"

"Brunts are kept beyond the perimeter. The chances that your friend is still alive—"

"He's there. I know he's still there."

"Even if he is, the Tomb is chaos. You'll never find him."

"I can find him."

"The gates are shut for the night, you can't even—"

"By midnight!" I turn and sprint for the fence line silhouetted against the flashfall like the spine of a wiry beast.

I weave around the glowing domes of the Delvers' quarters, past the barracks, telling myself I can do this, I will find Dram. The flashfall shivers along my senses like a mocking caress, and I shut out the doubts that rise up like gooseflesh.

I fit my hands to the cordon fence and climb, just high

enough to see the Brunts gathered twenty meters in the distance. I have no hope of finding Dram in the crowded pen of Brunts they call the Tomb. If I'm going to bring him to Fortune tonight, it will have to be because he sees me. I jump down and run toward the tallest thing in this place, the corral tower that marks the entrance to the cordons.

I leap for the bottom of the wooden structure. The slats are spaced wide, forcing me to jump to the next beam in order to reach it. The ground shrinks beneath me as I scale ten meters, twenty—my hand slips, and my fingernails claw the battered wood. I straddle a slat, leaning against an angled support beam.

See me, Dram.

In the distance, the flash curtain displays its splendor in towering ripples of fuchsia and emerald, moving across the horizon like a vertical wave. The colors smash up against the edges of its parameters, as if hitting an unseen boundary. There is time yet. I stretch my gaze, but I can make out only dark shapes moving beside the Tomb.

I need to get higher.

Standing carefully, I draw my axe from its holster and slam it in an arc above my head. The pick bites into the wood of the next slat and I pull myself higher, my feet scraping for purchase. My legs clamp the wooden slat, and I pry the pick loose for another swing.

The Brunts trudge toward the Tomb, its metal doors reflecting the glimmer of flashfall from a slab of ground dug out of the sand. They shuffle through the sand with heads bowed, like the ground offers the only solace. I climb higher, hoping to catch Dram's attention. I wonder if he still bothers to look up.

Rotted wood snaps, and I slam against the corral, legs

dangling. Breath pushes from my lungs, parting the ash-filled air. I clutch the corral post, scanning the cordon for a lifted hand—anything that would indicate that Dram sees me, that he's still alive out there. I take a flare from my pack, rip the cap off with my teeth, and light it one-handed. Smoke lifts as I hold the flare high and sparks nip my face and hand.

See me, Dram.

I close my eyes, willing someone to notice—just one Brunt at the Tomb to point out the girl hanging off the top of the corral. Wind whines through the tower, and the flashfall stirs a golden-orange, like flames being stoked with a bellows.

"Brunts in!" a Strider shouts.

Doors lift from the ground with a mechanical groan, and figures lumber toward the refuge, shoving in their haste to get inside, safe from what's coming. I scan the shadows for the stragglers, the ones who find the Tomb more terrifying than exposure to the curtain. There's just one. A Strider murmurs something in low tones and raises his weapon. The shape turns and faces the soldier; he lifts his arm, where an amber indicator flashes. My breath catches.

Dram.

They shaved his hair off. I almost didn't recognize him. The flashfall illuminates his dirty, bruised face. I can't see him clearly, but I sense the emotions he's holding in check.

"It's almost midnight, Brunt," the Strider says. "Get down with the rest."

"It's not time yet." His tone is flat, dead as the land he's standing on.

"Get in the Tomb," the Strider commands.

I hurl the flare toward them. It sails over the fence, and the Strider whirls toward me, rifle raised.

"Delver?" He squints up at me.

I barely look at the man. My gaze collides with Dram's. He takes an unsteady breath, like he's not sure the air is safe.

"You're not supposed to be this close to the perimeter," the Strider calls, lowering his weapon.

"I have Fortune," I shout. "And so does he."

"No Brunt gets Fortune."

"He does."

"Not tonight." He shoves Dram toward the Tomb, and Dram shoves back. He connects with the Strider's armor. Current ripples through him.

"Dram!"

His body spasms, and he collapses. The Strider checks to make sure Dram is still breathing, then drags his unconscious body to the edge of the hole and shoves it over the side. The doors grind shut, and he jogs to the fence.

I cling to the corral, frozen in horror. Then, a taste like metal on the back of my teeth as the first orange bands spiral down. I'm too late.

"Orion!" a voice shouts.

I sigh against the wood supports, ignoring the metal brace cutting into my cheek. I stare toward the curtain, where a wave begins to crest.

"SCOUT!"

Wood explodes beside me as a bullet tears off a chunk of the corral. I glance down and see Greash shouting up at me. I toss my axe to the sand and scramble down as fast as I can.

"Run hard," he calls, taking off toward the Strider barracks.

The flashtide ripples downward, bathing the Overburden in the shades of a flame. I hesitate, my gaze straining toward the place where Dram was pushed into the Tomb. If I don't survive, neither will he.

I grasp my axe and sprint for Fortune.

The metal badge I wear is a key. Attuned to my biometric signature, it opens places to me that most people can't enter. At least, that was how it was explained to me before I ran off, climbed the corral tower, threw a flare at a Strider, and got stuck in the flashtide. I pound up the pathway to Fortune's indistinct, rounded door and collide with the metal-enforced wood. A remnant from Old Alara, Val told me, referring to the entrance that looks more like it should lead into a secret fairy garden than an underground fortress.

I slam my hands against it. Right now, I don't care if it leads into the underworld—I just need to get out of the flashtide.

"I'm a Delver with Fortun—" The door opens, and I stumble through, into a dark alcove. It closes and locks behind me.

"Welcome, Orion," Val calls. "The lights are at night-dim. I'll help you find your way."

"Dram's stuck in the Tomb—"

"As he should be. No Brunts get Fortune. I told you to forget about him."

"I told you I wouldn't."

"Then we're at an impasse." She smiles like she's offering me a gift. "Come out of the vestibule, and I'll show you to your quarters."

I clamp my lips together and remind myself this is where I

need to be. I've never been closer to the cure. I need this woman to trust me. I swallow the arguments simmering behind my teeth, and follow. My boots echo off stone tiles that gleam in the faint light. They're painted, etched with designs, spreading across the floor, up the walls, to the low ceiling arching above us.

"You must decon before descending into Fortune," Val says, directing me toward a pod. "We preserve Protocol at all costs. Especially here."

I want to tell her what I think of her Alaran Protocol. Instead I step past her and seal myself into the pod. Air whips around me, and I will the chemical to sear away my thoughts along with the curtain's particles. Every thought but one.

I'm where I need to be.

The pod opens, and I stride to where Val waits beside the entrance to a narrow tube-like shaft. Blue lights illuminate its cylindrical metal bars.

"Fortune lies thirty meters beneath us," Val says. I step inside, and the bars close around us with a soft groan. The inside of the shaft is bare earth, compacted in ways that tell me Conjies helped form it. "The early Subpars devised Fortune with a series of interconnected shafts," Val says. "This port leads to the Grand Hall." Tech illuminates and we drop. I count down the meters instinctively, mapping the place in my mind.

"You have hands," I say. "Are you a Gem?"

"Subpar. Outpost Two."

"You were a caver?"

"Second Ray. The Congress brought me here to test in the gorge when I was sixteen."

Metal sighs as the port slows to a stop. We step out into a

massive cavern with walls of gleaming white stone, lit by crystal lights suspended from the vaulted ceiling. Balconies rim one side of the hall, and alcoves veer off from the main room. I realize I've stopped walking, that I'm gawking at portraits lining the wall.

"A long ways from Outpost Five," Val muses. She lifts a candelabra off a table and turns down a corridor. "Have you heard of Vestiges, Orion?" I shake my head. "They are people dedicated to preserving the heritage and traditions of Alara as it formed after the flash curtain fell. They are esteemed for the history they preserve—the reason our culture survives. Meredith grew up a Vestige. It's why she's so tied to this place—and why it remains as it is."

"Meredith?"

"You'll meet her tomorrow. She's the Subpar commissary, fifth member of the council. She lives and works here." She turns an ornate metal handle on a door. "This is your room."

I step past her, working to conceal my shock. It looks like something pulled straight out of my imagination. A canopy arches above a huge bed piled with blankets, and beside it are a small table and chair, a shelf filled with books, a wardrobe with clean clothes and Delver's suits. Val sets the candelabra on a low table.

"Fortune is powered by much the same tech as Alara—but Meredith prefers the old ways." She turns down a coverlet and ushers me toward the bed, as if it's a normal occurrence to get tucked into a lush bed in the Overburden. The candlelight casts leaping shadows over the stone walls. Like monsters. I can practically sense them, stirring in the bowels of this place.

"The beautiful things are usually the most dangerous," I murmur, my gaze slipping over the room.

"This isn't the part of Fortune you should fear. That will come tomorrow down the tunnels."

I climb onto the bed. "It can't be worse than tunnel nine."

Val smiles, and I'm reminded again of monsters.

"You had to leave your family?" I ask. "When you came to live here?"

"Congress needed a new Prime Delver, and Subpars make the best Primes." She douses the candles, shrouding us in darkness.

"Don't you need the light?" I ask.

"You spend enough time underground, you learn to see in the dark." She turns to go.

"What happened to the Prime Delver? The one you replaced?"

"That's the part of the story you know." I can hear it in her voice—she's smiling again. Dread crawls through me as if the shadow monsters peeled off the wall and slid beneath my skin.

"I don't know what you're talking about."

"She didn't tell you about any of this?"

"Who?" My heart pounds as if it's trying to escape my chest.

"The girl I replaced. Your mother." She walks from the room, and I stare after her, gaping.

I was wrong—the shadows aren't inside me. I'm becoming one of them: formless, void, absent without light.

I'm not sure I've actually won anything by getting into Fortune.

It feels suddenly like a trap.

NINETEEN

7.2 km from flash curtain

"MEREDITH," VAL SAYS, "may I present Orion Denman, your newest Delver."

An older woman turns, and color drains from her face. "You'll have to forgive me," she murmurs, shaking her head. "It's just that . . . I feel I've stepped through time. Ferrin was your age when she came to us. You look just like her."

The white-haired man at her side steps forward, scrutinizing my features. "You're indeed Ferrin's daughter," he says. "You have her features."

I like to think I have her heart or her courage.

They stand before a wall of ports, each marked by a tiled pathway etched with a number. Meredith stands atop a chipped 3 carved into the stone.

"This was your mother's tunnel." Her words pierce me, like a knife slipped past my armor.

"My mother mined the Barrier Range," I say. "Seven was her tunnel."

"Before that. Before she was sent to Outpost Five. She grew up here, in the Overburden."

Mom is preserved in my mind in hazy, light-filled images, snippets of memories that are painted with feeling more than visual representations. Her smile, the way her hand felt on my cheek, and now—like it's been summoned by Meredith's words—a sort of lost look in her eyes, when she'd stare toward the curtain. But now I know—she wasn't looking for the curtain at all. She was trying to see her home. The Overburden.

"Why didn't she tell me?"

"Because it's a dangerous thing to know. Her silence kept you safe, Orion."

"I'm not sure that lies keep anyone safe."

"No, but they keep people alive. And in a world like ours, that's often the best one can hope for." She ushers me into the port and a cage-like door slides behind us. It descends, and scents of earth and musty air rush up around us.

"Why did she leave?" I ask.

"Our system is a careful construction of roles and boundaries. One must adhere to them, or we are no longer effective. She could not comply."

She could not comply.

I picture Mom dressed as I am now, the Congress's Delver. Noncompliant. I feel like I'm retracing her steps and it's bringing her back to life, a moment at a time.

"Your mother is a bit of a legend. She was the best Prime Delver we've ever had. I'm hoping you possess her same skill."

"She died before she could teach me to mine."

Meredith cocks her head and studies me. "Biology is an

interesting thing," she murmurs. "I'm hoping you've inherited your mother's . . . instincts. Things she understood that no one ever taught her."

"I won Fortune because I captured a gull and followed it out of the cavern. I tracked moles to the soil. I cheated."

Meredith nods. "That's precisely what I'm talking about."

The port groans to a halt, the sound echoing in the cavernous depths. She lifts her chain of office before a sensor and the metal bars pull away to reveal the yawning maw of a tunnel. Bare bulbs flicker from the rock ceiling.

"The Congress is busy finding ways to survive in a world with flash curtains. We are focused on taking back the world." She touches a pulse transmitter projecting from the stone. "We reclaim this land one passage at a time, mining eludial soil in an effort to control the flash curtain. If we forge a path to the eludial seam, it will be possible to destroy it altogether. It is essential work. The most important work."

A Delver approaches us, a girl my age, with curly black hair streaming beneath her skullcap and skin a shade darker than the dust smeared across her cheek.

"This is Cora, our Prime Delver," Meredith says. "She'll show you what you need to know."

Cora's gaze flicks down my body and up. "This is the Scout?"

Meredith's eyes bore into the girl. "This is Orion Denman. Ferrin's daughter."

"Huh."

"Teach her how to survive down here, Cora. Train her as if she's the next Prime."

Cora lifts a dark brow. "Well, then. I'll try not to let her get eaten by a termit."

"Cora," Meredith says, her tone a warning.

"Right." Cora waggles her fingers at me. "Future Prime, come with me." She turns down a narrow corridor. She's tall, and I have to double my pace to keep up with her.

"Did I do something to upset you?" I ask.

She huffs a snide laugh. "I get that you're a Subpar, so you've got mining and climbing skills, but I'm curious about your level of sense. It doesn't take much to figure out why I'd have a problem with you."

"Enlighten me."

"Ah, well. It's like this, Ferrin's daughter: there's only one leader here, and it's not you." She points to the short cloak hanging halfway down her back. "I've earned this Prime's cape, and I'm not giving it up. I don't care who your mom was."

"I'm not trying to steal your cape," I mutter.

"It's an honor."

"I'm sure it is."

"You do realize that if you're made Prime Delver, it means I'm either dead or severely indisposed."

"I suppose that puts a dent in our budding friendship."

"No friends down here, Subpar. It will go easier for you if you remember that." She lifts a black rectangular instrument from a heap of equipment piled on the ground.

"Depth gauge," she says, dropping it into my hand. "And pulse transmitters." I clip the tech to my belt. She lifts a flash rifle and caresses the barrel. "Meredith is a purist. She doesn't believe Delvers need the tech Ordinance provides." She tosses me the weapon. "She's wrong."

Lights illuminate at my touch, the gun's biotech reacting to my heat. This is way beyond the Dodgers' guns. This looks more like something a Strider would use. It feels foreign in my grip, but Cora's going on about some creature, and I remind myself that any weapon is a good weapon.

". . . and it will shoot the head off a termit at thirty meters."

"A termit?"

"Self-camouflaging mammal. Sharp teeth." She lifts a brow. "They don't have those in Westfall?" I shake my head. "Huh. Lucky bastards. Well, you won't see them unless you're wearing these—" She draws a pair of goggles from the crate. "They're heat-sensing." I loop them around my neck, and she walks away.

"Let's go," Cora commands.

"What about the . . ." I glance over the rest of the gear. Rope, harness, bolt gun, flares, medkit, and nutri-pacs.

"Leave it," Cora calls. "I want to see if the stories about you are true."

Whatever myths this Delver's heard about the Scout, I'm not above food or med supplies. I stuff them into my pockets, strap on the bolt gun, and jog to catch up to her.

"Whatever you did to get here," she says, "none of it matters. Only this tunnel matters. Try not to die. I hate training new Delvers." She catches hold of a lip of stone and pulls herself up. Beneath her Prime Delver designation, she wears a patch with a wave on her sleeve.

"You were in the Trades?" I ask.

"If you understand the Trades, then you know what I've done to get here. Ferrin herself could return from the dead, and I'd still not let her take Prime from me."

A sudden thought occurs to me. "Was my mother commissioned in the Trades?"

Cora's expression hardens. "No. Her family bought her

commission, like everyone else down here. Well, everyone but me and the Ghost."

She's enjoying my confusion. I can tell by the way she drops bits of information as if she's slapping ore mites on me and waiting to see if they'll explode.

"Ghost?" I ask. *Boom.* She grins.

"How do you think we carved these passageways? Congress uses adapted Conjies like rock plows." *Boom.*

"Adapted Conjies," I murmur. "Those who can conjure this close to the flash curtain? I thought that was a rare ability."

"Technically, they're called Forgers. But it hardly matters now. There's only one left. I'm taking you to her."

"A Conjuror? There's a *person* down here?" She shrugs and pushes her goggles up on her head. "What happened to my mother?" I ask. "If she was some important Delver here, why did she leave to go mine in Outpost Five?"

"She didn't ask to leave. No one volunteers to serve in the outposts. She disagreed with Meredith—questioned things. When she was discovered with that Conjie, it was—"

"What?" I feel as if she's suddenly speaking underwater. Her lips move, but I can't make out the meaning of her words. "What Conjie? What are you talking about?"

"I don't know his name. Anyway, they sent her away after that."

Sent her away.

"And the Conjie?"

"What happens to all Conjurors, I suppose." She reaches for the ledge.

"Cora." I grab her arm. The girl is a blur of motion, and I need her to be still this one time. She knows things. Things more important than flash rifles and termits. "Who was the Conjuror to her?"

"Her Ghost."

Her Ghost.

My mother grew up in the Overburden. She was commissioned as a Delver. And she had a Conjie slave.

Cora is climbing again, which is fine, because I'm not sure I want her to see the emotions flashing across my face. Truth is a commodity here, and I'm not ready to trade mine. I follow her up the rock face, mindlessly gripping handholds, hungry for more. I barely register the slick stone beneath my fingertips, the water seeping through a tear in my glove. For the first time since she died, I feel like I'm getting Mom back, instead of losing more of her each day. By the time we reach the top, Cora's gasping for breath. We settle against the wall, our knees drawn up.

"Well, they didn't exaggerate your climbing skills," she mutters.

"The outpost director sent me down tunnel six when I was nine. I learned fast." She tilts her head, as if she's trying to process this new thought with what she's been told. I realize I may have something to offer Cora, after all. The girl is as starved for information as I am. "Ask me about Outpost Five. I'll tell you anything you want to know."

Her gaze shutters. "I told you, nothing from before matters. These passages are all that matter now."

"That isn't actually true," I say. "If you really believe that, then I'm sorry for you."

"Says the Westfaller who's never come eyes-to-nose with a termit." She tears open a nutri-pac and squeezes the rations into her mouth.

"You made it sound like there was more between my mother and her Forger than finding eludial soil."

Cora shrugs. "Ferrin wasn't the first Delver to fall in love with an adapted Conjie. He was all she had—for months on end. It would have been more surprising if they hadn't formed a bond."

I think of Dram and me. What we forged down the tunnels of Outpost Five went far beyond the partnership of scout and marker. When you've held someone's life in your hands that many times, you end up holding all the other parts of them too—mind, body, and soul. Dram was my lifeline, and I was his—and we are indelibly linked.

This Conjie Ghost was Mom's soul mate.

We pass beyond the dripstone, the last jagged point scraping along my back.

"What happens to the Forgers now?"

"Fern's the last of them. Besides her, there aren't any more. Haven't been for years. Because your mother was Prime, she was assigned one of the few left. Adapted Conjies were rare then; now they're nonexistent."

An image of Roran comes to mind, how he forged a passage beneath the Range. He saved me when he first revealed his hidden ability during a flash storm and then saved our team of cavers when we fled Outpost Five. If the Congress had had any idea what he was capable of . . . they would've turned him into a Ghost.

"You ready?" Cora asks.

"For what?"

"To meet a Ghost." She strides around a curve in the stone, and my heart stops. Before us rises a cube of cirium, a shiny metallic box smaller than my bedroom at Outpost Five.

"What is that thing?" I murmur.

"The Box. Half-meter-thick-cirium-walled containment cube. Fern's home." She strides forward and sets her hand to the side of the cell.

"Why doesn't she just use her ability to overpower you and escape?"

"She's tried it—twice. Now we're life-linked." She pulls back her glove and points to her wrist. "A bit of tech inside there. She has it too. Now if I die, she dies. Also, they've promised her freedom if she complies."

"Are Forgers ever given their freedom?"

"What do you think?" Cora asks. She lifts her hand before a sensor, and bolts slide open with a hiss. "What did they promise you cavers in the outposts?"

"A place in the protected city," I say. "If we mined four hundred grams of cirium."

Cora's eyes darken. "And how is our fair city?"

"I couldn't tell you. I earned four Rays, and Congress sent me to Cordon Four."

"I guess in that way, Eastfall and Westfall Subpars are the same," she says. "Congress flashes us both." She lifts a lever, and the heavy door grinds open. In the frail light of a single bulb, a girl sits on a cot, her hair streaming down her back.

"Come, Fern," Cora says.

The Forger stands, a young girl—maybe thirteen or fourteen—and draws on body armor that matches ours. She wears no equipment, save for a headlamp. A girl with her abilities has no need for rope. She tucks her hair beneath her skullcap, and I remember all the times Dram did that for me.

The girl is pale, her skin like the smooth white skin of ore mites. She moves with a sort of animalistic grace, like she was born of these caverns, her strength rooted in the earth as surely as the stone.

I smile at her. "I'm Orion."

"I've heard of you." She doesn't smile back. Her face is passive, like it's unaccustomed to expressions of emotion. I search her eyes, expecting to see desperation, a place to funnel all the pity I feel welling up within me, but her eyes—a strange mix of brown and blue—remain as empty as her face.

If she was ever a normal girl, that person has been lost to this perpetual darkness, her humanity absorbed by the walls of a cirium prison.

"Do you wish to proceed, Prime Delver?" she asks Cora.

Cora nods, but she's watching me, like she's enjoying my reaction to this strange, captive girl. Fern walks past us, and Cora leans in close to me.

"Now you understand."

I slip the goggles over my eyes, blocking my despair from Cora's prying gaze. "What do I understand?"

She looks after Fern. "Why we call them Ghosts."

TWENTY

7.2 km from flash curtain

I WATCH FROM the shadows of the pricking tent, the only place where the different stations mix. I slipped away from the rest of the Delvers—at the front, lingering near the crowd of Miners. It's been two weeks since I began my work at Fortune, delving paths alongside Fern and Cora. Two weeks of arguing with Val, but she refuses to take my pleas to Meredith, insisting that Brunts have no place in Fortune. I can't offer Dram solace, but I'm desperate to see him, to know that he's still alive.

"Can I borrow your neck cloth?" I ask a woman still clutching her pail and sifter. I show her the small orange clasped in my palm: a trade. We get real food in Fortune.

"If you're trying to blend in, it will take more than that, Scout," she says, eyeing my white Delver's suit. She unwraps her torn coat and drapes it around me, her eyes darting to the Striders lining the tent.

"Thank you," I murmur. "I'll give it back."

I stall as long as I can, keeping my head down, my body hidden amongst the group of Miners. If they notice I don't belong with them, no one says anything. Finally, I'm the last in line. The tech raises his brow when he sees me.

I'm too clean to be a Miner. That was my first mistake. I'm missing a pail and sifter, too. And there's no hiding my white Delver's suit and boots poking out beneath the dirty coat.

The tech grins. "Good fortune to you, Delver." He has an accent, a strong one. His hands are cirium.

"And you." I'm unused to the Conjie greeting. It feels stiff on my lips.

A needle jabs my arm, and I welcome the burn that tells me I'm safe for another day. Brunts enter, and I strain to see each face. Then, behind a wall of ragged bodies, dark, newly shorn hair and a set to the shoulders I would know anywhere.

Dram shuffles forward, his eyes scanning the tent like he's bracing for attack. My heart twists. Gone is the tenderness, the easy smile. Ice-cold clarity stares out of a face stark with an emotion that's several degrees beyond desperation.

"I've seen him out there," the tech says, following my gaze. "He's the maniac they call Weeks."

"Weeks?" I ask.

"Brunts usually just live a few days if they're charmed, but not that one. He slays anything that gets close—the only Brunt that's lived this long. Not days, but weeks."

I stare at Dram. *Weeks.*

I barely recognize him, his hair cropped close, skin reddened and bruised, a hollow despair filling up his features. *Just a little longer*, I tell him in my heart. *I have a plan. Hold on. Keep fighting.*

His eyes lift suddenly, and his gaze bounces off me as if I'm just another Miner, then flies back.

"Rye . . ." His voice is rusty-sounding, like a wheel trying to turn with a broken axle.

I push my way to his side, but he steps back as I reach for him.

"Careful," he says, lifting his arms.

He wears armor made from the skin and feathers of flash vultures, and long cuffs on his wrists formed by the overlapping feathers of tunnel gulls. Tiny silver blades, like deadly scales. He's done more than protect himself; he's turned himself into a weapon. Even his spear is wrapped in cordon brush, so that both ends are barbed. There's a cordon rat impaled on the thorns.

"You know there's a dead rat stuck on your spear?"

He doesn't grin like he would've before. He just stares a moment, then nods. "They don't always feed us," he says, his voice hoarse. "Forget to give us nutri-pacs sometimes."

My mind catches up to his words. "Oh, fire," I whisper. I see the furry brown body with new eyes: as a meal held in reserve. This is Dram surviving. This is why he is Weeks.

"Your dad was right. The cactus with gray spines and red fruit is really bad." He says it with that scratchy, stripped-raw voice I don't recognize, but a hint of his outpost humor lies beneath his words. It all comes back to me, the conversation Dad had with us before Dram and I were first sent to the cordons. It seems like a lifetime ago.

"The paralysis was temporary," he murmurs, a trace of the old Dram lighting his eyes. "At least it kept me from feeling the pain in my stomach."

"Miner's compass," I answer, fighting the tears swimming

in my eyes. "The cactus with yellow fruit. He told us that was good. The pulp, I think he said."

Dram nods. "Found some. Followed the dogs to it."

"Miner!" a Strider calls. "Back to your squad."

"I have to go," I say, pulling off the coat I borrowed. "Look for the Miner wearing this. She'll share her orange with you. She knows who we are." Dram's gaze slips over my Delver's suit and chain.

"Who are we now, Rye?"

The truth of his question slams into me.

"More than what the Congress says we are."

"I feel like a Brunt."

"I see a Subpar. A Fourth Ray caver." I lift his hand, avoiding the barbs of his cactus armor, and draw my finger across his palm in two slanted lines. The caver's mark that means we've found the way out. He curls his fingers over mine.

"Maybe not this time, ore scout."

"Soon," I whisper, but I'm not sure he hears me over the sound of a Strider's armor as I'm pulled away.

Days, I assure myself. A few more days, and Bade and Aisla will show up with an army. Just a few more days for Dram to keep proving that even a Brunt can survive the Overburden.

———————

My mom was reckless. Impulsive. Possibly more than I am.

Definitely more, I decide, as we forge our way through craggy tunnels reeking of termit scat.

"This is mad," I grumble, sliding past a trail of bones.

"Right, and you've never done anything like this before," Cora murmurs.

I glare at her through my goggles. "How do you know my mother went this way?"

"She and her Ghost marked it."

The light of my headlamp catches letters the length of my forearm. "What does it say?" I ask.

"Conjies have five words for freedom," Fern answers, her gaze trained on the wall. It's the most I've heard her speak. The first four words inscribe the rock in bold, looping script etched with flourishes. The last is all raw, jagged lines, cutting across the stone. I can't read them, but it's like I can feel them.

"How far does this passage go?" I ask.

"Right up to the edge of a termit den," Cora says. "No one has forged past it."

"They didn't try?"

"They didn't survive." She shines her light against the base of the wall, illuminating a dust-covered, cracked piece of tech. She lifts what looks like an old, shattered pulse transmitter and curses. "We need to replace the transmitters that were damaged here. This passage is probably overrun with gorge moles."

Fern freezes suddenly. She draws a handful of dirt from her pocket and shifts into the shadows.

"What is she—"

Cora clamps her hand over my mouth. The heat-sensing indicators to the right side of my goggles paint an object in orange light. A hulking body, shoulders packed with muscles that bunch and shift as the creature nears. The termit lifts its stunted snout and scents the air, rising onto its hind legs. It stands taller than a man. A sound—like a blade sliding from a sheath—and its claws extend.

Fern presses her palms to the earth. A tremble of vibration and a wall of rock erupts before us.

"Hurry, Fern!" Cora shouts. "It's climbing!" She reaches for her rifle.

Rock scrapes and clatters, meters above our heads, but the sounds of the termit are louder. A gorge mole suddenly darts from the shadows, and the termit lunges for it.

"RUN!" Cora shouts.

A tree bursts up from the stone, roots thrusting beneath our feet. Stone rains down on us, and I cover my head. A screech, a startled cry. I can't see them, but their pain echoes back to me.

The ground gives way. We cling to a ledge, our feet dangling near the gulf that's opened beneath us. Cora's sobbing, the sounds tearing from her lips.

"How bad is it?" I call. I can't see her clearly, but I know the sounds of a serious injury.

"Glenting mole," she bites out. "Conjured s-straight through us."

"Fire," I breathe. I shove my goggles off my head and stare. A branch juts through Cora's palm, splaying her fingers wide. But it's nothing compared to the limbs impaling Fern. The girl teeters at the edge, half her body conjured roots and bark.

"I've got you!" Cora holds tightly to Fern. "Conjure! Fix yourself!"

"Can't. Not . . . this."

"Orion!" Cora's voice shakes more than her arms. "She needs the earth of the provinces. Find some!"

I pull myself up and stagger over the crumbling ground. "Cora—"

"You're the glenting Scout—*find some!*"

I crouch and grasp her arm instead, using my weight to anchor her.

"Give me . . . knife," Fern gasps. "Life . . . linked."

"Can you get the tech out?" I ask softly.

"Yes," Fern says.

Cora sobs, her arms straining to hold on to Fern. I set the handle of my knife into Fern's trembling hand. She digs the blade into her wrist and levers it beneath her skin, grimacing. She pries a narrow chip loose and says a word I don't understand.

"From the . . . wall," she says. A chill spreads over me. Her accent strengthens around the syllables of another Conjie word, then another. Words for freedom my Ghost father conjured along this tunnel. "The last one"—she gasps—"wasn't conjured. It was carved."

Carved. Ghosts don't have knives. But Delvers do.

I meet Fern's eyes, and she answers with a sad smile.

"*Sarcoom*," Fern says. And I repeat it, like my voice can keep her in this life.

Blood streaks down her arm, and the linktech drops from her fingers. She is gone when Cora lets go.

———

I leave the branch in Cora's hand. She tugs at it, her face drained of color.

"Keep going," I mutter as we crawl through bones and scat. She mumbles beneath her breath, a litany of senseless murmurings.

Before we left, I secured the passage with every pulse transmitter we had. And I drew a chalk circle with Fern's name beside the words for freedom. Cora moans her name over and over, but she didn't see the girl's eyes at the end. The relief there.

I haul Cora to her feet and stagger toward the tunnel entrance. I sense the solid cirium of the Box and direct my steps toward it like a beacon. Fern's prison.

Not anymore. She's free now. *Sarcoom.*

We collapse into the port, and I direct it to the infirmary. The physic settles Cora onto a gurney, and I numbly recount the events of the past hour. Meredith grows still as I reach the part of the story where we got between a gorge mole and a termit. She shakes her head in disbelief when I tell her that Fern is not locked in her cell. That she never will be again.

"You secured the passage?" she asks.

"Yes."

"Then we continue to move forward." She thrusts Cora's bloodied chain into my hands. "You're Prime now." As if to further her point, she drapes the Prime's cape over my shoulders. "I'll send Val to acquire a new Delver."

"No," I say, securing the clasp. "I'll go."

TWENTY-ONE

6.9 km from flash curtain

THE STEEL DOORS grind on hinges that sound like they're a hundred years old. I race toward them, my boots kicking up trails of sand. Since Delvers don't wear neck cloths, I press my glove over my nose and mouth so I don't inhale emberflies. They illuminate the darkness, twirling on drafts of air like the fireflies Mom once told me about.

"Wait!" I shout. The doors are halfway closed. "I'm going in!"

"No Delvers with Brunts," the Strider says. He braces his legs apart and crosses his arms, but makes no move for his weapon. I think he's curious to see how far I'll actually go.

I sense the shift in the curtain, like a nocturnal beast stirring to the hunt. Over his shoulder, orange bands ripple down from the cloud cover. I'm dead if I don't get belowground. I sprint forward, and the Strider reaches for his gun, uncertainty flashing across his face. Shooting Delvers is not something he's been trained for.

"You can't—"

"Flashtide!" It's all I have time to say as I drop and skid

beneath the lowering door. I hear the man curse and the sounds of his footfalls as the metal seals shut above me. I stagger in the darkness, tripping down the first few stairs carved into the ground. My eyes adjust to the frail light. Old-fashioned bulbs drape the perimeter with just enough energy to reveal that there is nothing down here but desperate humanity and dirt. I descend, and hundreds of eyes follow my progress as I make my way to the rectangular pit below. The air is stale, but free of ash and dust, and I take cautious sips of it as I search the dirty, battered faces for Dram's.

Brunts watch me, hungry—not for me, but for the protective suit covering me neck to ankle. I'm a fool to come down here like this, practically flaunting my good fortune. If I don't find Dram soon, I might end up a dead fool.

A boy leans against the dirt wall, Tempered appendages crossed over his chest. He's the only one not eyeing me like I'm a flash wand that just rolled into camp.

"I need to find Dram Berrends," I say softly. "Do you know where he is?" He tilts his head, and my heart sinks. I know why he didn't notice me before. I'm not sure he's aware of anything at all. He stares over my shoulder into space. "Sorry," I whisper. And I am sorry. He's just a boy, a little younger than me. I look around and realize at least half the Brunts wear the same glazed expression. Their bodies are here, but the rest of them checked out a long time ago.

"Dram!" I call his name, no longer caring how much attention I draw. I trip over arms and legs, sprawled bodies of people who just collapsed on the ground. I hit a wall—no, a man. He reeks of stale sweat. He grabs my arms. For a second I can't think, can't understand why the wall is holding on to me. Then the Brunt beside him—*flash me, is that a woman?*—cracks a light stick—mine, she pulled it off my belt—and I see that Wall Man is missing half an ear, and the smell is coming from his broken-toothed mouth.

"Delver," he says, and the way he draws it out makes shivers ripple along my skin. I pull away, but he squeezes tighter. I reach for my knife, and a hand grasps mine, twists until I drop the blade.

"She's still got all her parts." The voice belongs to the man still twisting my knife hand. His Tempered metal hand pinches my skin.

"I'll take your weapons and lights," Wall Man says. He nods to the woman. "She'll take your clothes. And your chain. Payment. Then we'll take you to Weeks."

"You're insane."

"And you're dead if we don't help you."

"Help me? I can't give you my Delver's chain!"

"Nothing is free, here, Subpar. Especially not protection."

My gaze shifts to the shadows, to the pairs of eyes gleaming. I can't believe what I'm considering. A trade. Then Wall Man will take me to Dram, and when he does, I'll be alive instead of dead.

"Fine." My heart hammers in my chest so hard, I'm sure the woman can feel it as she unbuckles my suit with greedy hands and peels it off my body. I drag on her dirty, shredded rags and follow them into the dark.

The Scout who can find anything would not have found Dram. I'm forcing myself to move—one foot in front of the other—beside Wall Man when I walk right past him.

"That's him," Wall Man says. He's pointing at a hooded

figure leaning against the wall with his eyes shut. The Brunt is covered in filth and dried blood—and the twisted gray spines of a cactus. They cover his arms like a deadly warning.

"That's not Dram," I say. My voice sounds strangely monotone, as if I bartered my emotions along with my clothes.

"Subpar," he says. "From the outposts." He lifts the Brunt's arm and peels up the cactus armor enough for me to see a Radband with a familiar amber indicator.

I shake like I'm crying, but no tears come. "Dram."

The Brunt doesn't move. I kick his foot, the only place he's not studded in thorns and gull feathers. He cracks his eyes open and stares at me without reaction.

"It's Orion," I murmur, feeling suddenly as if I'm drowning. He closes his eyes.

I'm speechless. I've found Dram—bartered myself to get to him—but he's already gone.

"Why doesn't he know me?"

Wall Man shrugs. "I doubt he even knows himself. He's been here longer than any of us."

My legs give up, and I sink to the ground.

"Keep your back to the wall, Subpar," Wall Man says. "This is the Tomb, not a Delver's pod." He sits a few meters from me.

My defenses are broken, worn away by the horror of the past hours. I curl onto my side, draw my knees to my chest. Dram hasn't moved from where he leans against the wall. He's barely blinked. I have never felt so alone.

"Sleep," Wall Man says. "I'll make sure you're not harmed again tonight."

A frayed laugh bursts past my lips. "*You're* protecting me? From what, exactly?"

"From him." He nods toward Dram.

Dram's hollow gaze lands on me. His stare is like a flash vulture's. Curious. Feral. He lifts a spear into view, the metal tip gleaming in the sparse light. I shift closer to Wall Man. Dram turns and melts into the shadows. He draws something from his pocket.

"What is that?" I ask Wall Man.

"Venom spike," he says, "from the tail of a cordon rat." I peer closer and see the fluff of tail and fur. "The toxin paralyzes, but in small doses it can be used to numb the mind. Many Brunts do it."

I thought everyone was dazed from exhaustion. Maybe there was more to it. I can't tear my eyes from Dram, hunched in on himself. Tremors rack his hands as he tries to bring the pointed spike to his forearm.

"Stop," I order. Nearby, Brunts lift their heads. But not Dram.

Anger erupts from someplace deep inside me—a place torn open and exposed. It floods me from the inside, this rage born from pain. It engulfs me, so that I'm kneeling, then leaping to my feet, striding toward Dram like he isn't some broken thing ten steps from death.

"Subpar," Wall Man cautions, "you don't want to start a fight with him."

"Yes, I do." I feel hot, then cold. Maybe it's shock; maybe it's this storm of hate rising in me. Whatever its source, I embrace it, because for the first time in an hour, I don't feel the imprint of metal tines on my skin.

"Get up." I stand over Dram, daring him to give me that vulture stare again.

But he doesn't even look up. He presses the venom spike into his skin.

There is a sound I have never made bursting from behind my clenched teeth. In my periphery, Brunts stir, some jolt to their feet. I'm not afraid. I'm a banshee, screaming into the face of death. I have joined their ranks of dead things in this Tomb, and they should be afraid. Of me.

I tear the rat tail from Dram's fingers.

"What happened to fighting?" I shout. "What happened to finding a way out?"

"Leave me, Brunt." His voice sounds low, reedy.

"I'm not a Brunt," I whisper. But even as I say it, I know that's what he sees. Just another shadow, pulled away from this place of darkness. Another nothing. Like him.

Dram pushes himself to his feet. "Leave before I hurt you."

"Too late," I murmur.

He swings at me, and I duck. His cactus-barbed fist whiffs through the air above my head. Holy fire. He really is going to fight me. Other Brunts shuffle closer, forming a ring around us.

"Weeks, Weeks, Weeks!" they chant. I glance at Wall Man, but he backs away, shaking his head.

Fine.

Adrenaline surges through me, and my instincts fire along my nerves. Flash bats, tunnel gulls, vultures, termits—of all the things I've fought, this is going to be a first.

"Give it back," Dram says.

I follow his gaze to my hand, where I've clenched the damn rat tail in my fist.

"This is what you're fighting me for?" I'm wearing my Delver's boots with the steel toes, so it's with utter satisfaction that I fling the poison to the ground and pulverize it beneath my foot.

His eyes narrow. In the dim light they appear orange, gleaming like orbie water.

"Now give me the rest," I demand.

"You'll have to fight me for them, Brunt."

"With pleasure." I launch myself at him, ducking his barbed fist. He topples backward, and I follow him down, dodging his armor. I root through his grimy pockets, searching for more venom spikes. He nearly flips me over as we tangle on the ground.

"I'll kill you!" he growls. He doesn't recognize me, his partner and best friend, and I'm struggling to see anything of Dram left in this shell of a person.

It makes it easier to fight him. My hands are unprotected, so I use my legs, my heavy boots, landing kicks to his ribs, his face. More Brunts gather around, so close I can smell them. Some of them begin fights of their own, and the others make way, like this is a common occurrence. Maybe this is why Dram is so quick to fight me. Maybe he's had to survive every night down here like this.

I'm just another brawler to him.

I reach into the tangle of cordon brush at the top of his spear, heedless of the thorns, and grasp the dead rat. I throw it as hard as I can over the heads of the Brunts. Dram roars and dives at me.

I block his attack, my arms straining. "I'm trying to help you, you idiot!"

Dram would normally win this fight. He's taller, and heavy with muscle, despite weeks in the Overburden. But his senses are dulled from the venom, his reactions delayed. Which is good for me, considering that Weeks, the Brunt, apparently has no conscience.

"You want to cry about cordon rats?" I snarl. "Well I have glenting *termits* hunting me down!" I yank my hair free from his grasp and roll to my feet. "The Tomb is unbearable for you, I know. I have to delve tunnels where moles can conjure stone around me! I watched one of them turn a person into a *tree*!" I land a kick, and cactus barbs crunch beneath my foot. A tail rips from his pocket, and I grab hold of it.

"Give it back!" Dram roars.

"No," I answer, bobbing away. "This place is hell! But we were supposed to fight it together!"

Dram lurches toward me with his spear. *His spear!* Barbed with cordon brush and gull feathers.

"Dram!" I choke out his name—my heart is in my throat.

He whips it toward my legs, and I leap over it.

"Dram Berrends!" But this isn't the boy who etched *step in my steps* into our bonding cuffs. This is Weeks.

"That glass around your neck," I shout. "You remember who it's for?"

He catches me in the arm with his spear, and I cry out. The venom spur falls from my grasp as I set my hand to the stinging gash. He drops his spear and snatches the rodent tail off the ground.

Blood streams beneath my fingers, and I lift my hand to check the wound. Dram lurches at me. He yanks my hair back, baring my neck to the stale light. I barely recognize Dram's voice, laughter rumbling past his sneering lips.

"You want a taste of this poison, Brunt?" he asks, sliding

the venom spike along my throat. "A prick, and you'll escape this hell for a while." He presses it harder, and I gasp as it nicks my skin. "Any deeper, and you'll escape permanently."

Tingling pain radiates along my nerves, and I fight him, twisting in his grasp. The spike cuts deeper. Tears fill my eyes. Horror clenches my gut. It won't be the flashtide or a termit that claims me. It might be the person I trust most in the world.

"You were my marker," I gasp. "In Outpost Five." There's a fervor in his eyes that terrifies me, so I squeeze my eyes shut and invoke the memories of the Dram I know. "You had a sister. Lenore."

The spike stills against my throat.

"You wear her ashes, and your mother's—in the pendants around your neck."

"Stop," he says.

"You like outpost ale. And mountains. You love being a Conjie, even though you're a Subpar."

"Shut up!" he yells.

"You wore a talisman in your hair, for me!" He presses the spike, and I gasp, struggling against his hold. The poison sears through me.

Metal hinges screech, and everyone looks up at the doors opening above us. I use the distraction, leveraging my weight and slamming my head against Dram's face. He staggers back, clutching his nose, and sinks to the ground.

"You taught me that move, you glenting skant." I swipe his spear off the ground, twirl it in my hand, and point it at his throat. I lean down and snatch the remaining tails from him. "This—" I hold the barbs up so everyone can see. I am shaking, the venom tripping up my nerves, but I raise my voice. "This is not an escape. The only escape is out there! If you're going to die, do it trying to *live*!" I drop them. I can't even hold my arm up anymore, but I have just enough strength to crunch them under my boot. I taste blood and swipe my hand beneath my nose. I can already feel my cheek swelling from Dram's sloppy right hook. He rolls onto his side and spits blood onto the ground. I can't believe we've done this to each other.

"Anyone who lets this Subpar put more of this poison in his veins answers to me." I stalk toward the woman wearing my Delver's suit and point the spear in her face. "I'm a Delver with Fortune. Give me back my badge." She stares at me, wide-eyed, then hurriedly lifts it over her head.

Above us, the metal doors open, and the flashfall steals into the Tomb in shades of luminescent green. Particles slip into the air, pricking my lungs with a tease of danger.

"Strider!" a voice shouts.

The soldier descends into the Tomb. He wears his helmet and visor lowered, his suit charged so high it gives off a crackling sound. The Brunts step away as he nears.

"Keep your distance, and everyone lives," he says. "I've come for the Delver."

I know that voice. Greash.

He stops before me, suit humming. "You're alive."

"If you're here because of my noncompliance—"

"I'm here because I thought they might kill you." He takes in my Brunt's rags and bleeding face. "I see I was half right." His head shifts to where Dram is crouched, blood dripping down his chin. "Did you see what you needed to see?"

"Yes."

"Will you allow me to escort you back to Fortune?" he asks.

"Or do we need to see how your spear holds up against my flash rifle?" I look down and see that I'm still holding it raised in a double-handed grip.

I hand Dram's spear to Wall Man. I don't trust Dram not to try to stab me with it. "Give it to him when I'm gone."

"Whenever you're ready, Subpar," Greash mutters. Despite his bland tone, I can tell he's on edge. Armed and electrified as he is, he's still outnumbered, and these people are half mad and desperate, their bloodlust stirred by my fight with Dram.

He directs me up the stairs, guarding my back as we wade through the Brunts. We emerge into the cordon, and the doors lower behind us. I stagger a few paces and throw up in the sand. He doesn't say anything, but I hear him mute the charge on his suit as I wipe a shaking hand over my mouth.

"We need to go," he says. "We're exposed out here."

I feel the particles, the mercifully low Radlevels. I'm surprised I can still feel gratitude for something like a green indicator flag.

He hauls me to my feet, and I flinch away from his touch. An unnatural panic flutters in my chest, heavy as a body knocking me down. Greash releases me immediately. I can't see his eyes through his face shield, but I know he's scrutinizing my face.

"So, I take it Dram hurt you down there."

"Hurt is not a big enough word," I murmur.

He presses a code into his screencom and guides me through the turnstile. "You shouldn't have gone in there."

I want to shout, to rail at him. Of course, *of course* I know that now. But all the fight has seeped out of me. Everything I had left was used defending myself against Dram. I lurch to the side and heave again.

"Were you hit in the head?" Greash asks. "You might have a concussion."

"Toxin," I mutter. "From a cordon rat."

"What?" He lifts his face shield and studies my eyes.

"Not enough to kill me," I murmur. Blood patters on the sand at my feet, and he mutters under his breath, tearing the rags apart to see my arm wound.

"Spear?" he asks. I can only nod. He draws a tube from one of his pockets and opens it with his teeth. "This first part burns like a skant." He rubs the disinfectant over the gash, and I groan behind my teeth. He pushes the edges of the wound together with one hand and spreads the liquid over it. "Liquid stitches," he says.

"Thank you," I murmur. "For this, and . . ." I glance toward the Tomb.

"You can thank me by promising to never do that again." We reach the door to Fortune and he waits as the tech reads my badge. "That—Brunt—isn't Dram anymore, Orion. He's not worth giving your life for. Not now."

"You don't understand."

"Understand what?"

"Subpars." The door opens, but I don't step through. "When there's a cave-in, we don't protect ourselves first. We brace our axes over the head of the caver next to us." I lift my hand, try to bend my swollen, bloody knuckles. "I've done that since I was *nine*. That instinct we develop doesn't wear out over time. It grows stronger."

"If that's true, then why are you crying?"

"I didn't say it was easy."

I step inside, and the bolts slide home. The night-dim lights cast shadows over me where I shudder, safe behind Fortune's coded entrance. I've never felt more exposed.

I ache in too many places to count, though I know my senses are dulled and I'm not yet feeling the full effects of my brawl with Dram. The remnants of the venom pulse through me in a way that makes my head feel like it's hovering above my body.

The stink of the Tomb permeates my skin, my hair. I try to breathe past the lump in my throat. Slowly, my fingers shaking, I reach up and trace the cut on my throat.

"You want a taste of this poison, Brunt?"

Dram.

"I'll kill you!"

He'd snarled the words, spit the threat at me like an animal. And then he'd really tried to do it.

My throat works as I struggle to hold back tears; my shoulders shake with silent sobs. I slide down the door and fold in on myself, like I can shut out the memories of the past hours. I tear the Brunt's rags off and sit shivering. But I can't pull away what happened.

I could open this door and walk toward the flash curtain, and it would all be over. The pain. The loss. A few dozen meters for the flashfall to burn away every terrible choice I've made. Every failure.

Shame, swept away in ash and ember.

It would all just fade.

Memories from the Tomb rise up, until it's all I see, all

I hear. I press my hand to the door. A soft chime, the click of the bolt, the door opens. I stop at the threshold.

The stories about the Marker and the Scout can't end like this.

Dram couldn't shield me from the horrors of the Overburden. When the rocks fell, he wasn't able to keep his axe braced above me, and I feel the pain of every impact.

But I've still got my axe wedged above him. I'm damaged, bleeding, but I'm not letting go.

Whatever was taken from me down in that pit, I'm still a Subpar.

And we fight to save the people beside us.

TWENTY-TWO

7.2 km from flash curtain

I MAKE MY way to the baths through the silent compound. When I turn the taps and lift my face to the spray, there is no one to hear my deep sigh, nor the things I murmur aloud into the steam. I touch my scars, the flash bat bites on my thigh and my arm, where just months ago, down nine, Dram drew the venom from my body. My memories paint a canvas of images: his eyes, green from the effects of the venom, lips cracked, a bat jaw clamped over his arm.

I dry off and dress in a clean Delver's suit. I stuff a pack with rations and water and my sharpest knife. My hands still tremble, and my thoughts drag a few steps behind, but my legs are steady when I stand on the 5 etched into the floor of the Delvers' quadrants. It's crossed out with an X, an old caver's mark that means "unsafe passage—do not cross." According to Meredith, this tunnel is overrun with creatures; the outpost it once serviced is now inaccessible. I wedge my boot into the port door and force it open. It's not the first time I've pushed past the Congress's boundaries.

I climb into the pod and strap in, smoothing away layers of dust. The compartment allows a Delver to sit, because it moves horizontally, farther and faster than any of the other ports. I press my Delver's chain to a sensor, and the port hums to life. The pod lights flicker and die. I sit for a moment in the pitch-black capsule.

What is the most important thing we bring into the caves?

I click on my headlamp and release the lever. The pod shimmies along the shaft. It creaks and groans like it's protesting my unsanctioned Delver run.

And if our light fails?

The darkest places aren't down tunnels, or in cordons absent of moonlight and stars. They're inside us.

But then, so is the light.

My decision sparks inside me, a glimmer that grows as the pod skims above the track toward Outpost Five.

I'm not going to leave Dram in the dark.

I refuse to leave any of them to the dark.

———

Meredith was right about the termits. Evidence of them fills the passageway. As I move along the tunnel, I watch them through my goggles, though I think the moles did more damage than anything else down here. The pod won't make it all the way to Outpost Five—Meredith wasn't lying about that. The moles have cut off the passage with their own conjured pathways.

I check the map I found in the archives of the Grand Hall. I didn't want to risk using a screencom that could be tracked by Congress. I study the tunnel markings and try to find my bearings. I'm close, but I can't get as far as Outpost Five. There's no getting past this barrier of rock.

Iron rungs protrude alongside conjured steps that lead up from the tunnel. I grasp them and pull myself up through an old auger shaft. I work to turn the hatch's rusted crank handle, pushing past my exhaustion. On the other side of this barrier lies Cordon Five.

The glass cordon where I left my friends.

A place of flashbursts and broken promises.

———

I move quickly, leaning forward as my feet crunch over the glass crust. A narrow trench winds through the cordon, and I stay to the side of it, my only possible refuge. The sulfur clouds thicken around me, and I tug my goggles on, tighten my neck cloth over my nose and mouth, and push through the haze.

Lizards scurry over the scorched sand, chasing odd yellow insects and spiders. I watch them, hoping that the instincts that have preserved them will help me, too. Suddenly, they dart into crevices.

I dive into the trench after them, grasping hold of roots and rocks as I slide down deep. The roar of the flashburst echoes around me, and I clap my hands over my ears. Stone presses my cheek where I've wedged myself into a cleft of rock.

"I'm alive I'm alive I'm alive," I shout, to cover the sounds of the burst, and to cover the fear raging within me. The heat robs me of breath, and I press into the stone, willing it to be shield enough. Sweat drips into my mouth, and I realize I'm yelling again, roaring back at the flash curtain.

Silence. Heavy. Oppressive as the heat.

I can hear every one of my breaths, and I count them, telling myself that I am still alive. A sudden, irrational fear of the dark seizes me. I crack a glow stick and stare at its green light.

I'm so disoriented, I can't tell which way to climb. Maybe the curtain releases something—some kind of particles—when it bursts like that. Or maybe it's just that I haven't slept since I fled the Overburden.

I rest my cheek against the stone and clutch my light. This will not be my tomb. I'm not surrendering to the darkness.

"I'm alive." I say it until it sounds like a song. I sing it to my friends the lizards, and whatever else might be hiding in the shadows. We are allies, fighting the beast that is the flash curtain.

A spider inches toward me. Black, with bright yellow markings. Dram and I would have avoided it down the tunnels, but I can barely lift my head.

"We are allies," I murmur.

I set the light stick on the stone between us and sleep.

TWENTY-THREE

30.2 km from flash curtain

OUTPOST FIVE IS a husk of its former self. I walk the barren, ash-ridden patch of land, winding past scorched pathways peppered with smashed, burned-out cottages. The imprint of the lodge still marks the ground, and axes are scattered in the dirt where the Rig once housed the cavers' gear. Timber poles poke up from the ground at odd angles, like bones picked clean. Congress destroyed the only thing standing between the outpost and the burnt sands, offering the outpost up like a sacrifice to a hungry, merciless god.

And the curtain consumed it.

Something catches my toe, and I stumble. I look down at the rough-edged metal protruding from the sand. Realization steals over me, followed by a sort of eerie reverence. I smear the dirt away with my boot, but I already know what I'm standing on. I walked beneath this sign on my way to the tunnels nearly every day of my life in this outpost.

"We are the fortunate ones," I murmur, staring down at the words of our Subpar motto.

I've never been down the tunnels without Mom's axe. Maybe I'm more superstitious than I ever realized, because suddenly I'm desperate to find it, wasting precious minutes searching the rubble for a piece of gear that's just like all the rest I'm stepping over.

Only it's not like the rest. My axe—Mom's axe—has a handle indented from the press of both our hands. A handle that should've been replaced multiple times by now, but that I held on to—literally—because it was the only way I could still feel the curve of her hand against mine. Wood groans as I ease a fallen board aside and slip inside the leaning remnants of the Rig. Hooks still line walls covered with climbing rope and harnesses, standing by for cavers who will never come. I free a headlamp and click it on, searching the shadowed husk of the building for the one thing I need.

Part of the roof has collapsed, and steel rebar juts free like the shattered ribs of a beast. What I need is in its belly. I straddle a beam and wriggle past debris. The way the building's shifted, the hooks hang at an angle. I grasp them like the rungs of a ladder, pulling myself to the one I want. Suddenly I see it, hanging on Dram's hook. I exchanged it for his when I fled the outpost months ago.

Subpars never mined the cirium that lined the basin of the Sky. Our secret memorial was the one place we refused to mine, and it's that ore I need now to guide me to the tomb buried beneath the rubble, or the risks we've taken will be for nothing.

I drop to my knees beside the rock and debris. Congress detonated flash bombs inside the Range, so that parts of it have been reduced to sand. The Sky is beneath me, somewhere in this heap of stone that once formed tunnel six. I stretch forward, bits of stone digging into my chest. I lie prone, heart and palms pressed to the earth, willing myself to feel, to hear the song of the cirium deep inside.

"Help me, Mom," I whisper. I picture her telling me I did this as a child—a girl who loved the Range because I didn't yet understand the tunnels.

Use it to find a way out, Orion.

I imagine the last time I went to the Sky—with Dram and Lenore and Reeves. Memories flood my mind so powerfully, I can feel the cool blue water holding me buoyant. Then Dram held me, and for the first time I knew it meant more than just a marker assisting his scout. We wrote our names on the wall, and deep inside I made a promise to every Subpar. *I'll find the way out.*

Now Len and Reeves are gone, their lives sacrificed to give us a chance. And Dram . . . My chest tightens so hard I can't breathe. I shut out the image of his Radband, with its indicator the color of dried blood.

You're dying, Orion. All of us are.

Clouds shift and the flashfall glares over me in shades of pink and aquamarine. It licks my skin in ripples of heat, like a carnivore testing my taste. I roll onto my back and raise my sleeve, ready to see exactly how much of me the curtain has consumed. I understand now why Dram covered his Radband. It's terrifying, watching a color countdown to your own death.

I just crossed the cordons for the second time in my life. There is a cost.

Amber.

A soft cry escapes my lips, and it sounds too loud for this deserted outpost. My indicator is the shade when yellow ends and orange begins. And the Congress manipulated our bands, so I'm really at . . .

Red.

"Flash me." I stare at the light until my eyes sting. I can't bear to have it attached to me—to die with this shackle, marked as the Congress's slave. I grasp my double-bladed knife and wedge it between my skin and the band—the space created when Dad removed it. The skin is so scarred beneath, I don't even feel the blade as I pry at the sensors connecting the biotech to my wrist. Blood streams, but the wounds are shallow—just the few places the biotech had begun to adhere. My hand shakes as I work the knife, scraping against metal and skin and whatever else was used to mark me as an outpost miner. I won't be bound another moment by another of the Congress's lies—a tool they used to secure our compliance.

A scream builds behind my teeth, but I lever the band free, letting the pain sharpen my determination. Metal twists, biotech cracks, and the Radband falls to the dirt. Blood trickles past my fingers as I stand and stare at the shackle they promised would help keep us safe.

Lies.

I grip my mother's cracked axe handle and slam the axe down on my Radband. Bits of metal and biotech break off.

"I am not your slave," I say, bringing my axe down again and again. Tears fill my eyes, and the shattered Radband blurs, but I hammer at the pieces. For Mom. For Dram, and my Ghost father. For every Tempered Conjie. Every Brunt. Every Subpar.

The crack in my axe handle widens; I can feel it splintering apart—the wood that I've held in place of Mom's hand all these years. I collapse to my knees, weeping. I don't want to let go. Letting go of this shattered handle feels like letting go of my past, and Mom's past—the two woven together and forming the deepest parts of me.

And, too soon, I will have to let go of everything—this life included.

"AUGH!" I scream to the sky. The sky that isn't sky. The blanket of clouds and colors that have kept me prisoner my entire life. The radiation that kills and calls to me at the same time.

I let go.

Wood falls away, and my hands fill with dirt.

Dirt.

Splintered wood reveals a hollowed-out space carved into my mother's axe handle. I turn it on end, and more dirt pours out.

"Holy fire," I whisper. I sway on my knees, the weight of too much emotion sinking in—the possibilities burning in me more than the embers on the wind. No. Surely, not—

You have magic, Orion.

I study the dirt Mom hid inside her axe. It's not from the outposts or the cordons. This is Eastfall soil. From the mountain provinces. I know because its elements do not sing to me. They do not burn me. They contain no particles of cirium to contain me.

Slowly, like I'm reaching toward a mirage, I touch it. My mother's secret.

My secret.

The dirt is soft, with no sand or glass or bits of rock.

She could not comply. Meredith's words, describing why my mother was sent to the outposts.

And when she was discovered with the Conjuror . . . Cora, telling me that the Congress's best Delver loved her Ghost enough to be exiled for it. Or maybe she was doing what she could to get away from the Congress, protecting me even then.

The dirt sifts through my fingers, and I close my eyes, stretching my Subpar senses. Maybe more than what I've always thought of as Subpar.

If they're close enough, Conjurors can sense when elements are being shifted. Jameson told me that once. It was how he knew about Roran's ability. And now my heart pounds so hard I'm dizzy, my breath coming in erratic bursts—because *I've felt it.* I just didn't know what it meant.

Subpar *and* Conjuror.

Maybe. I stuff the dirt into my pockets—all but a handful.

"We are the fortunate ones," I say, pressing my palm to the ground. I envision the rock shifting, forming to the mental map I've laid out in my mind. Minutes pass, with the flashfall heating the air. I close my eyes and picture Fern shaping caverns with nothing but her hands. The wind kicks up, sending ash into my face, but the rubble remains simply rubble.

I am not a Conjuror. Just the daughter of two ghosts.

I slam my hands against the dirt, the cursed Conjie dirt. And it burns me. No—my hands are burning. They are suddenly a forge, altering the elements beneath them.

The earth shifts, and I tumble forward, flailing through darkness.

"Oof!" I land on my back and stare up at the flashfall shimmering above the crater I . . . carved. It can't be. It's not possible that I'm a Conjuror as well as a Subpar. My mind rebels against the idea, even as I stare at the proof.

Then I hear it—the faint hum of cirium, setting my nerves tingling. I need to get deeper. I imagine the ground shifting, opening a passage down to the Sky. And this time, I'm prepared for the burn. I feel the elements like they're strings on an instrument—I pluck the ones I need, and the melody is one I play by instinct.

———————

I wedge myself through a tight crevice, hands stretched before me. When they hit air and my headlamp reveals a vast drop, I know I'm getting close. I smell water.

Rock is relatively easy for me to manipulate. Vines—any living things—are proving more of a challenge. All I have to go on are the things I heard and saw while living with the free Conjies. And what I learned was that it takes time and practice to develop the sort of abilities they had. Even then, not all Conjurors are gifted equally.

I'm hoping desperation counts for something.

That, and Subpar instincts.

The dark is oppressive, a heavy thing that breathes in all the air and leaves nothing for me. I'm not sure any air caves survived the collapse of the Range. If that's not the Sky down there, I'm not sure how much farther I can go. I pull myself to the ledge and bathe my face in the musty air lifting from below.

This has to be it.

We used to follow secret markers to this cavern, ones only the cavers knew about. Now I find my way with nothing to guide me but instinct. My headlamp catches a white mark smeared across stone. I make a sound, not quite a sob. Maybe something more than instinct led me here. I turn, the path new but marked with guideposts I know by heart. And then—

A pool of luminescent blue water, its glow revealing cave walls.

"It held," I breathe, walking into the cavern. Elation swells . . . then crashes down.

It's empty.

I walk its length, hoping for a glimpse of gear, or the remains of a fire—some sign that they were here. I listen for voices, but all I hear is the quiet stillness of this memorial cavern.

I walk to the names written across the wall in chalk. "Goodbye, Mom," I say, touching the place where her sacrifice is remembered. It feels different this time, and I'm not sure if it's because I've changed so much, or if my understanding of her has. Her axe doesn't hang beside her name like the others. A sudden thought occurs to me. What if Mom's axe handle wasn't the only one hiding secrets?

I climb to the nearest axe and pry it from the rock. The end of the handle is bare. I check the one beside it. Two narrow lines are scratched into the axe handle. I crack it open, and a square piece of biotech falls out. I lift it in my hands, a mystery that's the size of my thumbnail. I study the coded diagram, trying to make sense of the illustration that shows a wrist and a device implanted beneath the skin where my Radband used to be. Alaran biotech hidden in a rebel's axe in order to give us access to the protected city. Not as a Subpar who earned four Rays, but as a scout who figured out that the only way into Alara was subversion.

I leap to the next axe and pull it down. Empty. The next falls with a clatter as I pry it free. Parallel lines.

A thin sheet of paper filled with words I've never heard before. Do Alarans speak so differently from us? A row of familiar words are crossed through with lines. These are words I know. Subpar phrases. Cavers' terms. Conjie curses and slang.

Words that would give me away.

I visit every memorial, every name marked with a flash date and a chalk circle. Less than half of the axes bear the cavers' mark and contain some other piece to a plan I am slowly beginning to understand. They intended to get a Subpar inside Alara. A Subpar who, disguised as an Alaran, would make a way for her people to get free.

I lay the treasures out on the cavern floor. A pile of secrets beside a heap of broken axe handles.

Clothing. Female. A dress of such airy fabric it fit into the handle of an axe. Another contained an embroidered robe marked with the seal of Alara. Something—according to the diagram—worn by a Vestige, a person dedicated to the study of Old Alara. A person who has access to the council's chambers.

A necklace that I hold up to the gleaming light of my headlamp. A dosimeter, beautiful, fragile-looking, but real. It's reading the radiation in this cavern with a visible meter worked into a silver backing, steadily gleaming through its levels: green, dark green, yellow, dark yellow, amber, rust, red.

Rust.

The color of my Radband before I destroyed it.

I'm dying. Dram is dying. All of us are.

The thought spurs me to action, and I stuff the items into my pouches.

Before I leave, there is one last thing I must do. I grip a piece of chalk and press it to the wall, tears pricking my eyes. I will honor them, the cavers I could not save, the friends I didn't reach in time.

I look for a place that will fit all their names together. There's space on the end, the far corner beside one lone name. I glance at the writing, and the chalk drops from my fingers. *Roran.* The flash date beside it—just weeks ago.

I don't read the inscription, but turn and bolt across the cavern—to a different wall. The one where an ore scout and her marker once drew their names when the world seemed full of hope.

I gasp and press a hand to my mouth. I read the names—they're all here: Owen, Roland, Marin, Winn—every Subpar who followed me into Cordon Five two months ago. Mere. She's alive, her name written in barely legible scrawl because she likely drew it herself with her one remaining appendage. This wall is for the names of those who got free.

"Scout?"

I whirl toward the cave entrance and peer past the light of a headlamp, a glimpse of broad shoulders and brown skin gleaming beneath layers of particle dust. "Owen?"

His stunned expression gives way to a smile. "Flash me, it *is* you!" He drops the water bottles he's holding and runs to me, crushing me in his arms.

Safe. I let myself savor the feeling I haven't known in far too long. This caver helped carry Dram and me up out of nine when our air tanks failed. He kept me running when the Barrier Range collapsed above our heads. Tears fill my eyes.

"You're all here?" I ask, my throat tight.

"Yes. We've been waiting—for you, for word that things have changed."

"Soon," I tell him, pulling away. I dash my hand under my eyes and take in his smiling face. "There's a serum—a way for us to live in the flashfall without sickening from exposure. I'm going to find a way to get it to you—to everyone." I smile as I secure my gear over my shoulders. "Tell Mere . . ." My throat closes, and I swallow hard. "Tell Mere her son's name is on the wrong wall." Owen's eyes widen. "Tell her he's with me—in the Overburden. And that I'm going to get him out." He crushes me in another hug. "And, Owen?"

"What is it, Scout?"

"Tell Mere I made the promise like a Conjie."

TWENTY-FOUR

WHEN DAWN ARRIVES, I'm standing at the fence, first in line to enter the cordon. I managed to convince Meredith that my exploration of tunnel five was necessary—that I was following instincts that led to a dead end. She grudgingly excused my actions, but she'd never approve what I'm planning now.

I watch the Tomb, waiting for the doors to lift. Trepidation prickles along my skin. It's been four days since I last saw Dram, facing him down over the end of a spear. I needed to get things in place before this final step, because what I'm about to do will push me over the edge entirely.

"Orion?" GM16 approaches with my old squad. The expression she wears fills me with dread. I search amongst the faces, half of them strangers. No sign of Roran.

"Roran?" I ask, panic fluttering in my chest.

"He's in the infirmary. He'll recover." She pauses, and I hear the other name in her hesitation. Dram.

"What's happened?" I ask.

"Roran got caught out in the cordon. The Dodgers wouldn't go after him. Dram volunteered."

"He went into the cordon—at night?"

She nods. "He saved Roran from the flashtide, but . . . he didn't make it back."

A night in the cordon. Without the dose of serum that keeps us alive.

"So he has flash fever." I sound like Dad when he makes a clinical observation.

"Worse than that." She slips a syringe into my hand. "We were going to find him this morning, but I have a feeling you'll be faster. One and a half kilometers northwest."

I search her violet eyes. "Worse than flash fever?"

"There were cordon rats. Roran could hear him. And the dog—Soma."

The buzzer sounds, and I push through the turnstile.

"No Delvers in the quadrants!" a Strider shouts.

"Shoot me, then," I call, shoving my way past.

I feel like one of the winged cordon creatures as I fly across the sand. I sprint harder than I did even from King and his crew. You run faster when it's to save someone else's life. I dodge bones scattered along the dust trail and barrel over cordon brush to the mining quadrant assigned to our squad. I scan the burnt sands, and through the flaming embers I catch sight of a figure slumped on the ground.

"Dram!" I scream his name, but the shape doesn't move. *Be alive, be alive, be alive.*

I kick something. Dram's knife, the blade stacked with rat bodies half consumed by the flashtide.

"Dram!" I drop beside him, crumpled on his side next to

Soma. I lift his head so I can see past his face shield. His eyes open.

I flinch. His retinas are burned, and he watches me through eyes the color of my Radband indicator.

"I told him to go," he says, his voice hoarse. His mouth moves, and a ragged cry escapes. "I told him to go."

"I know," I say, touching his face through the headpiece.

A thin sound pushes past his cracked lips. His face crumples, and I know if his body had any water left, there'd be tears. I push his suit up, ignoring the red welts blistering his skin, and shove the needle into his vein. "I'm treating you with serum, Dram." He doesn't hear me, or if he does, my words don't mean anything to him. His gloves are chewed through. Bite marks cover both hands.

"I pulled them off of him . . . but there were so many."

And then I understand—he was paralyzed with toxin. No wonder he couldn't keep going. But he's alive. Soma lay at his side like a bulwark and took the brunt of the attack.

Beneath the layers of cirium cloth, Soma looks like he's sleeping. If you don't look at the places his body's been chewed away. The way Dram's covered him, just his head and front paws peek out, and they are untouched. Sleeping Soma.

Dram rolls onto his knees and presses his forehead to the dog's neck. "You are free," he chokes.

His despair gives me hope. Weeks the Brunt didn't feel anything anymore. But this is Dram, the caver who saved a dog that saved him back. I untie Dram's neck cloth from Soma's neck and push it into his hand.

"He is free." I repeat the words Subpars say on Burning Days, the words we've said to each other too many times.

"Rye?" He looks up at me like he's just noticed who I am.

"I'm here." I drip water between his cracked lips. His eyes might be half blinded, but he sees me more than he did in the Tomb.

"I'm bad off, ore scout." His voice is even worse than he looks, like something clawed the inside of his throat.

"I'm taking you to Fortune. There's a Radbed." I slip my knife beneath the strips of cloth holding his armor in place. Cactus, vulture wings, gull feathers—it all drops in a decayed heap.

"Wear my ashes, Rye." He reaches for his memorial pendants.

"That's not our arrangement." I drag him to his feet, wondering how I'm going to cross the cordon with him amber-eyed and flash-fevered. When he staggers and stumbles, I pull both his arms over my shoulders, bearing his weight as we struggle to put one foot in front of the other.

"Walk," I command. "Walk, or we're going to die!" His head lists to the side, and I wonder if he can even hear me. "Come on, just a few more meters. Remember the air cave down nine? Keep. Going." I grunt as he collapses against me. I grasp him about the waist, but we tumble to the ground.

"Dram Berrends! If you ever loved me, get on your glenting feet!" I grab his arm and pull as hard as I can.

"I did . . . things," he murmurs. "Bad things. To survive."

"It wasn't you." His body slides along the ground. Two meters. Five.

"I hurt people."

"You saved Roran."

"Leave me. I'm good as dust."

"You are not *dust*, you glenting skant!" I drop his arm and crouch beside him. "Why are you smiling?"

"You sound like a Conjie."

Oh, fire.

I am. I want to tell him so badly. *I am one of the Conjies you love so much, Dram. Half of me, anyway.*

"I have something to show you," I whisper, my throat choked with emotion. "I can't save you as just regular Orion."

"You were never regular, Orion," he says, eyes drifting shut.

I tear into the seam of my jacket. Soil trickles from the hole and I wrench it wide, filling my hand. "My mother was a Delver, Dram. She fell in love with her caving partner—an adapted Conjie. When they exiled her to Outpost Five . . . I was with her. No one knew."

His eyes open, and he stares at me, then at the dirt I'm grasping.

"Fire, Rye, what are you saying?"

"I'm saying you're going to live, Dram Berrends, because the Subpar who loves you is holding the earth of the provinces."

His brows draw together, and I turn my focus to the elements in my hand. The compounds of the soil roll across my senses, and I hear them on some level, like the way I've always heard the flash curtain.

The same way I became Outpost Five's lead ore scout, the same ability that earned me four Rays, I understand now—it's the Conjuror in me, woven together with everything that makes me a Subpar. No one senses the elements like I do, and it enables me to distinguish the chemical makeup of what I'm holding, and alter it.

"Holy fire," Dram breathes, watching the first green shoots

twist up from the dirt. "I can barely see, Rye. Tell me I'm really seeing this."

The sapling lifts from my palm in a tangle of roots, fine as hair, that twist and thicken. Leaves caress my arms, twining around us as I direct the branches into a vessel that lifts Dram off the sand. Wood skims beneath him, forming a sledge with handles I can push.

He turns his head, and I stare into his wide eyes. They are full of awe, and for the first time since I dragged him off the burnt sand—hope. He murmurs something, so softly I miss the words.

"What?" I lean down.

"We are the fortunate ones," he says hoarsely.

"We are." I lean forward and run for Fortune.

I conjure as I run, reinforcing the vessel holding Dram, even as the curtain burns it away. Leaves curl and smolder, lifting on cordon winds as we skim over the sand toward camp. When the corral tower becomes visible, I drag Dram's arm over my shoulder and leave the sledge to the elements. I can't let them see what I'm capable of. Not yet.

Maybe it's a renewed sense of hope, but Dram finds his footing this time. He's able to keep pace with me all the way through the fence to Fortune.

He staggers a few meters from the door.

"We're here. Stay with me, Dram!" I lever his body through the doorway. He's no longer conscious. "Hold on. Just hold on."

"Orion!" Cora shouts. "What are you doing?"

"Help me, Cora!"

Her eyes skip from me to Dram's battered body. "You're breaking Protocol!"

"I'll tell Meredith I forced you to help me. Please!"

"You didn't force me to do anything," she grumbles, grasping Dram's feet with her good hand as well as her bandaged one. She hisses when his weight presses against her injury, but she doesn't let go. We tow him from the vestibule, bypassing decon. Cora shoots me a look but doesn't mention my second breach of Protocol. I'm not sure any Delvers have ever broken as many rules as I am now—except maybe Mom.

We descend the shaft and carry him to the infirmary—mercifully empty at the moment—and she releases Dram to open the Radbed. I grasp him around the chest and lever us both over the side. We collapse onto the medcot.

"Get out, Orion!"

"No time. Do it!"

Cora slams the lid and seconds later, serums mist over Dram and me. I close my eyes as the radiation treatment chamber hums to life around us.

Mom once told me of butterflies, fragile insects that lived before the curtain fell. They began as something without wings, crawling on the ground until they transformed inside a chrysalis. That is how I feel now, as the chamber fills with the fog of serums and my body trembles from exertion and fear. I hold Dram tighter, and will my strength into him. Will his body to take some of my remaining resistance, so that he can emerge from this chamber like those butterflies. Changed. Wings unfurling.

Alive.

"What are his levels, Cora?" I shout through the glass.

"Improving," she calls above the sounds of the Radbed.

Dram's body shakes, and I hold him tighter.

"You're safe. You're going to live!" His short Brunt's hair brushes my cheek as I tuck his head beneath my chin. I reach around him and unfasten his shirt, pulling it apart to expose his skin to the serums. My hands brush his memorial pendants. Something metallic dangles from the cord; the talisman he wore for me. They cut off his hair, but he found another way to keep it close.

The chamber hums around us. Whatever awaits us on the other side of this cocoon, we'll face it together. I hold on tightly to the boy who never stopped holding on to me.

———

"You brought a Brunt into Fortune." Meredith's clipped tone cuts through my thoughts as she walks into my room. I resume brushing my hair, watching my reflection in the mirror. She stands in my line of sight. "A nearly dead, *exposed* Brunt."

"I'm Prime Delver. It was my right."

"You went too far with this, Orion."

"He was one of the best miners at Outpost Five. He'll make a fine Delver."

"He must return."

"He'll die!"

"When one is made a Brunt, there is no going back."

I pull my chain off and drop it on the floor.

"What are you doing?"

"Giving up Fortune. Make Dram Delver in my place."

She laughs. "And where would you go?"

"To the Box. As his Forger."

She raises a brow like this is more amusement than she's had in months. "You can't be a Forger," she says with a grin. "You're not an adapted Conjuror."

I hesitate, my words catching in my throat. "What if I was?"

Her smile dies. "Then you'd be the most valuable person in the city-state." Her shrewd gaze flicks over me. "You're a Subpar. I've seen your Radband."

I lift my cupped hand, shaking with the enormity of what I'm about to reveal. This admission could cost me my hands. Possibly my life.

It's certain to cost my freedom.

A flower blooms against my palm, petals shifting over my skin. Meredith stares, transfixed. Then, slowly, her eyes lift, and she looks at me as something other than her Prime Delver.

I'm already a Ghost. The last one.

"I'll assign Val as your Delver."

"No, it must be Dram."

"He can't be Prime—"

"It's my one condition."

"You don't get to make conditions, Forger." The name cuts through my senses, severing the bond I shared with this woman. Any safety I once felt here is gone.

"We were caving partners at Outpost Five. First to earn four Rays. We accomplished the impossible, Meredith, and we can do it again. Make him Prime. I'll be his Ghost. And we'll find the eludial seam."

She picks up my Delver's chain. "I'm going to miss you, Orion." Her statement swings between us like a door closing on the future I once had. Now there is just the caverns and the Box.

"I'm going to miss everything," I say.

———

Meredith gives me three days. There's no sense in sending me to waste away in the Box if there's no Prime Delver to utilize my ability, so while Dram's still receiving treatment, I get a last bit of freedom. No one can know about me yet. That was her condition. And since she's commissary, she gets to make as many conditions as she wants.

But that doesn't mean I trust her.

I've taken to following her, silent and unnoticed as the specter she's commissioned me to be. The morning of the third day, she clicks down the hall with determined strides. Straight into Dram's infirmary room.

I linger outside the door, just out of view.

"Commissary," Dram says.

"What are your intentions concerning my Prime Delver?" Meredith asks. I hear the creak of a chair as she sits and risk a glance through the door hinges.

Dram grins. "My intentions."

Meredith's eyes narrow. "What is the context of your relationship?"

"What has she told you about us?"

"She held up her climbing rope and said, 'We're like this.'"

Dram's smile widens. "We're bonded."

"But you're not Conjurors."

"Then call it something else."

Her eyes widen, like she can't get his words to line up in a way that makes sense. "But surely, you clarify your relation-ships—"

"You Alarans and your need to define things that don't bear defining," Dram says. "There's just living and loving, and either you're at someone's side when it happens, or you're not."

"I'm asking if you're married!"

"What is marriage but a public pledge of commitment? In Outpost Five, when a couple marries, they sign a paper in front of the director and exchange tokens of commitment. They're given a house and a day free from caving."

"Answer the question, Dram."

"I've been pledged to Orion since I was fourteen."

"As her marker, you mean."

He shrugs. "Call it what you will. I'm devoted to her, body and soul. I've made no secret of it." His brows draw together. "Except outside processing, when they were going to cut our hands off and possibly execute us for treason." A hint of his smile returns. "That time, it may have been a secret."

Meredith sighs heavily. But this is Dram, and even she isn't immune to his charm.

"Sign this paper, then." She lifts a document and hands him a pen. "Orion already did."

"What is it?" Dram's eyes skip over the print.

"Call it my Alaran need for clarification," Meredith answers.

"This is written in your fancy council-talk," Dram mutters. "I can barely understand what it says."

"It pertains to the precise nature of your relationship with Orion."

Sign it, Dram. Don't sign it, Dram!

"If I sign this, can I see her?"

"Of course." Meredith smiles, and it reminds me of Soma baring his teeth before he loved Dram.

He scrawls his name on the form, and something inside me dies. I wanted him to sign—need him to. But now there is no hope for us. He has no idea what he just agreed to.

He hands her the paper. "Does this define our relationship clearly enough for you?"

"Oh, yes. Thank you, Dram." Meredith tucks the contract away. "What did you say couples were given in Outpost Five? A day free of caving?"

He nods, eyes narrowing slightly.

"Then you'd better get up. This day is yours." She turns toward the door, and I slip away, my bare feet silent over the stone, as quiet as a ghost.

TWENTY-FIVE

7.2 km from flash curtain

I'M DRESSED FOR a wedding. At least, that's what Meredith tells me. In Old Alara, she explained, as she buttoned me into the gown, a woman's worth was displayed in what she wore. All I know is this dress required two people to lift it from its box.

It sways at my waist with every step like it has its own momentum. I wear special undergarments to support it, as if I am not enough on my own to bear the splendor of Alara. The gown pulls me down, but it's got nothing on the weight in my chest.

I search for Dram, my gaze flitting over sparkling crystal. I sip the drink in my hand, and it fizzes down my dry throat, makes my dress feel lighter.

"Take it easy with the champagne," Cora says. She wears a blue gown overlaid with silver cloth. She sparkles in the light. We all sparkle like we've been pulled down from the night sky.

I tip back my glass.

Jewels are rare, treasured, Meredith told me, but the things sewn over my dress, refracting light like miniature sunbursts, are more rare to Alarans than any gemstone.

Cordon glass.

It makes me want to laugh.

I spent my childhood climbing the Range and staring out over the glass cordon, dreaming of Alara. Then, when the Congress destroyed the outpost, we escaped to that same cordon. I feel like I'm wearing my rebel flag. Or a gown made of memorial pendants. The thought presses on my chest, the place I store memories of Mom and Wes, and I swap my empty glass for a new one.

Meredith insisted on candlelight. I'm glad because it will hide the shadows under my eyes. I'm hoping Dram will be distracted enough by my makeup that he won't notice the pale skin it's hiding. I'm also hoping he doesn't notice the guns subtly pointed at me.

Meredith made that threat clear when she showed me Dram's signature on the agreement. "I want to give you a wedding celebration, but if you conjure so much as a leaf, I'll drop you where you stand. Is that understood? Good. What kind of cake do you prefer?"

I sense Val at my side. She and Cora appear to be hemming me in, blocking me from reaching for more champagne.

"Look who's back from the dead," Val murmurs.

It's impossible to miss Dram as he steps into the Grand Hall. He wears a Delver's uniform, the formal style I've only seen in paintings. He walks across the room like he stepped right off the canvas. He doesn't know that he is Meredith's prize, that he's been dressed for the part. There's an unseen stage beneath Dram's boots that no one can see but me.

He scans the room, and suddenly his gaze connects with mine. His lips part, like he's taking an extra breath. Then he smiles. The old smile that I'd see down nine after we outran flash bats.

The glass cracks in my hand.

"Fire, Orion!" Cora slides a tray beneath my shattered drink. "Why are you so nervous?"

I'm crumbling beneath the weight of so many emotions: a cave-in of relief and sadness, want, and despair. I wonder how good I've become at masks, or if Dram can see all of it on my face as he walks toward me. He walks differently. Not shuffling as when I last saw him out on the cordon, but there's a stiffness to his steps, remnant effects of venom from cordon rats he didn't fight off fast enough. We are both so changed. Outwardly and inwardly. I wonder if the parts of us that make us fit together are still there.

Cora and Val slip away as Dram nears. The physic shadows him, a few meters away, as if Dram could falter at any moment, his radiation poisoning returning all at once to claim him right here in the Grand Hall.

"The most beautiful things are the most dangerous," Dram says softly.

"Then this place is deadly," I answer. It's the truth. It is the most beautiful place I've ever seen. But then, I've never been to Alara.

"I wasn't talking about Fortune," he says, grinning. "I've never seen you in a dress."

"This would've been a tough fit through the neck of nine."

He smiles, but I catch his furrowed brow as he looks over the ornate walls flickering in candlelight. "This place is so strange. It reminds me of Sanctuary."

Sanctuary. The red house in the prison cordon, our only refuge from King and the dusters. A place where Dram and I forged something beautiful in the midst of the worst horrors we'd ever faced.

"Why does the Congress do this?" he asks. "Why not share some of this food and shelter and tech with the other people here?"

I don't answer, because he already knows the truth. Our society is built upon disparity. From the moment the flash curtain fell, it divided humanity, and people in power decided who was *less* and who was *more*. Then they named it Protocol.

"Ladies and gentlemen!" Meredith calls. "To the alcove, if you please." She sails between us, her black gown streaming behind her like a signal flag. I know what she is doing, even if no one else here senses her intentions.

She's keeping Dram and me apart, even as she orders us into place beside each other for the ceremony. She radiates with more than her usual manic energy. This is her world, and she alone is its master. I let her maneuver me, because I want her to believe it's true. She slides me a glance, pleased with my compliance. The mask I'm wearing for her at least is working.

The others surround us in a half circle. Four Striders, the physic and his assistant, Cora and Val. We stand beneath a cirium canopy, a fine mesh of iridescent metal. I try not to think of the Subpars who mined it and what it cost them to bring it up out of the tunnels.

Meredith wears her formal commissary robes, and her chain of office reflects the light of the candles Dram and I each hold. I join Dram beneath the canopy, and Meredith explains that this tradition symbolizes the protection of the shield and the covenant Alarans share as members of the city-state. Her brow furrows, and she pages through the rest of the book she holds, probably realizing that Alaran tradition doesn't apply well to Delvers in the Overburden.

"Did you bring tokens?" she asks. Alarans don't exchange verbal vows, Meredith explained to us earlier, but rather physical tokens of their devotion. Something from our "houses."

"I pledge myself to you," I say, opening my hand over Dram's. A single white bloom spills into his hand, the one thing Meredith allowed me to conjure. Dram looks up at me. It's identical to Roran's conjured flower—the one I gave Mere in Cordon Four. "May we always have hope," I say. His fingers close gently over it, and he tucks it inside his sleeve. Exactly where I placed Mere's.

"I pledge myself to you," Dram says. He sets a braided piece of cloth across my hand. It's the coarse, torn fragment of his Dodger's neck cloth. This belonged to Soma. The brave one. "May we always have courage," he says softly. But he's saying more with this, too. He's telling me he would lay down his life to protect me. My fingers tighten over the cloth.

Meredith reads from the book, but I'm no longer listening. I lower my gaze to the candle she's given me. Beneath this compliant veneer, I am a flame burning, burning.

Planning.

Filling in the details of what I must do while there is still time.

Dram nudges my foot. I glance up into blue eyes studying my face. He shifts his gaze to the unlit candle between us. Together, we dip our flames to the wick until it lights. We blow out our solitary candles, and Meredith reads something about two becoming one. I shut out her voice again, because all I can think about is two becoming separated by a cirium Box forty meters beneath our feet.

Meredith closes her book with a snap.

Dram draws me into his arms.

"That isn't part of the ceremony," Meredith says.

I smile against Dram's lips and kiss him again.

———

Meredith gave us the day, but not the night. She approaches Dram with the physic in tow, telling him he's to spend the night in the infirmary, for one last night of monitoring. When Dram tells them what they can do with that idea, she explains that she's preparing our future living arrangements, sliding a glance at me, a warning in her eyes.

No, Meredith, I won't say anything, my eyes tell her back.

So when Dram reaches for me, bristling with frustration, I hug him as tightly as I can. He doesn't know this is it. He doesn't know that, tomorrow, everything comes crashing down.

"Somehow, I think the outpost Subpars fared better on their wedding nights," he grumbles in my ear. An unexpected pang of longing grips my chest. For the life we might've had in Outpost Five—a simple caver's cottage and little blue-eyed toddlers.

Children who would've grown up enslaved.

I shiver suddenly, and his arms tighten around me. "It's all right," he murmurs. "What's one night, right?"

It's everything. My eyes go to Meredith, who watches us closely. "I'll see you in the morning," I say tightly, pulling away.

"Rye, wait." Dram catches my arm and draws me back. "We just married each other." His lips twist in a grin. "For what I'm pretty sure was the second time." He kisses me, cradling the sides of my face.

Later, the gown is lifted off me, and I'm freed from the undergarment supports. I'm left alone, and the door is not even locked. Meredith knows it wouldn't stop me. Not now.

I struggle against the urge to run, to fight. We would be caught. There's a better way; it's just not the easier way. I go over the plan the Subpars devised, over generations, with coded axe handles in a memorial cavern. I conjure white flowers, one after another, until the air fills with their perfume. I breathe it in. Hope.

Then I conjure them to dust so fine no one will see it.

———

Dram sits up in his bed as I breeze through the door. He sucks in a breath—the movement pained him—and touches the bandaged wound around his ribs.

"Still healing?" I ask.

"Nah, beat up and bruised is my body's new natural state." He smirks in a way that makes him look younger than his nineteen years. I let myself absorb the view of his bare chest, marveling at how quickly Fortune's restoring him. He pulls on his shirt as I drop a folded uniform at the end of his bed.

"What's all this?" he asks, sorting through the pile of clothes.

"They didn't tell you? You're going to be made a Delver."

"They told me, but these are . . ." He lifts the coat. "Fancy."

My heart twists. I can't tell him. Not yet. You don't go against Meredith's conditions—especially when you've asked for one of your own.

"They take commissioning very seriously around here," I say, holding the white jacket as he slides his arm in.

"Your hands are shaking," he says.

"Your eyes are blue again," I say, but it's not enough to chase the worry from his gaze.

"What's wrong?"

"What's wrong is your bruises don't match this uniform," I murmur, buttoning his jacket.

He covers my hands. "What aren't you telling me?"

I hate lying to Dram, but I am my mother's daughter, and I can keep secrets when I need to.

"It's these uniforms—the white. They remind me of how Congress dressed us for the prison cordon." His eyes soften, and he draws me against his chest, and I know I've successfully evaded him.

"I know this isn't what we dreamed of," he says, "but we can survive down here. We can be together."

A sound of dismay escapes my lips, muffled against his chest.

Not together. You will live here, and I'll be in a cell 132 meters deep.

Cora pokes her head into the room. "It's time."

Dram takes my hand. It's damp, my skin clammy with dread. We walk into the chamber, and the Delvers take their places at the tunnel entrances. The third quadrant—the Prime's quadrant—is vacant. I stop before the lines painted on the ground. Dram looks at me, confused.

"Take your place, Delver," Meredith says to him.

Dram stands rooted in place beside me. "This is Orion's quadrant."

"Not anymore. Step to the line."

His eyes dart to mine. "What did you do?"

"Delver—"

"Orion, what's happening?"

Val steps behind me and removes my Prime's chain.

"Did you really think a Brunt could earn Fortune and become a Delver?" Meredith asks. "The only way out for a Brunt is death. Someone had to die."

"Weeks died," he says bleakly.

"No." Meredith shakes her head. "Weeks is still buried inside the boy I'm looking at, beneath the veneer of civility I've given you."

"Then who died?" His tone is dark. Dark as the Brunt who survived the Tomb night after night.

"Orion did."

This isn't how I wanted to tell him. But I have no say in Meredith's schemes, no say in anything at all anymore. He and Cora stare at me wide-eyed as Val whisks my Prime's cloak away and hands it to Meredith. Next, she takes my jacket. I can't look at Dram—this is the part I've been dreading. I can't stand for him to see how much like the prison cordon this really is.

"Holy fire," he murmurs hoarsely, staring at the collar around my neck.

Cora gasps. "Oh, no, no, Orion . . ."

"I won't do this," Dram says, striding from the Prime's quadrant.

"It's already done," Meredith says. "You are now her best chance of survival."

"She told me what you do to . . . Forgers."

"We give them an opportunity to use their abilities, to serve honorably."

"They're nothing but slaves—prisoners in cirium cells!"

"She will be spared Tempering."

"She'll be a Ghost!"

"Orion is now the single most important person in our city-state, and you will be commissioned as Prime Delver only because I think you can protect her better than anyone else." She settles the Prime's cloak around Dram's shoulders. "You're not here because I need another Delver. You're here because I need Weeks, the Brunt who stayed alive against all odds. What you will face down there with her, beneath the curtain, is nothing that anyone has lived to tell about. I believe that, maybe, for the first time, a Forger and a Prime have a chance at succeeding."

I dare a look at Dram's face. Tears fill his eyes. The truth in her words has won him over, and he's grieving the loss of me, the loss of what he thought we might have had together.

"Don't make her a prisoner." He bites out the words. "Let her return here—"

"No. Conjurors are not permitted freedom—especially those with her capabilities."

"Then I'll stay down there with her."

Meredith shakes her head. "You are my Prime. I cannot risk your well-being."

"Then you better *glenting* well let me stay with her!"

Meredith signals Val. "We must proceed. The other commissaries will be joining us via com any moment. They've been apprised of the situation, and they expect your compliance, Dram."

"And if I don't *comply*?"

"Then you'll return to your Brunt comrades, and Val will take your place as Prime." *And Orion will die.* She doesn't say the words. Every person here knows it.

"I'll be your glenting Prime," Dram says.

"Good, because you've already agreed to it." Meredith holds up the contract he signed. "We don't force people to do things here at Fortune, but I needed to be assured of your compliance."

"That contract was about my partnership with Orion."

"So it was. Just not the way you thought."

The commissioning lasts half the length of our wedding ceremony and is witnessed by the council on the other end of a screencom. A recitation of words that I echo, but my mind has already moved beyond this moment, traversing tunnels, bringing plans into alignment. Even the Prime Commissary's voice isn't enough to pull me from my thoughts. Meredith drapes the chain of office over Dram's neck. He glares at her.

"Dram, as Prime Delver, it's your duty to escort your Forger to her barracks."

"Now?"

"A reminder—you can be replaced."

He sighs and strides into the port.

Cora pushes past Meredith and throws her arms around me. "You stupid, brave girl!" Her wet cheek slides against mine, but I can't look at her. Her tears will bring home the horror of what I've chosen.

I return to the map in my head.

I push past her and step into the pod. Val latches the door. She doesn't meet my eyes. I suppose, to her, I'm already a Ghost.

The port descends. Dram grips the rail and presses his forehead against the metal cage. It shakes, and air winds through the shaft as we drop so quickly my stomach flutters. This isn't like the smooth tech up in Fortune. This is raw; every meter we drop is another suggestion of danger. The pod stops, and still Dram doesn't move. I unlatch the door and step out.

"That was a long ride down," he says. "Over a hundred meters, I'd guess."

"You don't have to guess. You're wearing a depth gauge."

He shoves away from the pod and glares at me. He checks the glowing tech on his wrist. "A hundred thirty-two meters, but I guess you already knew that. It was one of the factors in your plan—your little mind map, right? The Scout, the *Hunter* who knows everything and leaves everyone else in the dark!"

I don't answer. Nothing I say can change any of this. Not yet.

He looks around at the passage entrance. "What is that sound?"

"An alert that lets us know if any of the high-frequency emitters have been damaged. They're the only things that deter the moles from getting close enough to conjure."

"When do you get to come up?"

"I don't."

He stiffens, and I know he's caught sight of the Box.

"Holy fire," he murmurs. Tension thrums between us, like one wrong word could set off an explosion. I adopt a neutral tone.

"As Prime Delver, you have biometric access to the cell. It can't be closed or opened from the inside." I demonstrate, and he opens the door. "You're not permitted inside. There are specific rules to preserve Proto—"

"Don't you dare say that word to me." His shoulders rise and fall, like his body is working to contain the anger expanding inside him. He steps past me into the cell. His gaze roves over the low cot in the corner, to the toilet and the shower spigot. "How could you do this?"

I don't answer. Meredith already told him. A trade.

"This is"—he swallows—"this is brutal. Worse than anything they've put us in."

It's not worse than the Tomb, but I don't say that. "It's the only way to contain someone . . . like me."

His eyes slide shut. "You should never have told them."

"They were going to send you back!"

"You could've gotten *free*, Orion! This wasn't the glenting plan!" He slams his fist against the cell wall.

"Our plan changed when they made you a Brunt!"

"I was already *dead*. Why didn't you just leave me?"

"You think because I don't wear my cuff I'm not still bonded to you? I feel your heartbeat, and I wouldn't feel anything, ever again, if it stopped!"

"Yes," he says brokenly. "You would."

My collar chimes. Time's up.

"You need to go," I say. "Close the door so it can lock."

"Tell me there's more than this—tell me you've got some sort of plan."

"I'm drawing maps in my head." I force myself to smile, but I can taste my tears. I walk into the cell.

"I can't stand this, Rye," he says, his face pinched.

"Do it now," I command softly. He grits his teeth, mutters

a curse, and shoves the cirium barrier closed. My collar chimes. It sounds just like the prison cordon. Congress has me in a cage once more.

Dram doesn't leave. At least once an hour, he knocks a pattern on the door just to let me know he's still there. I barely hear it through the walls, but I feel the vibration where I've got my back pressed against the door.

I lose track of time, but I'm still awake when I hear him bang a new rhythm—angry and desperate—onto my cell. My breaths come shallow, and I can't assemble my thoughts. Standing takes all my strength, and when I push myself to my feet, suddenly up feels down and down feels up. I press my hands to the wall to keep from falling. One clear thought forms from the impressions tangling in my head: they've cut off my air supply.

They are forcing Dram to return to Fortune.

Silence descends, heavy, with no intermittent knocking, no reassuring taps that tell me Dram's just on the other side of this dark oblivion. Fresh air pours through my vent.

He's gone.

I am well and truly alone.

"I am not a Ghost," I say aloud into the void. Panic tingles along my nerves, and for the first time, I understand the fear that seizes Dram in tight spaces. I am sealed inside a metal box, one hundred and two meters beneath Fortune, which is thirty meters from the surface.

I'm not a Ghost. Not yet.

I'm just the girl that Congress buried alive.

———

Somehow, I fall asleep. When the cell door opens and my collar chimes, I'm curled in a ball on the cot. Dram is there before

I've even opened my eyes. He pulls me into his arms, holding me so tight the buckles of his uniform dent my skin. He doesn't speak, and I just soak up the feel of him, warm and alive. But we're inside the Box.

"Get me out," I say.

"Oh, flash me," he murmurs, leaping to his feet. "Sorry, I didn't think—"

I stagger out, squinting up at the bulbs. Dram presses rations into my hands, and I eat, walking, putting as much distance between me and the Box as possible.

"I need to know the plan," Dram says. "I can't do this, Rye—lock you in that thing and then go sleep in the Congress's palace—"

"There is a plan. Not mine, my mom's."

TWENTY-SIX

7.2 km from flash curtain

EVEN DELVERS GET one day off a week, which means I spend an entire day locked in my prison. I knew this was coming, but there's nothing that prepares a person for utter isolation in a three-meter-square cube of metal.

The solitary light died a flickering death. Now I sit, my body aching from too many hours on the hard cot, holding the last of Dram's flares. The candle he stole for me burned down to a puddle of wax hours ago. And I was only lighting it when I felt I would go mad from the darkness—when it felt so heavy, pressing on me like a living thing, slowly suffocating me. I stare at the red flame, gold at the center, with a sort of manic affection. In a matter of days, I have come to love fire, when once I hated everything that reminded me of Burning Days. Now each flame is a gift beating back impenetrable darkness. Sparks hit my skin, and I cherish the sting that tells me I'm alive. Smoke fills the Box, but I pretend the ache in my lungs is from standing too close to a fire pit on a Friday night at Outpost Five. The flare burns out, and panic rushes in, the darkness presses . . .

I close my eyes to better imagine a mug of ale, held in one hand, my other warming above the fire. Voices spill from the Rig as cavers ditch their gear and join the raucous laughter of Subpars gathered on Friday night. Graham is there, telling stories in his graveled voice, calling me *girlie* and pouring me too much ale. My heart aches with a sudden stab of loss, but I push it away, back to memories of a time before he gave his life in the burnt sands.

The thrum of the flash curtain stirs inside me, raising goose bumps along my arms. I shut it out, imagining Roland tuning his fiddle, and the nervous feeling I'd get wondering if Dram would ask me to dance.

I open my eyes, and I can't see—I'm blind! No, it's like I'm dead. Buried. It's my day off. Dram's not coming. I've got thirty-six hours to go.

Thirty-six hours of nothing but the flash curtain whispering across my senses. My scout's instincts magnify the cirium on every side, so that I feel like the curtain has me contained in hands made of its elements. Hands surrounding me, squeezing me—

"Ugh!" I surge to my feet, hands pressed over my ears. I yell again, until I'm louder than the stirrings of the flashfall. I sway, my hands lift, and I turn to the patterns the cavers taught me. My feet tap to a rhythm Owen pounded on a barrel, a bawdy song about women and brew, with words Dram explained with a red face when we first became caving partners. I was twelve, and he fourteen, and the memory of it makes me smile and sing louder. I twirl and stomp and dance, with nothing to hinder me in this empty Box. I sing until my voice grows hoarse, until I've filled the Box with memories so vivid, I no longer feel alone.

My collar chimes, waking me from a restless sleep. The door slides open, but something's off—it's not time for Dram to be here. The tunnel lights are still at night-dim. I rise from my cot, tense.

"Ore scout? You awake?"

I leap for the figure pushing his way into the Box. Dram catches me against his chest with a soft laugh.

"What are you doing here?"

"I decided I was through being a compliant Prime."

Laughter bubbles up inside me, but it's tempered with worry. No one goes against Meredith. "How are you here?" My collar lets out a warning chime. "If you're caught—"

"It will be worth it." Dram slips a pack off his shoulders.

"We can't close the door from the inside." Red light blinks from the tech circling my throat.

"I worked that out," Dram says. He turns and speaks to someone outside the door. In the faint light, I can just make out her features. Cora.

"Be well, Orion." She nods to Dram. "We'll only get away with this once. Make it count." She shuts the door, and Dram grabs hold of me. He's kissing me when my collar chimes.

"Fire, I hate that sound," he murmurs. I catch his face between my hands and guide his mouth back to mine. He smiles against my lips, and his hands leave me long enough to pull something from his pocket. I recognize the cracking sound from a light stick just before the glow illuminates my prison. He tosses it onto my cot and draws me back into his arms.

I unfasten the buckles at his neck and waist, and our hands bump as we work his coat off. His Prime's chain hits the floor with a clank. He kisses my neck, and I pull his shirt free, throwing it aside along with everything else that marks him as a Delver. His mouth skims along my collarbones, and my head tips back. His lips bump my collar, and I want to scream at the reminder that I am not free, I am not my own.

"Shhh," Dram whispers. "There is nothing separating us, Rye. Nothing." He presses kisses over my throat, like that cursed piece of tech isn't there. His weapons belt drops to the floor, and I reach for the one holding his pants up. His breathing quickens.

"This isn't what I came for," he says, pulling away. "I mean—I love this, I want this—but it's not the reason I came." He grabs my questing hands and kisses my knuckles.

"What are you talking about?" My breath's as ragged as his.

He grins and brushes his thumb over my kiss-swollen lips. "I brought you gifts."

"I can't have anything in here."

"Just for tonight," he says, reaching into the pack he brought. He tosses me a canteen.

"Rations," I murmur, failing to hide my disappointment.

He laughs. "Not rations. Try it."

I twist the lid and sip. "Oh, fire." I take a longer drink. "Where did you get this?"

"Meredith keeps a hidden keg. Well, not so hidden, it turns out." He toasts me with his own canteen of ale. "Ready to hear something more than the flash curtain singing in your head?" He draws a screencom from his pack, and music fills the Box.

"It's like we're in the outpost," I say.

"Or the provinces." He grasps my hands and twirls me into a dance. "Do you still hear the curtain?" I shake my head. For the first time in months, it's drowned out by something louder, a melody born of laughter and hope and sacrifice and passion. The flash curtain calls to me so powerfully, I hear it inside myself. But now I know . . . love is louder.

The music changes. Something soft, quiet, not like we had in the outpost. "It's Alaran," he says. "I thought, even if you can't go there, you could at least hear—"

"It's lovely," I say, and we sway to the sounds of instruments I can't name. I can't think about never seeing Alara, about this Box being a permanent part of my life, so I tighten my arms around his neck and lose myself to the sounds of a city I still dream about.

"Will you step in my steps, Orion Berrends?" he asks softly. Tears prick my eyes. I haven't heard my name linked to his since we lived in the provinces.

"Always," I whisper. He slips something over my wrist, where my bonding cuff used to be. Braided rope threads, wound in climbers' knots.

"I figured this suited us."

I touch the woven cords. "A figure-eight knot."

"The strongest, most secure."

I can't speak right away, so I swallow hard and clasp his face in my hands. "Will you step in my steps, Dram Berrends?"

"For as long as this life allows." He lifts his hand, and I see the rope band circling his wrist, an exact match to mine.

I launch myself at him, and he catches me against his chest, laughing even as our lips meet. This time, he doesn't stop my hands, and they skim over his shoulders, his arms, pausing along the scars left by flash bats. I sweep my lips over his chest, all the places he was exposed to particle burn down nine.

"Remember the air cave?"

"No clear thoughts right now," Dram breathes. But his eyes meet mine, and I can see the memories lingering there.

"I thought you'd die—"

"Fire, Rye, if we discuss all the times we thought we'd die, that'll be a lot of talking." He kisses me, hands skimming over my body, touching every scar, every injury he knows by heart. "Sit down and close your eyes," he says. I raise a brow, and he smiles. "One last gift."

I sit on the floor and press both hands over my eyes. My skin smells like Dram, and it intoxicates me more than the ale. I sneak a glance. Dram stands on my cot, a broken light stick in one hand, his other stretched above his head. He studies the cirium ceiling, then presses the metal with his fingertip.

"Stop peeking," he calls without looking. I cover my eyes, trying to imagine what he's doing. I hear the sounds of him dragging my cot across the floor, and clicking that sounds like another light stick. "All right," he says. "You can look."

I peer up at the dots of light. We sit in darkness, illuminated only by pinpricks of chemical he painted across the ceiling. I look at the patterns, trying to . . .

Stars.

He painted the night sky just as it looked from the provinces.

"I drew it in the sand when I was first captured," he says. "And each day after that. So I wouldn't forget."

"Fire, I love you." The music is turned low, so I know he hears me, and again, when I say it just beside his ear, where my lips brush the side of his face. Soon, there's nothing of Congress between us—not my collar, our Radbands . . . not even this cirium prison. There's just Dram and me, our skin glowing beneath the stars he's given me.

He raises himself onto his arms, and his memorial pendants slide over me. We have this between us: life and death and all the ways we've fought to hold on to what matters.

He drops his forehead to mine, and our hands tangle.

Our bracelets press together, and I think how they're like us—pieces of frayed rope, woven into something stronger than they were before.

TWENTY-SEVEN

MEREDITH DOES NOT abide noncompliant Delvers. Especially a former Brunt who stole Alaran treasures from under her nose, tapped the keg of outpost ale she'd been hoarding, and sneaked into the Box.

These are the conclusions I'm drawing as Dram and I lie light-headed on the floor, sipping air like we're sharing a broken air tank again.

They cut off our air hours ago.

Dram's fingers curl around mine, and I squeeze back, wishing it didn't take so much effort. We stopped talking soon after the vent shut off in order to ration our oxygen, but neither of us imagined they'd leave us this long. I should have been let out by now.

As angry as Meredith is, she can't risk harming us. I am, after all, our city-state's last Ghost, and Dram, the only Delver strong enough to be my Prime. The flashfall is expanding, and there's no time for pettiness or punishment.

Or so we thought.

Dram's staving off claustrophobia. In all the plans he made to join me for my extended imprisonment, he didn't consider how it might affect him, being in the Box with no way out. For once, we weren't thinking about our circumstances; we had our minds on other things . . . at least until the air shut off.

We've used up all our light sources, so we look at the stars he painted, the chemicals deactivating so that our cirium sky grows dimmer, star by star.

"Sorry," he breathes.

I twist onto my side and rest my forehead against his. "I can still taste that Alaran cake you brought me," I say. He squeezes my hand. Music plays from the screencom, the soft Alaran tunes growing familiar to me. I turn it louder, so Dram will maybe think about that instead of the airless, dark Box we're sealed into.

"What do you think Graham would tell us to do?" I ask.

Dram laughs. "He'd say, 'What are you wasting time for, boyo—hurry up and kiss her!'" He turns, and though I can't see him at all, I can imagine the corner of his mouth lifting, the dimple it puts in his cheek. "He was always saying that to me. We'd be down eight, orbies all around, I'd ask him what I should do, and he'd be like, 'I'll tell you what you should do, boyo. That scout, she's something special . . .'"

"Graham was wise," I say, my hands finding Dram in the darkness. We lean toward each other at the same time. Our lips meet, and I turn my head to bring him closer. Dram brought me gifts, but what I cherish most is having him back—seeing the smile that makes me feel breathless and invincible at the same time. I thought I had lost that part of him, that it was destroyed while he fought to survive as a Brunt.

"Are you crying?" Dram pulls back, and I swipe my hand beneath my eyes. I run my hands over his shorn hair, but it's not a Brunt I'm holding in my arms—I've got my caver back.

My collar chimes, and the door grinds open. Cora stands with her arms crossed over her chest. "You're still alive. Good."

We scramble out and sprawl on the cavern floor, sucking in air.

"Three days' rations, extra weapons, Oxinators," Cora says, dropping packs beside us. "Meredith says don't come up until your gauge shows you reached eludial depth." I stare numbly as she tosses rope and a suspension tent onto the pile of gear. Three days.

"But the termits—"

"Are worth the risk. That passage is our best chance." She opens a pack filled with metal disks I've only seen on a screen-com, tech that's supposed to map the eludial seam. "These will automatically engage once you reach the perimeter. They're activated by the elements there."

Dram and I fasten armor over our suits, then take turns strapping on gear, balancing the weight of it all between us. He takes the tent and rope. I take the mapping tech. Both of us load up with weapons.

"Before you go, seal me in." Cora strides into the Box.

"What?"

"Did you think Meredith wouldn't punish me for helping you?"

"How long?"

"Till you return." I stare at her. It will take Dram and me three days of hard climbing to make it that distance and back. That's if we're lucky enough to find the eludial seam. "Three days . . . in the Box."

"If that's what it takes. Don't look at me like that. I sneaked down an extra pack for myself. I've got food, light, books . . ." She gives me a wobbly smile.

"I'm sorry." I catch her in a hug. "We'll go as fast as we can."

"Just find the seam," she says. "Don't get eaten by anything." She squeezes me tighter. "Do whatever Ferrin would do."

I can't watch Dram seal her in. I jog the passage, telling myself the faster we go, the sooner we can free Cora.

The sooner we can free everyone.

———

Do whatever Ferrin would do.

Cora's words slip through my mind in the darkest places—especially in the dangerous places. We pull ourselves onto a ledge, and I hand Dram a pulsating silver disk.

"What's this?"

"High-frequency pulse transmitter. It deters the moles. Wear it inside your suit."

He slips it beneath his armor. "Won't it draw the other creatures?"

"Yes, so be ready to switch it off when we come across bats, gulls, or termits."

"Maybe it's not worth the risk? They're just moles. So they conjure—we'll find our way."

I work to hold on to my patience. I remind myself that I had the same ignorant assumptions when I first delved these tunnels.

"This isn't tunnel nine," I say. "The moles are the worst thing down here. Worse than gulls, or bats, or orbies. Worse than termits. They're fast—" I break, off, sighing. "*Fast* isn't even the right word for it. They move quicker than the human eye can track them. They conjure defensively, that's true— they're not going to come after us—but you don't understand how dangerous their defenses are. They've conjured the ground out from beneath me. I watched one conjure a branch through Cora's hand—and the rest of the tree through Fern."

Dram nods. "Transmitter. Got it."

"Any new routes we delve will also need to be preserved with the transmitters—every hundred meters."

"Fine. Tell me again about the other things—the termits. Not as bad as the moles?"

"Termits are bad." I turn down another passage, follow- ing the map laid out in my mind. "Do you remember Ennis telling us stories about animals that used to exist? Remember 'lions'?"

"Yeah. Hairy mane. King of the jungle."

"Well, termits don't have manes, and they're smaller, but otherwise—lion. Except they can climb rock faces. Really well. They have semi-opposable thumbs and retractable claws."

"Climbing lions," Dram murmurs.

"That has one of the strongest bites of any creature, ever."

"Like flash bats."

"Except their molars work like *scissors*." He blinks at me behind his goggles. "They have self-camouflaging fur that helps them blend into cavern walls and water. I'm talking *invisible*, Dram."

"Not with these." He taps his goggles.

"They prefer to fight standing up, supporting their bodies with their tails, so they can use their hands and feet to attack—Fire, Dram, why are you smiling?"

"Because I would rather fight one of these demon creatures with you at my back than be alone as a Brunt. Any day." He smiles again, and something inside my heart fractures. "Today is a good day, even if I have to face a termit's semi-opposable thumb claw."

I drop my goggles over my eyes. "Semi-opposable *retractable* thumb claw," I mutter, sliding past him.

His laughter fills my earpiece and I think, *Today is a good day*.

———

We suspend our tent so that it forms a triangle stretched across the water. At each of its three points of contact, a transmitter gives off high-frequency emissions we can't hear. That will keep the moles from conjuring over us, or through us, while we sleep. The other creatures we had to get more creative about.

"I have to say, I didn't see this day ending with me holding a pile of poo."

I smile, despite my exhaustion. I have missed this Dram—the boy who can find humor in a desperate survival situation. I smear termit scat beside the tent anchor.

"What about *glowing* poo?" I ask.

"Nope. Before today, I didn't even know that was a thing." He finishes spreading it beside his anchor and tosses the branch he was using into the water. "It's from the fish they eat?"

"Yeah, something to do with their bioluminescence."

"And this will keep the gulls away?"

"Well . . . if I'm right. It's sort of a theory-in-progress."

"Ah. And we'll know if you're right by whether or not we are attacked in our sleep by tunnel gulls?"

"Pretty much."

Dram slides into the tent beside me. We leave our armor on, even our headlamps. Both of us hold weapons.

"Dad taught me to look for scientific solutions to problems," I say. *Dad.* My heart squeezes thinking about him. I may share someone else's genes, but I can't think of him as anyone other than Dad.

"When I was trying to win Fortune," I continue, "I captured a tunnel gull so I could use it to find my way back out of the gorge. It refused to eat the ghost fish I caught for it. It ate earthworms fine. So, I think there's something in that fish they don't like. Maybe it makes them sick or something."

Dram blinks. "You captured a tunnel gull."

"Yes."

"Then you fed it. Willingly."

"Well, yes. I wanted her to have enough strength to fly back to her nest." Dram's eyebrows creep toward his hairline. "But only after I covered her feathers in glow chem—so I could follow her. Then I had to break through a mole's conjured rock so she could reach her younglings on the other side."

"Fire, Rye."

I smile. It's exactly the way I imagined him absorbing the story. "Is today still a good day for you, Dram?"

"Yes."

"Then I won't tell you."

"Tell me what?"

"Your hand is glowing." He looks down at it, and I can tell

he's trying to think of what he might've touched that would leave bioluminescent residue. I bite my lip to hold back a laugh. "It's where you were holding on to that branch—"

"*Fire*," he curses.

I hide my grin and roll onto my side.

———

We give ourselves four hours of rest. Then we hydrate and eat our rations, and I show Dram how to dig for earthworms. Since the passage is protected by pulse transmitters to repel the moles, the ground here is filled with fat, wriggling worms.

"This is how we know we're on the right path," I explain, holding one up. "Their skin is slightly translucent, and you can see if they've been consuming dirt with trace elements of eludial soil. They glimmer a bit."

"Glimmering worms," Dram says, dropping a handful into his ore pouch. "Better than light markers. And this will help us with the termits?"

"I hope so."

We pack our tent and our gear, and take the passages at a run—something we could rarely do down the tunnels at Outpost Five. These have been carved over decades, by Conjies. The passages are smooth stone, just the right size for humans to traverse, with stone bridges and steps, even a bioluminescent lighting system. Some Conjies took the time to embellish the walls with patterns carved into the stone. Our headlamps reflect over them, and I wonder about these artist Forgers, who made something beautiful out of their prison. We stop at the place the words for freedom are carved, where I added my own writing when I wrote Fern's name.

"This is the most dangerous part," I say, muting my lights as we near the termit den. "If we make it past, we should find a passage to the eludial seam. At least, that was my mom's theory."

"That was years ago," Dram says. "Why hasn't anyone tried this route?"

"They have. No one's made it past."

"Great," Dram mutters. "So, on a scale of flash bat cavern to gull's nest, how bad is this?"

"Let's focus on the positives," I say, adjusting my goggles. "Termits can't fly. They can't conjure. They're usually solitary creatures—so you usually only have to take them on one at a time."

"Unless you walk through their den—"

"Or encounter a place where there's a major food source. Like the eludial seam, where their favorite meal—moles—will be concentrated."

"This isn't positive."

"Right, well, let's hope my idea works."

"Fire," Dram mutters.

We approach the den, silent, our transmitters switched off. We smeared our flash blankets with termit scat, and we wear them draped over our packs. We reek of termit, so that we will reek less of human. Dram's idea.

I disengage the transmitter protecting the tunnel and wave my arm once, a signal to Dram. We fold ourselves into the shadows, him holding his flash rifle, and me with my gloves off, ready to grasp a bead from my bracelet if I need to conjure.

A termit lumbers into a dim patch of light from the passage.

I feel Dram tense beside me. It must be worse than he imagined. I want to tell him this one's small—a female. I reach into my ore pouch and lift a handful of earthworms.

Please work, I think, dropping them along the ground. *Please let this work.*

Dram makes his way to the other side of the cavern, scooping worms from his pouch, and I feel every step he takes away from me. It's one more step I'll have to take if I need to get to his side. The shadows hold him, and I can only see him through the infrared of my goggles, his shape and biometric reading separating him from the termits.

Three of them. My tech registers the signatures of three—no, now four of them. Two mothers, two younglings. I drop more worms. *Come on*, I think. *Come get them.*

If Val is right, the moles sense even the barest of seismic shifts: like a transmitter pulse that's no longer a barrier or fat earthworms exposed for the taking. The ground shifts near my foot, and a mole tunnels up. It hesitates, scenting the air, then zips past, a blur of motion. I don't even see it catch the earthworm; I just see it hunched over, chewing.

A termit lifts its head. They too, sense a shift in their surroundings. They scent the air. A low growl rumbles up from a mother's throat. The sound must be a cue to her young, a sort of warning. Her skin ripples, and her fur changes to the slate color of the rocks. The youngling yips, sniffing the ground. Its skin shivers, but it can't seem to match its coat to its surroundings. The others disappear. The light is frail, but there's enough for me to see the ground erupt around them as dozens of moles surface in pursuit of the worms. They don't see the camouflaged termits watching. I empty the rest of my pouch.

My goggles illuminate with the signatures of three more termits approaching.

We have to get out of here. Now. A meal of gorge moles will only distract them for a time.

I can't risk conjuring in here. Any shift of rock would draw attention. This cavern is craggy, with sharp overhangs of rock and ledges we have to crawl beneath. These are like the caverns Dram and I grew up with. Stone slides beneath me, and it is so familiar, it's almost a comfort. This is not the first time we've sneaked past deadly creatures. We developed a talent for it, instincts that will help us evade what no one else could. I tell myself this as more termits enter the den, their claws clicking over stone. They already have them out, poised to attack.

I hold my breath as I pass within meters of them.

Do whatever Ferrin would do.

Somehow, deep inside myself, I know she's done this. Maybe she didn't make it all the way to the eludial seam, but Mom made it this far. And she lived.

I reach out and carefully place the pulse transmitter. We need this passage to hold. I look across the cavern, my movements slow, and confirm that Dram is in place, awaiting my cue. Once I engage the transmitter, the moles will try to burrow and tunnel away. If the termits haven't attacked by then, they will.

And then we will run. Dram holds his rifle at the ready. I hold the earth of the provinces in each hand. From here on out, we will shoot and conjure as needed. There will be no hiding our trail after this.

I engage the transmitter.

The termits roar.

We run.

The curtain thrums in my head. I can't think. I can barely breathe. Whatever connection I share with the flash curtain—the ability to sense its elements or its call—is detrimental to me down here. We wade through eludial soil; it covers our boots and coats us in glimmering dust. Still, we haven't reached the heart of the seam. The mapping devices won't function until we get close enough.

Our coms don't work. Our earpieces are useless this close to the seam. Dram and I have used hand signals for the past hour, but I can't lift my hands any longer. When he has a question, he grasps the sides of my headpiece and stares at my eyes.

Is this the right way, Scout?

Blink. *Yes.*

Do you need to stop?

Stare. *No.*

I lose track of time. There is only one breath to the next. An orbie pool. Massive. So many, their orange color bathes us in luminescent light. Dram helps me sit.

He presses his face shield to mine.

Worried blue eyes meet mine. *Do we have to cross it?*

Stare.

His brows lift.

We made it, I tell him.

He shakes his head, like he can't understand. I'm probably squinting too much from the pain. Slowly, I lift my pack of mapping devices. It lightened as we approached the pool, the tech responding to the elements. I push it into Dram's hands.

We made it, I tell him again with my eyes.

He smiles.

———

We stay only long enough to open the pack and watch the disks lift free of their own accord, dozens of them, shooting across the orbie pool toward the seam, faster than pulse trackers. Meredith said they could transmit data back to Central Command in Alara, and that techs could map the eludial seam down to millimeters. Within days, we'll be ready to send an autonomous mining device to scour the seam.

I'm not sure I will live to see that happen. I taste blood, and I'm not sure if it's dripping from my nose or my eyes. Dram carries both our packs and hauls me up through the passage. I conjure when we need a path, but even that is getting to be too much for me. If we had to climb our way back, I'd never make it.

"Let's go, ore scout," he says. I can hear him again in my earpiece, but we still haven't regained communication with the techs at Fortune. I stare down at the ground, bewildered, until I realize Dram's carrying me over his shoulder. How he's managing my weight plus our gear—

"I ditched the tent," he says, like he's reading my thoughts. "And your pack. My rations will have to be enough. I've got ammo and a medkit."

"But . . ." I think of all the supplies we used getting here.

"It was you or the skanty flash blankets. You were the less smelly choice." Dram usually jokes when our situation is most dire.

"What aren't you telling me?" I ask.

"Something in the seam zapped our equipment. Everything that wasn't protected inside our suits. Our comlink to Fortune is fried—same with the infrared goggles. We won't be able to see any termits—not if they're camouflaged."

The termits. How will we camouflage ourselves when we crawl through their den? And now we're going through *blind*.

Dram shifts me on his shoulder, but as the minutes pass, I feel his body shake from the strain. We've gone too long without rest.

"Dram. Put me down." I can't walk more than a few meters, but I can conjure. I conjure a tree, with a winding bower of leafy branches for us to sleep in. Then I conjure a wall of rock to shield us.

I fall asleep conjuring.

———

Dram and I ditch our remaining gear. Whatever particles we encountered near the eludial seam, they took our strength with them. We haven't spoken today, not since he handed me our last nutri-pac a kilometer from the termit den.

We stand outside it now, reluctant to enter, but knowing we can't afford to delay. We're out of rations, out of time. We dosed ourselves with our daily ration of my father's cure, but I feel like we need Radbeds. I still hear the echo of the curtain in my head.

There are things I should probably say to him. In case. But fear sends tremors rioting through my body. I can't even unclench my jaw enough to speak.

"I wish I could kiss you," Dram says. "Before we, you know, encounter the invisible cave lions."

I smile. "Kiss me after."

We turn off all our lights and crawl inside.

––––––––––

We make it through. We're so jubilant, we actually remove our headlamps and kiss. We follow the passages back; hungry, exhausted, but alive.

It's the termit just outside Fortune that we're not prepared for.

The one we don't see coming.

TWENTY-EIGHT

7.2 meters from flash curtain

I DREAM OF freedom.

And fire.

I wake inside the Box, to utter darkness. My only light shattered when they forced me inside. But that fire. It stirs within me—worry for Dram formed of molten fear. I roll a wooden bead in my palm, over and over, and all the while that fire blazes, builds, expels from me—

I conjure fire.

I stare at the flames in my hand—light that illuminates the cirium walls around me. This shouldn't be possible. Not even Forgers can conjure within this prison. But still the flames burn, and the energy swells within me, fed by something more powerful than fear.

I used to wonder if Conjies needed to feel an exchange with the elements, the way Naturals need air and light. Now I know. We do.

And so my flames burn, burn—

Burn.

And when I sleep, the fire is there again, awaiting me in my dreams.

———

The door vibrates at my back, and I stir. In the haze between sleep and waking, I think it's Dram, knocking on the metal, reminding me he's just a wall away from me. Then images invade: a termit leaping . . . biting.

The door slides open, but I don't turn. I'm paralyzed with dread.

"Dram's all right," a man says. Something about the voice triggers a feeling of recognition. "His armor caught most of the termit's bite. Did you hear me, Orion?" Whoever he is, he doesn't breach my solitude with anything more than his voice. I roll over and see his boots, just beyond the cirium floor. "He said to tell you *you don't need to take his axe to the Sky.*"

Tears leak from the corners of my eyes, and I laugh into the floor with a sound like sobbing. I push myself up, my stiff muscles protesting the movement. It doesn't feel like my arms shaking under my weight, or my head throbbing and dizzy from lack of food, lack of everything.

"I tried to get you to the infirmary, to see him," the man says. "I'm afraid that not even I can get a Ghost that close to Fortune." There is gentleness in his tone that seems at odds with the forceful command of his words. I know this voice . . . I look up.

"Jameson?" He doesn't answer, just stands there, holding my questioning gaze with one of his own.

"Meredith tells me it's been four days. Four days since

you've been in the light or heard another voice." There's anger in his tone. Anger at the commissary. He steps inside the Box, eyeing the doorway like he's stepping into a gulls' nest.

Slowly, he crouches beside me. His eyes track my features like he's reading a map, and when he finally meets my stare, it's with the shadows of memories lingering there. "Four days in this hell," he muses. "The longest I ever went was five."

The words hang between us, his admission like a bridge to a place inside me. A place I didn't know was there.

"You were a Forger?"

He nods. For the first time, I see that his eyes are not dark, as I've always thought, but the sort of hazel that changes depending on the light and the color one wears. He wore black in the outposts and cordons, but his uniform now is a muted green, and his eyes—

Are like mine.

"I saw you on the screencom," he says, handing me water and rations. "Meredith didn't use your real names when she reported your commissioning status. I think she was afraid the council would insist on sentencing you for treason or perhaps hold you to gain access to Arrun. But she forgot that I've seen you and know you well enough to recognize you from a brief glance during the commissioning.

"At first I was shocked. We'd lost you, and then there's Dram, a Prime Delver. I couldn't make sense of it—I kept waiting to see you standing before one of the other quadrants . . ." He looks at me with sorrow in his eyes.

"I had to pretend I wasn't feeling anything." He laughs, a sharp bark of sound. "I'm sitting there—in the council's high chamber, this *objective commissary*, and I didn't know where you were. I knew nothing could keep you from Dram's side. So I looked away the whole time Meredith prattled on about her new Prime, thinking you were dead. But then she dropped her grand surprise. A new Forger.

"And I . . . flash me, Orion, somehow *I knew* before I even looked. There you stood, brave and foolish, with that damned collar. It didn't seem possible you're a Conjie and Subpar both—but then I realized . . . it *is* possible. I had to get up and leave the chamber, because I was afraid that someone would see the Conjie inside the commissary." Tears gather in his eyes. His hazel eyes that look just like mine.

Neither of us says it.

Mom is our link, and she is gone.

"What happened to you?" I ask. "After they sent my mother to Outpost Five?"

"Few people had seen my face besides her. I'd been a Forger since I was twelve. After she and I . . ." He swallows. "This is hard—sorry. I've never talked about this with anyone." He sits beside me and leans back against the cell wall. "Meredith hired a tech from Ordinance to upgrade the security down here. He asked me to plant a monitoring device close to the seam so Ordinance could run their own tests. In exchange, he smuggled me out of the Overburden, gave me a new identity, and shielded me inside Alara. When I was older, they arranged my commissions—I held various posts on both sides of the curtain—until I worked my way onto the council."

"Did you know about me?" I ask. "When you came to Outpost Five—was it because you knew who I was?"

"I knew you were Ferrin's daughter. I didn't know . . . that you were mine." He sighs and drags his hands over his short hair. I wonder if he used to wear talismans. "You look just like her," he says, a sad smile playing about his lips. "Not . . . me."

"I guess the parts I have of you are on the inside," I say, lifting my hand.

He makes the laugh sound again, but it is filled with pain. He scrubs the heel of his hand over his eyes. "Ah, flash me," he mutters. "I'm a glenting weeper-lily." I wonder if he realizes he's slipped into his accent. He swallows hard and looks up, his face red and blotchy.

It surprises a laugh from me. "I get the same way when I cry," I admit, gesturing to his face. He smiles, and I realize it's the first true smile of his I've seen. The commissary didn't bring his mask into the Box with him. This is the man my mother knew.

"Before you became a Forger, who were you?" I ask.

"Carris Imber." He hesitates, like he's waiting for a barrier—a protective guard on his history—that doesn't come. "Bade's my brother. My youngest. He was a baby when the Congress put me in here."

Bade.

Bade is . . . my uncle. So many questions storm my mind, but the one that makes it out is—

"Can you make fire too?"

His brows lift. "No. Can *you*?"

I smile, and he laughs.

"No wonder Meredith's afraid of you. My father—your grandfather—could do it. Of all the Conjurors, only he and Bade . . . but now . . ." He looks at me, shaking his head like he still can't believe I'm real. Then he looks at the Box, and his brow furrows. "But forging all the way to the seam . . . No one, not a single Conjie could do that. That part of you comes from Ferrin."

Mom's name. Spoken from him to me. There is something to it that feels like more than word, or breath, or sound. It feels like the last scrape of chalk on the circle drawn beneath her name.

"Because she was a Subpar, you mean?"

He shakes his head. "Because she could do impossible things."

"You're the Ghost who became a commissary," I murmur. "Maybe I get some of that from you, as well."

"I guess we'll find out," Jameson says.

"What do you mean?"

"The devices that you delivered worked. They've transmitted back the data, and techs have mapped the seam. We're ready to proceed with the next step." He stands and helps me to my feet. "Time for you to meet the *Luna*."

A sleek metal craft fills the tunnel outside my cell.

"The Congress named it for the moon," Jameson says. "Since it's the only way we can hope to control the flashtide."

"How do we mine eludial soil with a ship?" I ask.

"We don't. The *Luna*'s just a vessel to drop this off at the seam." He presses a code into a panel, and the floor of the craft slides away, revealing a narrow pod. "The real technological marvel is this: the SAMM. Semiautonomous Mining Module. Just get it to the eludial seam, and the SAMM will take care of the rest."

"Get it to the seam . . ." I touch the side of the craft.

He opens the door, and I clamber inside as he directs me to the control panel, discussing technology that I barely understand. He trails off halfway through his explanation of underground altimeter readings. "You won't have to know these things. Techs in the city will monitor the instruments."

I touch the throttle. "You want me to *fly* this?"

"The *Luna* practically flies itself."

My gaze skips over the illuminated screens. "This isn't what I know. I was raised to rock and earth and instinct."

"So was I," he says. "But we adapt, Orion."

"What do you think my mom would say?"

Something shifts in his eyes. He looks past me to the hold of the ship, and I wonder which version of her he's remembering. "She'd tell you that nothing is impossible—unless you convince yourself it is."

Tears prick my eyes. She used to say that all the time.

"When do we start?"

Jameson steers me into the seat before the console. "Right now."

Instead of tunnels and termits, my days fill with belowground flight training.

The Congress prepares Dram and me both. I'm the lead on this mission, but any good plan has a backup. As Dram recovers from his injuries, he logs hours in the *Luna*, testing, prepping for a mission we're not likely to survive.

In one of the rare moments we're left alone, Dram shows me his new scar from the termit bite. I show him the flames I can make dance in my palms. It's good to see him smile again.

We spend the day talking about all the ways my abilities

could've helped us down nine. I don't tell him what I've come to believe—that without all we went through in the tunnels and cordons, I might not have discovered the fire within me. I think maybe Dad was right. What breaks us can also make us stronger.

Finally, Jameson returns to inform us that we're ready. Or, more accurately, that we're out of time. He's pensive, his demeanor gruff. "Techs have tracked an approaching solar storm. They're concerned its effects could fry the transmitters, that we'll lose the passage."

My stomach flutters like I'm falling. "I'm not ready."

His features tighten. I know him well enough now to recognize when he's trying to rein in his emotions. He looks away, running his hand over the instrument panel. "You are capable of this, Orion. I wouldn't send you if I didn't believe that."

"What will happen to me when this is over? If I succeed and deliver the SAMM, am I still the Congress's Ghost?"

He doesn't say anything, and I have my answer.

"There's nothing I can do that will result in your freedom," he says. His stark hopelessness slams into me.

"I can't spend the rest of my life in the Box."

"I know. So when you find a way out—take it."

TWENTY-NINE

7.2 km from flash curtain

I DON'T HAVE to look very far to find my way out.

Mom's plan sits in a heap in the middle of my cirium prison.

What I told Jameson was true: I can't spend my days locked inside a cell. I didn't escape the caves and cordons just to end up buried alive beneath them.

Ideally, I'd complete my mission, demolish the flash curtain, save everyone I care about, and then turn my attention to my personal escape options. But there's one factor preventing this.

Dram sits across from me in the cell, breaking Protocol. He watches me absorb the news. He even stole it from the tech room in order to show me: a thirty-centimeter, reinforced-cirium, electrified circle of horror. My new Forger's collar.

They've modified the sensors. This one will attach and adhere with biotech, like our Radbands. If I try to remove it, it will literally be the last thing I do.

"When?" I ask.

"As soon as you return in the *Luna*."

Tears splash my hands, where I clutch the glenting thing.

He pulls the tech from my grasp and sets it behind him, then he clasps my hands, right over the tears. "You have to go. Before night-dim, before flashtide."

"If I go now, who will deliver the SAMM?"

"I will."

I'm trying so hard not to cry, but a tear plops right on the back of his hand. "You might not come back. The eludial seam—"

"Rye."

I nod. Breathe. My voice shakes, but I say it anyway: "I was supposed to free everyone."

"So do it from the other side of the shield," he says. "I'll do it from here."

I conjure a leaf and swipe it beneath my running nose. Dram laughs.

"There's nothing funny about this."

"You just conjured a flower to wipe your snot. That is weirdly funny." His smile slowly fades. "You have magic, Orion." He knows these were my mom's words to me. That day she first set my hand to a tunnel wall. He clasps the sides of my face. "You have *magic*. Don't you dare let them contain it."

My past and all the possible outcomes of my future collide into this single moment that is just *now*. "I'll go."

He nods, and I can tell that now he's the one trying not to cry. "Good," he says. "That's good." He presses the heel of his hand against his eye.

"Let me know if you need me to conjure you a flower," I murmur.

He laughs and slings an arm around me. "Fire, I'm going to miss you."

"I'm not gone yet." I grasp his head and bring it down to mine. He resists me, so I swing my leg up around him and use it to bring him closer. He sighs against my mouth, and then all at once he's melting into me, and we are two halves of one body.

Tears wet my cheeks, and I'm not sure if they're mine or his. It doesn't matter. What matters is his skin against mine and our hearts pressed together this last time. We let our bodies say the words that we can't.

You are mine.

I am yours.

Always. No—not always. Not anymore.

There is only now. He says my name on a breath, and I respond, kissing him, memorizing him with my touch. His hair winds through my fingers—his short Brunt hair that's growing longer now. I won't see it long again—the way he wore it in Outpost Five, or longer, when he adopted the free Conjies as his family.

I will only know this Dram. Not the Dram who is finally free. If I succeed, it will be because I'm enmeshed with Congress, utterly removed from all that I once was—everyone I knew before. To save Dram, I have to give him up. I've known this since that day in the Sky, when I stood beside those broken axe handles and pieced together my mother's plan.

My life for theirs. It's how Subpars have always served. Sacrifice is in my blood.

But so is Dram.

He cradles my face, and the amber glow of his Radband reflects off the wall. *This is why I'm doing this*, I tell myself. This light that signals the end for Dram. If I hold on to him now, it won't be for much longer. I lose him either way.

I draw him deeper into my arms, knowing this is it—the last time I will lose myself and find myself at the same time—in this boy who shows me the stars, even when there is only darkness. His eyes open, and I can't look away. We kiss this way, once, twice. He tips his head, and our foreheads press together. His eyes are a storm of emotion—passion, anguish. Love.

Before Congress sent me to Cordon Four, Dad told me to look after Dram—that he was part of what made me strong.

Now I must let him go and be strong enough for us both.

I love you, Dram.

You know I love you, Orion.

I read the truth in his eyes, the blue depths that first reminded me of safe water and, later, the sky. Then I give myself over to the places we take each other that have no names, where strength and stars are born and the Congress can never reach.

THIRTY

3.2 km from flash curtain

I LIFT THE dress over my head, and the material floats down around me, delicate as a flower petal. These are clothes not made for protection from the elements—clothes created with no thought to the need to blend in to a cave or forest. I turn, and the fabric waves around my legs, a material that would be useless at soaking up blood, that would snag on cavern walls. Talons would sink right through this gown.

"No talons in Alara," Dram murmurs, and I realize I must've spoken the thought aloud. He studies me, a sadness in his eyes I can't bear to acknowledge. He's losing me one layer at a time, and we both know it.

He holds his hand out for mine and works a lace glove over my fingers. My hands are a giveaway—caver's hands, callused and scarred with bite marks.

Dram stops. The glove hasn't made it past my fingers.

"What's wrong?" I ask.

He shakes his head, like he's trying to clear it. "Nothing, I was just remembering that day down nine with the orbies."

The pad of his thumb brushes the back of my hand, where the glowing leeches dug past my veins. "That's when all this started."

"It started long before that, Dram." I pull the glove over my hand.

I feel anger building inside me—anger at these people who wear protection they don't need and style themselves after the cavers and cordon miners whose hands burn from exposure.

This is what I'm worried most about hiding—the resentment I will have to conceal from the Naturals we are dying for. They tell themselves we are all victims of the same sun, but they are nothing like us. The flash curtain they know is a tamed creature, kept beyond reach with a protective shield. We know the beast it truly is, have felt its claws and known its bite.

I haven't set foot behind the cirium shield, but I'm already gone to Dram. I can see it in the way he holds his arms rigid at his sides, touching me only out of necessity, like now, when he adjusts my silver necklace, so the dosimeter hangs down the middle of my chest. He steps back, as if even that touch brought him too close to a creature of Alara. I'm not a Natural, but I may as well be.

"You look like a Vestige," he says, the Alaran term slipping like another barrier between us. "They'll never guess. If you're careful to speak like them and act like them—they won't see the truth."

There's no mirror, but I don't need one to know he's right. I have never felt less like a Subpar. The fabric hangs feather-light over my skin, but I'd feel more comfortable in my old caver's suit, shielded within its coarse cloth and padding. For only the second time in my life, I'm wearing something for style more than functionality.

Beneath it all, I'm still me. I have dirt from the provinces sewn into a hidden pocket of my dress, and another pocket concealing my old double-bladed knife. Either would give me away in an instant. Both remind me who I am.

———

There are two quadrants we Delvers are not permitted to enter. Since I already breached quadrant five, I think it's only fitting I explore the other forbidden tunnel. Quadrant one. Designed exclusively for the council's use.

I'm going to ride it straight into Alara.

"My Prime's chain isn't unlocking it," Dram whispers. "I'm not sure how Meredith gets past the door."

"I think I know." I lift the small chip I found tucked inside an axe handle, and step onto quadrant one. The pod door slides open. Dram smiles, and I know he feels like I do: as if we're being helped by Subpars we never knew.

"Ready?" he asks.

I climb past him into the pod. We need to hurry so that Dram can get back before anyone realizes we borrowed Meredith's ride. The pod glides through the passage, more smoothly than anything I've ridden before.

"It barely feels like we're moving," Dram says. But we are—quickly. Too soon I'll be on my own. "Don't," he says softly, watching my face. "We said our good-byes." He tugs my Vestige robe into place. "You need to be an Alaran. Let the Subpar go for now."

"Never," I whisper.

The pod slows. An alarm sounds.

"What's happening?" Dram asks.

"I don't know—we're not there yet! This was supposed to take us into the city—" The pod's screencom indicates we're beneath the perimeter, just outside the shield.

"There must be some kind of security clearance we don't have!" The alarm blares over our voices.

"We can't go back," I say.

"No. Come on, I have an idea."

We open the pod and climb out into the tunnel. It's lit with lights I've never seen before. It's too bright. I feel exposed.

"Orion!" Dram calls. He's climbed a ladder to another hatch, this one equipped with tech. "Hand me that chip."

I ascend the ladder, and as soon as I reach Dram, the tech chimes and the hatch lifts.

"I think that tech works for Striders," he says. "Not commissaries."

"So where does this lead?" I ask, following him up through the hatch.

I freeze. The cirium shield rises up directly before us. We've been here before—only this time we're not wearing camo-cloth cloaks.

"You there!" a Strider shouts.

"Trust me," Dram whispers. I stare at him, trying to make sense of the determination overshadowing the stark pain in his eyes.

I don't answer. I don't need to.

"Strider!" he shouts. He grabs me and turns me, hoisting me up in front of his body like a shield. He shoves a gun to my head.

"Take him out," a voice commands.

"He's holding a girl. A Natural."

"Let me in, or the Vestige dies," Dram calls. His arm tightens, and I struggle against his hold, trying to breathe. *Oh, fire, Dram, what are you doing?*

"A free Conjie?" a voice asks.

"No, a Subpar—look at his wrist."

The door grinds open, silver, flashing in the sunlight.

"Let her go," the Strider commands.

"Let us pass," Dram says. "I'll release her once we're inside."

"I can't let you in. Protocol—"

"Then she dies. Right now." Dram cocks the hammer, and I flinch. I can feel the barrel of his gun bruising my temple. "You want to explain to the council how you lost a Vestige?"

The Strider curses beneath his breath and motions us forward with his rifle.

Dram pulls me through the metal passage, his arm across my chest. He lifts the gun from my temple the second we pass beyond sight of the guard. We walk through the shield our people mined and died for. It's wide as my cottage back in Outpost Five, and lit with suspended lights, so that it feels less a tunnel and more an entryway to someplace grand. The corridor fills with the sounds of our steps and his sharp breaths. I realize I'm holding mine.

We pass through the shield.

Towering buildings rise toward the sky, their walls made of glass that reflects the dying light of the day in pink and golden hues. Dram and I have finally made it to the protected city.

Weapons click all around us.

"You made it, Rye. Your city," Dram whispers. "Now go live for us both." He shoves me from him, and I stagger, trying to find my footing as shots fire from every direction. My lips clamp down on a scream. I nearly shout his name. But I'm not supposed to know him.

I'm not supposed to love him.

I sprint forward, not looking back. I swallow my tears before they give me away.

Go live for us both.

The gunfire ceases, and a silence more terrifying than anything I've ever known replaces the shouts. I look back—and have to clamp my teeth into my lip to hold back my cry. Dram lies in a crumpled heap, unmoving. The ring of Striders closes around him. One of them looks in my direction and I turn, slipping past a crowd of onlookers. I run blindly forward, a foreign pathway beneath my feet, toward a park with a stream, reflecting the sunlight like diamonds. I'm finally here—I made it to Alara.

And Dram is dead.

They can't see me crying. *Act like a Natural, Orion!* No one can know who I really am. *What* I really am. Or he will have died for nothing. My pace slows, and I force myself to breathe around the sobs squeezing my chest.

"Miss?" a man asks. "Are you all right?"

"I was frightened by the disturbance," I say, waving my gloved hand toward the place where Dram took the Congress's bullets.

"Ah, it's rare to witness such an intrusion. It's charmed you weren't hurt."

My eyes fly to his. *Charmed.* A Conjie word. He reaches up to adjust his hat, and his cirium wrist peeks out from the edge of his sleeve. So he's a Conjuror—was, anyway. But not the kind I am.

"Excuse me," I murmur. I touch my cheek with shaking fingers, the Alaran custom I practiced with Dram.

Dram.

I have to get away from here before I'm recognized as the girl the rebel brought through the shield. The man touches his fingertips to his cheek, watching me with concern.

I turn and walk as quickly as I dare toward the one thing I recognize. A building I've seen once before when Dram stole a cordon guard's screencom and showed me Alara. My instincts tell me to burrow deep belowground and hide. Instead, I walk the path alongside a shallow canal, toward the building no Westfall Subpar has ever been.

Central Tower. The heart of Congress.

———

I bury my grief.

Years down the tunnels developed my miner's ability to compartmentalize things like pain and fear—to push them away in order to complete the necessary tasks—so I do the same now. I yield control to this part of myself, and it is brutal, tamping down every thought of—

Stop.

I will not think *that* name. I cannot remember—

Stopstopstopstopstop!

I have a job to do.

And then.

Then.

My heart twists; I feel it, like a fissure opening inside my chest.

Don't think about him!

I close my eyes and imagine my heart hardening, freezing

into ice, ice filling me up until every thought and feeling and ache is frozen so that I can't even sense them. Until a time— later—when I'll let it thaw. And I will feel it all.

For now, I continue to conjure inside myself, and it is rock layered over with ice. I give free rein to the analytical parts of my mind, sorting through the ramifications, making course corrections to plans that must now change.

————

This world is made up of boxes.

Sometimes it's the beautiful ones you must work hardest to escape.

I walk Alara's pathways, and no one seems to notice the Vestige girl staring at everything with wide eyes. For the first time, I breathe air that is free.

But it's not free. Not when it was gained through blood and ashes. Not free—because it costs more pieces of my soul the longer I inhale. Guilt has a weight, heavier than my pickaxe after hours down nine. Heavier than cordon shards.

I would trade all this air for life back in the boxes. The ones all Subpars are born into, on the other side of the shield. In the flashfall.

I would trade this heavy, blood-bought air for the walls that hemmed me in all my life. Then maybe—this time—I could figure out how to take them all down. Every dividing line. Every boundary.

I didn't know then that escaping the boxes wasn't the point. Destroying them was.

Because a captive world can only be broken apart one way.

From the inside.

THIRTY-ONE

I WATCH PEOPLE enter and exit the building until I know how to mimic their confidence, the ease with which they stride through doors that have never been closed to them. The woman in front of me tilts her head so that sunlight glints off the delicate metal links woven over her hair. I suppress the urge to snatch them off and shove my Radband scar in her face.

Naturals wear pretty reminders that they are safe—while Subpars wear tech that displays the depth of their radiation sickness. None of what I'm feeling shows on my face. I know it's true because the woman smiles serenely at me, and my lips part in a matching smile.

"Lovely day," she says.

My teeth are gritted, so I just nod in response. Then I angle my chin so light winks off my hair adornment and stroll past her through the open door.

————

There's a spot of blood on my dress. Dram's blood. I cover it with my hand and make my way to the council's chambers.

My mind is a tangle of thoughts—most of them clouded with grief.

How could he do this?

The thought simmers, and I clamp onto it, like the anger is a lifeline, pulling me from the sorrow I'm drowning in. We had a plan. He lied to me, put into motion plans of his own, at a cost he knew I would never agree to.

Dram sacrificed his life to protect me, but I can't stay here.

Not at the expense of everyone living beyond the shield. If the SAMM isn't delivered in time to the eludial seam, the flash curtain will continue to expand, and with Dram gone—

I'm the only one who can do it.

"Miss?" A woman is staring at me with wide eyes. "Your glove is on fire."

I gasp and pat the smoldering cloth.

"That's a sure way for them to take your hands, Conjuror," she whispers.

My delicate glove is scorched where I conjured fire. I've been here less than a day, and already I'm giving myself away.

"Here." She pulls off her gloves and shoves them into my hands. "Whoever you are, you need these more than I do."

"You're not afraid of me?" I ask.

"Should I be?"

In her response I see what it feels like to have grown up here. Protected. She has only ever known control, order, and security. Like the Tempered Conjie on the street, she doesn't wear the innate fear, the readiness to fight like all of us beyond the shield. She knows there's a flash curtain, but she's not felt it scorch her skin or watched it turn someone she loved to dust.

"Thank you." I hand her back the gloves. "But I actually

need you to turn me in." The girl's eyes widen. "Inform the Prime Commissary that Orion Denman is here and that I'm conjuring in the lobby."

————

They question me for days.

At first, they're gentle about it. I stick as closely to the truth as possible when I tell them why Dram and I tried to escape into Alara. I assume they have tech that can determine if I'm lying, so I weave a tale about a girl who is terrified of the Box.

After this, they employ tactics less kind to get at the truth. I don't have to convince them of my story after that. I simply let them see my terror. In the times I'm present—in mind and body—I convince them of our mutual need. With Dram gone—

————

I lose myself when they speak his name—fire, if I even *think* it— but I must. I am the only other person trained to deploy the SAMM. With solar storms approaching, there isn't time to properly train another Delver—not one who could find her way to the seam.

I swim up through pain and make them believe that my resentment is not for them, but the flash curtain. They test me with equipment designed for Naturals, but I am not natural. Like any creature of the flashfall, I adapt.

I tell them that I don't hate the Congress—only the flashfall.

And they believe me.

THIRTY-TWO

THE CURTAIN IS so loud that from this far beneath the earth, it sounds like groaning. Or maybe that's the *Luna*, the strain on its aluminum and rivets as it carries me closer. I pull sound cancellation devices over my earpieces and watch the meters tick off on the instrument panel. Almost there.

"Approaching curtain threshold," a voice says in my earpiece. "Shields in place in five . . . four . . . three . . ." Cirium panels descend over the viewing window, obscuring the caverns blurring past outside my craft. Cabin lights illuminate, flickering with those in the cockpit.

A warning suddenly flashes from one of the gauges, one that monitors the energy spikes in the curtain. *Not now. Please, not now.*

"Detecting particle interference," a voice crackles in my earpiece. The stall warning goes off, a droning sound that spikes fear into my blood. The ship wobbles, and I stare at the controls, waiting for the remote pilot to do something.

"Central Command!" I move my mouthpiece closer. "I could use some help here!"

"Auxiliary power commencing in five . . . four . . ." The cockpit plunges into darkness. I hold my breath as the craft whines, as if it's struggling to catch its breath. It slows, banging into cavern walls like a bird with one wing. It nicks a wall of rock, jolting me off my feet. I grasp the console, holding tight as the craft spins awkwardly off its axis.

"Central!" I shout.

No response. Just the grinding of steel on stone as the *Luna* careens to a stop.

The craft is suddenly too quiet, and in the silence, I'm made aware of exactly where I am. I feel bared to the elements, the meters of rock my only shield from the radioactive particles crashing down overhead. The curtain presses on me, its energy pulsing inside my chest like a second heart. I don't need my gauges to tell me how close I am. With shaking fingers, I tug free my sound cancellation earpieces. I try to hear the curtain's song, but it sounds like screaming.

Maybe it knows it's about to die.

I have to hurry. The release point lies half a kilometer from here. The caving suit they created for me will protect me long enough to get the SAMM into place. I'll have to do this like a Delver.

I slide along the wall, following the hum of cirium in the fabric of my suit. My hand glides over dents in the aluminum where rock nearly penetrated the fuselage. A sinking sensation settles in the pit of my stomach. This really is going to be a one-way trip. I stumble against the tube of glass housing my gear. My fingers slip over the locking mechanism, and the door opens with a hiss. Cirium hums its melody as I drag the suit free. It has its own power cell, and I engage the perimeter lights.

It reminds me of the spacesuits I saw pictures of in Alara. Only this is more compact, with built-in armor, and it's black, silver, and gray—the shades of cavern shadows that I insisted upon. I lift myself into the suit and seal it at my wrists and neck. It's warm inside the suit, and I engage the auto-adjusting body coolant and the air intake, but what I need most right now is contact with Congress.

They designed my headpiece with a screen that shows text in case I can't hear anything more than the curtain. It's compact, with a 360-degree viewing shield, so I won't have any blind spots. I settle it over my head and lock it into place. The silence is a welcome relief. I activate the screencom.

"Congress? Can you hear me?"

"Luna—" The garbled voice cuts out.

"You're not transmitting," I say. "Too much interference. Auxiliary systems failed. I'm ditching the *Luna* and delivering the SAMM manually." I can't understand the response. The words that scroll across my screen don't make sense either.

Something stirs in the darkness, and I look past the jumbled words on my visor. I lift my palm light, and a shape moves just beyond the glow.

"Who's there?"

A friend

The words display on my screen.

"I came alone!"

You're not alone

My heart thunders in my chest as I peer through the dark

cabin. This isn't possible. I would have known if someone had slipped onto this craft with me. "I told the Congress I don't need a Delver."

Not a Delver

I stare at the words. Whoever this is, he's using a private comlink. Congress isn't hearing any of this.

"If not a Delver, then what?" I whisper the words, but I know they're coming up on his screencom. I search the darkness for the glow that will give him away.

If you're going to find your way back, you need a marker

The words stop me cold. There's no sound but the flash curtain, but I swear I heard Dram's voice in that com. I scan the cabin, turning in a slow circle, breathless. Hope is a flower, blooming in my chest, poison if I'm wrong.

"There are no markers anymore," I whisper.

Right behind you, ore scout

The lights flicker, the auxiliary power struggling to find life. In the flashes of light, I catch glimpses of his face. The visor of his helmet is clear, so nothing blocks the blue eyes I thought I'd never see again this side of life. The *Luna* shifts, and we both stagger. Dram catches my arm, but I feel like I'm falling still.

"I watched you die." My words flicker across his screencom.

He shakes his head. "You saw Striders shoot me." He removes his helmet, and I stare numbly as he unfastens mine.

The curtain screams inside my head.

I cry out, but I can't hear myself. The sounds of the flash curtain are like fingers raking across my mind. Dram grips my arm and shoves a bit of biotech behind my ear. A pinch of pain, but I am numb, and the curtain is all I feel, its voice filling every part of me until I explode—

Silence.

My eyes fly to Dram's worried gaze. He did something. The device he inserted shut out the curtain somehow. I taste blood on the back of my tongue. He grips my face in his hands and wipes my tears with his thumbs. Not tears. Blood. I can see it on his fingers, even though his suit is black like mine.

He touches the device behind my ear. "This will block the sounds of the curtain. It transmits only the frequency of my voice."

I try to make sense of what he's telling me, but his fingers brush the side of my face, and I can't think at all. I'm suddenly a creature of sensation. Touch. Sight—though I'm still doubting what I see. And now I *hear* . . .

Dram's voice, calling to me. Not on a screen, not in my memories, but right . . .

Here.

"Rye? You all right—"

I crush him to me. His arms steal around me, and a sound escapes him—like he was stuck too long underwater and just came up for air. His lips move beside my ear as he murmurs my name in a choked voice.

"Orion."

The way he says it is like no one else. He knows what it means to me—a girl named for some of the brightest stars, who lived in a place of only ash and embers. Even when I earned the title *scout* and the cavers stopped laughing about my name, he called me Rye—to remind me of who I really was. To remind me there was more beyond the flashfall. I never thought I'd hear my name like that again.

"I don't understand," I murmur. "There were Striders surrounding you. I heard the shots."

"Only one of them actually shot me. A . . . friend intervened while they were transporting my body."

"A friend." The word sticks on my tongue like a sour taste. He doesn't offer further explanation, and I sense an edge to his emotions, like he's holding them in check as much as his body.

"We need to move." He glances to the right of his visor, and I know he's reading something—time, or depth gauges, maybe. Or communication from *a friend*. "It's not particle interference," he says. "I jammed the coms myself. They can't know I'm here."

Apprehension tingles along my nerves. "Why are you here?"

"For the mission—the real one." He hoists a pack over his shoulders and fastens it across his chest. "I'm going to destroy access to the eludial seam."

"What are you talking about?" I ask. "What happened in Alara?"

"Ordinance . . . recruited me."

Ordinance. My mind spins through the implications.

Something nags at me, like a hand tapping my shoulder. I look closer at Dram. He's different, and it's not just his allegiance that's changed.

"Your Radband's gone."

He lifts his sleeve, past the place where the tech's been removed, and I gasp. It's not a stretch of scarred skin like mine, but smooth, with the brand of a Codev glowing beneath it. Numbers and symbols, the luminous blue of safe cavern water. But he is not safe.

I recognize the symbol pulsing from his arm. Vigil. They've made Dram deadly.

"Glenting hell!" I lurch back, an instinctive reflex at the sight of that symbol. "How?" I ask, staring, as if my eyes will give me some explanation.

"I don't even understand it myself," he says. "Ordinance tech is . . ."

Gems are engineered from conception with biologically predetermined features and characteristics, and genetically synthesized resistance. Dram is not a true Gem. But Ordinance has modified him like one. A million questions jump to mind, but only one matters now.

"Why are you here?"

"To save you." Something in the way he says it—like there's a message in his words I'm not getting. It's how Gems speak, like their thoughts are beyond ours. I shiver. I didn't feel truly alone until this moment. I step back, feeling my way through the fractured darkness with caver's instincts.

"You jammed my coms. You did something to the auxiliary power." He doesn't respond. I back away, bumping into things. I have never been afraid of Dram Berrends, but this isn't the same boy I grew up with at Outpost Five. "Fire, Dram, why are you really here?"

"To stop you." There's no hidden meaning in his words this time. He walks toward me, this Dram who is not Dram. He was always graceful in the way he moved, but his stride now is efficient. Predatory.

"What did they do to you?"

"Set me free."

"You're different."

"And you're blind, Orion. You don't see what's really going on. Mining eludial soil is what's causing the flashfall to worsen. We have to stop the delving. Permanently."

"You can't stop me."

A pained look crosses his face. "I already did." I touch the place where the biotech earpiece pricked me. I felt the stab of it inserting, but in the pain of the flash curtain tearing through my senses, I didn't register the additional prick of a needle. Even through my glove I feel the swollen skin at the side of my neck. The place where Dram stuck me with . . . my thoughts turn inside my head, like flurries of snowflakes in a gust of wind. Where he must've . . . I stagger against the console, suddenly exhausted. *What was I doing?*

"Serum 5," Dram says, his voice echoing strangely. "Conjie inhibitor. Your dad's creation."

Dad. Dram. Betraying me. My legs forget what they're for, and Dram catches me, easing me to the floor of the ship. "I'll be back as soon as I can."

"You won't . . ." My words stick inside my mouth, and I work to push them past my lips. "Make it . . . without me . . ."

"This is the only way." He pulls a space blanket from a pocket of his suit and covers me, then goes through every one of my pockets, removing the dirt and seeds I'd stored there. "I'm sorry, Orion."

My name again, only this time, the sound of it is all wrong. My eyelids refuse to stay open, and part of me is wondering why I even care. I should just sleep. Another part of me is screaming that I have to stay awake. There is something . . . something I need to remember . . .

Dram says something else, but it sounds like I'm hearing him from underwater. He touches my face, but I can barely see him through the slits of my eyelids that are heavy as rocks. Lights flicker as I watch him climb out the hatch, and I sink deeper, down, down.

Water cradles me. I'm floating, weightless in the Sky. I stare up toward the cavern walls, where chalk circles glimmer like stars above me. Mom. Her name, her chalk circle. She is safe.

You're not safe!

My brow crinkles. That other voice intrudes . . . but I'm happy here, floating—

Orion!

My name is the stars, and I am floating with them, far beyond this—

Ship. Crashed. The Luna!

The water pulls me down, but I can breathe underwater. I am a creature of the cavern, resting along the cirium basin. But something's missing. Dram should be here.

Dram. Betrayer! He left me here to float away—took everything that would let me conjure.

I force my eyelids open, but I still see the Sky. There is something—

Conjure!

No, I'm a creature that sleeps at the bottom of safe cavern water—

Conjure!

I can't conjure anything. Dad drugged me, and Dram took the earth of the provinces—

No.

My hands fist, and my eyes open wide, seeing the damaged cabin. Dram didn't take everything.

He didn't know about the dirt in my gloves.

———

He left the medkit. It rests against my thigh in the large pouch on my left leg. I can only seem to hold one thought at a time, so after I grasp this realization, I set it aside for another.

I can't lift my arms.

Whatever serum Dad made, it relies on knocking me out hard. I have no idea what adrenaline will do to me now, but I have to try. And fast. Some part of my mind is awake, but it's losing the battle to the rest of my head that feels like it's being stuffed with gauze.

My hands. I just need one to move. I concentrate, pushing every last fragment of energy into the fingers of my right hand. The pouch of dirt and seeds rests against my palm, ready to be broken open. A thin barrier of cloth rests between me and freedom.

Oblivion beckons. Meds pulse through my body, weighing down my veins, my bones. I'm so, so tired. I'll just rest a moment . . .

Orion.

Mom's voice. Or the way I remember her voice. It's been so long.

I'm here.

She hands me her axe. The handle's cracked, but she's smiling. Why does her broken axe make her happy?

Use it to get free.

She said that to me. I was just eight. She's saying it now. Her voice fills the cabin, and I feel the wood handle crack beneath my fingers. Bloody fingers. Conjie blood. Subpar blood. I'm back in Outpost Five, shattering my Radband with Mom's broken axe. I slam it into the ground, and dirt explodes beneath my fingers.

No. There is no axe. Just my hand, hitting the floor of the *Luna*. But the dirt against my palm is real. Soil from the provinces, its elements alive in my hand, slipping like threads along my fingers.

Roots tease my palm like soft hairs. Like little Wes, when I used to comb his hair and those baby-fine strands would wind through my fingers. The roots thicken, pushing against my palm, restrained by my gloves. The vine thrusts from my palm, stretching the fabric, tearing through with a rending I can't hear, but feel all the way to my bones. Serum 5 winds a cocoon around me, snuffing out all sensation, all thought, until I can't—

"Augh!" Thorns pierce my skin, clearing my mind enough to focus my ability. I conjure more thorns along my vine, long enough to pierce my suit and make pain penetrate the haze of serum. My vine lifts, green shoots tangling, thorns thrusting past leaves, and I center every remaining bit of energy I have on directing the vine, like a hand to my pocket. The thorns poke me, like teeth keeping me awake in nips and bites, as the vine wraps around my medkit and carries it to my outstretched hand.

My vision is fading. I direct the vine to pry into the kit, because I can barely move my arm. Adrenaline. I uncap the syringe with one hand. I don't have the strength to drive the needle into my thigh. The world spins away; I am falling through a galaxy of stars, where I can rest with the sound of my heart loud in my ears . . .

"Water," I whisper. My leaves shiver and morph. I can't open my eyes to see them alter, but I feel it. Droplets of water splash onto me, drip down my neck. I gasp, jolted from my dozing half sleep. I send vines shooting around me like arms, turning me on my side while my shaking hand holds the syringe. Vines shoot upward, widening to limbs and branches; roots shudder against the fuselage, flipping my body. I slam down, the needle piercing my thigh. I sob into the floor of the ship, wet and shivering, thorny vines tangled around me.

It's not enough. Whatever Dad composed this serum with, adrenaline's not enough to—

I gasp, long and hard. My breath shudders through my lungs like it's shaking out cobwebs. Blood races through my veins so fast—too fast. Now I'm breathing like I've run for hours. I tear free from the vines and stand.

Dram took my guns but not my knives. I find two of them, along with a pickaxe. I strap them on, secure my suit, and step from the *Luna*. As I scout my way to the seam, I consider my options. Part of me wants to take the ship and leave Dram here, but he's out there in the seam—engaging a device that will wipe out all the transmitters. If I don't stop him, every passage we've delved will collapse, and the seam and its eludial soil will be inaccessible once more. Besides, I'm not sure the *Luna*'s going to be able to take anyone up out of here. As I pass the craft, I can't help noticing the damage.

Dram left a trail of bloody corpses. I wind my way through the cavern passages, my lights turned low, the pungent scent of termit blood thick in my nostrils despite the headpiece. I can't believe how many there are. I've stepped over five already. That means only one thing—there's a food source for them down here, large enough to draw multiple termits to the same territory.

The thought should scare me, but I'm numb inside and out.

Dad and Dram betrayed me, and my body is mine to command only so long as the adrenaline lasts. Even now, I sense Serum 5 teasing the edges of my mind.

An orbie pool glows orange, illuminating the slick walls like flames of fire. I cross the water, my feet slipping on stones. I'm slow. Too slow. Orbies clamber atop each other to get to me—the hope of a meal stirring the pool into a frenzy. These orbies are fast, so numerous they rise from the water in growing towers. They won't leave the water, but I still have ten meters to cross before I'm back on the ground. I should conjure a bridge, but I've barely enough energy to walk.

A rock path suddenly forms close by, arching across the pool. I race to follow the mole that's conjuring it. The orbies shoot up toward us, reaching from the water like glowing hands. I've never seen them move this way, fast, linking to each other to form chains that reach—

I unfasten my glove, gritting my teeth against the sting of particles. They burn—but not as much as the orbies would. I grasp dirt and conjure fire, throwing it at the towers reaching our bridge. The orbies let out shrill screeches as they burn up. I'm almost across the pool. I keep throwing fire, hoping the mole doesn't conjure this path to dust the second it reaches safety. My aim is terrible, and I stagger as I run; the serum feels like hands pulling me back. The rock path glows orange as orbies spill onto it. Then it dissolves.

I leap across the remaining distance and crash onto the ground. I'm not sure I can get up again. Serum 5 is a door closing me into the Tomb. I feel like I could sleep and never wake. But my ungloved hand presses against the dirt, and without having to look, I know it's eludial soil. I've made it to the seam.

I curl my fist around it and shove it into my pocket. My arms shake, but I manage to lever myself off the ground. The soil is so thick that I can see each one of Dram's footprints. *Step in my steps*, I think bitterly as I follow his marks.

He doesn't hear me as I approach from behind. He's leaning over some sort of device: tech that glows with a Codev.

I could stop him right now—take him down with fire from my hands. I reach for dirt, and eludial soil glitters in my palm. Flame sparks.

I can't do it. Not with his back to me.

He didn't fight you fairly, a bitter voice reminds me.

"I followed your marks," I say.

He whirls around, shock written across his face. "Orion." He holds a flash rifle, aimed at me.

"You going to shoot me, Dram?"

"Don't make me. Please."

"What you're doing is going to kill everyone."

"It's going to *save* everyone! The delving is making the curtain expand, the flashbursts—"

"You're wrong!"

"When did you become so *compliant*, Orion?"

"I'm not—"

"You do everything you're told, like a good little Forger— Meredith's obedient *Ghost*. When did you stop questioning things?"

"Jameson said—"

"Jameson did this to me!" He lifts his arm, where the clear sleeve of his suit shows the Codev glowing beneath his skin.

"Why?" My voice is a choked cry.

"So I'd survive long enough to finish this. So I'd be capable of stopping you."

Better that Dram had died than be turned on me like some brainwashed mercenary. I thrust my hands toward him, conjuring vines that slam into him, knocking him off his feet. He hits the ground, and I pin him down, weaving the vines into thick roots. I crouch beside him and remove every knife, every gun. "You're not able to stop me. Even with your damned modifications."

"Oh, fire, Orion, I really am." He looks forlorn, like he's being forced to stab me, but his hand is empty; I've kicked all his weapons aside. His gaze shutters, in the way Vigils have, like they're reading internal data. A wave of energy bursts from his Codev, cracking apart the roots I conjured. He grasps my wrist.

Pain.

Ripping.

Tearing.

Can't. Breathe.

Makeitstopmakeitstop.

My vision blurs, but I can still see tears in his blue eyes.

"Stop. Fighting me." I read the words from his lips, because I can't hear anymore. My eardrums are outside my body, somewhere beyond the

seizing

choking.

I try to speak, to scream all the thoughts knocking around my head, but only bubbles of drool form on my lips. What is he doing to me? The force of it makes his arms shake where he grasps me, as if a current pulses from him into me.

I have to make my words count, then. They're the only weapon I have left.

"You put poison . . . inside me." My voice is so soft, but I see the words flash across his screencom. "When you were . . . Weeks." He stops—whatever he's doing—and I gasp a breath. I sound like an old caver, wheezing through particle-filled lungs.

"What are you talking about?"

"You didn't know . . . it was me." He sits back on his heels, like he wants to escape what I'm telling him. But he can't; the truth writes itself across his headpiece in glowing text. "We fought . . . in the Tomb."

"That's not possible."

"You attacked me . . . with your spear . . . and a venom spike."

"That was a Brunt . . ."

"Me. I became a Brunt . . . for you. To get to you." His breath is ragged. I can't hear it, but I can see his shoulders rising and falling. He shakes his head.

"No." The single word flashes on my screencom. "I was . . . gone . . . out of my head."

"I know."

He reels back, like I hit him. And I have, I know it. I've rocked him to his core with the one thing I know he can't handle. Not even modified Dram can manage this horrifying truth.

"I *hurt* you," he says, the words somewhere between a question and a statement.

I thought I had forgiven him, that I had placed the blame for his actions on Congress. But now resentment claws its way from the deepest parts of me, from the part of my soul that died that night on the dirt floor of the Tomb.

"You *attacked* me."

He stares, like I've impaled him straight through the gut with a spear. He slowly shakes his head, but I've got my hands clenched on the other end of that spear, and I'm coming in with the death twist.

"I traded my clothes. Payment. To get to you."

He yells so loud I have to press my hands to my ears. He yells like I'm stabbing him with my truth spear again and again, but I've stopped. I'm all out of revelations.

Some part of him—the deepest part that contained Weeks— remembers. Maybe not my face, but the girl, broken and brave, staring him down inside the Tomb. The yelling stops, but these sounds are worse. He's crouched, arms over his head, but he can't escape himself.

He doesn't ask for forgiveness. He doesn't explain away what he said and did that night.

I don't tell him I understand, that Congress took his human- ity one gram of flash dust at a time.

We don't say anything. I've mortally wounded him with the truth, and now we can only kneel here, bleeding out all our broken pieces. Serum 5 takes me farther under. I can't muster the strength to fight it any longer.

"Orion," Dram says, his voice raw. Tear tracks streak the grime on his face. His eyes are red-rimmed, making the blue extra bright. "I need you to trust me."

"Trust you?" If I had any strength at all, I'd laugh.

"There is no chance that you will outmaneuver me. Not with that serum in your veins." He says it as an apology, with a look of such remorse that it's like he's sorry about the Tomb also, and everything that's happened to put us on two different sides.

"Please, Dram." I can barely move. "Finish my mission." He looks at me, hard, as if he's looking for his answer in my face.

"No." And now the spear is in his hands, the tip twisting in my gut. He lifts my hand and examines the holes a vine tore through my glove. "It was in your gloves." He pulls off my glove, and I gasp as particles tingle along my exposed skin. He shakes out the earth and seeds.

Tears burn the back of my throat, and anger rises past the drugs in my system. As he empties my pockets once more, I lift my exposed hand to my mouth, grip the rope bracelet he gave me with my teeth, and pull it off. Dram watches me grasp the bracelet with shaking fingers, the bonding cuff he wove for me, the figure-eight knot that symbolizes the strength of our union.

I drop it over the ledge.

I feel him tug my glove back over my hand, wondering why he cares about protecting my skin when he's utterly destroyed me. I want to curse at him. I want to be back on my feet, fighting him with everything I have. But he stands and walks away.

Text glows across my screencom, too blurry to read—the words sway to the slowing of my pulse. Darkness crowds the edges of my vision. I'm paralyzed, as if I've been hit with the barbed tails of cordon rats, and I ache, like they've chewed right through to my heart. I stare at the ribbon of words until it stills enough for me to read it.

I love you, Orion.

The pain is too much. Darkness pulls me down.

THIRTY-THREE

0.23 km from flash curtain

METAL GROANS.

My body hums with vibration that has nothing to do with serums—I'm on a ship. Part of a crushed metal hull pushes into my side. The *Luna*.

I try to sit up, but I'm strapped down. I'm in a medcot, an IV trailing from my arm to a drip suspended above my head. The bag of fluid sways with the ship. I twist my neck and see that beneath the blanket I'm dressed in a fresh under-suit, my particle-exposed hand bandaged. The door of the decontamination chamber bangs against the fuselage; who-ever used it last didn't even bother to close it. I look at my skin. Particle-free.

The *Luna* groans again, a shudder that ripples up from the engines and shakes the cabin. Dram stands at the controls, still dressed in his suit, coated in particle dust. He wears a com unit and is speaking to someone, his tone strained, the words soft but urgent. Somehow he's blocked the sounds of the curtain from the cockpit. But he couldn't block the sounds of the *Luna*, and she sounds like she's dying.

"The straps are for your protection," he calls, and I realize he's talking to me. "Hang on!"

We dive, and my stomach leaps. We should be headed up, not down. The thrusters must be damaged.

"What have you done to us, Dram?" I pull free of the restraints and slide the IV from my arm. The hull shakes, and I grasp hold of the medcot.

"You shouldn't be up," he calls. The lights flicker as the ship lurches, and I hold my hands out, feet braced as I make my way to the cockpit.

"What did you do to my ship?"

"Not me. The curtain." The lights go out, and for just a moment, the only illumination is Dram's Codev. I follow the glow. The instrument panel flickers to life above the console, illuminating his anxious expression.

"Another flashpulse?" I ask.

"Not a flashpulse," he mutters. "Ordinance is bringing the device online. They warned me the curtain could destabilize momentarily."

"Momentary destabilization . . . of the *flash curtain*? We're traveling the eludial seam!"

"Yes, Orion," Dram mutters. "I'm aware of that."

He presses a button and speaks in an undertone. I can hear only his side of the conversation. He says my name more than once. A knife sits on the console beside him like a dare.

"Don't, Rye," he says without looking. "I won't fight you again."

"Well, then this should be easy for me."

He hands me a screencom. "Jameson intercepted these. Projections on the device the Congress ordered you to deliver."

"I made a deal," I say behind my teeth.

"You made a *mistake*."

"The *cure*, Dram. Freedom for our people—"

"They were going to be *dead*, Orion! Of course the Prime Commissary made that promise—it cost her *nothing*!" He slides his finger over the screencom, and a projected image illuminates above it. It takes me a moment to understand what I'm seeing—image after image of the curtain expanding. Maps of predicted outcomes.

"Look at it!" Dram says. "You think I'm lying? You think Jameson would help me—your father would help me—if it wasn't the truth? Open your eyes, Orion! The Prime Commissary did not make some *deal* with a seventeen-year-old caver from the outposts! She tricked you. *Used* you."

I sink to the floor and draw my legs to my chest. The holo-projection plays on repeating loop.

"Who knew about this?"

"The Prime." He looks at me. "And Meredith. I think she has some fantasy about restoring Old Alara. Ordinance is changing our society. They saw this as a way to take it back."

"They would start a war with Ordinance."

"Not if it seemed like an accident. They planned to pin this on you. Rebel intervention."

The ship heaves and stops, slamming against the side of the tunnel. We catch ourselves against the floor of the craft. "What happened to the *Luna*, Dram?"

"They didn't trust a remote detonation—too many variables affecting the tech. I had a window of time to get back and get out of the seam before it went off. I didn't plan to—" He breaks off, a look of stark hopelessness in his eyes. "I took too long getting back to the ship."

He didn't plan to have to carry me. That's what he's not saying. I run through the passage in my mind—the termits, the massive orbie pool. My memories of it are hazy, but enough to paint a startling picture.

"How?"

"How what?"

"How did you possibly carry me all the way back?" He doesn't say, and I know it has something to do with the Codev glowing on his arm.

"It doesn't matter. The ship's dead. We're not getting out of here." Whatever Gem modifications he's had, they didn't fix his claustrophobia. I can almost see the whites of his eyes.

"I'm glad they didn't make your eyes purple," I murmur.

"What?"

"How much do you trust me?"

"Completely. Not at all. It depends."

"You're not thinking like a Conjie." I search the dark hold for my clothes and start dragging them on.

"What are you talking about?" Dram asks. He watches me secure my suit and stuff my feet into boots. "We can't just conjure a path. We can't survive this close to the curtain without cirium shields, and the ship's dead."

"We'll have cirium shields," I assure him. "But we're not riding the ship out of here. We're taking the SAMM."

———

As far as tight spaces go, this ventures into Dram's nightmare territory. The SAMM was designed to hold eludial soil, not Subpars. We managed to secure ourselves inside the vessel and launch it from the crippled *Luna*. The autonomous controls kicked in immediately, and the craft self-pilots itself along the eludial seam, faster than the *Luna* in her best moments.

"If this doesn't work," Dram mutters, "at least we'll die quick."

I barely hear him. Even with the tech he placed behind my ear, I'm struggling to block the sounds of the curtain slamming down around us. We brace ourselves against the rounded metal walls as the SAMM rockets through the passage. It's stifling. There's no ventilation. Our suits are the only things keeping us from suffocation.

The metal collection doors strain to open. The seams groan where I've conjured them shut. Eludial gems ping against the metal, and it sounds like rocks hitting a tin roof. They sound like they will hammer right through the cirium shields.

The SAMM was designed to collect ore, and it seems to resent being forced to transport people. It begins to rattle so hard it shakes the breath from my chest. I brace myself, but my teeth clack together. The door motors grind, smoking as the gears spin uselessly, the sounds adding to the cacophony pounding through my skull.

Please end soon, please end soon, please end—

We hit the seam bed, and my head slams against the inside of the pod. Dram wedges me against him, gripping me tightly with one arm, the other braced against the metal wall, his legs splayed to keep us secure.

"I'm going to tell you about my talisman," he says loudly in my earpiece.

"What?"

"The promise I made you. The secret one." The craft rattles so hard that it makes his words vibrate in his chest. I feel them better than I hear them.

"I'm listening." Anything to get my mind off the rattling, jolting—

"Home," he says. "I vowed to give you a home. One you didn't have to keep running from."

Home. The word resonates in me, stronger than the curtain. I try to paint an image in my mind, but come up blank. So I hold on to the word, as if it's a thing with doors and windows and shields enough to shut out the flashfall. And I cling to Dram as we rattle through the passage.

All at once, the collection doors cease their clatter. We've left the seam behind. The SAMM glides through the delved passages. I don't give myself time to catch my breath. We have only moments before we reach the tunnel entrance, and whoever's awaiting the SAMM beside the Box. I tear my gloves off and drag my hands across the inside of the module.

"What are you doing?" Dram asks.

"I didn't seal it completely. I left it open—just a crack."

"Why?"

"A theory. An important one." Rock forms beneath my touch, and I concentrate, focusing on the elements. I have to get this right.

"Are you conjuring rocks?" Dram asks.

"Tunnel shale."

"Is there a reason you're filling this very small space with worthless stone?"

"I'm thinking like a Conjie."

"Great. You're talking like one, too." The SAMM slows to a crawl. "Whatever you're doing," Dram says, "you'd better hurry."

I conjure away the places where I sealed the opening, then carefully slide my gloves back on. The module stops with a hiss. "Let me do the talking," I murmur.

"Part of your theory?"

"Step in my steps."

The collection unit opens. Techs in Radsuits hover at the opening. They stare at us, their instruments hanging slack from their gloved hands.

"Commissary?" one of them calls. "You'd better come see this."

Meredith strides forward just as Dram and I sit up, dusted in glinting particles of eludial soil.

"Striders," she orders, and four soldiers raise flash rifles at us.

"The *Luna* failed," I announce, unfastening my headpiece and stepping free of the pod. "I had to ride the SAMM out of the seam."

"And him?" Her wide eyes shift to Dram like he's a flash bomb about to detonate.

"Ordinance sent him to assist me." Always best to lie with the truth.

"He died in Alara."

"Not completely," Dram says, taking off his headpiece. He turns his arm so she can see his Codev.

"Restrain him!" Meredith commands. She turns to a tech. "Get the council on the screencom. Now!"

"We can't transmit from down here—"

"We'll go up. Bind her," Meredith orders. I don't fight as a Strider forces cirium binders over my gloved hands.

Meredith pushes past the techs and peers into the pod. "This isn't right," she mutters, lifting the small boulders of tunnel shale. She tosses them on the ground. I watch where each piece lands.

"Where's the eludial soil?" she demands.

I meet her hard stare. "Beyond your reach."

Her gaze flicks to Dram, then to the Striders holding him. "Take him up. We'll question him before the council." They drag Dram into the port.

"Where do you want the Forger?"

"Put her in her cell," Meredith says. "We'll find out what happened, then deal with her." They guide me into the Box, and she hovers at the entrance.

"Your mother played her tricks with me," Meredith says. "And it gained her nothing. She died beneath a heap of rock at the bottom of a cave. It seems you're following in her footsteps, after all. The physic will be coming for you to fit your collar. If you survive the procedure, you will probably wish you hadn't." She steps away and nods to the tech.

"There's no light," he says, glancing past me at the dark bulb.

"Seal her in," Meredith orders. "Ghosts don't need light."

The door slides shut. Darkness holds me in its grasp.

"I'm not a Ghost," I say.

I wait for the vibration that tells me Meredith and the techs have ascended the shaft. Then I turn my focus to the eludial soil pressed against my palms, hidden beneath my gloves.

Flame sparks and flares in my hand. They have consigned me to darkness, but I have my own light. I study the flame leaping through the cirium binder. I shouldn't be able to conjure through cirium. It's not possible. Not unless I'm right about eludial soil . . .

I stop conjuring fire and turn my focus to the dirt pressed against my hand. My Subpar senses pick apart the elements until I can identify every trace of rock and eludial gems. I'm already attuned to the cirium—there's so much of it—surrounding me on all sides and binding my hands. An image fills my mind: the flashtide swirling in spirals through the flashfall, like it's being drawn down from the atmosphere. I feel the eludial soil pulsing with similar energy, a sort of compulsion to draw the cirium back into itself.

I told Dram I had a theory—and I know, as the binders fall away, that I was right. I conjure fire with both hands. The gloves are burned away, but the eludial soil remains. I crouch and study the metal binders. Iron. I turned them into iron.

I start laughing. The Congress thinks they have me contained. They have no idea what I'm capable of, but I'm figuring it out, inside their carefully designed prison.

Meredith and the Prime Commissary may understand the power of eludial soil, but not the people who have the ability to wield it.

"I'M NOT A GHOST!" I shout. They can't hear me. No one can hear me.

The flame wavers in my hand, dancing in a draft of air. I lift it, examining the size and shape of the air shaft. No other

Forger would have seen it—not without light. Even if they had, the vent is high up, with no possible way to reach it.

Not for a regular Forger.

I don't speak aloud my next thought, but I hear it echoing from my past, from the tunnels of Outpost Five, and the dust of the cordons . . .

I'm Orion, the Hunter, the Scout who can find anything.

And I just found the way out.

THIRTY-FOUR

7.2 km from flash curtain

I NAVIGATE THE ventilation system like a gorge mole, conjuring my way up and out of Fortune. I dangle from bioluminescent vines forty meters up, pulling myself up the narrow shaft. I'm not sure how long they planned to leave me in the Box, but I feel like I'm on borrowed time. Every second that cirium door stays shut is another second to put my plan in motion.

Before crawling up through the ventilation system, I conjured a narrow crack in my cirium cell, just wide enough to slide through. I filled my pack with every last piece of the tunnel shale left discarded beside the SAMM. Hefting that thing onto my back made me grateful for every time Reuder made me carry a pack full of rocks. I know just how to shift and balance the weight. I'm strong in ways I wasn't before. I didn't realize it then, but every time I shouldered that extra burden in the cordon, I was practicing—for this.

The final air duct leads through some sort of decontamination system and a massive fan with an air intake valve. I conjure my way around it, tunneling up through the ground into the Overburden. I spit dirt and sand from my mouth and drag myself into the shadows. I study the flashfall and try to guess the time.

I feel like a literal ghost, moving unseen amongst the rest of the camp.

I need to get to my old squad.

I choose my moment, watching the barracks from beneath conjured concealment. The lights switch to night-dim in anticipation of flashtide. If Dram's right, it won't come tonight, or ever again. But the squad doesn't know that. Any moment now, they'll be opening the door. GM16 might lead them now, but I'm betting they still do initiation.

Shouts erupt, muffled, followed by a scramble up the steps. The door flies open, and I slip past the startled newcomers. I trudge down the stairs of my old squad barracks.

"Orion!" GM16 gapes at me, and I throw my arms around her.

"They told us Dram was killed, and that you were—"

"Not dead." I pull away and clasp her arms. "How compliant are you feeling?"

"Tell me what you need."

"You know Greash—the Strider?" She nods. "I need you to bring him here, along with anyone else you think will help us."

"But the flashtide—"

"No flashtide anymore. Ordinance destroyed the tech that was causing it. Most everyone will be seeking shelter, but tell Greash to trust you. Tell him I said to 'run hard.'"

"I will." She glances at the squad members staring at us with wide eyes. "Do whatever she says. She's squad leader now!"

"Gear up," I tell them. "Make sure you're dressed for the cordon and your rifles are loaded."

"Rifles? What kinds of creatures are we supposed to fight in the middle of the night?"

"Not creatures. Striders."

"Our weapons won't fire on humans." The voice comes from the back of the barracks, weighted with scorn. My heart lifts. Roran.

"I think I know a way around that," I answer. I turn to the Dodgers and Miners. "Prepare your gear with extra rations and anything you want to take with you. We're leaving the Overburden." They rush to comply with my orders, and I walk to where Roran sits at the table.

"You're alive." He tries to make his voice sound flat, but his expression is giving him away. Especially the hope in his eyes.

"Dram's alive, too," I say. "So is your mom."

"GM16 told me you said that."

"It's true. You'll see her soon." I heft the pack of rocks off my shoulders. It clatters to the ground. "I've been practicing." I toss a chip of metal onto the table.

"What is it?"

"My talisman. The piece of cirium you gave me our second day in the Overburden. It chipped off from the end of your wrist, remember?"

He lifts it, tilting it in the light. "This isn't cirium."

"No," I say softly. "Not anymore."

His eyes dart to mine. He looks back down at it, then slowly fits it to the divot in the metal. The uneven edges align perfectly, only the metal's a dull gray instead of silver. His hand trembles, and when he looks back up, his eyes are filled with wonder.

"You did this? With the earth of the provinces?"

"Eludial soil," I say. "It has properties that allow Conjurors to manipulate cirium."

"You can conjure cirium?"

"I can't create it. I can only change it into something else. But, Roran—Ordinance sealed off access to the eludial seam. It was the only way to stabilize the flash curtain."

Roran's face falls. "So you're saying it's gone?"

"Not all of it." I open my pack and lift one of the rocks out. "I couldn't let the Congress take it, so I used—how would a Conjie say it? Scammer's tricks. This is tunnel shale, the most worthless rock a miner can bring up out of a cavern." I conjure the rock away to reveal eludial soil cupped in its hollow center.

He laughs. "You *are* a Conjie!"

I press my hands into the eludial dust, and my palms glitter with glinting chips of gems. I clasp them over the band of cirium at the end of Roran's wrist. "My dad told me that Conjies instinctively conjure new tendons and bone—everything—once the cirium isn't a barrier." My entire body shakes. So does his.

The elements shift beneath my hands, and I sense energy in rivulets of current, like I'm swimming in the blue water of the Sky.

The Sky, where his mother waits.

He makes a choked sound of surprise, but I'm not sure what he's seeing, what he's feeling. My eyes are clenched shut so I can focus—

"Orion." He squeezes my hand. With fingers. Not appendages.

Now I'm the one who makes the choking sound. Tears break behind my eyes before I even open them and see—

And see.

He flexes the fingers of his hand.

"You have magic, Orion," he says.

"It's the curtain in my blood," I answer, echoing the words he said to me months ago, at Outpost Five.

"Yes," he says, lifting the piece of shale. "And something more. Maybe something there isn't a name for."

I slide the bag of rocks toward him. "Your turn."

———

"You can't be serious." Greash lifts his face shield. "Brunts. That's your plan?"

"It has to be now," I answer. "While the Striders and compliance regulators are sheltered from the flashtide."

"Why do you think I'll help you?" he asks.

"You have a chance to trade the life you have for the one you want."

"I fought to earn this," he says, pointing to the Strider designation on his sleeve.

"So fight for something more."

Cora strides up with Dram and I release a pent-up breath.

"You got my message," I murmur.

"*Sarcoom*," Cora says. "Conjie word for freedom." She holds up my note, where I scrawled the word before dropping it through her room's air vent.

"I wasn't sure you'd remember."

Sadness fills her eyes and I know we're both seeing our last memories of Fern.

"I'd never forget," she says. "Though the rest of your message was less clear." She taps the note where I wrote *Dram* and *spear place*. "I got to Dram and he took down the Striders guarding him without a sound." Her wary gaze flicks to him, and I see that she's as unsettled by his new Vigil abilities as I am. "He understood the rest of your message and knew it meant to meet here. He told me about the flashtide, and we walked right out the door. No one expected us to try to leave. Not after night-dim."

Dram stands watching me, and I can tell he's putting the pieces together—forming a theory as to how I escaped the Box. "You conjured through the binders?" he asks.

"I transformed them into iron, then conjured them away."

His eyes gleam. "The eludial soil." It's not a question. He studies me, in that new Gem way he has of analyzing information. Suddenly he grins. "Your gloves. It was hidden inside your gloves." My smile matches his. "And the tunnel shale is actually—"

"Quite valuable once you conjure the stone away," I say. "I gave it to Roran."

"Who has—hands—again?" He hesitates, as though he's afraid to hope that much. My eyes well with tears. I nod. "Fire, Orion," he breathes, and the smile he gives me is one that I know, a part of him Ordinance didn't touch.

"We need to get going," Greash says, "if we're going to follow through with this plan." He gives Dram a hard look and sets his hand to a panel beside the Tomb. The doors begin to lift, and Greash glances at me. "You remember your last encounter with Brunts, right?"

I feel Dram tense beside me. "I remember," I say.

"And you're really going back down there?" Greash asks.

"She's not." Dram says, stepping past the doors. "I am."

"They'll tear you apart if I'm not with you."

"Not if I'm leading them out."

―――――

There are only a handful of Brunts left who remember Weeks, but every one of them has heard the stories. Dram's past is legendary to them, and seeing him now—strong, healthy—resurrected from certain death—gives them the faith to leave their only shelter during flashtide. They emerge onto the cordon, many wearing cactus-barbed armor. Some have cordon rats trapped in their spears or flash vulture carcasses dangling from their belts.

Dad would remind me that testing theories is all part of the scientific process. This is what I tell Dram as I aim a Dodger's rifle at his chest and squeeze the trigger.

It locks. A yellow error light glows in the periphery of my eyeshades.

"It won't fire on a human biometric signature," I call to the Brunts, Dodgers, and Miners gathered tightly around us. "But it will shoot through a cordon rat, or flash vulture. Effective, if we can get them close enough. Lift the spear," I command. The Brunt positions his spear so that a flash vulture carcass hangs in front of Dram. I engage the gun's safety and squeeze the trigger. Green light in my eyeshades. The familiar high-pitched tone of a flash rifle ready to fire. I lower the weapon. "That's how we fight them. But only if we have to."

They pair off—Dodgers with the Brunts I selected. They form a ring around everyone else.

"This isn't right," a Dodger says. "Dodgers protect the Miners."

"You protect them all," Greash commands.

"We'll load the transporters and take them out of the Overburden, into the Mod station. The Striders there will be sheltering. They won't be expecting us. We'll force them to take us out on a hover."

Dust rolls in from the cordon, shielding us as we jog toward the transport conveyances that first carried us into the Overburden. All at once, we're met with a contingent of Striders.

I raise my rifle and point it at Nills. "Stand down."

Nills sneers at me. "You can't shoot a Strider with a Dodger's weapon, you stupid girl."

A Brunt shifts his spear so that a cordon rat is positioned over Nills's chest. My rifle emits a high-pitched tone.

"You sure?" I ask.

Nills curses. "Stand down," he commands the Striders. They drop their weapons.

Suddenly, the air fills with a droning rumble.

"We've got hovers incoming!" Greash calls.

Sand lifts from the dust trail. Massive dark shapes descend through the clouds of flashfall. I have never seen so many hovers at one time.

"Holy fire," Dram murmurs.

"We're going to need a lot more cordon rats," a Brunt mutters.

"I don't think so," I say. Dram looks at me, anxiety carving lines on his face. "Trust," I say softly. "Your dad's message— *morior invictus*."

"Your faith in him is misplaced, Orion."

"You held a gun to a Vestige's head and stormed into Alara. You were surrounded by Striders, and yet you weren't killed or captured."

"Ordinance—"

"Ordinance doesn't command the Striders, Dram."

"If my father had any power at all, he would've—"

"He would *wait*," I say urgently, "at all costs, until he knew we could *win*."

Dram shakes his head. "Fire, Rye—I hope you're right." He lifts his rifle, and we take up positions as the hovers land.

"Trades Striders," Greash murmurs beside me, peering through the dust. "They're wearing the Trades on their sleeves."

Nills dives for his rifle, emboldened by the reinforcements. Shots fire, and suddenly the Striders are up on their feet, tackling Dodgers to the sand. Through the dust and the dark, I see Nills press the muzzle of his weapon to Greash's back.

"Hands behind your heads!" he shouts.

I've got the earth of the provinces in both hands, ready to make the ground crack apart and swallow Nills. Instead, I drop my rifle and kneel in the sand, directing the others to do the same. The heat of the cordon burns up through my padded armor as the Striders flank us.

My hands fist around the dirt, but I tell myself to wait. To trust.

The Trades Striders approach in a synchronized manner, oddly quiet, their armor muted. They don't reach for their weapons.

One of them breaks rank and walks toward the Striders surrounding us. "Stand down," he commands.

"I'm not taking orders from a tradesman!" Nills growls.

"Yes you are." The Strider lifts his arm, and something glimmers with the blue symbols of a Codev.

"What the hell?" The Overburden Striders look down at

their armor, buzzing with odd hums. A flash of blue light, and they drop—every single Strider with a weapon pointed at us.

"They're just stunned," the Strider says, stepping over Nills's unconscious body.

"What was that?" Dram asks.

"A bit of tech I borrowed from Ordinance."

"You're a Gem?"

"No. I'm more like you. A lot like you, actually." He lifts his face shield.

Dram lets out a shaky breath. "Dad," he says hoarsely.

Arrun nods, swallows hard. He crosses the distance and claps his arms around Dram. "I'm sorry I couldn't come sooner." His words are muffled against Dram's armor.

"Ordinance helped me in Alara," Dram says.

"No," Arrun says. "*Sooner.* Outpost Five. Before you and Len—" His voice breaks off at the mention of Dram's sister. Lenore. Arrun was far too late to save her.

Dram hugs him tighter. "You're here now."

The Trades Striders load everyone onto the hovers with brutal efficiency. The sooner they deposit everyone in the mountain provinces, the sooner they can cross the curtain and back up the other half of their force, already infiltrating the cordons of Westfall.

As the first hovers lift, Arrun explains how, with the support of Ordinance leaders, Jameson approached the council with the truth of the flashtide and the dangers of mining the eludial seam. Operations in the Overburden have been suspended, and the Prime Commissary and Meredith stripped of their positions. The Congress of Natural Humanity is in a strategically organized state of chaos, and Jameson's at the helm.

"However, this—what we're doing now—is a rogue operation," Arrun says. "Unofficially sanctioned. The Congress would never agree to simply liberate everyone in the cordons." He smiles. "But we've got at least an hour before they figure out we borrowed a few hovers and some of their Striders."

"What about the cure?" I ask. "Serum 1?"

"We took everything the Prime had in Central. It's enough to treat everyone here."

"What about the Westfall Subpars and Conjies?"

"Enough for some. Not all. It's not a perfect plan, but it's all we have—" His brows pinch together. "Where are you going? This is the last hover. I need to get you and Dram out of here."

"I can get into Fortune. I know where they keep the serum."

"The Commissary barricaded herself in there. She's got a handful of techs and Striders who refused Jameson's orders to leave."

"I can avoid them. We need the serum."

"Jameson can get it later—"

"There won't be 'later'!" I whirl to face him. "The device that Dram detonated in the seam knocked out every high-frequency transmitter beneath the surface. The creatures down there can conjure. They'll erode the structural support. I'm sure they've already begun to."

Arrun sighs and looks back at the waiting craft. "Jameson can only stall the council for so long. I'll send the hover on, and come with you—"

"I'll stay with you," Greash says, striding up. "You'll need a pilot. I can manage one of the Skimmers. I'll help you get out with the cure."

"I'm staying too," GM16 says.

"Go with the hover," I tell Arrun. "Get everyone free. When you do, I'll have more Serum 1 waiting."

"Dram?" Arrun asks.

"I'm staying to watch her back," Dram says. "This is what we do."

"So I've heard," Arrun says.

"When I see you again"—Dram lifts his arm, where his Codev glows—"will you show me how to zap Striders with this thing?"

Arrun grins. "I'll show you more than that."

———

The hover lifts as we reach Fortune, shredding the clouds of flashfall above us. It rumbles off into the night. The Overburden is eerily still.

"You didn't have to stay," I say, looking at GM16.

She smiles. "You're my squad leader."

"You're an Unaccounted now," I tell her. "You should be running as far from here as possible."

"I'll take my chances at your side."

I sudden thought occurs to me, and I turn to face Dram. "How much do you owe them?" I ask. "Ordinance."

He looks away. "We need to get the Serum 1 and get out of here." He jogs toward Fortune, and I follow, right on his heels.

"Dram Berrends."

"Orion—"

"How much is that Codev costing you?"

"They require my service."

"Everything we've done to get free, and then you go and—"

"I would've *died* without their intervention!"

"How many years?"

"Rye—"

"HOW MANY?"

"ALL OF THEM!"

I stare, openmouthed, trying to breathe past my shock.

"They gave me the years I would've lost," Dram says. "A trade."

"You traded one form of slavery for another!"

"I don't see it that way."

I slide into the ground, into the dirt hole I conjured up through Fortune's ventilation system. Dram crouches beside me.

"I get it, you know," he says. "You use anger like armor. I'm fine with that—rage at me if you have to—but I'm not letting you go back in there alone."

"I wasn't planning on it," I growl. "I can't bring up all the serum by myself." I give him a hard look. "GM16 told me that her blood repels the rodents. Does yours?"

"Yes."

"Fire," I grumble. "Then step in my steps. Closely."

I lower myself into the hole, and Dram follows.

———

I can barely manage the pack digging into my shoulders. I like to think I am strong, but as we leave the infirmary storage, winding our way up through Fortune's air shafts, my arms begin to numb and my spine convinces me it has all the strength of a toddler.

"It's the particles," Dram calls. "From the eludial seam. Your body's still recovering from exposure."

I roll my eyes. Dram keeps sharing these new tidbits of knowledge he gained through . . . whatever devil's bargain he's made with Ordinance. I have twice considered dropping the Dram of All Knowledge down this last, longest ventilation shaft. But he's hauling two packs filled with Serum 1. I'll have to keep him around for now.

"Still mad at me, aren't you?" he calls.

I grumble something about *idiot choices*, and push my body up.

We've rigged a system of pulleys with my conjured vines, with loops for our hands and feet that enable us to propel ourselves upward. It's similar to what we used to do with ropes and ascenders in tunnel nine.

"We'll still be free of this," he says, levering his weight over the final ledge after me. "It just might not look the way we imagined."

"Will it look more like a glowing blue symbol for Vigil?" I frown at him over my shoulder and lumber toward the air intake fan.

"I can help people."

I shove my pack into the hole I conjured and push it forward. "You'll have to *hunt* people—people like GM16. She's an Unaccounted now, Dram. And so is Aisla."

"Ordinance offered me an alternative," Dram says, his voice muffled by dirt. We pull ourselves free and shake off.

"What are you saying?" I ask. "An alternative to what?"

"To Alara."

"I don't want to live in the protected city."

"I mean *all* of Alara. The city-state." He slides his two packs onto his back. "You could come with me, Orion," he says, his voice filled with urgency. "To places they don't have maps for—"

"Don't move!" Greash shouts. He's standing beside GM16

a dozen meters away in a ring of lit flares. "They're coming up through the ground. The ones that conjure!"

I look down. A ring forms around Dram and me—the creatures tunneling up through the ground avoid us, repelled by whatever Dram's modified biology emits.

"Transmitters!" I pull two of the devices from my pockets. "I grabbed these from the infirmary. They were still working!" I activate one of them, and the ground clears.

"Hurry!" Greash calls. "They're changing the surface. I'm afraid we'll lose the Skimmer before we get her off the ground."

I toss him the other device, and we all run for the craft. They reach the Skimmer and clamber in. I'm struggling with the pack, suddenly wishing Reuder had made me carry twice as many rocks into the cordon. My legs fold beneath me, and I hit the sand.

"I've got it," Dram says, loping back to my side. He hefts my pack, clasping it to his chest. I push myself up and race after him.

Engines whine, and my heart pounds with sudden exhilaration. Almost there. Almost free. Dram and I will get this serum to our people, and then—then—talk about places without maps. He loads the packs into the Skimmer and leaps into the hold.

"Come on!" he shouts.

I climb into the Skimmer and collapse into a seat.

"I'm taking us up!" Greash calls. The door seals shut, and the Skimmer lifts. We rise above the cordon, and my gaze settles on the packs of Serum 1. More than enough. For everyone.

"Where are we headed?" Greash asks.

"To the outposts," I answer, my gaze sliding to Dram's. "One last time."

THIRTY-FIVE

35.6 km from flash curtain

THEY SECURE A boat for us.

Well, not a boat. A floating structure, half organic, half Ordinance tech, that will traverse the ocean on its own photosynthetic power. This biostructure is the first of its kind, designed to navigate seas altered by flash curtains.

We call it the *Outlier*, naming it for its crew, people set apart from others. Also for its mission to assist others like us—those on the fringes of fragile societies, trying to survive this world and shape it into something better.

Our first encounter will be aiding the miners on SeaPod One, an aquatic mining outpost. The council received a distress call from its techs shortly before they lost communication. Cirium, Jameson explained, is still the best shield we have against flash curtains, and our people aren't the only ones who figured that out.

Jameson replaced the Prime Commissary and has begun to reshape the Congress of Natural Humanity in ways that protect the futures of all Alara's people, Natural and otherwise.

The agreements he reached with the leaders of Ordinance will help ensure a partnership between our city-states.

I hug Mere, and her new commissary's chain presses against me. "Go shake things up," I say.

She smiles. "I never stopped."

Winn clasps her arms around my waist. "Bring Roran back safe," she says. I brush my hand over her long black hair.

"I promise."

"Conjie promise or Subpar promise?" she asks.

"Both." I lift my hair and show her the shell talisman conjured into my hair.

"The outboard vessels are in place around the *Outlier*," Bade says, lifting his gaze from a screencom. "They're ready to depart."

"And the Subpars from Outpost Five?" I ask.

Bade checks his screencom. "Owen, Roland, and Marin. All confirmed."

I smile, imagining my friends seeing the ocean for the first time. "Before we go, there's one last thing I need to do."

———

Greash opens the shield door nearest Cordon One and I step through, into white sand. I wear a Dodger's suit, and over it a Strider's electrified armor.

Serum 1 doesn't protect us from everything.

The flash curtain shimmers in the distance, a luminescent wall, the end of it dissipating in waving tendrils of energy. I jog toward it.

As I near the curtain, something moves beneath the sand. I adjust a sensor on my armor, and a transmitter pulses out a frequency I can't hear, modified from the devices Delvers used down the tunnels. I told Jameson that I had a theory. If I'm right, this will repel cordon rats as well as moles. One last suit to test for the Congress.

But that's not really why I'm out here.

The screencom on my wrist chimes a warning. I've reached the edge of the Exclusion Zone. Every step past this point exposes me to the flashfall.

I stand at the invisible boundary line, one that used to signify freedom and safety on one side, danger and oppression on the other. Now, all Subpars and Conjurors have Serum 1 and protection from the curtain's particles. They can live within the flashfall without sickening from exposure. Or they can choose to leave. Freedom and safety.

On both sides.

"We did it, Mom," I whisper. We broke apart the box the Congress had us contained in. Whatever stories Alarans choose to tell in the Honor Hall, I know the truth.

I step past the boundary. *One last time*, I tell myself.

Violet auroras fade to blue and collide with garnet ripples, shimmering above the sand. I close my eyes as I walk, not to shield my eyes—I'm wearing eyeshields beneath my Strider helmet—but to better hear it, the call I have known and answered all my life. No one would understand the ache rising in my chest. Not even Dram.

The flashfall dances over me. I turn beneath it, stretching my hands upward. Energy swirls around me, in me, a part of me. It has taken so much, but it also made me who I am. Something like loss hollows my gut. I feel as if I'm leaving Mom and Wes behind, and Graham and Lenore, and all the Subpars I've loved and lost here. All of my memories are tied to the curtain. The flashfall has touched every one of my days, and leaving it behind feels like leaving them behind.

Good-bye.

I will make new memories in places they have never been a part of. It aches to breathe, and for once, it has nothing to do with the flashfall.

"Quite a view," a voice says in my helmet. "Now that it's not cooking our insides." I turn to see Dram walking toward me in a matching suit and armor. I leave the heaviness of the curtain and join him where he stands, halfway to the shield.

"Electrified armor," he murmurs, glancing down at his suit. "Is it strange that I actually *want* a vulture to attack me?"

I grin behind my face shield.

"I stole something for you," he announces, reaching into his pocket. "Well, stole something *back* for you." He holds up my memorial pendants. The ones I traded to save Roran.

My breath catches. I can't speak as Dram clasps them around my neck. The glass pendants hang down my chest, right where they belong above my heart.

"What did you fill them with?" Dram asks.

"The earth of the provinces," I say.

"Can you mute your armor so I don't kill myself when I hug you?" Dram asks.

"Strider armor works on a repulsive charge. We can't shock each other."

He draws me into his arms. Our suits crackle and spark.

"You ready to go places that haven't been mapped?" he asks.

"Always."

We turn away from the flash curtain and walk toward our future. With each step, I realize that memories aren't tied to places, but to the people who made them. Wherever we go, I'll bring the best moments with me.

———

Dram and I stand in the greenspace at the top of the vessel, watching the shoreline disappear. The flag illuminated above us is a holographic image, a blend of the seal of Alara and Ordinance's Codev-like symbols. It's intended to project our intentions as a research and aid vessel, representing the best parts of both our city-states.

Still, we're not taking unnecessary risks. Greash leads the contingent of Striders and Untempered Conjies making this voyage along with us. We wear the Trades on our sleeves. Honorary Outliers, Arrun said. I was familiar with the symbol, but I had to ask him to translate the Latin motto.

Invictus maneo. I remain unvanquished.

A powerful statement, as far as mottoes go. Whatever trouble we may get into, I've vowed to keep the patch clean and the words clear. I may not carry an axe, but I haven't left my Subpar ways behind.

"Orion . . ." Dram grips the rail. "There are things we need to talk about." The ocean air snatches at his words, so I lean in closer. "What I did in the Tomb—"

"It wasn't you. You were out of your head with venom."

"Sometimes, pieces of that night come back to me," he says gruffly. "It's like I'm reliving the moment in someone else's body, because I can't believe what I'm seeing, what I'm doing—" His voice breaks and he squeezes the railing so tightly I'm expecting it to crack under his Gem-supplemented strength.

"I forgive you."

Tears fill his eyes, and he pulls me close, so tight against him, I feel his heart beat with mine. I thought I forgave him in the cordon when I found him beside Soma, but this is different. *More.* Like now that everything's been exposed, all the ugliness and pain is burned away by the light.

He pulls back, clasping the sides of my face. He looks into my eyes and nods, as though he's found what he needed to see. His lips move, but no words form, as if *sorry* is too small a word for what he's trying to say.

"It's all right," I whisper. He wears a lost look, like he's unsure he can cross to the other side of this bridge we're standing on. So I show him, reaching across and pressing my mouth to his. He exhales—I feel it against my lips—a shuddering sigh that turns into a kiss. And then he fills me, and I him, and we are all touch and taste, banishing the empty places.

I touch the climbing rope he still wears around his wrist in the place his Radband used to be. Blood stains the fibers, but the figure-eight knot is still woven tightly against his skin.

"I wouldn't let them take it off," he says. "Not even when they . . ." He doesn't finish. *Not even when they took away the Subpar and replaced him with something that I still don't understand.* For a moment, I'm back beneath the curtain and Dram is fighting me. I wait for the anguish to come, for the bitterness of betrayal to harden. But it's only sorrow that I feel now, tempered with understanding. What Dram did then, he did to save me.

"I wish I hadn't destroyed my bracelet," I murmur.

"I'll make you a new one," he says, and the light is back in his eyes. "I'm good with knots."

I take a moment to savor those eyes, free from shadows. Then I cross the bridge again, to where I am strong, and he is strong, and together, we are invincible.

ACKNOWLEDGMENTS

I'm honored, dear reader, that you cared about what happened to Orion and Dram, even after the last pages of *Flashfall*. It's you I have to thank most of all for this sequel.

I'm grateful for every encouraging e-mail, post, video, and tweet from those of you the story touched, who wanted Orion to see the stars as much as I did. You are honorary Subpars, and whether you knew it or not, you had my back while I was deep in the writing cave on this one. Thank you. *Nos sumus fortunati!*

To my amazing editor, Kate Farrell, who guided me so skillfully as I waded out into Book Two waters: I still pinch myself that I get to work with you. Thank you for believing in me and throwing your support behind an ore scout and her marker.

Once, I was just a girl lost in the land of Slush Pile, and a very extraordinary agent plucked me out and dusted off this quirky mining story called *Subpars*. She made me change the name and add more "light" to the "dark places." I will always be grateful to you, Sarah Davies. Here's to more adventures to come. . . .

To all the wonderful people at Macmillan, especially the amazing team at Henry Holt: so many of you helped bring *Flashtide* to life and I'm grateful. Special thanks to Rachel Murray for the early read, support, and all-around awesomeness; Kathleen Breitenfield for the gorgeous cover; and Brittany Pearlman, along with the rest of the publicity and marketing teams who have been such a vital support.

Special thanks to the teachers, librarians, booksellers, and book bloggers who have shared their enthusiasm for the Flashfall series. Thank you for all the ways you've helped this story land into just the right hands.

Very special thanks to Anissa de Gomery of FairyLoot, and Korrina Ede of OwlCrate. You both are amazing, and your support means more than I can say!

To my friends and family who have supported me in countless ways, and shared this publishing journey with me: I love you and I'm so thankful for you.

I couldn't have written *Flashtide* without the incredible support of my husband, Jacob, and our boys, Caden, Landon, and Hezekiah. You encourage me to explore the wild places in my mind, then give me the best place to come home to.

And finally, to the dreamers: Orion's story was born in my heart at a time when I thought my publishing dreams were beyond reach. I decided to write a character who got knocked down again and again but still believed there was a way through, and who had the resilience, courage, and faith to get back up.

Her journey inspired mine, and I hope it encourages you to keep reaching for the stars, even when you can't see them.

Run hard, you dreamers and Outliers, and never give up.

Invictus maneo.